# Out By Five:

## The Freshman Chronicles

A story told by Nicholas R. Lemon

ISBN: 979-8-9993193-0-2

Printed in the United States of America.

Edited, Formatted and Published by Empower Her Publishing, LLC

empowerherpublishing.com

To Nas, everything I do is for you. And to my parents, Earl Lemon and Ramona Jones-Lemon, thank you.

# Table of Contents

# Out By Five:

# The Freshman Chronicles

# Scene 1
## Friday Night Lights

The alarm clock blared as Sly rolled over in bed, simultaneously slapping the clock and covering his head. "Daddy gon' be mad if you don't get up," his little sister, Mina, yelled to him as she left the bathroom already dressed and heading towards the stairs. Sly rolled back over and looked at the clock: 7:43 a.m. As he struggled to sit up, he heard his dad from downstairs, "If I have to get you out of that bed, you not gon' make it to that game." Sly sat all the way up and turned off the alarm clock for the final time. He yelled down, "I'm up, I'm up!" As he dragged himself into the bathroom, he heard his father utter matter-of-factly from the bottom of the steps, "Yea, that's what I thought."

After he got dressed and made his way downstairs, Sly turned the corner quickly, almost running into his dad. The two paused in front of each other to figure out which way the other was going. At that moment, Sly's father, Alonzo, looked Sly up and down and shook his head. "I'll never understand why you dress like that for school on the days of your games." Sly was dressed in his practice shorts from the summer, a black thermal with his jersey on top, and socks in both team colors with his slide sandals. "Dad, I've been wearing this for gameday for the last three years. I'm not about to break tradition today." His father shrugged his shoulders and turned to walk away mumbling, "Fair point, I guess." Sly headed into the kitchen, hoping to find something to put on his stomach before heading out the door. Halfway up the steps, his father yelled back, "And take that towel out the back of your shorts. That's only for the field." Sly quickly threw the towel over his shoulder, grabbed an apple, and headed towards the door. He ripped a chunk of the apple out as he opened the door. The alarm system beeped and he heard his dad call from upstairs, "You ready?" Sly smiled ear to ear before responding, "Yes sir." Overly excited, he ran outside, but still careful enough not to slam the door.

Sly drove slowly up the street towards the Stop sign and saw the neighbors with small kids waiting to wish him luck. The neighbors in the last house on the left anxiously waved him down, so he stopped and lowered his window. A tall, rigid man in his state trooper uniform stood beside the car. "You boys ready for a fight tonight? You know White Oak isn't going to lay down like these other teams you've played." Sly confidently responded, "Yes sir, Mr. Woods. This is what we've been working for." Mr. Woods shook his head in understanding and pride. "Since you all were about six, right – time to make it come full circle." Sly nodded with a grin. Mr. Woods turned to walk away as Sly rolled his window up. But suddenly, Mr. Woods whipped back around, "Sly, one more thing." Sly stopped raising the window and with eyebrows raised, he looked at Mr. Woods. "Can you ease up on the bass as you go by the elementary school?" he asked. "The principal won't leave me alone about it. Just clear the school zone. Then you should be good. Here's a tip: from my house to the end of the school zone is 12 seconds, driving the speed limit. After that, you'll be clear." They both laughed before Sly responded, "Yea, I can do that. No problem." They laughed again as Sly rolled up his window and crept to the top of the hill. Twelve seconds, he thought, as he shuffled through all of the CDs he had burned. "Ahhhhh!!!!" he exclaimed as he pulled one of the disks out and placed it in his deck. While stopped at the top of the hill, he turned the volume down to let the first track play for a moment to make sure he had the right CD. He smiled, switched the track to number four, then looked up to make sure he was clear to make his left turn. He cleared the intersection and slowly turned up the volume, as the kicks from the beat started. Approaching the school zone, he slowed to 25 miles per hour and coasted through with a quick wave to the traffic guard as he sped up to 30 miles per hour. Just as he passed the line, the bass dropped and he glanced in the rear view to see the crossing guard shaking his head.

After listening to nothing but Three 6 Mafia and Young Jeezy on the ride to school, he had just about released all the energy from his dad's questioning this morning before leaving.  Just as Sly parked the car and got out, he heard someone yelling from near the school, "Aye, I heard 5's make plays." Sly turned around to see Sam, a lifelong friend and teammate. "All goddamn day," Sly replied with a big yell. "But I hear 7's make it look easy." Sam laughed before correcting Sly jokingly, "Nah, nah, nah... 7's make it look pretty, which just so happens to make it look easy." They both laughed and dapped each other up. Then Eugene and Reggie approached and all the players greeted each other. They discussed the magnitude of the game happening later that night as they strolled into the building with the rest of the student drivers and late buses.

As the four walked up the ramp, they saw Coach Cassidy, the wide receiver coach, waiting at the top for the bell to ring for the late students.

"You fellas loafin' already?"

"No sir," they all said in unison as they sped up the ramp.

"Y'all got five minutes to get to class and none of y'all better be late."

"Oh that's light work, Coach C," Sam responded only to hear Coach C reply, "That's funny coming from the third fastest player in the group."

"Ohhhhh!!!" Sly and Eugene said as Reggie laughed. "I don't know what y'all 'Ohhhhh'ing about," Sam said, pushing Sly and heading down the hall towards his class. "I'm 'bout to dip 'cause Coach C not wrong; that joint a hike!"

"That's 'cause you slow. Still gon' be late wit cho slow ass," Eugene responded as both fellas laugh and Sly heads towards the gym to go back outside. When Coach Cassidy turned back towards the bus ramp, Sly flipped Eugene the finger on both hands, "And same to you sir." They both laughed harder going their separate ways. Coach C yelled from the bus ramp, "Aye, y'all need to focus on the task tonight. And get to class, Jones."

Sly slid through the threshold as the morning announcements began. "Nice for you to join us in such a prompt fashion, Mr. Jones," Coach Granger said sarcastically while chuckling. "Of course, Coach G - it's my pleasure." Various chatter and giggles echoed throughout the class and Coach Granger attempted to get everyone to settle down. "Alright, alright. That's enough." As Sly sat down, he dapped up his teammate, DK. "You a trip man, you're lucky Coach ain't try to give you some sprints or somethin'," Sly laughed. "You right man, but I'm so hyped up, I wouldn't have cared, bruh. You ready for tonight?" Sly replied while trying to keep his voice down. "Nigga, is water wet? We been working for this day since little league bro. Since Laurel bro. It's time to put up or shut up tonight." Sly nodded in agreement, and the two dapped each other up again, just as the announcements concluded. Coach Granger stood up and started a video. Sly and DK continued to talk about the biggest game of their season, and potentially, their lives. Between talking about the game and dozing off from sheer boredom of the video, the class flew by. Once the bell rang, everybody hurried to the door as Sly and DK slowly made their way out. Right before they reached the door, Coach Granger barked from his desk, "You boys need to tighten up before White Oak wipes the smiles off your faces." In unison, they replied, "Yessir," understanding the gravity of the game.

Sly and DK returned to the main building of the school and went their separate ways for class after doing their wide receiver handshake. As Sly hustled towards the History hallway, he took a detour to the guidance office to check in with his counselor about his college aspirations. Obviously in a hurry, he yelled, "Hey, Mrs. Reeves! Hey, Mrs. Kinsley! Can I come back and talk to y'all about colleges?"

"Not if you're late to class, Mr. Jones."

"I won't be. I'm in Ms. Graham's class."

Sly sprinted out of the office, and heard Mrs. Kinsley say, "we'll see," chuckling with Mrs. Reeves.

The bell rang as Sly gave a high five to another one of his teammates in the second row and took his seat in front. "Look at you today, Mr. Jones, on time. This game has really got all you players on your P's and Q's," said Ms. Graham

"Yes ma'am," all the players in the senior History class responded, trying not to say too much.

"Well, I'm glad to see it. I wish you all the best in tonight's game."

As Ms. Graham turned to take her seat, there's a knock at the door. Annoyed, she opened the door and a student handed her a note. "Mr. Jones, your presence is requested in the Guidance Office."

"Oh, ok cool."

Sly grabbed his bookbag and slung it over his shoulder. As he headed towards the door, Ms. Graham looked at him puzzled, "Uhhh, Mr. Jones, I think your timing is off. You're going to the Guidance Office."

Sly responded, "I know Ms. Graham, but I'm going in there to talk about college. With my future hanging in the balance, you wouldn't want me to rush a decision like that, right? Plus, I already have an A in this class."

As Sly finished his sentence, Ms. Graham approached him to have a more discrete conversation. "You have a 91.6, Mr. Jones," Ms. Graham clarified, clearly irritated by Sly's attempt to skip class participation.

"Yes, Ms. Graham, that's my grade. But a 92 is an A, if you'd be willing to round my grade up. I pay attention, Ms. Graham. Even when I'm always joking, I'm paying attention."

Ms. Graham shook her head in agreement, "Fair point Mr. Jones, fair point. Take your time, but please try to make it back to class."

Sly nodded, "Yes ma'am." Sly understood that Ms. Graham was from an old school generation of educators and parents and she enforced that on all of her students.

Sly arrived back at the Guidance Office and he walked in upbeat and excited about the conversation regarding his future. "Hey Shawna, thanks for dropping off the note," Sly said to the student aide, as he passed the office receptionist's desk.

"No doubt, Jones. Y'all gonna handle business tonight? I got a cousin at White Oak that's been talkin' cash shit."

"Yea, that's what I heard. But we been playing against these same niggas since we were kids, and it's always been a tough game. We been working though, so we gon' be straight."

"No doubt."

As the two dapped each other up, Mrs. Reeves opened her office door, "Hello Sly, how are you?"

"Hey Mrs. Reeves. I'm doing good, just trying to get to tonight!" Sly expressed with the utmost excitement.

"I get that," Mrs. Reeves said as she waved Sly into her office. "Well, just in case your football plans don't work out, let's try to put together a plan for life after football."

"Mrs. Reeves, I told you. After last year, I have some big walk-on invites, and I can earn a scholarship. I wanna go somewhere that is going to give me a chance."

"Again Sly, I get that, but let me put it to you this way. Let's say you go out there tonight and you get hurt and then you're forced to never play again. What then? You need this plan to secure a future, any kind of future. What would you want to do if you couldn't play sports?"

Sly pondered the question as he stared at all the college pennants on the wall. "I really like video games and animation, but I can't draw. I guess I'd like to get into the back end of the gaming world."

"See, that's a step in the right direction," Mrs. Reeves said, expressing her relief that her message was getting through.

"But, I always had that as a plan, Mrs. Reeves. I wasn't going to college just to play football," Sly reassured her.

"Okay, but a walk-on invite isn't anything set in stone, Sly. You have to be ready to pursue different interests with these possibilities in mind."

As Sly listened to the spiel he had already received from his parents countless times, he stared harder at a red and black pennant that caught his attention. Interruptedly, "Hey, whose pennant is that?"

Obviously offended, "Uh, rude. But ok, I'll let it slide since you asked about a school. That's Fulton-Harley University," Mrs. Reeves said proudly, only to catch Sly with a confused look on his face. "You know that tunnel before you get to Virginia Beach?" she asked.

"I think so, but..."

"Where all the traffic is."

"Ohhhh, yea I know what you're talking about."

"There's a college right beside the highway."

Sly, still confused, asked, "Why is it that I've never seen anything about them or anything? Are they D1?"

"They're D1 double A like University of Richmond."

"Hmmmm ok, but they can't be any good though. I've never heard of them and they're in the state."

"Sly, again, we're talking schools, not sports."

"Ok, I'm sorry. Well what would they have for game design?"

"That's the beauty of college, Sly. You can make your own curriculum and cater it to what you want to study. Your advisor could help you customize a plan that is under Computer Engineering, or Computer Science, or maybe even Information Technology. There are countless possibilities. You just have to choose a path. I know you want to play football, but the reality of it is that most of us don't get to do what we want, but the earlier we try to decide what we want to do, the better prepared we are for the opportunities that exist."

"Thanks, Mrs. Reeves. I get what you're trying to say, but I feel like that kind of pushed me more towards football," Sly said laughing as he stood to stretch.

Mrs. Reeves laughed too and attempted to further explain. "You know what I meant. Start your plan for life now and things will sail a lot smoother, instead of hanging on to a dream that may never come true."

"That's some pretty harsh guidance, Mrs. Reeves."

"Reality is, Mr. Jones, once you walk across that stage in June, the next chapter of your life begins. You have to decide how the story unfolds."

"Thanks, Mrs. Reeves."

Sly headed out just as the bell rang for lunch. He passed Ms. Graham who was on her way to lunch duty. "Are we any closer to a decision for a university, Mr. Jones?"

"I still want to go to Virginia Poly to play, but everyone is saying that I should just focus on going to school to learn and get my degree."

"You should never abandon your dreams, Mr. Jones, but only a fool doesn't prep for possibilities." Sly stared at the lady. He pivoted by thinking about the place he was currently in and the fact that he was having these conversations on this day. As he tried to pull himself back into a focused space for the game, he approached the cafeteria and saw a table with fellow players discussing the shit talking that had been happening on both sides.

"Aye bruh, fuck them White Oak niggas," Sly overheard Brandon yelling to some of his other teammates. "They still think shit sweet since they beat us last time."

"But none of us were even in high school when that shit happened," Shaq responded with a face of confusion.

"But they fucking laid into us last time we played. That's why Coach Thomas is here. Y'all know what happened to the last coach right?" Johnny chimed in, looking for someone to give him the go ahead to tell the story. "The last time we played White Oak, they scored on purpose on the last play of the game, after already being up by 50. The coach of White Oak tried to shake hands after pulling that shit, and Coach J swung on him."

"Coach J was a real one," Sly said before Brandon jumped back in.

"Man, if we had Coach J, we would've gone to states last year."

"Aye, kill all that noise, y'all need to focus down on what the fuck we got going on tonight. Fuck all that last year or years ago bullshit. We strapping up with these same niggas that used to play at Glen Lea and Highland Springs. We all got some get back coming tonight," Reggie explained with the fire of a pre-game speech. Reggie was the star of the team after his breakout during  Junior season.

"I know a couple of y'all remember playing against them teams and never getting that W but that all ends tonight!" he yelled.

"Hell yea, fuck White Oak!" Brandon exclaimed once more, as all the players at the table cheered in agreement while eating their lunch.

Sly left the cafeteria and headed to his home room. On the way, he ran into Reggie and Domo. "You think them niggas ready man?" Sly asked the two as they all turned the corner towards the classrooms.

"They better be. This is easily the biggest game of all of our lives," Reggie said and Domo agreed.

"We got one chance to shock the world bro. We gotta get it done."

Sly felt the same way. "Nah, you right, but I can't wait man. I'm ready to play now." He had been jittery and full of extra energy all day.

"Keep that because we gon' need it and then some for the game tonight."

All the fellas dapped each other up before splitting to go to their respective home rooms.

Sly strolled casually into his home room as the bell rang. "Eaasssyyyy, what's good bro? You ready for tonight?" Sly yelled at

Eugene as he took his seat. Ms. Green snapped at Sly, "Mr. Jones, please lower your voice and take your seat. I get you football players have a lot going on tonight, but the world will continue to spin when that game ends."

"Maybe for you," Sly said under his breath.

Eugene chuckled, "Yea man, I'm ready. You know the game sold out, right?"

Sly said, "Yea nigga, this what Friday night lights are all about man. We trained for this for four years bro. Shit finally 'bout to pay off."

He and Eugene whispered and nodded their heads to something that the teacher had asked but neither one could tell what they had agreed to. While Sly and Eugene continued their conversation, their friend Dean chimed in.

"All the White Oak basketball players have been talking cash shit, even the ones that don't play football. Y'all niggas better be ready."

"Nigga who side you on?" asked Eugene, giving Dean the side eye as all three laughed.

"Aye bruh, don't shoot the messenger. They say that their main running back, the Michigan commit, isn't even 'bout to play against y'all, and they not worried even the least bit," continued Dean.

"That's fucking disrespectful. We bussin' heads tonight," said Eugene.

Angered by the trash talking, Sly replied, "Aight, Mr. Ray Lewis, I hear you and that sounds good. We gon' see."

Dean responded with laughter, "Yea we are."

"Gentlemen, would you like to share what you're talking about with the class?" Ms. Green asked.

"I don't mean no harm Ms. Green, but I'm sitting back here with two football players on game day. Of all days, I know you know what we're talking about," Dean said as the rest of the class, nodding in agreement, tried not to laugh.

"Fair point, Mr. Chester. Sly and Eugene, do you guys feel ready for tonight?" asked Ms. Green.

Both Sly and Eugene confidently nodded their heads yes. Sly had been trying all day to view that question as a positive versus negative, but no one had ever asked if they were ready for a game before this. He was growing more and more annoyed by everyone's sudden curiosity. As he tried to come to grips with this realization, Eugene snapped him out of his moment of frustration. "Hello...Sly!" Half the class had already cleared out and he hadn't even realized it. "You good, man?" Eugene asked. "Yea, I'm good man. Just had a moment, that's all." He and Eugene gathered their things, did their handshake, and left the room. Sly headed to his last class for the day located in the tech center part of the school.

He was about halfway there when he came up on a window in route with a clear view of the practice field. It reminded him of all the work he and his team had put in through the summer, through the scrimmages, and through the first two games of the season. His confidence was renewed, knowing that the hard work they put in showed what they had accomplished so far and what they were capable of accomplishing later that evening. Sly smiled a little as he opened the door to go down the steps to reach the sub-level of the high school. As he entered the classroom, Mr. Finland, who was also the track coach, called out to him. "Juice, you're almost late." He pointed to the clock above his head. Sly scurried over two more steps and landed inside the threshold just as the bell rang. "But I'm not, Coach. I'm not." They both laughed as Coach Finland cracked back, "Oh, so you can move fast? Ok." Sly stopped laughing and gave Coach Finland the side eye, which only made him laugh harder. "You know I'm just picking. Go ahead and take your seat."

As the class settled in, Coach Finland had just begun explaining an engineering concept when he was interrupted by the fire alarm. "Ok, let's all line up at the door so that we can get outside," Coach Finland said to the class before putting on his coat and heading towards the door himself. As the students lined up, Coach Finland asked the class, "Isn't there a pep rally today too?" The whole class responded like a mass choir, "Yes!" Coach Finland, obviously annoyed, mumbled under his breath, "Why do both on the same day? That just eats up the whole period." In an attempt to lighten the mood, Sly said, "But that's ok because it's for school spirit," with a thumbs up and a smile. He and Coach Finland both laughed with the rest of the students. The class went and stood outside for about five minutes before the administrators marked the area safe. "No firetruck and no fire. Every time," Derrick said, shaking his head. "Try not to look so disappointed by it," Coach Finland said. This time, him trying to make light of the situation. As everyone walked back into the classroom to take their seats, Sly raised his hand before he even sat down. "Yes, Sly?" responded Coach Finland. "I know we typically get to leave a little early before the pep rallies, and I have to go get something out of my locker. Can I go now?" he asked. "It's like...You know what, you can go Sly. But if you all don't win tonight, I have some sprints waiting for you next season," responded Coach Finland. "And that's why I'm playing basketball," said Sly, as he and the rest of the class laughed. He grabbed his stuff and headed towards the door. "There's always Spring," Coach Finland joked as Sly left the classroom.

The halls were cleared, except for the varsity football players who had all used the same excuse to get out of class. It was sort of a rite of passage for the senior players, especially for a game of this magnitude. Sly opened the door at the top of the stairs and saw a group of his teammates passing headed towards the gym.

"Time to get to it fellas," he yelled. As he shuffled his way to the middle of the group, he could feel the energy shift of his teammates from earlier. No more joking around. Everyone was now more focused. "I'm ready to get this shit over with. This ain't for us. This is for everybody else. Tonight is for us!" Brandon yelled. "You know they gon' make a spectacle of it. We just gotta lock in." Everybody agreed as they approached the gym.

When they went inside, the rest of the starters were already there. The underclassmen starters had already earned their stripes from the year prior and their deep playoff run. There was an eerie quietness in the gym before all the students and administrators poured in from the school. As the rest of the squad arrived, the team all joined together on the gym floor at the back of the gym, some of them posted against the wall. As the gym grew more and more crowded, the athletic director, Mr. Bowman, attempted to get everyone seated for the pep rally to start. Students continued talking until Mr. Bowman threatened to revoke students' admission into the game. The crowd instantly became silent and you could hear a pen drop in the gym. Finally, Mr. Bowman continued, "Thank you. As I was trying to say, 'Welcome to game day at the Dennnnn!!!!'" The whole gym erupted into cheers. "And tonight, for the first time in twenty years, we'll face the White Oak Wolves." All the cheers quickly turned into boos at just the mention of their name. All the football players, very aware of the gravity of the game, perked up when the opposition was mentioned. They all stood. Some even began jumping around to get hype. Mr. Bowman suggested, "Hey fellas, not yet." Some of the linemen started egging on the crowd, chanting "Lion's Den! Lion's Den! Lion's Den!" Mr. Bowman, though visibly annoyed, remained calm while stating that his threat from earlier wasn't empty and would be valid through the whole pep rally. Everyone calmed back down again, and he proceeded to introduce the soccer team and the rest of the Fall sports teams.

When Mr. Bowman finished introducing the volleyball teams, Sly shuffled over to Eugene, who was posted on the wall at the end of the pads. "Yo, you ready?" Sly whispered in a somewhat nervous tone. "Yea, man, you…. You okay?" Eugene replied subtly, but slightly off put by Sly's shakiness. "Yea man, it's just such a big game man. This is that opportunity we been talking about. Just can't believe it's here."

"Man, that's all you been talking about. Me, I'm trying to show out and reap the benefits," Eugene said, acknowledging the girls in the stands trying to get his attention.

"Bruh, you a trip," Sly said as he elbowed Eugene. They both laughed and Sly turned back around to face Mr. Bowman. "Now it's time for this year's Denali Lions football team." The crowd exploded with screams of excitement and anticipation. As all 22 starters made it out to the middle of the basketball court, Mr. Bowman continued to spew stats about the team. "Starting this year 2-0, outscoring their opponents a combined 83 to 21, and the #1 ranked team in the city of Richmond, give it up for your Lions!" Mr. Bowman then proceeded to announce all of the starters on both sides of the ball. "Our starting tight end, Sly Jones." As Sly turned and waved to both sides of the gym, he felt surprised by the overwhelming amount of admiration he received from his classmates when his name was called. The rest of the team joined him and his teammates in the middle of the court after the safety was introduced.

The crowd was still going wild and the team was just soaking in all of the praise. Suddenly, Doug walked towards Mr. Bowman and the rest of the team looked at each other slightly confused. Mr. Bowman then announced, "Our starting quarterback has some thoughts he would like to share before tonight's game." The team muttered smart remarks to one another and chuckled. "Last night I had a dream…" Doug began, then took a slight pause, as if he was waiting for a response. As the pause grew longer with the silence, Sly tried not to laugh with the rest of his teammates. Instead, he looked over at Sam and noticed he had his face in his palm, just shaking his head. "I dreamed that we crushed the Wolves!!!!!!" Doug screamed as the electricity came back into the gym. He handed the microphone back to Mr. Bowman and went back to the center of the court, while enduring several jabs from teammates. "They didn't see the movie. That's all. They just didn't see the movie," he quipped. They all had one last laugh.

Once again, the crowd in the gym went quiet. Brandon gathered the team in a huddle so only they could hear, "Aye fellas, it's put up or shut up time, aight?! No more practice, no more talking about it. Fuck all that the paper calling us the best. We prove that shit tonight. Let's get it." As several members of the team let out a Jeezy "yeah" they echoed their team chant that had been a traditional staple of the varsity team for years. In the midst, Brandon yelled, "Red!!!!! Grey!!!!!" and the rest of the team yelled back, "Red!!!!!! Grey!!!!!" The team yelled the chant repeatedly with Brandon as their leader, "Red!!!!!! Grey!!!!!!" and the team responded, each time faster and louder, "Red!!!! Grey!!!!!" Finally, the crowd joined in and the team moshed in the middle of the court to keep the momentum going. The student body was in a chaotic frenzy of enthusiasm.

When the pep rally ended, Sly got together with Doug, the quarterback, to head towards the locker room. "How you feelin' Dougie Fresh?" Sly asked, while pushing Doug. "Sharp man, I'm throwing darts tonight so have your hands ready," he said. "Boy, don't you know I was born ready?" Sly responds. They both laughed a little as they approached the trailer where their pre- game meals were normally served. "Look man, I put that intro on the CD you asked for. You'll have about 45 seconds to speak before the song starts. You know what you're gonna say?" Sly asked, as he handed Doug the CD. "Not exactly." They both laughed, then Sly responded,

"Let's stay clear of the movie references." They laughed again. One of the teammate's mom popped out and waved. "Hey, Ms. Snelling," the guys greeted the woman holding serving utensils. "Hey fellas! We have turkey, stuffing, green beans, cornbread and a brownie for dessert." Sly rubbed his stomach as Doug responded, "That sounds so good. We need something hardy. The temperature is supposed to drop in the game tonight." As Doug and Sly grabbed their food, they greeted some other teammates coming in. They were all sure to thank Ms. Snelling before leaving.

After grabbing their food trays and trying to get the team mothers to give them extra portions, the team members headed on into the locker room where Coach Thomas came from out of his office. "Doug, come here please." As Doug went to speak to the head coach, Sly proceeded to his locker to put his backpack down to get ready to eat. As soon as he took his first couple of bites, his phone rang.

"Hey Sly, ready to crush your game tonight?"

"Ha, yea Ma."

"Sorry I won't be able to make it tonight. They have me on a crazy shift, but I know you all are going to do amazing. Tell everyone I said good luck!" his mother said.

"I will, love you Ma."

He ended the call and Eugene, Reggie, and Lenny all came to sit at their lockers. There was small chatter here and there about the day and the pep rally, but for the most part, everyone was trying to get into the headspace they needed to be in for the night. Sly wrapped up the last few bites of his meal and pulled out his MP3 player to listen to his gametime playlist. He bobbed his head to Three Six Mafia's "Who Gives a Fuck Where You From" while putting his pads in his pants. He remembered playing against these same guys as kids and always being on the losing end. Back then, his teammates were intimidated by their trash talk or aggressiveness, but not tonight. No, this team was built with that same kind of grit as him. Although they hadn't been tested yet, Sly knew that with their experience from last year, they would be able to overcome any challenge. He put on his game pants and flak jacket just as Coach Cassidy was coming out of the coach's office. For the most part, all of the receivers sat together, and Coach C was a man of very few words. He simply pointed to the group and pointed outside. We knew that it was time for the position meeting.

Gathered back in the trailer where the meals were served, Coach C cut off the lights and turned on the projector. He played a couple of clips of the team against other schools. The players were able to see multiple pass breakups, interceptions and even a pick 6. "They are not going to press you. You have to sell your route. They are fast. They are aggressive and they are well coached. If you make a mistake, they will make you pay. But I feel this group can contest the ball at the highest point with the best of them. We say it every Friday, and the shit doesn't stop because #2 comes in our backyard. We own the skies!" Coach C exclaimed. "We own the skies!" The receiver core responded.

By the time the receivers came back into the locker room, the rest of the team was pretty much ready to hit the field for warm-ups. Sly put on his shoulder pads and wiped his visor one more time before putting on his helmet. As the team lined up to go out onto the field, you could hear everyone yell, "Don't forget to touch the sign!" The 'Hard Work Brings Championships' sign had been hanging in the locker room since it was built. It was considered the ultimate disrespect and bad luck to not touch it before touching the field. As the team jogged onto the field, it was eerily quiet. People were coming into the stadium but there was a calm on the playing field. White Oak wasn't on the other side of the field warming up, which was unusual, but the team didn't pay it much attention. When all the positions were finished warming up and heading back into the field house, the team noticed that only their side of the stadium was filling up, but they could hear staging buses in the parking lot.

Despite the questionable start of the evening, they all gathered back in the locker room and took a seat in front of the whiteboard or their lockers. The coaches gathered at the front of the room and each one discussed what the key assignments would be for each position and how it would play into the overall scheme. After the defensive coordinator, Coach Polly, finished creating bloodthirst for his linebackers, Coach Thomas was up next. "Gentlemen, we've been preparing for this game since last season. For some of you, this is the culmination of all of your hard work. You all are the #1 ranked team in the city, and you've earned that ranking. Now, it's time to go prove it. Let's go!" as he pointed to the door. All the players stood up, screaming, ready for battle!

As they lined up to head out, they could only hear their band initially. But as they moved out, they could see the other half of the bleachers filled with white shirts. "There they go!" someone in a white shirt yelled. The yell seemed to start a telephone effect amongst the White Oak faithful. When the Lions approached the field, they could see that all the way down to the goal line, there was no team on the other end of the field, only a heavy fog that had rolled in due to the incoming rain. As they got closer to the field, the horns from the White Oak band started to play. The Denali players started to chatter. Then one player said, "Wait, is that the intro to 'Patiently Waiting'?" The team looked up at the band as they entered the end zone, already on edge. As the sound faded, White Oak's band started back up. This time, with the assistance of their student section. They clapped and chanted in unison, "We some East End Wolves, and we running this shit." With every clap and chant, it grew louder and louder. The Lions then started their chants, enraged that a visitor would try such a stunt. The White Oak Wolves walked from out of the fog behind the field. Their quarterback, #2, was the only person in the county cleared to play with a black visor. With his speed, and his slim 6'3" frame, he earned the name, "The Slim Reaper". They slowly walked onto the field, pointing at Denali's head coach. The Lions ran onto the field, all the while eyeing the other sideline. This is going to be a blood, sweat, and tears type of game and both sides were ready for it.

The teams lined up across the field from one another and the captains met in the middle of the field. The referee greeted both sides. "Gentlemen, we're here for the biggest game of the season so far in the Richmond area. I hope you all are ready for battle. White Oak, you're the visitor." The Reaper replied, "No we're not." His other captains laughed and within seconds, Brandon replied, "I can't wait to see the fear in your eyes even with that dark ass visor on. Give 'em the ball."

"Ok fellas, let's stick to the game. Call it White Oak."

"Tails never fails."

As the referee tossed up the coin and watched it come down, all three sides leaned in.

"The toss is tails. White Oak, would you like to kick or receive?"

"What he said," The Reaper replied, taking every chance he could to talk a little trash.

"Oh, I'mma come visit you #2. Don't worry, I'll see you real soon," Brandon responded.

"Ok, ok fellas, enough. Denali, which end are you defending?" the ref asked.

Reggie licked his finger and put it in the air, looking for the wind for our kicker, and then pointed to the south end of the field. As the referees put the captains in the proper spots and signaled who would be receiving the ball, the crowd roared in anticipation. As the kickoff team gathered on the sideline, Sly moved into the middle of the circle where the kicker, Dexter, was getting loose right outside the circle. "The time is now fellas. Dex gon' boot it deep and they not gonna bring it out. This our chance to smack a motherfucker in the mouth. You see the disrespectful shit they doing on our field? In our house? They got us fucked up," Sly said just above a whisper, yet firmly, for the team to hear. Reggie ran over, adding fuel to the fire. "They said they not visitors here. They said it's their house." Sly chimed back in, "Fuck no! Aye fellas, they can't talk if they're unconscious. Let's put 'em out. Bang on 3, Bang on 3. 1,2,3!" And the whole group yelled, "Bang motherfucker!" Hyped, they ran out onto the field for the kickoff. Everybody took their positions while Sly stayed on the sideline. He was only on the offensive side of the ball. He could see and feel that all of his teammates were ready to take a head off. As the whistle blew, Dex approached the ball, and the rest of the team went for the 40-yard line with a full head of steam, ready to destroy anything in their way. The White Oak front line was made of what appeared to be all linemen, but as soon as the ball was kicked, they moved like running backs across the field. They were trying to create crackback lanes and clear the middle of the field. The collisions sounded like a multi-car pile-up on the highway as the ball soared overhead. As it landed in the end zone, and the referees blew the play dead, there were still some hits happening because of the crowd noise. After multiple whistles were blown, the play was finished.

When the special teams' players cleared, the Slim Reaper and the White Oak offense came onto the field. Brandon had been silent since coming back from the captains' coin toss, which was highly uncharacteristic of him. He is usually the first player on the field when the Denali defense hustles on the field. As both teams huddled, Brandon made it clear that he was going to be hitting #2 every play he got a chance. His eyes bore into his teammates' as he took a moment to look each one of them in their eyes, "He's mine." Everyone in the huddle nodded in agreement. "Bishop, you with me the first time. Just tap the side you want me to go," Brandon barked. "We headbussin' today," Bishop excitedly replied. "We're cover 2 on the back-end fellas. Ready!" Bishop yelled. The rest of the defense responded, "Break!" The defensive backs all fanned out to their respective positions, as the defense took shape. When the rest of the defensive linemen took a knee, Brandon stood in the middle, almost pacing, and waited for the White Oak offense to line up. When their offensive line approached the ball, the center looked at Brandon with a grin and yelled, "No help, no help, I got lil' man and his chump ass MLB." "Word nigga?!" Bishop quickly yelled back. The rest of the White Oak line laughed, as they got in their stance. The quarterback approached the line and locked eyes with Brandon one more time and smiled before starting his cadence. Brandon dug in. At the snap of the ball, Brandon punched the center in the sternum, stunning him. After he discarded the center, he had a clear path to #2 who had his back turned. He wrapped him up and drove him into the ground. Brandon popped up, pounding his chest. The Reaper rolled over laughing. "What's so fucking funny?" Brandon asked. "You ran past the play dummy," the Reaper laughed. Brandon turned and saw the running back getting up from a 30-yard carry. "That won't happen again," Brandon scuffed. "Then you won't hit me again," the Reaper replied as he got up. "You can either hit me or stop the play. You can't do both. Shit, you probably can't do either. You just got lucky that play. Pick your poison big boy," he teased. "We gon' see 'bout it, itty bitty bitch," Brandon barked back. Both players stared each other down and returned to their huddles before the referees could intervene.

After a few more plays, the first drive for White Oak stalled and they punted it to Denali. As the offense got set to take the field, everyone gathered around Doug and Coach Thomas. "Alright fellas, showtime!" Doug yelled and fist bumped the whole offense. Sly was so busy jumping up and down that he only half listened to the call. He was too focused on seeing who was on the field. "Alright fellas, pro right, 32 dive is play one, and pro left 32 trap is the second play," Coach Thomas yelled into the huddle. The crowd's noise was deafening. "Both on 2 guys, let's get some free yards." Doug chimed in. "Ready..." Doug shouted. The offense responded, "Break!" and ran onto the field.

Denali's center approached the ball, and the referee stood over it, waiting for all the officials to be ready. After he received the signal, the referee blew the whistle and Doug proceeded with his cadence. "Blue.........Blue.....Settttt.........Hit!!!" He finished the first of the two cadences, and the defensive tackle lunged through the line, trying to grab Doug as he just back peddled and smiled while pointing at his head. "I'm gonna beat y'all up here." The defensive linemen backed up slowly, while being pushed by Denali's linemen, nodding his head. After the referees moved the ball forward, the Lions lined up and ran the plays called on the sideline and got a first down. After those two plays, the Lions offense met back in the huddle. "See fellas, just like any other game. Now let's go give them their ass whoopin'. Reggie coming your way. Pro right, back motion, 303. Pro right, back motion, 303. Ready?" Doug barked excitedly after he received the call from the incoming receiver. "Break!" yelled the team. They broke the huddle and raced to the line of scrimmage. Denali got set at the line. Sly spaced out a little for the release for his route. Doug started his cadence again, "Blue…..Blue….Set………Hit!" He got back into his drop, twisted his shoulders over his left side, delivered a dart to Reggie while he was in stride, then he zipped past the cornerback. With one man to beat, Reggie did a stutter step and caused the defender to dive short of his feet, just outside of the 20-yard line. "Denali Touchdown!!!!!!" the announcer screamed as the crowd erupted. "But there appears to be a flag on the play." The referees conferred for a moment, then the head referee came to the middle of the field and signaled Denali for holding. Coach Thomas was furious on the sideline, "What's the number, What's the number?" he yelled, as Coach Cassidy tried to pull him off the field. "69 coach. Left hand was outside the shoulder pads."

The offense huddled back together. Everyone looked at Rico, "You good man? Shake it off," Sly said and he tapped him on the back of the head.

"That call was bullshit."

"We know man. We know, but lock back in. Alright fellas, Slot left, 35 waggle, slot left, 35 waggle. Ready?"

"Break!!" The offense yelled and they hustled to the line as the crowd roared. Doug started his cadence again, taking a second to scan the defense. "Blue……Blue…….Set…….Hit!" The Lions fired off the ball, and Sly broke into his 15-yard mid-route, anticipating the chance to throw a haymaker of a crackback block. He sprinted to that mark and made his move at the top of his route. He turned to see the ball in the air, but it wasn't the pretty spiral that Doug usually throws. It resembled a dead duck. The whistles blew and the ball was called incomplete. Denali's offense hustled off the field and the punting team headed on. Doug seemed dazed and stumbled as he came off the field.

Toliver, the school's sport's trainer, pulled Doug over to the side. "Hey Doug, you here with me buddy? You good?" Seemingly annoyed by the question, Doug replied, "Yea, I'm fine." He sat on the bench next to Sly and Eugene on the last play. "Ok, I'm glad you're ok. Doug, where are you right now?" Toliver asked. "Why would you ask me that? Do y'all hear that bell ringin'?" Both Sly and Eugene looked at Doug, and then looked at Toliver, then looked at Doug again. "I mean, I'm at the White Oak game. I just had a baseball thought." Toliver looked at Doug again and checked his eyes to make sure he was still good to play. "You're not showing signs of a concussion, but I need you to tell me if anything about how you feel changes." He yelled at Doug who stared back with a blank look, like he had forgotten about everything that had led to this point. Finally, Doug shook his head in agreement, strapped his helmet back on, and went and stood beside Coach Thomas for the Denali's offense to get the ball back. "For the glory?" Eugene looked at Sly as they took one last swig of water and got off the bench, "for the glory." They fist bumped and headed towards the edge of the sideline.

After fighting hard for what felt like eternity, Sly looked up as the final seconds ticked on the clock. "Man, what the..." as the final buzzer sounded. The final score was White Oak Wolves 44, Denali Lions 10. As the teams lined up to shake hands, all Sly could think about was how his whole plan had gone out the window with this single loss. The team went back into the locker room. They discussed meeting for film the following day. The series of events leading up through the game continued to linger with Sly. Even after arriving home, his dad could tell that something else was bothering him besides the loss. "You alright man?" Sly answered just above a whisper, "Yea Pop, I'm good." Elaina couldn't wait to chime in, "Y'all did get smoked though." His dad felt sorry for Sly. "Elaina, cut it out," his dad pleaded with his youngest. "It's a fact though," Elaina continued. "Once you all were down 20 and it was raining…" Sly became increasingly annoyed. "Elaina, stop!" he leered at his sister. He went upstairs to shower hoping to shake the feeling of loss.

## Scene 2
# A Meaningful Conversation

The weekend was over in a blink. On Monday morning, Sly arrived early to Denali and waited at the guidance office for Mrs. Reeves to get there. Before she could even ask, Sly shrugged and asked, "So due to recent events, could you tell me more about Fulton-Harley?" Mrs. Reeves started to laugh, and Sly tried to find humor in the situation himself, but didn't feel much in the mood.

Sly shuffled his feet into Mrs. Reeves' office and she turned to him and said, "Well it's only one game. They can't drop you all that far. Y'all will win this week, and everything will be back to normal." Sly plopped down in the seat in front of Mrs. Reeves' desk. "I hope you're right," then slid down in the chair and rested his head on its back. "I've never seen you like this, Sly, but I promise you it's ok. You can get into those same schools based on your grades." Sly, still hopeful about his future, responded, "I know, I know, but I wanna play. I get good grades so I can play. But with the last game, and not even being recruited, the chances of me getting to play at the next level are slimming, Mrs. Reeves."

"Well…" Mrs. Reeves turned away from Sly and looked at the Fulton-Harley pennant. "What about them?" Sly asked, intrigued and annoyed at the same time. "Ok, hear me out. They aren't a power five school, but they are a D1 double A school. So, the same as University of Richmond or VCU. You could still get to play D1 football and still get into a good school." Sly tried to be patient and replied, "Mrs. Reeves, I remember you telling me all that." Mrs. Reeves interjected, "But what I didn't tell you is that it's an HBCU." Confused, Sly said, "Ummmm, ok. I'm kinda lost on what that's supposed to mean to me?" Mrs. Reeves said, "It means that the majority of the people on the campus would be African-American." Sly looked at Mrs. Reeves with reservations for a moment and replied, "Ok...That sounds good. But from what I know about all black schools – at least the high schools in Richmond – that's not typically a good thing. Y'all remember taking us to that one city school? I literally didn't see a student besides the students that were in the classroom we were going to meet." Mrs. Reeves tried not to laugh, while Mrs. Kinsley in the next office could be heard giggling. "This is completely different, Sly. HBCUs have a rich tradition in molding young black minds across many industries. You'd be able to thrive amongst like-minded individuals – not only intellectually, but socially as well." Sly tried to be open-minded. "I mean...I hear you," Sly started, "but, wouldn't I be around like-minded individuals if I attend a school to be an engineer? We're all studying the same thing." Mrs. Reeves took a moment before answering to make sure it was worded so that Sly would get the bigger picture. "You're not wrong to think that way, and it's great that you do. But what happens when something happens that's outside of the engineering school, outside of school in general, when just life things happen? How many people do you think could relate to you? College is a great learning arena for not only knowledge of skill, but also for life. White Oak showed you that life isn't fair, no matter how hard you work, right? This is just a way to hedge your bets with Tech and still give yourself a chance to play ball."

Sly sat back in his seat, stunned by the lecture Mrs. Reeves had given him, since no one in his last 12 years of school had framed life that way. Meanwhile, in the next office over, Mrs. Kinsley chimed in: "Message!" Sly felt a bit more optimistic now. "Aight, aight, I get it," he said, as he chuckled and sat up in his seat.

"Ok, so what has to happen for me to apply to Fulton-Harvey? I guess it'll be good to have a back-up school, and I can still play ball there, right?" Sly asked with reservations. Mrs. Reeves exhaled, "You're dead set on playing, so yes. You can walk on there and you can talk with Coach Thomas about putting together a tape for you." Sly gave Mrs. Reeves the mean side eye as he sat all the way up in his seat and planted both feet firmly on the ground. "I don't rock with Coach Thomas like that. After he moved me to tight end this year, I'm kinda good on him." Mrs. Reeves cocked her head back, "What's wrong with tight end? Don't you start?" she asked. "Yea, but I'm 160 pounds soaking wet with two bricks in my pockets. I don't belong on anyone's line in Henrico County. I'm not getting no kinda look playing tight end, especially after we got our ass beat by White Oak."

"Language, Sly!" Mrs. Reeves exclaimed, surprised by Sly's sudden expression of emotion.

"Sorry, but it's true. But I can put in that app, and I'm sure I can do it with or without him."

"Ok…" Mrs. Reeves, slightly thrown off, tried to refocus.

"Well if you put in the app now, their admissions staff will actually be here in December granting on-site admission."

"What's that mean? Like they'll be able to tell me on that day if I got in or not?" asked Sly.

"Exactly," answered Mrs. Reeves. "So at least you'll know if you got into one college before Christmas."

"Ok, that's a bet!" Sly exclaimed. "But don't college applications cost money? How much is it for this one?"

"They gave us vouchers since they're coming here so I can give you one."

"Word. Thanks Mrs. Reeves. Would you need anything from me?"

"No, just stay optimistic about the season and going to school and playing at the next level," she replied.

"Thanks Mrs. Reeves, I appreciate it. I'll catch you later."

The bell rang for the day as Sly got up to leave. "I'll write you a note for class. Just make sure you don't make any stops along the way," Mrs. Reeves advised. Sly looked at Mrs. Reeves with a smirk and she gave him a stone-cold look back. Sly quickly changed his stance. "Yes ma'am," he said, and shook his head on the way out of the guidance office. "Bye, Mrs. Kinsley," he said as he passed her office. "Bye Sly," she said, "and you would love FHU by the way." Sly looked over his shoulder, while taking the note for class and replied before walking out of the guidance office door, "Yea, I guess we'll see, huh?"

## Scene 3
# Lemme Find Out

After the football season concluded, Denali had been on the outside of the playoffs for the first time in five years. Sly, while relieved that the season was over, was disappointed by the way that things had played out. Knowing that the season wouldn't help his prospective walk-on journey, he skipped his senior year of basketball to train for football full-time. He also joined the indoor track team.

It was around November when Sly walked back into the guidance office. "Hey, Mrs. Reeves! I got that application filled out," he exclaimed loudly. "Uhhhh....volume. And good morning," Mrs. Reeves responded with her head peeked out of her office on the phone. "Oh, my bad," Sly mouthed as he sat down in her office. "Aight girl, one of my students is here early, really trying to go to college...Yea, he's thinking about Fulton-Harley...He doesn't need to know that part." Mrs. Reeves laughed as she hung up the phone. "I don't need to know what part?" Sly asked, intrigued by what he thought he heard. "You'll learn if you go visit. So you finally got your application completed, perfect. The administration team from Fulton-Harley will be here next week." Sly sat back in his seat, "Dag, already?"

"Yea Sly. I know you forget but when you all typically end football season, it's basically the end of the first half of the year. In less than a year, you'll be in college."

"I mean, when you put it like that, it sounds like I've been slacking." Sly responded, feeling like Mrs. Reeves was implying that he hadn't been taking applying to college seriously.

"I know you had your plans Sly, but the reality is, you don't have any offers, and this application you just handed me only makes two schools that you've applied for."

"But I have good grades. Getting in shouldn't be a problem. I do things outside of school."

"The only thing you do is sports, Sly. You not fooling nobody. You have to try to get more involved in more social aspects of school. It'll benefit you in the long run."

"I hear you, Mrs. Reeves, but all that stuff feels forced."

"Well, do it until it doesn't. That's the only way to fix that." Sly slid back in his seat again, dreading the requirement of being social outside of the comfort zone of his teammates.

"It's not that bad, Sly. Plus, college has a ton more social experiences so you'll be able to find something that fits what you want to get into."

"Mrs. Reeves, I really hope you right."

As she laughed, "Sly, relax, the FHU admissions office will be here next Thursday during lunch; I'll introduce you, and you can get your decision."

Sly left the office feeling a little more confident about his college outlook, but still had reservations about the little information he had about Fulton-Harley.

As the days without sports flew by, Sly arrived at school on Thursday morning just waiting to get to lunch. Sly's first period class, a lifting class, was primarily for football players, but the course was made for anyone who wanted a period to lift. As the football players sat in class, they all contemplated what their next steps would be now that the season was over.

"Man, I can't believe we don't have a game this week," Brandon said, after racking 245 on the bench.

"Aye B, where you going next year?" Sly asked, as everyone looked at Brandon for his response.

"Man, I don't know for real. This JuCo was talking about something, but they said my grades bad."

"But if your grades are good enough to play, then they would be good enough for college, right?" Butch chimed in.

"Well..." Brandon said, as he laughed and winked at one of the female basketball players in the class, "I had a little inside help here, so my grades weren't bad this year. But my overall GPA for my time at Denali is garbage."

"I think you hypin'," Sly said, laughing it off. "It can't be that bad." He was thinking about his own situation.

"Nah, you need a 2.0 to accept a scholarship, and I am half of that right now. Might be able to pull it out at the end, but we gon' see."

"You got it bro, just stay at the work," Damon joined in.

"What about you Sly? Where you going?" Brandon asked.

"I ain't got no offers. Why you ask me that?"

Brandon laughed, "So, don't you still want to go to school? I know you don't wanna stay in Richmond."

Several members of the football team turned and answered in unison with Sly, "Hell nah!!" They all laughed.

"I wanna go to Tech. They invited me to walk-on after last year and for the engineering school, but after this season, I don't know for real. I been talking to Mrs. Reeves about Fulton-Harley."

"What is Fulton-Harley?" Brandon asked.  Butch leaned in as well.

"Think of it like, University of Richmond meets Virginia Union."

"So…..that statement didn't really make sense. Those things couldn't be more opposite," Brandon responded, and he and Butch looked at each other puzzled.

"Yea, it didn't make any sense to me either when she said it, but she said I'd find out more if I go for the visit. I'm supposed to find out today if I got in or not."

"Oh, word? Like they coming here?"

"Yea, their admissions staff supposed to be here at lunch. I think they're gonna be accepting people on the spot. Shit, it's still a D1 school. Maybe you can get in there."

"Bet that! I'm in there at lunch," Brandon responded and he dapped up Sly.

"You gonna come over there too Butch?"

"Nah, I already know my calling. Y'all can catch me on The Food Network."

"That's word, Butch. You gon' be cooking or eating?" Sly laughed, knowing Butch was full of jokes.

"Shiiiittttt, both."

The whole team laughed as they racked up the rest of the weight, since class was ending.

Sly ran into Eugene on his way to his second class of the day. "What's good bro? You going to the Fulton-Harley table during lunch?"

Sly was taken aback by the question and responded, "Yea, but how did you know that?"

"You know Mrs. Kinsley can't hold water. She gave me one of those applications too."

Sly exhaled, relieved to know that he would at least know one person if he did end up there.

"That's a bet, so what do you know about Fulton-Harley?"

"Not a damn thing, but I did hear they got the prettiest women of all the HBCUs," Eugene grinned, while nudging Sly in the ribs.

"Stop man, I struggled with that shit in high school. I don't wanna hear about that at college. Give me something useful," Sly replied, only half-jokingly.

"They're a D1 school and a D1 AA football team."

"Knew that, next?"

"Academically, they rank in the top three of HBCUs in the nation."

Sly turned to Eugene with a huge grin on his face. "Oh word! They're a top three school. That's all I need to hear. You know how Ma Dukes is, but if the school has something like that to stand on, it's gotta be good, right?"

"That's what I'm rolling with."

They both laughed as they walked into their third period classes.

When class ended and they came out of their respective classrooms, Sly and Eugene anxiously headed towards the cafeteria. Along the windows of the senior courtyard were three tables set up for the Fulton-Harley Admissions team. Sly and Eugene approached the side of the tables where Mrs. Reeves and Mrs. Kinsley were sitting.

"Hey Sly. Hey Eugene. You guys ready to hear your application results?"

"Oh...uh yea. I thought there would be a little more to it," Sly said nervously.

"Just tell me I got in," Eugene added.

Mrs. Reeves handed both young gentlemen their respective letters.

"Aye, this said I got in, but I have to go to summer school. What kinda bs is that?" Eugene asked after reading his letter.

"Don't look at it as summer school, but rather a way for you to get a head start socially," Mrs. Kinsley responded to Eugene, trying to give a positive spin.

"It states right here I have to take two courses, that's school," Eugene shook his head. "Well at least I'm in."

"That's the way to look at it," Mrs. Kinsley laughed, continuing to be encouraging.

"Well Sly?"

"I got in. I know that's good, but I really don't know what I was just accepted to."

"Don't overthink it, Sly. As of right now, you're a prospective college student with a good school you've already been accepted to."

Sly forced a smile, but without knowing if he had the option to go to Tech, he wasn't as excited as the rest of his classmates who had been accepted.

When Sly got home from school, his mom, Ria, was home to his surprise. "Hey Sly. How was your day?"

"It was ok. I got into Fulton-Harley," Sly said in a kind of melancholic way.

"Why did you say it like it's a bad thing? I mean I'm not a huge fan, but they are a really good school."

"Oh, you know about them?" Sly asked, surprised.

"Of course! I'm from Virginia, and they're a Historically Black University. Just because I didn't want you to go to those particular schools doesn't mean I don't believe in what HBCUs stand for and achieve."

"Ok, wow, my mistake Mom. I really thought you hated HBCUs," Sly laughed, relieved that his mom didn't just shoot down the idea of him attending Fulton-Harley.

"No, I don't hate them, but all of them are party schools."

"I feel like that term isn't fair. Every movie I've watched with college, people party, whether it was about a black school or not."

"Yea, but there is a stark difference between going out on the weekend, and someone throwing a party on a Tuesday, just because. When someone says party school, they are talking about the latter." Sly's mom stated while looking at Sly, who she could see was still trying to process the information.

"Wait, there are parties on Tuesday in college?"

"You were paying attention to the wrong thing in that statement, Sly." Ria shook her head at Sly and he grinned and kissed his mom on the forehead before heading towards the door.

"Dinner will be done shortly."

"Oh, I was gonna shoot over to the Von Dutches' house. You know Auntie Deb is a Fulton-Harley alum. I know she's gonna be hype."

"You can't just give her a call?"

"And miss Mr. and Mrs. Von Dutch's reaction to this in person?......Nah!" Sly laughed and headed toward the door.

"Be safe and tell them I said hi. And don't go to the plaza," his mom yelled.

"I will and I will!" Sly replied before heading out the door.

"Don't go to that plaza, Sly."

"But that's where people meet up over Southside," Sly yelled.

"You are not from Southside. You don't know those people, and neither does Andre. Y'all don't need to be over there."

"Ok, but......." Ria looked at Sly one last time. "What if I'm not driving?"

"Then you need to get out of the car, walk back to your car, and drive home."

Sly laughed at his mother being crystal clear about not wanting him in the plaza. "Ok, yes ma'am."

"Thank you sir, be safe. Love you!" she yelled just as he walked out the door.

"Love you too!" Sly yelled back as the door closed behind him.

Sly cruised through the city over to the Southside. He couldn't help but take notice of everything that his city had endured – between the increased crime to the more broken parts of the city being neglected. Sly then recalled what Mrs. Reeves had said about attending Fulton-Harley and what it would mean to go to an HBCU as a black student. It also caused him to look at the communities he rode through with a different mindset. He knew that Church Hill had always been a black community. Sly also knew that unless you knew someone from Church Hill or you stayed over there yourself, there was no reason to be over there at night. But that couldn't have always been the case. As Sly rode past his great - grandmother's house, he heard gunshots in the distance. "Shit man, I hate it here." As a tear fell down his cheek, he was angry he couldn't go see his grandma June anymore. Those cowards who took her away from him were still out there.

After about a 25-minute drive, Sly arrived at the Von Dutch house. His cousin called from the upstairs window as he got out of the car. "Aye bruh, I'll be down in a sec. Don't ring the doorbell, the old man sleep. You know how he get."

"Aight, word," Sly responded as he approached the front door.

Dre opened the door and the two dapped each other up and walked into the living room.

"I could hear ya yelling from down here witcha loud ass," Mr. Von Dutch exclaimed as he sat up on the couch for a moment to see who had entered his home.

"Hey, Mr. Von Dutch. How you doing?" Sly asked, trying to be polite.

"Mmmm Hmm…" Mr. Von Dutch responded.

"Duke be nice. Hey, Sly. How have you been?" Auntie Deb came down the steps and tapped Mr. Von Dutch on the shoulder.

"I'm good, I'm good. I just wanted to come over and give y'all the news that I'm going to Fulton-Harley."

Auntie Deb took a step back and looked at Sly like he had just grown up right before her eyes.

"Oh really? Let me find out my nephew gonna be a Fulton-Harley man. You know my Sorors have some daughters that will get there at the same time as you."

Sly, seemingly happy but nervous about his aunt's statements, just kind of laughed. "Uhhh ok……" Sly stuttered over his words before Andre could step in. "Don't worry Ma, I'll make sure he gets a proper introduction."

"So do you already know these people?" Sly asked, confused about Dre's comment.

"Why, yes, cousin, I do. Not only that, but I'll be down that way attending the local community college before transferring over to Fulton-Harley."

"Oh word, that's what's up. Eugene gonna be down there with us too."

"Oh, so y'all gonna have your whole little clique down there cutting up, huh? Don't come back with no baby," Mr. Von Dutch bellowed from the couch.

"Are you done sir?" Dre asked, kinda fed up with his father's outbursts.

"Boy, don't make me get off this couch and embarrass you in front of your little friend."

"He's my cousin and your nephew."

"Mmmm Hmm."

Dre and Sly shook their heads. They looked at Auntie Deb and she just laughed. The two then went upstairs to Dre's room.

"Aye bro, I know you didn't drive all the way across town to tell my moms you were going to FHU?" Dre asked while changing his shoes and picking out a shirt.

"Why can't I just be happy to be sharing that information with the family?" Sly asked, with an innocent look on his face.

"Because I know you think more like me than you'd care to admit, and you know the plaza be jumping on Thursday with bad joints."

They looked at each other for a moment and then bust out laughing.

"Yea, yea, ok you right, but nah, I can't go over there tonight man. I think my moms got hip to me coming over here for that."

"Uhhh, duh nigga. You over here every Thursday night since you not doing sports anymore."

"Well my guidance counselor said that I would need to be more social to round out my college resume."

"And even though I've never met them, I can almost promise you that this isn't what they were talking about," Dre responded and they both laughed and headed downstairs to Sly's car.

"I'll be right back Ma," Dre yelled to his mom.

"Ok, be safe. And congrats again, Sly."

"Thanks Auntie."

"Don't bring back no kids," Duke yelled before the door closed.

Dre and Sly pulled up to the plaza through the west entrance. They searched for the optimal parking spot as they drove past the rows of cars. The goal was to be close to the action but also far away enough just in case something happened. When they found that perfect spot, the two hopped out of the car and walked over to the group of people congregating.

"What's good, Dame?" Sly called out to a fellow football player who was also from West End. The two dapped each other up. "What you doing out here bro? This is even further away from you than me."

Dame laughed, "You know the city small as shit bro, and football is over, so I'm just out here going with the breeze man."

"Nah, I feel it.  Shit looks like it's packed tonight," Sly replied as the two of them scanned the crowd together.

"Yea it's deep. It's that time of year right before Christmas. Everybody trying to bag them something. Where you going next year?" Dame asked as he took a swig from his bottle.

"Right now, it looks like I'm going to Fulton-Harley."

Dame looked at Sly over his glasses. "Oh word...Nigga you bout to have a good ass time."

Sly was instantly interested in what Dame had to say since he was the one person his age who had had some type of experience there. Every other person he had talked to about Fulton-Harley was older than him.

"Bro, I went down there on a track visit. I think one of the guys said that the ratio was 10 women to every guy. Or some shit like that? They were loving a nigga." All three of them laughed as Dame added, "But all jokes aside, that HBCU shit is like that.  It feels more like a family than anything. Shit should be a good look."

"I can respect that. Thanks, Dame."

The two dapped up again before he slid into the crowd.

## Scene 4
# Some Decisions Make Themselves

After what he considered to be his worst semester in high school, Sly turned the corner in his college pursuit and knew that he was either going to attend Tech as a walk-on or at the very least, he would be a freshman at Fulton-Harley. As the spring semester rolled on, Sly became increasingly more nervous about his potential spot at Tech.

Because Sly wasn't super serious about any of the Spring sports, he took that time to train for football and really tried to learn more about his options. While the school days were winding down, Sly periodically popped into Mrs. Reeves and Mrs. Kinsley's office to check-in with them and let them know that he still hadn't heard back from Tech.

"Hey, Mrs. Reeves! Hey, Mrs. Kinsley!"

"Hey Sly. Any good news yet?" Mrs. Kinsley asked, as they prepared for another day, just days before Spring Break.

"Not yet, but I feel like it's coming soon. Spring Break is in a couple days, and I know for the state, it's done by the end of the month. That only gives us a month before school's out. I'm thinking that they have to let me know before then, right?" Sly asked, looking at both counselors. They both looked at each other and shrugged. "Super helpful, y'all. Thanks so much." Sly laughed as the two counselors rolled their eyes, having a laugh with each other.

"Don't get cute, Sly."

"Sorry Mrs. Reeves. I'll let y'all know when I learn something."

Sly waved as he left the office and headed to the next class.

After school, Sly went to track practice and then rushed home in hopes that he would have some good news waiting for him. Once he pulled in the driveway, he hopped out of the car and heard his sister yell down from their parents' bedroom, "It's here!" Sly hesitated for a moment and then burst into the house. His mom was holding an envelope while his dad sat at the dining room table with anticipation. "It's a big packet," Ria said, "And you know what that normally means…"

"Yea, yea, let me open it first," Sly said, with a huge grin on his face. As his mom handed him the packet, he could tell that although it was a large envelope, it seemed light. Sly ripped the top of the parcel open and pulled out the singular piece of paper that was in it.

"Dear Mr. Jones, we really appreciate your application, but we regret to inform you…….." Sly stopped reading out loud and threw the paper on the table before running upstairs in frustration and disappointment.

He was lying on his bed when his father came up to sit with him and give him some words of encouragement. "You caught a bad break, Sly, but you can't pout about it. You've still been accepted to college, and if you're that set on going to Tech, you can always go the community college route. Either way, this isn't the end of the world. The way you just reacted was a bit dramatic." Sly sat up for a moment to respond to his father.

"I've worked essentially my whole life to get a shot Pop, just to get a shot, and I couldn't get it. Even with my grades being good and everything. Why wasn't I good enough?"

"That's not the question you should be asking. The question that you should ask is what did they not see that Fulton-Harley did? You don't have to change you for anybody. If they don't like what you're doing, find someone that does."

"But I don't even know what Fulton-Harley is."

"None of us do, really. Your mom and I know about it, but nothing extensive."

"Hey, you got another letter down here, Sly!" Mina screamed upstairs. Sly and his father went downstairs and Mina handed her brother the regular mailing envelope that was already partially opened. Sly looked at his sister and she responded, "What? I was curious. Plus, you already know what you got in there." Sly looked down again at the envelope, not realizing initially that the letter had come from Fulton-Harley. He hastily opened the letter and there was a single sheet of paper. In the letter was an invitation from the Fulton-Harley Admissions Office for their Next Class Up program. "Hello Future Buccaneer. We hope that you'll join us on April 7th, 2006 at 8 am EST for Next Class Up. Come meet your fellow classmates from across the country and upperclassmen that can more accurately paint the picture of what it means to be at Fulton-Harley." The invitation pictured the football team and mentioned that the school's Spring game would be on the same day at 2 p.m. Sly looked at his dad as he finished reading the letter. "Oh, that's perfect, and I might be able to speak with the coaches after their game." His father just smiled and nodded at him in approval. Sly then looked at his mom and sister for approval as well. Both were excited about Sly just being accepted and going to college. "Looks like we're going to Fulton-Harley next week!" Sly's parents were excited that he had reached this point, but, admittedly, they were both a little skeptical of what was to come next.

*Scene 5*
# Next Class Up

As the days of Spring Break slowly dwindled away, Sly anticipated Friday, while searching the internet for anything he could about Fulton-Harley. Besides Auntie Jill, Sly's other aunt, Auntie KJ, had also attended an HBCU. With the two of them being the closest in age of all of his uncles and aunties, Sly always knew he could get it straight from Auntie KJ. To help pass the time, he continued studying up on the University he would be attending. After he thought he knew a decent amount about Fulton-Harley, he gave Auntie KJ a call to get a better idea of the situation he was walking into to be better prepared for everything to come on Friday.

Sly pushed away from his computer and picked up the phone to dial his aunt.

"Hey Auntie. How you doing? How's Grandma and Knight?"

"What's up nephew? And they good, just in here driving me crazy. What you got going on?" Auntie KJ responded. Sly could hear his grandma in the background, "She's being so dramatic. We are not doing anything, Sly. Knight and I have been sitting here on our best behavior all day."

Sly laughed as Auntie KJ, faked a laugh, and whispered on the phone, "Lord, I need a drink! What's going on Sly?"

Sly continued laughing, trying to put together his sentence. "I... I've been looking into this Fulton-Harley school, but everything they have on their site is basically what every school has on their site. I know all these schools have an education to offer, but would you know what it's like? Like what are the people like?"

"They booooouuggiiieeee!!! Boy they bougie. But they earn it though, so no hate, just an observation." Auntie KJ laughed as she exhaled. "But, I'm bougie, so I would've fit in there so perfectly, but can't get this Aggie mixed up in that."

"Bougie?" Sly responded, a bit confused and not as familiar with the term. "Ever met a person that swears they are God's gift to Earth, and demands the best of everything, and if they don't get it, they act a way?"

"Of course, I'm in high school." They both laughed.

Then Auntie KJ stopped laughing abruptly and said, "Some people never outgrow that, and that's a real thing."

Sly stopped laughing. "Oh…." His voice dragged out and turned into a question. "So wait, everybody that goes to the school is like that?"

"No Sly, come on. Nowhere is everybody the same. You know better than that. But a Tuesday will be a fashion show, and the administration will have something to say about your appearance and your clothes."

"Yea, I saw there was a dress code. I thought that was just a public high school thing. They have that in college too?"

"Yea, in private colleges," Auntie KJ laughed. "But don't worry Sly, you're gonna get a feel for it on Friday and you'll see."

"Well what made you go to A&T?"

Auntie KJ paused for a moment, almost as if she was reflecting and then chuckled. "It's the people. They had amazing people who gave my tour. They really answered all my questions and everything I wanted to know about the school and made me feel comfortable.

As someone as socially awkward as me, that's all I needed to make my decision. With your personality, you'll fit right in."

"I'm not so sure Auntie, not after what you just said. You know I spend my money on games and tech. I was looking forward to wearing sweats every day."

"Yea nephew, don't do that and don't say that again. And you'll be fine, trust me. Have I steered you wrong yet?"

"No, not yet."

"Why you say it like that?" They both laughed.

"It just hasn't happened yet. Is that not a true statement?" Sly answered.

"I guess..." Auntie KJ laughed again, but Sly could feel the side eye through the phone. "Give me a call on Saturday to let me know how it all turns out, but like always, I know what you like and you're gonna love this."

"Thanks Auntie and I'll let you know."

"Love you nephew."

"Love you too. Love you Grandma," Sly yelled as they disconnected the call.

Sly tossed and turned Thursday night, as he felt conflicting feelings of nervousness and excitement about his visit to Fulton-Harley the next day. When he finally fell into a deep sleep, his mom came into the room.

"Wake up Sly. We have to get ready to leave."

"What? What time is it?" he asked, hardly bothering to open his eyes.

"It's 6:30. Come on, get up. If we're going to be on time, we have to get going."

Sly moved sluggishly towards the bathroom and Mina chuckled.

"You got 30 minutes or so, you got this."

"Easy."

Sly fist bumped his sister and went into the bathroom. He smiled and closed his eyes again, feeling confident that it was going to be a good day, but accidentally walked into the closed bathroom door.

Mina shook her head while laughing, "Hopefully that woke you up."

Sly stumbled back, laughing, and opened the door to the bathroom.

After everyone made it downstairs and gathered by the door to leave, Alonzo asked the family, "Everybody got what they need? We're going to the beach afterwards, so Sly, you got your trunks and stuff to change into?" Sly pointed at his backpack, "Yea I got it." They all filed out the door and into the truck. Mina and Ria slid in the back seat, Alonzo took the driver seat and Sly hopped in shotgun. As they headed for the highway, Sly turned on his GameBoy and Mina pulled out her phone. Alonzo turned on the Smooth Waters jazz station for Ria and him to ride in peace. Considering this was Spring Break time around the country, there was a lot of traffic going down the highway. Before Sly knew it, he had turned off his GameBoy reluctantly, regretting not bringing another set of batteries. They were making good time, but with nothing to occupy his mind combined with the soothing jazz, Sly easily drifted back off to sleep.

Sly was awakened to his face pressed against the freshly baked glass window from the rising sun. They had come to standstill in traffic for their exit to Fulton-Harley.

"Are we there?"

"Kinda, but I'm assuming these are all your soon to be classmates," Sly's father joked, as they crept towards the exit.

Once off the highway, there was a light and a couple of officers directing traffic, allowing more people onto the campus that was right beside the highway. As the officers waved the Jones family through, Sly saw people walking around the campus and also saw boxes randomly placed in a few locations. As they moved further onto the campus, more police officers were in place waving cars into a sprawling parking lot that had an entrance from two sides. As Alonzo pulled into a parking space, Sly stretched before opening his door to stand and stretch again. He was sure to take a good look around in the process. Still trying to get his feet under him, he heard a loud scream. "Welcome to FHU, Essence of Excellence 5, Class of 2010." Sly turned around to see where the commotion was coming from while the rest of the family got out of the car.

"I really like the police presence. And they seem excited about school," Ria mentioned as she took in the surroundings for her baby boy.

"They're excited about your money. I mean, our son is coming here," Sly's dad joked. Sly and Mina laughed, but all of it stopped with a side eye from Ria. In the distance, they could see a big arena where the invitation indicated that the initial presentation would begin. As the Jones, and several other families, moved toward the building at various paces, from zombie-like to that of entering an amusement park, Sly was sure to take all of it in.

Once they reached the edge of the parking lot and crossed the street, they could see a small bridge with what appeared to be representatives of the school jumping and screaming at the top of their lungs. As they got closer, they realized that the representatives were actually students. There were a lot of them on and surrounding the tiny bridge. Sly leaned over and whispered to Mina, "They do know it's eight in the morning, and this is about school, right?" They both laughed. Their laughter caught the attention of one of the representatives who stepped towards the Joneses. Lowering his megaphone, he asked Sly, "Hey, what's your name and where are you all from?" Caught off-guard, Sly paused, took a half step then answered, "Sly, from Richmond." Without hesitation, the representative stepped back, raised the megaphone, and what seemed like the volume as well to Sly and said, "Let's welcome Sly and his family from Richmond, VA." All the other representatives started cheering and Sly tried to hurry the pace of his family to get to the other side of the bridge. He looked back at his family and they looked at him a little puzzled.

"Y'all don't think that was a bit much?" he asked.

The rest of the family just looked at Sly with a slight shrug, then his mother replied, "They want you to be excited to be here. They are."

"There has to be some kind of perk of being part of this," Sly quickly responded as they approached the building. As they turned the corner, Sly continued, "This school is ranked amongst the top HBCUs in the country from what I read. They are getting noticed from somewhere. I mean…" Suddenly, they're met by even more representatives and another megaphone. Sly knew  not to say or do anything other than smile and nod accompanied by the occasional wave so as not to draw too much attention to himself. They hurried past the last group before entering the building.

Once in the arena, the Joneses made their way up to the second tier of the seating and sat near the steps. As they watched the rest of Sly's prospective class file into the arena, they noticed four people sitting on the stage, with a choir sitting directly behind them. The floor of the arena had already been filled and so had the lower bowl of the arena. Sly couldn't help but feel a little nervous, just by the sheer number of people, but he remembered that the only other option was staying at home and going to the local community college. He took another look around and then shrugged. "What was that for?" His mother watched him observe the school. "I'm trying to convince myself that this is a good idea. I still think you should've gone to VCU, but that's just me. But I like their campus so far, and they seem excited about this school, regardless if they're receiving anything or not. I think you'll like it here."

"I guess," Sly replied. "Beats staying in Richmond," he added under his breath so as to not upset his mother.

After about ten minutes of being seated, the Joneses and the rest of the arena grew silent as a woman approached the podium. "Good morning, Class of 2010, Essence of Excellence 5, and our future Fultonites." When she was finishing her sentence, all of the student representatives that had been outside, plus more, erupted into a cheer of celebration for the incoming class. "My name is Dr. Denise Chandler, and I am the director of the Office of Admissions at Fulton-Harley University. Let me be the first to formally welcome you to our Fulton Family." The student representatives cheered again before the director outlined what today would be about and encouraged us to be excited to have such an opportunity in front of us. "Our admissions office is very focused on selecting the best students to allow our campus to thrive and push us to new heights. You all are here for a particular purpose or reason. Take that in while you're here. Thank you." Sly and his family applauded. Ria and other parents throughout the arena even gave Dr. Chandler a standing ovation as she took her seat. Then, one of the gentlemen on stage approached the microphone. He was a smaller fellow with a deep bellow of a voice and a beard to match. "Good morning. My name is Mr. Stokes, and I'm the choir director here at Fulton-Harley University." He stepped back and the student ambassadors cheered, but there wasn't much applause. He stepped back quickly to the podium and grabbed the mic, "Could we all bow our heads for a moment of prayer? Dear Lord, we come to you today, thanking You for waking us up this morning. Allowing us to all make it here safely this morning. Allowing us to see what tomorrow may hold, and for us to gain purpose through the path You have chosen for us. For we follow in your steps, Lord. Thank You for bringing us this excellent class of scholars and allowing them to be here with us on this day so that they can learn of Fulton-Harley for themselves and gain a first-hand experience of what our campus is all about. You make all things possible, Lord, and so in your name we pray. Amen."

As the people of the arena raised their heads and repeated a unified "Amen," Sly felt a chill. He looked out the side of his eye to see if anyone had noticed his reaction, and couldn't tell, but he was conflicted by what he had just experienced. "And now for a selection from our choir," Mr. Stokes said. The choir walked behind the seats as the arena grew even more silent. Mr. Stokes raised his hand and the choir stood up on the hidden stand. With one down stroke of his hand, it seemed like the song had both started and ended. The choir director took his seat, and there was a brief pause before the other gentleman on the stage made his way to the podium. "Good morning, my future fellow Fultonites! My name is Dr. Waldo Francis, and I'm the President of this glorious, glorious institution." He waved his hands as the whole arena exploded with cheers from current students, prospective students and parents alike. Dr. Francis continued, "For years and years, we've strived for greatness, pushing the envelope of excellence to its limits. With your class, we feel we'll turn a corner and break into a whole new stratosphere or relativity. I'm so excited to see what you'll create, discover, learn, and achieve while you stroll throughout our halls and campus. Breathe in that crisp ocean air as you triumph, not only academically, but also socially. Allow yourself to fall in love by the waterside. To the parents, I have children of my own so you can take comfort in knowing that the campus is a gated community, and your children's safety is my number one priority." As he took a second to look around the arena, every attendee was on the edge of their seat, captivated by his promises. "More than anything, I want you all to be comfortable. Welcome to our home by the sea." The entire area rang in celebration as Dr. Francis stepped away from the podium. It was as if he had lit the mic on fire. The thunderous cheers continued until the last occupant on the stage stood up and walked towards the podium. The cries died down, curious to discover who the last person was and their role on campus.

"Good morning, Essence of Excellence 5 and welcome to your future!!!!" The last lady bellowed with excitement and all the student ambassadors joined her. They were even more excited than they had been for the President. Noticing this, Sly perked up thinking who could be more influential on students than the President of the school? "My name is Alexandra King, the Director of Student Intake and Outreach. The excited, charged-up students are my proud Fulton-Harley Student Outreach Team. Give them a hand." The team cheered as the rest of the arena tried to reciprocate the energy the team had been giving all morning. "This team helped me, and the admissions office, put together this whole day so I want to make sure we show them appreciation. I want to be the last...and best to introduce you to our beautiful campus. Please take it all in and ask our students anything. They'll be honest about what they are experiencing. We have students giving your tours so that you can get a candid view from their perspectives. Don't be shy, have fun and we love that you're here. Our students will come up to a section of you all and you can follow them on your tour around the campus. Enjoy your time, and I hope you fall in love with our school as much as we all love it. Class of 2010, Essence of Excellence 5, we salute you. We welcome you with open arms, and we embrace you. Welcome." Everyone continued to cheer as the ambassadors went to their respective spots in the arenas to corral a group of skeptical teens.

Sly and his family excitedly stood and they saw a tall, slender, caramel-skinned woman approaching the section they were sitting in. He tried to stand up as straight as possible. The young woman gestured to the area and said, "Y'all gon' follow me out, then once we get down to the bottom and recollect, we'll start our tour, 'kay?" Slightly confused, because he was expecting a southern accent, Sly was more intrigued than he had been all morning. He couldn't figure out where the young lady was from. As the group made their way down the stairs, Sly, not so subtly, made his way to the front of the group. The student tour guide turned around to make sure the whole group was present and then addressed the group again. "Hello, my name is Layla. I'm a sophomore from Oakland, CA, and I'll be showing you around the campus today. If you all have any questions, please don't hesitate to ask." Sly just stood in awe as the group proceeded to follow the guide out of the building. "Alright, alright, remember we're here for school," Sly's father whispered while nudging him to keep up with their group.

As they exited the building, the sun beamed on the lush, almost too green lawn and trees. The group started up the walkway. Sly's ears perked up when his guide asked the group in what could only be her loudest voice, "So where are you guys from?" Sly started to shout an answer, but hesitated so as to hear the other responses first. "Atlanta," "Miami," "Maryland," "Virginia Beach," "LA." Sly looked around the group after hearing all the responses, realizing the great distances that some people had traveled to get there. "How about you in the back?" Layla asked, pointing to Sly. "Richmond," Sly replied, trying to be heard without yelling. "Ahhhh, another local. You could probably give this tour." Layla laughed as the group laughed along with her. Mina looked at Sly as he chuckled and shook her head as she gently tapped Sly on his side.

"Duchess is gonna be so mad at you."

"What? I didn't do anything but answer a question," Sly responded, shrugging his shoulders.

"It wasn't the answer. It was the school girl giggle afterwards." Mina shook her head, and Sly walked back up to her side, shocked at what his little sister had just said.

"I'm not out here doing anything other than enjoying this tour," Sly responded to his sister, standing up tall from his previous position.

"Mmmm Hmmm," Mina replied, giving Sly a side eye but with a grin.

"She is pretty though."

"And from California, I wonder what that's like."

The two continued their side conversation until the group came to a stop.

When Sly looked up, a gentleman was standing on a crate or box, preparing to address the group. "Can everyone hear me, ok?" he projected, as the crowd muttered back yes in varied tones.

"Good morning, my name is Xander Reginald McGill, from Baltimore, Maryland. Any DMV people out here?"

The rest of the group looked around, confused as the girl from Maryland shouted in excitement, "PG County!"

He shook his head, "Ok, ok glad to see y'all made the trip. Welcome to Fulton-Harley University everybody. Our glorious school was founded in 1863 by Christian Attucks."

"The first guy to die in the Revolutionary War?" one of the parents asked.

The group looked at each other in confusion, as Xander tried to reel them back in. "No, Christian...Christian Attucks. This was a white guy, although that's a common confusion." The group collectively understood they had misheard the tour guide. As Xander bid the group farewell, he yelled to the top of his lungs, "And if I drop dead...." And every Fulton-Harlanite, even the parents with their kids, within earshot screamed back, "Bury me in that black and red!" All who had participated laughed and pointed at each other in a collective moment. The rest of the group followed behind the tour guide, looking around trying to figure out what they missed.

When the group reached the next stop of the tour, Layla turned around to address the group. "There are sooooo many sayings that you'll hear while you're here on campus, but they are all to celebrate how much we love being a part of the Fulton-Harley family. That particular one is a little dark but it shows how deep the love is we have for our FHU." Layla continued the conversation while guiding the group throughout the campus where there were several other students on boxes. With each box, Sly grew less and less interested in the history that the school offered and started looking around the campus and at the other tour groups.

As they walked past one of the freshmen dorms, one student yelled out of their dorm room, "Don't come here, it's a scam!"

"There are some students who have their reservations about the school, yes, but that can be said about every school," Layla quickly addressed the group to steer them away from the ranting student. "Plus, he can't hate it that much. It is the second semester, after all." The whole group laughed and continued walking. Sly lagged behind and stared at the window the deranged student was yelling from. He took a couple of exaggerated steps to get back connected to the group, all the while glancing back at the dorm. As they approached a main road on the campus, Layla waved to the group across the street as she stood in the middle of the road. "So, before you ask, yes that's a cemetery. And one other thing, pedestrians do not have the right-away on campus."

"Wait, what? Why not?" the guy from Virginia Beach asked. The students from Atlanta and Miami laughed.

"Private campus, and there's a sign." As Layla finished her statement, she pointed over to the sign that was pitched right in front of the entrance to the graveyard. "Directly behind me is our Student Center and that will be the completion of our tour. There are food vendors outside, as well as other vendors inside, along with a DJ. We also have our Spring football game going on at Royal Field. I always recommend the vendors, even though we have good restaurants because they're usually really good. Did y'all have any other questions for me about anything?" As she skimmed the group for any raised hands, the young lady from Maryland asked, "What made you stay here? You're so far from where you came from, and you said you hadn't been home in like two years."

"Honestly, I can say I have a family out here. This school is so much more than a school. The connections and experiences that you have with the people on this campus will be so unique to you and your friends that you'll be bonded for life. I know that may sound deep or even a little cheesy, but I promise you that's why I love it here. That, annnnnd that ticket home is north of 500 dollars, and I ain't got it." Everybody shared one more laugh before entering the Student Center and dispersing.

As the Joneses walked further into the Student Center, Alonzo turned to the rest of the family and asked Sly, "So where do you wanna go?" Sly shrugged his shoulders and they waded through the crowd. Sly had his head on a swivel trying to take in as much of the sights and sounds as he could. As the family reached the other end of the Student Center, Ria stopped to look at some handmade jewelry by one of the students.

"I really like these earrings. How much are they?"

"They're $7 for one pair or 2 for 10."

"Ok, let me get these and suggest one other pair for me."

The student looked down for a moment at her inventory before selecting a pair of green and gold earrings. "I think these would look perfect with your skin tone."

"Why, thank you."

Sly's mom slid the young lady $10 and they continued out of the back of the Student Center. As they opened the door, they were met with the smell of fried fish. There were five different food trucks with everything ranging from Jamaican food to pizza. As Sly observed the students socializing, he still couldn't get the student that had been yelling out the dorm window out of his mind. "So what do you think?" Ria asked Sly, as she tucked her new earrings in her purse. "I like it, but I still don't want to come here. But I'm also not staying in Richmond, so I'll learn to love it."

"Staying at home is not that bad," Ria nudged Sly laughing. He turned to his mother, stone-faced, and she laughed even harder. Sly walked ahead of the group towards the stadium where the football game was being played. Before the rest of the family could catch up with him, he gazed through the cracks in the fence and heard the quarterback call out the cadence. When he turned the corner to approach the entrance of the stadium, he noticed that the coaches were on the sideline and this Spring game was just an inter-team scrimmage. Sly, going back and forth in his head, stumbled towards the gate before quickly veering away. *They're in practice. I can't go over and interrupt practice, especially not as a scholarship athlete*, Sly thought to himself. *But you'll need to make that introduction at some point to make sure that your work gets noticed*. Sly's father, who was a standout quarterback in the 70s in Richmond, placed his hand on Sly's shoulder. "You'll be here every day soon. You'll get a chance to make a proper introduction then." Sly shook his head and they headed back in the direction of the family. Ria and Mina had been distracted by all of the vendors selling different Black-inspired products, from t-shirts, art pieces, makeup, and everything else.

The four regrouped and headed towards the car. While the other three conversed, Sly continued looking around the campus, observing the people and his surroundings. In his head, he could tell that his dad wasn't impressed after previously touring some of the power five schools. His mother, although initially expressed reservations about HBCUs, ironically seemed super excited about all aspects. Sly's sister could take it or leave it, since she was years off from college. She did make comments about all the food smelling good and the shrimp she had gotten were good. Most prominently, Sly couldn't un-see the guy yelling out the window not to come to Fulton-Harley. On the other hand, he also reflected on the feeling that he got when he saw the high stepping band, the cheerleaders, and dance line walking down the main street of campus. He also recalled seeing a couple, and what appeared to be groups of current students, casually pointing and laughing at not only his group, but also other groups, touring the campus. Not at anyone specifically, but more so at the idea of the day that was happening, and he didn't quite understand that. After contemplating all those things silently, his mother turned to him and asked, "So Sly, what did you think?" Sly paused for a moment, breaking his own mental sidebar, and snapped back into his family's conversation. "Looks like I'm coming to Fulton-Harley next year!"

*Scene 6*
# The Check-In

After Spring Break, Sly returned to his senior classes, only for them to fly by. He graduated in just a short month and a half later. The Joneses started summer vacation the same as they did every summer – in the house. Sly was the only exception as he was usually out of the house training for sports during the summer. This summer, he was in complete lounge mode for the first time in his life. After a long day of doing absolutely nothing, he came downstairs on a weekday evening while the family was watching the evening news.

"Look who decided to grace us with his presence this evening," Sly's mother said in a wily tone to let him know that she was not pleased with his recent behavior. "I apologize Mom. I'm just realizing though that I don't actually have to do anything right now. I can't remember when that was ever the case," Sly laughed. When he fully opened his squinted eyes, his mom was staring at him with a straight face and shaking her head.

"You actually have more to do now than you did before."

"How? I already got the grades and got in. What else do I need to be doing?" Sly looked at his mother completely baffled.

"You've done a lot while you were in high school, but now that you're headed to college, some of the background processes will require you to do some leg work."

Sly looked at his mother as she completed her sentence in sort of disbelief. "I mean, I applied to all the scholarships that everyone told me to apply to…"

"And you may have," Sly's mom rebutted. "But what scholarships have you looked up on your own? What initiative have you taken besides applying to the schools? I know high school was easy for you, but college will not be the same. You'll have to put in more of an effort in order to succeed at Fulton-Harley."

Sly, with a slight look of shock, just shook his head in agreement with his mother. "Yes, ma'am," he agreed, although in his head, he had put in enough work to get to this point. Sly looked back at his mother to ensure she had gotten everything off her chest. The family resumed their normal conversation Sly retreated upstairs, feeling somewhat defeated and overwhelmed by his mother's comments. As he reached the top of the steps and went into his room, he continued thinking about the words his mother had used, along with a conversation that he had with his football coach. The words of each exchange seemed to be themed around hard work. Sly fancied himself a hard worker, based on the compliments he had received on the field from various coaches throughout his football career. In his mind, that was the only reason he earned a starting position senior year. With all of the swirling in his head, he plopped down at the desktop in his room, spun around in his chair, and wiggled the mouse to wake up the slumbering computer. Right as the computer loaded, and he opened the browser, his father bellowed upstairs, "Dinner's ready!" Sly stared at the screen he had opened. It  had a bunch of random yearly scholarships, from a scholarship just for being left-handed, to one for wearing a duct tape outfit, to your prom that would get you money. "Ok, I'm coming," Sly yelled back. He looked at the list once more before slowly walking away to head down for dinner.

After a few weeks of filling out nothing but scholarship applications, Sly's mom had some more advice for her college-bound son. As he came downstairs one summer afternoon, Ria stopped Sly before he headed into the kitchen.

"Have you thought about getting a job this summer? I know you never had one because of football in the summer, but this would be a great opportunity to make a little extra money to take to school with you."

Sly was annoyed by her gesture, but realized his mom did have a valid point. He, indeed, didn't want to go to school broke. He looked at her and asked, "What kind of job should I try to get? I don't have any work experience or anything but school." Sly was already discouraged.

"Look for jobs that don't require any experience. They'll train you on what you'll need to be able to do. You just have to show some gumption and hard work, but that's no different than any of your sports. You didn't know how to play when you first got out there and now you've played enough to know pretty much every situation."

Sly listened to his mother's reasoning. He understood where she was coming from and nodded to agree. "But I was like five, Mom," he laughed, but suddenly stopped when he realized just how long it took him to get decent at his sports. "Yea... I'll start looking at different openings near the mall later today, and I can go from there."

"Ok Sly. Make a list of all the positions that you apply for and we can keep track and follow-up that way." Ria was more excited for her son to join the workforce than Nas, and Sly didn't waste any time letting her know.

"This sounds like homework, Ma. Do I have to do this?" Sly complained as he started to walk away from the conversation.

"You don't have to, but me and your father aren't lining your pockets when you go to that expensive school, so it would be in your best interest to be able to create some money on your own."

"How much is Fulton-Harley a year?" Sly asked since he had never looked into the numbers for Fulton-Harley.

"Let's just say you should've stayed home and went to VCU, and you'd have so much more flexibility."

"But is it really that much?" Sly asked again, slightly more concerned.

"Don't worry about it," his mother responded, "as long as your grades are good and you're working hard, it'll all work out in the end."

"Thanks Ma. Love you." Sly walked back to his mother and kissed her on the forehead before heading back up to his room to start on his job applications.

After only about a week of filling out job applications, Sly landed a position at the local skating rink as a laser tag technician. When Sly first received the offer and the training for the job, he realized that this was going to be in a completely different atmosphere than where he had spent his previous summers of high school. The staff at the skating rink were really laid back, and even the training that he had received was done by another worker who had just been hired a couple of weeks before Sly started. The job paid decent, from what Sly could gather, but it wasn't anything that he was super excited about.

Sly rolled into his job, seemingly, just to pass the time of the summer. While working, he had a couple of races with some of the hockey kids that would come up to the rink. He also had taken up a hobby of punishing bratty, unruly kids at their laser tag parties if they were bullying their guests. As the end of summer approached, Sly went to his manager, Kat, to inform her that he would be leaving for college.

"Well, we hate to see you leave, but you know you can always come back on break, and we'll have a position open for you. Where are you going to school again?"

"Fulton-Harley," Sly responded more confidently as the school year ended and the time for him to go to campus grew nearer.

"Is that like Hampden-Sydney?"

Sly laughed in his head, knowing that everyone who had made that reference previously, hadn't heard of the HBCU. "No, this school is down by the beach area, and it is a co-ed school," Sly laughed without giving too much detail about the school.

"I'm sure that you're going to do great," Kat said, as she looked in the opposite direction and signaled to another manager to go outside for a smoke break. "Let me know if you need me to do anything like a reference letter, and I'll make one for you."

"Thanks Kat, I appreciate it." They both headed towards the door, along with the other manager that Kat had signaled. They crossed the threshold and Sly headed in the direction of his car, waving goodbye to his managers and co-workers who were outside.

When he arrived home from his last day of work, of which his mother had to remind him to put in his two weeks' notice, he realized he had completely lost track of time. It was only a couple of days before Sly needed to report to campus. The summer was basically over, and Sly had worked it all away, except for a couple of pool parties that were thrown by his twin cousins, plus some time spent with his girlfriend, Deondra, who was lovingly called Duchess. The two met during his cousins' Christmas party their senior year. Duchess was also headed to an HBCU, as she was set to attend Howard that Fall. Sly had volunteered to go help his girlfriend and her mother when they traveled up to DC on her move-in date. He knew that it would be very similar to his experience that would happen later in the week, but Sly had never been to the historic Howard University.

Once they arrived on the campus, Sly wasn't sure what to expect. The traffic was heavy, but there were so many people moving around on the streets and right past the cars that were waiting for the lights to change. Duchess and Sly both looked out the window, as if they had been transported to another world. Once they arrived at Duchess' dorm, Sly saw a bunch of women outside in red who appeared to be coordinating this large moving effort. As they parked, he noticed that they were wearing the same symbols that Mrs. Kinsley had in her office. Sly also recognized the symbols from his mother's best friend when she would visit. He had no clue what it was but they seemed like a real team. Duchess, on the other hand, knew exactly who the women were. "These women are the distinguished, devastating, divine women of Delta Sigma Theta." Sly looked at Duchess, slightly confused, as she stared at the group. "So is it like a club?" Sly asked, trying to make better sense of what he was witnessing. "No, it's a sorority," Duchess answered, short and quick, giving Sly a side eye, as if he had just embarrassed her. As the two went around to the back of the car to start unpacking, Sly asked rather loudly over the city noise, "Oh, so are you going to join them?"  As he asked the question, a couple of them stopped and turned as Duchess then turned towards him with a death stare. Completely clueless, Sly looked at Duchess, then to the women of the group, who were still staring in their direction, and then back at Duchess. No one was speaking. About 20 seconds after Sly asked the question, things appeared to go back to normal. "Uhhhh, what just happened?" he asked Duchess, even more confused than before. "As a freshman, you can't pledge anything. So it's best not to express interest until you're ready for the process. You don't know that? Don't you go to Fulton-Harley next week?"

"Yea…" Sly responded, not so confidently, as he was slowly learning that there were nuances to college life that he hadn't seen in any of his movies. Sly began to unload the car, taking the heaviest stuff first. He asked Ms. Dawkins for Duchess' room number so he could begin making his way. A few of the ladies in red came over to the car and asked Sly what room they were going to. Sly simply pointed the ladies to the direction of Duchess and her mother, because he already felt he was in hot water and didn't want to upset Duchess before leaving her campus. "Room 334, ladies," Ms. Dawkins called out to the group ready to assist with moving Duchess in. Each one of the ladies grabbed what was left in the car and marched up to the room, allowing Sly, Duchess and Ms. Dawkins to just follow their lead. With a single trip, and about 13 people, they pulled everything out of the car at one time and Ms. Dawkins went back downstairs to move the car.

"Welcome to Howard. Where are you guys from?" one of the ladies in red asked.

Sly looked at Duchess and waited for her to respond. When he turned to her, however, she appeared to be trying to figure out a riddle, like she didn't trust the girl's line of questioning. To save another awkward moment, Sly quickly responded, "We're from Richmond."

"Oh ok, so not too far away. And are you going to Howard too?" Sly's eyes got big. Duchess' eyes went from the girl asking the questions to Sly. Even though he hadn't turned his head, he felt Duchess' glare searing into the side of his face.

"Nope, I move into Fulton-Harley next week," Sly answered quickly, thinking he may have just dodged a bullet.

"Ohhhhhh, you're bound to be a Fulton-Harley man? Ok ladies!" As the group of women in red celebrated Sly's proclamation, he felt even more awkward standing beside Duchess. When he finally looked at her, she appeared to be smiling. He had seen that smile before and he knew that there was nothing positive behind it. "Make sure you hold on to him, sis," one of the ladies in red said, as the group made their way out of the room. Sly and Duchess waved bye, and Sly slowly turned to Duchess. Her smile left as soon as the last lady in red was no longer in the room.

"Oh so you think you cute, huh?"

"What did I do?" Sly asked, confused.

"Bound to be a Fulton-Harley man, huh? Don't let them sorority girls get you hurt out here."

Duchess stepped back and looked him up and down. Before she could say anything else, Sly picked her up, placed her on her elevated bed, and stood in between her legs. They both laughed for a moment, before Duchess eased up. She looked Sly in his eyes and grabbed his hands. "I'm serious, Sly. Your campus is going to look a lot like this. I'm trusting you."

"I know, I know, and I got you. You know this, right?" Sly said, looking directly back into her eyes.

"I don't know Sly. You like the attention."

Sly took a step back, still holding Duchess' hands, but no longer in a close embrace. "I'll speak to anybody who speaks to me, yes, but I'm not going to be talking to anybody at FHU. I'll just be waiting to see you again."

Duchess looked down, shaking her head. Sly picked her chin up, only to see tears rolling down her cheeks. He wiped them away and wrapped his arms around Duchess. He rocked her slowly and whispered in her ear, "Hey, hey, don't cry. You have nothing to worry about. I'm going to school and I'm coming home. Mind you, I didn't, and still don't want to go to Fulton-Harley. We're going to be fine, okay?"

She looked at him and smiled as they shared that moment of reassurance. As the two sat intertwined, Ms. Dawkins re-entered the room. "Mmmmm Mmmmmm, no sir and no ma'am. The dorm director said that there must be three feet on the floor at all times." Sly and Duchess looked at one another confused. "Three?" Duchess asked. "Why three?" Ms. Dawkins looked at her daughter, then looked at Sly, and then back to her daughter. "I know Sly is a good kid, but I also know he's a teenage boy." Sly didn't know if he could blush or not, but if he could, he was pretty sure he was doing it at that moment. Duchess looked confused at what her mother was alluding to. "So I know both of you know why there has to be three feet on the ground at all times. And at the moment, I only see two, so uhhh, yeah let's get to fixing that. How 'bout it?" Ms. Dawkins exclaimed, staring at her daughter without blinking. Sly moved towards the front of the room, and Duchess hopped down and proceeded to stand next to Sly, the two holding hands. "Ok, you got everything up here? You good and ready?" Ms. Dawkins asked, as she glanced around the room one more time to make sure that everything she deemed essential was in the room.

"I guess," Duchess, who had been so excited to come to Howard was suddenly hesitant, said as she looked up at Sly. The two stared at each other for a moment before Ms. Dawkins interrupted.

"Ok baby, we're going to get on the road before it gets too late. Don't want to have to drive in the dark if I don't have to."

Duchess nodded and seemed sad to see the people closest to her leave. As all three of them walked down to the car, Sly and Duchess walked hand in hand the whole way. As they approached the car, Sly let go of her hand, and Duchess and Ms. Dawkins shared their final hug before leaving, "Ok, my princess." Ms. Dawkins, who had been pretty stoic throughout the move in process, had a couple of tears welling in her eyes as she held her daughter. "You're going to do great things here and be amazing. Just work hard like you always do."

"I will, I promise," Duchess responded. Now they both were on the verge of tears. As they released one another, Duchess walked back to Sly for him to wrap his arms around her and kiss her gently on her forehead.

"I love you Sly."

"I love you too, Duchess."

The two kissed, then Sly kissed her forehead once more before getting in the car. As Ms. Dawkins and Sly drove off, waving to Duchess, Ms. Dawkins turned to Sly while they were at a stop light.

"When do you head down to Fulton-Harley, Sly?"

"This coming Monday," Sly responded with some excitement, since this had been the only time he had been out of Richmond the whole summer.

"You make sure you keep your head on straight when you go, ok? Make sure you always remember why you're at SCHOOL, ok?"

"Yes ma'am," Sly responded, receiving his girlfriend's mom's message loud and clear.

The two continued to chat a little as they made their way back down 95 towards Richmond. Once they arrived back at the Dawkins' residence, Sly hugged Ms. Dawkins and let her know that he was available to help her with anything she needed while he was still in town. He then hopped in his car and drove back to his parents' house.

After waiting for what seemed like an eternity, Sunday had arrived for Sly to finally become a Fulton-Harley student. Unlike Duchess' move-in, Sly's check-in was early in the morning because it was the start of Fulton-Harley's orientation. His whole family had taken part in packing everything for his room over the weekend and had stuffed it in the car. They jammed into the car, with seats moved all the way to the front, and headed down towards the beach area. As they had experienced when visiting the campus for the first time, there was virtually no traffic until reaching the exit for the school. "Ok, this is the last time we're doing this," Alonzo declares. "There's gotta be other ways to get to this campus." Sly's dad surveyed the roads and could see the exit from the line of traffic ahead of him. The rest of the car was just waking up. Sly lifted his head off the windows with the sunlight shimmering from the river below. As traffic inched slowly towards the exit, the lanes started to split, and Alonzo kept the family in the lane going straight. "We're supposed to drive onto the campus this time, right?" Sly's father glanced at Sly, as he was waved through the light onto a two-way street. "Uhhhhhh, sure," Sly responded, completely unsure of what they should be doing. He realized then that he had known about the date to move-in but none of the real details of what would be happening. "Yes, we're going on the campus, and we need to go to the Student Center to check-in," Ria said from the back seat, giving Sly a side eye as he looked back at his mom. Sly grinned and shrugged his shoulders.

"You know that I won't be here to bail you out of things like this. You must pay closer attention to the things you need to do down here," Sly's mom pressed him as her demeanor went from lighthearted to serious without a breath.

"Yes ma'am," Sly responded, no longer smiling. He recognized the seriousness in her voice.

"I wonder if they'll be people standing outside, screaming like crazy again?" Mina threw out her question, breaking the tension.

"God, I hope not. That can't be a normal thing that people do here." Sly responded, smiling as they approached the front gate of the campus.

Alonzo rolled down the window and the security officer approached the front of the truck and wrote down the license plate number. "You folks here for the move-in?" the officer asked.

"Yes sir," Alonzo responded, while placing his hand on Sly's chest, who had leaned over to more than likely make a smart remark.

"Aight now. Welcome to Fulton-Harvey. You're gonna go straight to that second Stop sign and make a left. The Student Center will be on your left side. You'll go inside to the ballroom for registration."

"Thank you, sir," Sly exclaimed from the passenger seat. He smiled at his father as he slowly sat back. Alonzo gave Sly a glare that wiped the smirk off his face.

Once they had parked the car, there were signs situated outside of the Student Center instructing new students to go into the ballroom. As the family walked towards the building, Sly noticed that there weren't as many people checking in or moving in compared to what he had seen on his girlfriend's move-in day. When they reached the doors of the Student Center, the doors to the ballroom were open, bustling with people who were trying to get situated in their new lives away from home. Sly opened the door for the family and the muffled noise turned into a moderate barrage of chatter coming from all directions. Still, to Sly, it seemed like there weren't a lot of people arriving at the school. The group looked around at their surroundings, noticing the letters that were attached to the tables that were lining the rooms. "Looks like our table is going to be over there," Sly pointed to the table that had a piece of paper on the front of it that read "J-K". As the family made their way across the room to the table, Sly looked around at the moderate amount of people in the room. Once at the table, the lady sitting behind it looked up at Sly, and then at Mina, before doing a double-take and asking Mina, "What's your last name, honey?" Sly paused for a moment, then responded as Mina looked at the woman confused, "She's thirteen and the last name is Jones."

The lady looked at Sly only to look at his sister one more time and back to him, "Hmmm ok. Well Mr. Jones, do you have a first name?"

"Allister," Sly whispered under his breath.

The lady at the desk smirked as she sat back. "I'm sorry sweetie. You're gonna have to speak up. What did you say your first name was?"

"Allister," Sly said just below his normal voice, looking around to make sure no one else heard it.

"Awww, that's cute. Different for sure," the lady commented as she looked through the documentation for Sly's name. "Ahhhh, I've got you right here. And it looks like you already pre-selected your roommate. You'll be staying in Jackson Hall. Here's your move-in notice. You'll be able to take this to your dorm and they will provide you with your keys for your room. Did you have any questions?"

As the lady handed Sly the package, he looked around again and asked, "Why are there so few people here?" The lady looked around, apparently confused by Sly's question, before answering.

"We broke up the move-in process according to the area you were coming from. We did Richmond and the Beach area last so you all are the last ones to arrive on campus."

Sly took another look around and then shrugged.

"We got everything?" Alonzo asked.

"Yea, we got everything. Now we just need to head towards Jackson Hall and unload the car."

"Sounds like a plan to me."

Alonzo headed out of the ballroom as the rest of the family followed. They jumped back in the car and followed the signs that the University had laid out for incoming students and their families.

"Next stop, Jackson Hall!" Sly shouted while clicking in his seat belt.

# Scene 7
## Welcome to Jackson Hall

Alonzo drove to the dorm and Sly looked up at the building. From the outside, it looked just like the biggest house that he'd ever seen. Alonzo pulled onto the lawn that was directly in front of and across the street from the dorm entrance. Once parked, Sly texted Eugene before collecting the documentation that he had just been handed and a couple of light bags. As the family got out of the car and headed towards the dorm, they could see a gentleman standing right next to the dorm's entrance with a clipboard. They crossed the street and the man greeted them with his deep voice, "Good morning, good morning. How are you fine folks doing today? This was a big man, around the same size as Sly's father.

Sly, who was leading the way, responded, "Doing well, thanks. Just trying to get moved in today."

"Ahhhh, yes we've got a few openings left. Do you have the piece of paper that they provided you with in the ballroom?"

Sly handed the paper to the man. He looked at the paper then back at Sly before looking at the paper again and asking, "What do you go by?"

Sly laughed and then responded, "Most people call me Sly or Jones."

The big man rubbed his beard. "Well we already got about five Joneses in the building, so it sounds like we're rolling with Sly. My name is Mr. Parnell, but most of the guys in the dorm call me Mr. P, and I'll be your dorm director for the year." He extended his hand for what Sly perceived as a handshake before the two ultimately dapped each other up. Turning his attention to Sly's parents, "Mr. and Mrs. Jones, I want you to know that I take having the boys here as a serious responsibility. As dorm director, I've appointed my R.A.s to inform me of any issues that arise. The boys' safety and grades are the main concerns." Mr. P paused for a moment as Ria shook her head in approval. "There will be a curfew of 11 pm from Sunday to Thursday, and a 1 am curfew on Fridays and Saturdays. Missing curfew is a punishable offense and can carry a penalty of being out by 5." Mr. P continued his explanation as Ria interjected.

"I'm sorry, but what do you mean by out by 5?"

"Uhh, yes ma'am. Here at Fulton-Harley, if you're found to be in violation of the school policies, you can be expelled from the University. If it is determined that this is the case, you would have until 5 pm of that day to remove all your belongings from the campus or you could be arrested for trespassing because the campus is private property."

Sly looked at Mr. P and then back at his parents before looking back at Mr. P, "Just by missing curfew?" Sly asked, confused. "That has to make this the most strict college of all time."

Mr. P laughed. "Each case is examined by itself. So it would have to be something pretty extreme, but there are some cases where it only takes that one time and they are gone. But if you're here doing what you need to be doing, you won't have to worry about this," Mr. P said in response to Sly. Then he turned his attention back to the Jones parents. "Look, these are teenage boys, and we're here to help them become young men. We're going to allow them to grow within themselves and take their lumps, while guiding them to find their purpose on and off our campus. We got a good mix of guys from all over the country,  and everyone appears to be getting along just fine. If you take your paperwork inside, they'll get you squared away with your room key and your roommate assignment." Mr. P finished and opened the door for the Joneses, guiding them into the space where the table was set up for check-in.

Sly approached the table, his family bringing up the rear, and handed his registration paper to the residential assistant that was sitting behind the table. As the R.A. looked down at the sheet, he then opened a small case that was sitting on the table. "Your room number is going to be 406. Looks like your roommate has been here since the summer."

"Yea, we went to high school together," Sly replied. Just then, Eugene came from out of the stairwell into the lobby of the dorm. "What's going on Easy?" Sly asked as he reached out to dap up his friend.

"You know I'm cooling man. How y'all doing today?" Eugene responded as the two dapped up.

Eugene then shook Mr. Jones' hand who replied, "We're doing well today man, just trying to get your partner situated down here." As Eugene greeted the rest of the family, Sly looked down the hallways and then into the stairwell that Eugene had come out of.

"Uhhhh, where's the elevator?" Sly asked, still looking around. The front door of the dorm shut as Mr. P came towards the table and yelled, "There is no elevator here, Mr. Jones. You're a young man, and your roommate is on the football team. You all can move your belongings in here with no issue." Unbothered, he then went into his office. Sly looked at Eugene who looked back at him. "It wasn't that bad," Eugene shrugged and said under his breath to Sly.

"Plus, you wanna play football too. Think of this as your first unofficial workout on campus," Alonzo said with a chuckle. Sly gave his father the same look he was given earlier, although it didn't possess the same effect. "Ok fellas, well let's get to it. We're out here wasting time and we can't do that. Eugene, are you going to help us unload the car?" Eugene nodded in confirmation as the whole group headed back out of the dorm and to the car.

After collecting all that they could grab, Eugene led the way back to the dorm, followed by Sly, with Mina and Sly's parents bringing up the rear. They finally reached the fourth floor and Eugene made a slight left at the top of the steps before opening the door to their room. Sly walked in after him, placing all of his belongings on the floor, on the left of the room, where his bed was. Alonzo tossed Sly the keys to the truck and he and Eugene headed back to the car to grab the remainder of Sly's stuff. When they returned to the room, Sly's mother had already organized everything and made the bed. Alonzo was setting up his desk and computer and getting it connected to the internet, while Sly's sister had already opened some of his snacks.

"Dag, I couldn't even open my own snacks?" Sly asked Mina, as he placed another bag under his bed.

"I'm hungry, and this is one of those big packs. You'll be ok," Mina responded before grabbing another bag of chips and stuffing it in her book bag.

"I guess we do need to go eat some lunch. Kinda lost track of time since we got started so early. Eugene, you hungry? Figured we'd give this knucklehead one more solid meal before we head out." Alonzo said while rubbing Sly's head.

"I mean, if you all are going to twist my arm and insist, I guess I can make that work," Eugene responded jokingly.

"Before we leave, Sly, is there anything that you are forgetting or don't have?" Ria asked, looking around the room herself. Sly checked under his desk and under his bed and saw all the things that he had remembered to bring.

"I got everything I can think of. Eugene, is there anything on the list that wasn't on the list that you think we need?"

"Shower shoes," Eugene said without blinking.

"I'm sorry, what? What are shower shoes?" Sly asked Eugene, before looking back at his parents, who both shrugged their shoulders.

"Like some slides or flip flops you can wear in the shower. People that were in the shower barefoot during the summer were getting athlete's feets and stuff like that. So I went and got some shower shoes. I suggest you do the same," Eugene said with a straight face, as if this was completely normal.

"Uhhhh, ok. I guess we need flip flops for the shower," Sly said to his mother, still not understanding the logic behind the necessity.

After lunch off campus, Alonzo pulled back up in front of Jackson Hall. He parked the car and turned on the hazard lights as everyone exited the vehicle. "Alright son, you're going to be great here. You're going to enjoy it here," Ria said as she held her son's face before embracing him with a hug. "Let me know how it is," Mina said as they quickly hugged and she hopped back in the backseat. Sly approached his dad, "You know I'm gonna make the team." Alonzo nodded, "Look, don't focus on that. Focus on school and bringing back those grades. Everything else will fall into place. Promise me you'll take care of the grades." Sly smiled and said boldly, "I promise," as the two shook hands and shared a brief hug. Sly's parents joined Mina in the car and Sly stepped back on the curb with Eugene. Alonzo honked the horn as the Jones family drove away. Sly and Eugene waved them off.

"Sooo.....what do we do now?" Sly turned to Eugene genuinely lost and confused. "Wanna hoop?" Eugene responded casually, as if there was nothing else to do. "Shit, you know I'm always down to ball," Sly said. The two headed back to the dorm.

Sly opened the door and then followed Eugene inside. As they approached the steps, Eugene made a sharp right turn. Unsure of where they were going, Sly still followed along, speeding to make up the ground he had lost. Finally, he asked, "Where we…" but before Sly could get out the full question, the pair made it around a corner, and Eugene knocked on a door. There was some shuffling behind the door before they heard, "Hold up. Ahh shit, I'm coming." Shortly after the commotion settled, the door cracked open to a dark room, "What up?" the tall light-skinned guy said with an accent that Sly couldn't place. "Nigga, were you sleep? It's like 2:30 in the afternoon," Eugene asked while chuckling. "I be tired bro, don't judge me," the half-sleep guy replied, slapping the braids under his wave cap. "You trying to hoop?" Eugene asked to which the guy in the doorway responded, "Now?"

"Yes, nigga now," Eugene replied, full out laughing at this point.

"It's cool bro, just let him sleep," Sly responded, not wanting to disturb anybody.

"Oh, my bad, Kevin. This is my roommate and boy from back home, Sly."

"Word," Kevin responded as the two dapped up. "Let me wake up and change, and I'll come up to y'all room." He closed the door and Sly headed back towards the way they came only to turn and see Eugene wasn't beside him. He saw him in another stairwell.

"Look man, just follow me," yelled Eugene, still laughing at Kevin and now Sly as well. Eugene started up the steps and Sly turned and followed.

After reaching the fourth floor, Sly looked at Eugene and asked, "And we gotta do that just to go to sleep every day?"

"You get used to it quickly. It's nothing for real. You an athlete, right?"

Sly looked at his friend with a straight face then cracked a subtle smile. "Yea, something like that," he said. The two laughed as they walked past their room. Sly, after noticing they passed the middle stairwell, "Ok, now I'm following you."

"Right," Eugene replied, and he knocked on the door diagonal from theirs. The door swung open as an energetic southerner stood in the doorway, "What up, my boy?"

"Not much man. Look, this my boy Sly from back home. You trying to go hoop?" Sly reached out as Daryl slapped his hand giving a hard dap.

"What's good man, I'm Daryl. And yea, I'm game, just let me throw my shit on."

"Word, what up Cole?" Eugene threw up the peace sign to the other guy who was laying on the bed.

Cole threw it back and responded, "Not much, man. What up fellas? Headed to the courts? You know it's bout to be packed."

"Don't matter. We not losing," Eugene said with a quiet confidence.

"I second that," Sly quickly added.

Sly and Eugene returned to their room and took out their clothes and shoes that they planned on playing in. After a few moments, there was a knock at the door. While Sly was still putting on his shoes, Eugene opened the door to a massive individual. Upon first glance, Sly couldn't tell if he had scarring or tattoos. The large man came into the room, "What up bo'?" Eugene dapped up the big guy before introducing him.

"Sly, this is Mack. He's here on the football team."

"No shit. No offense," Sly responded sarcastically.

"None taken. But I made my grades. Shit, so now it's crunk," he responded hyped up by his own response.

"I'm with that." The two dapped up.

"Y'all bout to go ball?" Mack asked, looking at both their outfits. "Man, y'all lucky. If I wasn't in season, I'd come out there and show y'all something, but y'all just gon' have to wait and see. E'll tell ya. Won't ya E?" Mack nudged Eugene.

"Yea, he pretty quick for a big man with a soft touch," Eugene quipped, giving Mack his due.

"Word, looking forward to it in the Spring," Sly responded.

Simultaneously, there was a knock on the door, followed by a flurry of knocks. Eugene opened the door again, and Kevin and Daryl were standing in the doorway. Sly looked at Eugene and Mack, both of whom shrugged their shoulders.

"Y'all ready to go?" Daryl asked, already turning around to head downstairs.

"E, let me stay in here and play Madden. Come on bro," Mack asked as Sly and Eugene headed out.

Eugene handed Mack the key to the room. "Don't eat all my snacks, Mack."

"I don't need your snacks, bruh," Mack said jokingly as Eugene started to close the door. "But I can't make no promises bo'," he let out quickly before the door was completely shut.

As the four fellas made their way down to the entrance of the dorm, Sly turned to the group and asked, "So we got some hoopers in our class?"

"A few, but nothing like back home," Eugene responded as he opened the door so the rest of the group could file through.

"Don't matter for real. We not 'bout to lose. Eugene was already talking that shit so now I'm with it," Daryl said with a laugh as the four walked towards the courts, cutting between the other two male freshman dorms.

"So Sly, your boy Eugene tell you about this summer?" Kevin asked.

"I mean, y'all were just here for classes, right?" Sly asked, confused by what more Eugene failed to share with him.

"Aye, chill out," Eugene nudged Kevin, while Kevin and Daryl looked at each other and burst out laughing.

"Nah, we gotta tell him," Daryl said while trying to keep a straight face. "Ya boy was out here loving on this girl that got pissy drunk in the Wharf," Kevin said as Daryl struggled to stay upright while laughing.

Eugene made a face of slight embarrassment before he shrugged his shoulders. Sly looked at his high school friend in confusion and disappointment. "I have so many questions. Like, what's the Wharf? And Easy, was she just drunk or really pissy drunk?"

"To answer your first question, the Wharf is the apartments in front of the library when you come on campus," Eugene promptly responded before Daryl could jump in and answer the second question.

"Nigga, she was pissy drunk. Like she smelled like she pissed herself."

"She was bad though," Eugene quickly quipped, to which Daryl nodded, agreeing, while Kevin and Sly just shook their heads.

"You said, was. Is she no longer here?" Sly asked, trying to gather all the information.

"Nah, she was a scholarship student and once her parents found out what happened, they pulled her out of school themselves. Forfeited the scholarship and everything. She was from my state, I think," Kevin stated as he attempted to clean up the conversation.

"Someone should've told her to drive slow," Eugene added and the whole group laughed as they approached the basketball courts.

As they walked onto the courts, Sly counted the people on the side of the court. "Who got next?" he yelled. The guys that were sitting at the other end of the court yelled back, "You got it." But before Eugene and Sly could figure it out, there was a voice that spoke up from behind them.

"Y'all some hoes. I got next but y'all can run with me." As the group turned around, all but Sly responded to the guy's voice.

"Oh shit, Melo. I ain't even see you there," Daryl exclaimed as he dapped up the tall, lanky dude who was standing with another guy of similar build.

"Dennis, you not playing?" Kevin asked the other player standing next to Melo.

"K Skip, nah man. I tweaked my ankle in the last game. New York niggas either super nice or hack the shit out of you. There's no in between," Dennis explained before limping over to the bench to sit down for a minute.

Melo shook his head at his friend as he went to sit down. "Dude just ripped you when you was trying to get fancy on him. He probably was trying to prevent you from dunking on him. You know you wouldn't be hurt if we were playing back in the D."

Melo laughed as Dennis shook his head and threw his arms up in frustration. "They were hacking bro."

"But they still on the court, so...." Melo replied as Dennis gave him a side eye.

"Well you gon' beat them this time? You were the one blowing layups."

Both laughed as Melo commented on his play, "That shit slipped out my hand, but you right. That shit ain't even graze the rim."

Everyone laughed as Sly wandered off to find a ball to put up a couple shots while the teams were down at the other end of the court. He signaled to one of the guys sitting at the end of the court and they rolled down a ball that was under one of the other player's feet. As Sly scooped up the ball and put up a shot just inside the three point line, the shot came off the rim to the right as Melo called out, "Coming down." Sly grabbed the ball before it could hit the ground again and scampered off the court. Eugene threw his hand up while the game was going on at the end of the court, where they had all previously been standing. As the game transitioned back to the other end of the court, Sly threw the ball to Eugene, watching the game for tendencies of those on the court. Sly and Eugene's team continued to shoot around while the other game was taking place. They stepped off the court as the game came their way. When  the two teams came down, the most athletic wing playing in the game pulled up in transition and fired a three while screaming, "Gametime!" As the shot rattled in, the player that shot it yelled, "This is my backyard, bruh. Y'all not beating me out here." The athletic built hooper continued talking, "Who on next? We get 'em on then we get 'em gone." Sly and his team stepped on the court, while the player who hit the game winner and is still talking, started to check the ball with Melo. "Everybody ready? Game thirteen. Ball live," Melo yelled. He looked over both shoulders before checking the ball back to the other team. The player from the other team passed the ball in, only for it to be swung back to him at the top of the key. He jabbed right, forcing Melo out of position, and drove left straight down the lane before laying the ball up and slapping the backboard with both hands. "It's too easy," he screamed. Kevin inbounded the ball to Eugene, as the rest of the team headed down to the end of the court. Sly set a screen for Daryl, who popped out and received the ball from Eugene. He made a quick pass to Melo, who was in the corner for a three and hit nothing but the net. "Two-one, our way.  You coming off the court this time DJ?" Melo called out, as he jogged back on defense. "Aight, aight, you went and found some hoopers Melo? Or we 'bout to put you off the court again?" The athletic player yelled out as he brought the ball down.

The game was super competitive and there were several jabs of trash talking going on while the score stayed even. DJ rolled the ball to the other end of the court where Sly and his team were waiting on defense, "Y'all tired huh?" Sly asked, standing straight up, only panting a little while picking up the ball and bouncing it back.

"We've won like four games. Y'all still not nice," DJ responded as he caught the ball in stride.

"Count's eleven tight," Sly called out and looked around. DJ tossed him the ball. "Ball live! No twos, no twos!" Sly yelled as he checked the ball back and got into his defensive stance. DJ passed the ball to one of his teammates. Just then, Eugene stepped in the passing lane, grabbed the ball and headed back down the court. One of the New York players stepped in front of him, and Eugene swung the ball back up to Daryl. He made a quick pass to the other wing, where Sly received the ball and squared up against DJ in a triple threat. Melo came and set a pick, but Sly waved him back into the right corner. Sly looked down at DJ's feet. He had his left foot up. During his assessment, he heard DJ comment, "You ain't been left all game. You can't go left." DJ crouched down more, continuing his rant, until Sly looked up and smirked. Sly took two dribbles to the left before crossing over to his right. He stepped past DJ at this point and the guy guarding Melo stepped over to help. Just as the other player came into the play, Sly kicked the ball out to the corner where Melo shot the three pointer. "Game time," he yelled as the shot went in, barely moving the net.

Sly looked back at DJ with a smile, "You know us Richmond boys run the state."

"Oh hell nah, you from Richmond? Eugene this your man?" DJ asked as he dapped up Sly and the three shared a laugh.

"So that's where all y'all hoopers are? They in Richmond?" Melo asked while DJ was making his way off the court.

"Don't do that. Act like you know. Best football player and basketball player both came from the seven five. You betta act like you know."

Sly shrugged his shoulders and said, "I mean, he's not wrong," to Melo as he waited for a response from DJ. DJ stared at Melo as he pondered what he had said before concluding, while walking off the court, "Yea them niggas cold, so you right." With everybody in agreement, Daryl checked the ball for the next game to start.

# Orientation

The following morning, Sly woke up a little before 8 am to the sun beaming into their dorm room. When he fully opened his eyes, he could see that Eugene had turned and faced the wall and placed his comforter over his head. As he started to get out of the bed and gather his things to go to the bathroom, Sly whispered to Eugene, "You going to breakfast?" Eugene, never removing the cover from his head or even turning around, responded, "No, it's too early. And you don't have to whisper. It's almost 8, not 6." Eugene tossed his pillow around, never making himself visible to the rest of the room before laying back down and falling back asleep. Grabbing his toothpaste, wash cloth, and toothbrush, Sly made his way to the bathroom to get ready for the day.

After getting back from the bathroom, Sly proceeded to get dressed. He had already packed his book bag. He took a moment to pause and shook his head at his eagerness. As he sat down to tie his shoes, there was a knock at the door. Sly looked at the door and wondered who it could be. He glanced over in Eugene's direction to see if he had popped up. After not seeing any movement, Sly got up and spoke through the door, "Hello?"

"Nigga, stop being scary and open the door."

Recognizing the voice, Sly opened the door, "What up Daryl?" The two dapped up as he walked into the room.

"Eugene, get yo ass up. You not still sleep." Eugene rolled over and uncovered his eyes for just a moment.

"Get up for what? They done already gave us the whole schedule for orientation, and nothing said I had to be up at 8 am. So I'm gon' take my ass back to sleep. Y'all do what you want."

After his short rant, Eugene turned back over towards the wall, covered his head back up, and threw in a fake snore for good measure. Daryl and Sly laughed as they headed out of the room.

"Yea aight, Sleepy Brown. Catch yo ass later."

Daryl and Sly made their way down the steps and noticed there had been flyers hung all throughout the dorm with dates and times for the week. Sly slowed down to read one, "Wait, this is the orientation schedule? This shit is a whole week," Sly said, confused. He remembered talking to a couple of his football friends and he recalled their orientations were two days at the max. "Yo, why is this shit so long?"

Daryl looked at Sly with a nonchalant shrug, "Who cares? Look, there's a party on Friday."

Sly looked back at Daryl, copied the shrug he just did, and the two laughed as they walked out the front door of the dorm.

The pair traveled to the other side of the campus and arrived at the cafeteria right behind another student who towered over them. Sly and Daryl attempted to look around the lanky fellow before he turned around, "Oh, my bad y'all."

"Oh shit! What up Nino? I thought you were one of the basketball players," Daryl said as the two dapped up.

"Yea I've been getting that more and more as more people get to campus. But nah, that ain't even me anymore."

"Nah, I can dig that. After high school, I knew I wasn't playing football anymore. This is Eugene's roommate, Sly."

Daryl and Nino laughed and Nino dapped up Sly.

"They got anything good for breakfast this morning?" Daryl asked, sounding optimistic.

"The same options they served us all summer. Soooooo a waffle?" Nino replied with a bit of sarcasm.

"So wait, are the waffles not good?" Sly asked, confused.

"You ever had food at another college?" Nino asked Sly with a straight face.

Without hesitation, Sly responded, "Yes."

"Ok, well this ain't that," Nino said, cracking a smile again.

"Uhhh ok," Sly said, not looking forward to the experience as much now.

"But, it is easily the best meal they do here," Nino said, rubbing his hands together, as the three approached the serving line.

Sly paused for a moment, even more unhappy about his circumstances since he forced his hand to come here. He wanted to at least try the food before he held judgement though. When it finally reached his place in line, he glanced down at the various breakfast options. They had the typical offerings for breakfast that you would expect: pancakes, bacon, sausage, potatoes, and eggs. Sly was impressed to see that they also had corned beef hash. He always thought it was something super country that his family ate because of his father's Georgian roots. "Well, at least it looks good," Sly said confidently. Nino smirked and responded, "Looks can be deceiving. I mean, just take me for example." Sly laughed and pointed at the corn beef hash to the line cook. She scooped some onto his plate and handed it back to him as he went to the end of the line and gave his student ID to the cashier. The cashier swiped his card and handed it back to him. Sly followed in the rear as Daryl led the way for the three to find a place to sit. As the gentlemen settled into their seats, Sly said his grace silently and then proceeded to dig in. After a few bites, Sly stood up with a puzzled look and walked over to get a cup of orange juice. He returned to the table with both guys looking at him and chuckling. Sly sipped the juice and ate a few more bites before saying, "Is it just me or is it weird to be at a black school with food that has a lack of seasoning?" Both Daryl and Nino burst out laughing after Sly's comments.

"I tried to tell you."

"You right, told me not to get my hopes up too high."

Sly acknowledged Nino's wisdom while shaking his head in defeat. Sly picked over the remainder of his plate as Daryl wiped syrup from his face before asking, "Aye bro, what made you come to breakfast so early?"

Nino had his head down before realizing that no one had answered Daryl. "Oh you talking to me? I scheduled a class at eight in the morning, so I need to be able to train myself to get up. Shit, in Jersey, high school didn't even start til 8:30. Gotta make sure I don't be out here just missing class."

"Nah, I can respect that," Sly chimed in. As the three finished their food, they collected their plates and dirty napkins and headed towards the exit of the cafeteria. As each person took their time clearing their tray and putting the silverware in the correct place, Daryl asked, "What you about to do?" He dapped up Nino.

"Shit, I may go to the Student Center to get a legitimate breakfast. What about y'all?"

Daryl shrugged, while Sly responded, "I guess go back to the dorm until that freshman event they were talking about during move-in."

"Yea that's wild to me that our orientation is for the whole week. I know some people that went to other schools and theirs wasn't longer than a couple of days," Daryl chimed in and Nino nodded in acceptance of that fact, "Same."

"Oh well, maybe there is something more to it that they just haven't told us yet," Sly said after the fact, still trying to stay optimistic.

"I hope you right, but I'm not 'bout to hold my breath," Nino commented back, as they laughed while walking out of the cafeteria.

When Sly and Daryl arrived back at the room, Mack was playing Madden on Eugene's TV, while Eugene was still lying in bed. He appeared not to have moved at all since Sly left for breakfast.

"What up bo'?" Mack greeted them as they walked through the door.

"Who trying to catch this dub real quick?"

Sly shrugged and Daryl responded laughing, "You talking a lot of trash for someone who had the record they had over the summer."

"Oh, I had to learn how everybody play, but now none of y'all can beat me."

Eugene sat up in his bed, only to turn to Mack directly and say, "You won't play for the bread though...."

There was a brief silence before Mack responded, "Nahhhhh, you got it E."

After that acknowledgement, Eugene laid back down.

"But everybody else can catch this work," turning his head back towards Sly and Daryl.

"Oh, that's how you feel? That's word, some fruit snacks on it then?" Daryl responded as he grabbed the second controller.

"Aight, you're on..." Mack responded but before he could get the second part of his response out, Daryl replied with, "Bet, I got Atlanta."

"Hold up, bruh. We not even on the selection screen yet. And no one should be able to use Vick."

"You can't just be making up rules for the game man."

Mack and Daryl went back and forth. As they continued figuring out the terms of their bet, there was another knock at the door. Sly opened the door and dapped up Kevin.

"What up Kev?"

"Shit, what y'all doing?"

"Not a damn thing, in here trying to see if Daryl and Mack gon' actually play this game they bet these fruit snacks on."

"Oh y'all playing for snacks? How much?" Kevin asked intrigued.

"We playing for 2 bags, but Mack wanna add all these rules because he knows if I pick the Falcons, it's over."

"Nigga, that's not just you, that's everybody. You can't play for snacks and shit with a cheat code on your team."

As Daryl and Mack continued their argument, Eugene rose up again. He wiped the crust from his eyes and yelled, "Y'all two just don't play for snacks and then play the game you were going to play." Everyone in the room paused, confused by Eugene's wording. "Y'all niggas not playing for snacks, and damn sure not playing for money, period. Now just play the game." He covered his head and attempted to go back to sleep again.

"Nigga, what's wrong with you?" Kevin asked Eugene as he shook him awake. "Nothing, I just know that once school starts, I won't be able to just lay here so I'm taking advantage. Me and Mack already gotta go do some football shit before the freshman event." Kevin, Daryl, and Sly all looked at each other as they computed the information Eugene had divulged.

"Well shit, what time is that freshman event anyway?" Kevin asked.

"It's at one this afternoon and you gotta be blind bro. Either way you come upstairs you have to pass like four flyers that have the information on it," Daryl commented back, never breaking away from the screen.

"If it didn't say anything about food or a party, I wasn't paying attention honestly," Kevin said nonchalantly, shrugging his shoulders. The rest of the room nodded in silence, agreeing with the sentiment.

"Oh well, shit, what y'all bout to do 'til then?" Kevin asked. Sly climbed into his bed, as Daryl stood after scoring a touchdown.

"Make him the dub club coach!" Daryl yelled, looking directly at Mack as he tossed the controller on the bed.

"Hold up! Nah I won, so you gotta come up off those sticks big fella."

Daryl continued his rant as Mack handed the controller to Kevin. Sly watched for a moment until he eventually slipped back into sleep.

Sly was awakened by nudges from Eugene. "Nigga get up. We gon' be late." Disoriented, Sly looked around the room until he could spot a clock, which read quarter after noon. "Oh we got plenty of time," Sly said as he rolled back over. "No, remember you gotta get dressed up," Eugene reminded his roommate, as he pulled out the ironing board. Sly flipped back over, "Shit, shit, shit. Ok, shit," Sly repeated as he frantically hopped out of bed and began putting his outfit together. He made his final selections, motioned to the ironing board and iron, and Eugene nodded almost like a proud father. Sly placed his shirt on the board and sprayed it with starch as he glanced back at the clock. After pressing his clothes, getting dressed and brushing his hair for a moment, he was about to rush out of the door before he noticed how much time Eugene was taking to get ready for the event.

"Who you trying to impress?" Sly asked, puzzled as to why his friend was not phased about the reality that they could be late.

"Can't just go in there with our whole class looking any kind of way," Eugene replied, spraying some cologne on his wrist and wiping it across his neck.

Sly looked down at his outfit and shrugged. "With Duchess at Howard, I really don't have to worry about impressing anybody here. I'm in a perfect space," Sly said confidently.

"Yea, until one of these chicks decides that her not being here gives them a pass."

"What you mean?" Sly asked naïvely.

Eugene just shook his head, "If you don't know, I can't really explain it, but just know these girls here don't care about Duchess," he explained to his high school teammate. He could see the gears visibly turning in Sly's head. Eugene shook his head again, "Just make sure that you are paying attention bro. Things aren't always what they seem."

Sly nodded, observing the truth in what Eugene was saying.

As they left their room, they saw that the majority of the dorm was headed to Armstrong Hall. There was a small crowd at the front door of the dorm with people waiting to walk into the summer heat until they absolutely had to.

"I don't know how you southern niggas do this heat with the humidity. I'd never go outside if I lived down here," a distinct New York accent complained within the group standing by the door.

As Eugene parted the crowd, he looked over to the New Yorker and said with a laugh, "This is slight. Welcome to the south," then opened the door.

"Y'all got it. This shit for the birds."

The whole crowd laughed as Eugene and Sly walked out of the door. Before the door closed fully, they heard Mr. P yell out of his office, "The event is at one gentlemen, don't be late. I promise you, you don't want to be late." With his last announcement, there was a pouring out of the last freshmen of the dorm.

When Sly and Eugene approached Armstrong Hall, they could see the majority of the class arriving at the building at the same time. Sly also noticed that there were students standing outside of the doors as they walked in the building. Eugene pulled out his phone to text Kevin and Daryl and Sly observed the building that he only walked past during his tour. While looking like a complete tourist, Sly flinched after being tapped by Eugene as they headed up to the balcony level. As they ascended the steps, Sly looked back to see that they were closing the doors and appeared to be locking them. Confused, Sly turned back around and continued up the steps until they reached the seats.

"What up fellas? Y'all cut it kinda close, didn't you?" Daryl said quietly as the lady from the Next Class Up walked on the stage. Sly and Eugene shimmied down the row to get to the open seats dapping up Daryl, Kevin, and one last person that Eugene spoke to.

"Ay Corey, this Sly, my man from back home."

Sly dapped up the guy after sliding by to his seat. "So what could they possibly have us meeting in here for four days straight? There isn't that much to school," Sly said.

The rest of the row collectively gave a response aligned with no one knowing what exactly to expect.

Ms. King approached the microphone in a somewhat urgent matter, "Good afternoon and welcome, Essence of Excellence 5, Fulton-Harley University Class of 2010." There was a start of a celebration before Ms. King raised her hand to cut it short. "While we are all excited to have you all here, there are some ground rules that would need to be made clear in this very instance. Not obeying these rules in certain situations can have dire consequences. Do I make myself clear?" The congregation confirmed in a unified voice, "Yes ma'am." As she goes into her spiel, Eugene leaned over to Daryl and asked, "Aye, where is Link?" Sly looked around as if he knew who he was looking for. Another guy towards the other end spoke up, "He was still asleep when I left the dorm, and that was like fifteen minutes before the hour." Just as everyone turned back around wondering if the student ever made it to Armstrong Hall, there was a shout followed by laughter. "Oh shit, Lincoln's on stage," Corey shouted as he pointed, and the rest of the group laughed. Ms. King brought out a group of students that were standing behind her as she continued to speak on the acceptable practices at Fulton-Harley University. "Now, here at Fulton-Harley, we preach that time is a commodity. One that once it's spent, you can never get back. So for you to be prompt and timely is beyond key to your success on this campus. Repeat after me. To be early is to be on time…" Ms. King paused for the rest of the student body to repeat the words. "That includes you all standing behind me as well. To be early is to be on time…" She paused again allowing the whole building to repeat. "To be on time is to be late…" she paused once more before finishing with, "And to be late is unacceptable." The freshman class repeated the last of the mantra as Ms. King shook her head in approval. "Glad to hear you all picked up on that one so well. In order to further drive home the point, we like to make this a very pertinent priority of every engagement. With that being said, the students standing on stage behind me were all late to this event. Even though the flyers were hung up in all the common areas in the dorms, along with all of the buildings across campus. To help students not forget to be on time, your fellow classmates will sing one of your class songs until I say they can stop." All of the students on stage mouths dropped and their eyes just followed Ms. King off to the side of the stage. She glared back at them with a smirk and started to sing, "E of E back up in this..." The students on stage picked up with the Soulja Boy rewrite about their class unenthusiastically which led Ms. King to reply with, "I'm sorry, I can't hear you. Sing it proud."

"Look, look, he's down there doing the dance and everything," Corey nudged both Wale and Danny and Danny responded, "He gon' be tight as shit when he gets back to the room."

The whole row of fellas had a laugh at their classmate's expense before Ms. King dismissed them and allowed them to find a seat before continuing with the beginning of orientation.

When the stage cleared, and Ms. King peered into the crowd, taking a deep breath before starting, "Here at Fulton-Harley, we're family, which means we do a lot of things differently because we are different. We are held in higher esteem. We hold ourselves to a higher standard. And we expect all of you to uphold that same standard." She paused for a moment as there was a small ovation. "Our mission is to create an environment where you all feel safe to become the entrepreneurs and CEOs of tomorrow."

"Damn that shit sounded cliché. She knows she doesn't have to sell us, they already took our money," Melo chimed in from the row behind, as a few of the fellas laughed.

She continued to elaborate on her spiel, informing the class on how people should act on campus. "Gentlemen, I've seen how you all look at our women on campus. They are all queens." She paused for a moment as men and women alike responded with praise to her claim. "For this reason, no woman should be walking this campus alone once the sun starts to go down. Gentlemen, if you see a young lady walking alone, you are to ask her where she is headed and escort her the rest of the way. Is this understood?" She posed the question to the men in the congregation, and they responded with a consensus, "Yes ma'am."

"Ok, now ladies. Since we've placed you in such a high place, this needs to be maintained by you and no one else. Is that understood?"

"Yes ma'am," the ladies of E of E 5 responded.

"I'm glad to hear it. To maintain this appearance, we ask that all young ladies refrain from wearing their bonnets and head wraps outside of your dorm. Gents, this is the same for your wave caps and durags."

The whole class looked around at each other as Ms. King stood at the front of the stage looking back and forth. "I said that there will be no bonnets, head wraps, wave caps, or durags worn outside of the dorms. Do I make myself clear?"

Still disappointed, the class mustered up the weakest "yes ma'am" it could manage after her announcement. As Ms. King continued to prepare the class for their time at Fulton-Harley, from resume building and teaching students how to tie a tie at the Student Services building, to the hours of the library, Sly at some point, had slowly dozed off. Ms. King's slightly raised voice woke him like an alarm clock, "And lastly…" He quickly shifted back upright in his seat. "When attending an Armstrong event, you will be dismissed by the person on stage." Everybody in the crowd looked at each other, and Ms. King pointed into the crowd on the ground floor, "Yes?" The murmurs grew quieter as people tried to hear what the student was asking.

"I was asked, 'So if the event is over, we can't just leave?'" Ms. King said mockingly. "No ma'am, you may not just leave. These are the rules of this building and have been a part of this institution for over 75 years and you all will respect that tradition as will everyone else that comes on this campus. Is that understood?"

"Yes ma'am," the class said in unison. In a brief moment, to further drive her point home, she stood at the front of the stage before glancing around the auditorium for what seemed to be an extensive time before raising her hand with a gracious smile and announcing, "You all are dismissed. Have an amazing day." She exited stage right. The rest of the freshman class followed suit flowing out of Armstrong Hall in several different directions.

Sly, Eugene, Kevin, and Daryl came out of the building and headed back towards Jackson Hall. They caught up with Danny who was joking with Lincoln about being late.

"Nigga, how you oversleep?"

"My alarm didn't go off on my phone," Lincoln responded.

"But I woke you up before I left," Danny said laughing uncontrollably, impersonating Lincoln.

"Nigga shut..." but before he could get his last word out, Daryl called out, "Yo, Linc," also mimicking him doing the dance on stage. Everybody continued laughing as Sly and the group caught up to the other two.

"Nigga, that shit was hilarious," Kevin said. Everybody continued laughing.

"Bet yo ass won't be late again," Danny said half joking.

103

"You right though," Linc replied, not hesitating at all.

"What y'all niggas 'bout to do?" Danny asked the guys as they approached the male side of the campus.

"Shit, maybe go to the courts. What about y'all?" Sly responded as everyone looked at him.

"Nigga, it's hot as fuck and the middle of the day. You gon' be by yoself nigga," Eugene said as everyone laughed along.

"Shit, we 'bout to go through Fin room."

"Who's Fin? Or what is Fin?" Sly asked, not so quietly.

"You were right with who," Kevin responded.

Danny chimed in, "He's another one of the bros. He be cuttin' niggas hair and shit."

Sly nodded his head at the dopeness of a college side hustle. Eugene rubbed the side of his head as he headed towards Danny and Lincoln's dorm, "I could use a little touch up before this afternoon."

"What's going on this afternoon?" Sly asked again, seemingly lost to the world.

"My nigga, I need you to pay attention," Daryl said, only half joking. "There's another event this afternoon where we're assigned our big brother or big sister."

"Well, to Sly's defense, I didn't see that event until walking out of Armstrong Hall just now," Kevin added.

Sly nodded his head, still slightly confused. "What time?" he asked.

"I think it said it was at 6, but it's at the stadium," Kevin added.

"Oh so we got some time," Sly replied, not as worried about having to be late to an event.

They all followed Danny and Lincoln into their dorm, as Sly grabbed the door and held it open for his new friends. He read the dorm name that was engraved on the side of the building, "Roberts Hall".

Sly followed behind the rest of the group as Danny pushed the Up button on the elevator. Sly side-eyed the fact that his friends wanted to take the elevator before his gaze was interrupted by a smaller statured man with a large afro.

"Good afternoon, gentlemen. How was the engagement at Armstrong Hall?"

Sly stared at the man, surprised by the deep voice coming from the modestly sized man.

"All good, Mr. Gooden," Linc replied with a thumbs up.

"Sounds good, but I bet not catch you being late to another one or you gon' have two punishments to deal with. Am I crystal, Mr. Duggin?"

Lincoln replied not so confidently the second time, "Absolutely."

The rest of the group tried their hardest to hold in their laughter until they boarded the elevator.

As they reached the fourth floor of the dormitory, the elevator doors opened and the group exited and headed to the right. Eugene, leading the way, knocked on a door that was maybe three feet from the end of the hall from where Sly was standing.

"Who the fuck is it?" a high pitched voice said with a very distinct New York accent.

"Yo, Dunn open the door, it's Eugene," he replied as the others chimed in, "...and Danny," "...and Kevin."

"Nigga it's a bunch of us. Just open the door," Eugene said at the end before Dunn finally opened the door.

The group walked into an already crowded room while dapping up their host. There were guys seated on each of the gentlemen's beds and in the seats and desk in front of the window. Sly found a place to sit down amongst the group as they joined in the group discussions. As time went on, it began to feel hotter and hotter in the room. Eventually, Fin stopped cutting the guy in the seat's head and announced, "Look, it's like twenty niggas in here and some of y'all already got y'all cut. Y'all niggas gotta go. It's too damn hot."

"Why the fuck is the heat so bad down here? This humidity is terrible," Dunn chimed in.

A few people exited but when it wasn't enough to Dunn and Fin's liking, they started hand selecting more people to leave.

"Nigga, you were one of the first people here," Fin said to one as he pointed to the door.

"And nigga you lost on the sticks like an hour ago and never tried to get back on," Dunn said to another also pointing at the door.

After their evictions, they had cut the number of occupants in their room to less than half. Sly moved to a seat at the desk. As the last person got out of the chair, Eugene sat down immediately. He reached back, dapped up Fin and slid him a twenty dollar bill. He mumbled to Fin, "Go head and get me right."

"You know I got you Easy."

Sly undid his tie as he looked around at the room. Although it had basically emptied out, you could still feel the heat of every person who was in there.

"Why is it still so hot in here?" Sly asked, trying to push up the window beyond its metal limits.

"Because y'all got the AC and we got the elevator," Fin replied, never raising his eyes from Eugene's head. Everyone nodded in agreement with this truth.

"Trust and believe I'm gon' have a fan by this time next week. I'm gon' have a fan. You can bet that," Dunn said, fanning himself with one of the programs from Armstrong Hall.

"Yea, nah, I don't know how y'all do this shit. I'm over this bitch cooking," Kevin added as everyone gave a half-hearted laugh.

"Yea bruh, I'm bout to head back to Jackson. Y'all can have this heat," Daryl said and he stood up and headed towards the door. "Easy, let me know when you get back so we can get on some Madden before the event at the field."

"Yea man, I'mma see you back at the room," Sly said hesitantly before getting up, dapping up the room, and heading out behind Kevin and Daryl.

Upon re-entering Jackson Hall, Kevin dapped up Sly and Daryl before splitting off from the group. He yelled back down the hall, "Aye, one of y'all text me when y'all start playing Madden." His voice faded as he turned the corner. Daryl and Sly got to their floor, slightly out of breath. "I'm not gon' lie. I hate those steps, but I'm glad we have AC," Daryl said, as they walked through the threshold, out of the stairwell, and went their separate ways. "I'll be over there shortly," Daryl said, unlocking the door to his room. Sly walked to his door and opened it. After he made it inside, he took a moment to close his eyes and take a deep sigh. The cool air pumping from the unit above the door was refreshing. He entered their room fully and flopped down. It was the first time he had been in his room by himself. He took it all in. These were his new surroundings for the year, his new "home". After that realization, he walked over to his closet and picked out some basketball shorts and a t-shirt to put on. After changing his clothes and lying back down for a moment, he could hear keys jingling at the door before seeing Eugene and Mack come through.

"Whew, that boy fresh ain't he," Sly said as he approached Eugene and brushed off his shoulders.

"You know how I do," Eugene replied with a short pimp stroll to his desk chair. "Had to get right before we go out to the stadium."

"I ain't mad at it," Sly said, rubbing his almost bald head.

He understood the importance of a good haircut, but he also knew he didn't know anyone in the area. Before leaving Richmond, Sly had gotten a bald fade in hopes to go as long as possible without having to go get a haircut.

"Damn, he did a good job though," Sly said, inspecting Eugene's head as he and Mack started up the PlayStation.

"Yea, you know I'm particular about my shit. I sat in that hot ass room in the middle of July to watch him cut hair before I let him touch my head," Eugene said proudly.

"Is that because you let that girl you thought was cute cut your hair that one time back at Denali?" Sly said jokingly.

Mack turned slowly to face Sly with a huge smile, "Bo' tell me you got a picture of that shit."

"Nah, he wouldn't let us get a good one, but that shit was funny as hell," Sly said, trying to hold back his laughter.

"Aye, chill out, or do we gotta talk about how you being pigeon-toed caused you to miss three weeks last season?"

"Aight, aight, you got it," Sly conceded to his former teammate.

As they laughed, there was a drumming knock at the door. Mack stood up briefly to open the door before unpausing the game and continuing his barrage of smack talk. Daryl walked through, "What's good niggas? I got next." He pointed at Sly and he shook his head, declining the offer.  Mack moved his chair to the side to allow Daryl by and moved up to Eugene's bed to sit and wait for his game. Before he could hop up, there was another knock on the door. Everybody looked at Daryl, and he looked all three guys in the eyes and said, "This ain't my room."

Eugene replied, "But you were the last one in and you not sitting yet."

Daryl looked at Eugene for a moment, then turned to Sly who shrugged his shoulders, before answering the door.

"What up fellas? Shit, Eugene, I didn't know you were in Jackson Hall too."

When the door opens, Sly could see Kevin, but the voice didn't match. As the guys walked through, he could then identify the unknown as Corey, from Armstrong Hall, behind Kevin.

"Bruh, all the athletes from our class are in this dorm," Eugene responded.

"That's not true. Some of the track guys, and I think a basketball player, stays in Roberts."

"Ok, well all the football players stay in Jackson, and we play football, so…." Eugene snapped sarcastically.

"You got it Easy," Corey said, raising his hands and falling into Sly's computer seat.

"Who's got next?" Kevin asked as he popped up on Eugene's bed next to Daryl.

"I do, so I'll be who you'll be losing to," Daryl said proudly, wrapping his arm around Kevin.

"Yea right nigga, you bout to get dubbed," Kevin rebutted.

"Shit, for real for real neither one of y'all may get to play. It's already 4. Daryl might get a game, but..."

And before Eugene could get the rest of his thoughts out, Kevin responded with, "I got first when we get back in here after the stadium."

Everybody looked at him for a moment before busting out in laughter, "You got it my nig, you got it," Eugene responded to the somewhat random outburst.

After all the laughter subsided, Sly noticed Corey looking around the room. "Aye man, you ok? What are you looking for?" Corey slowed down the rolling of his eyes and head for just a moment, "Y'all don't have a clock in here?" Sly looked around the room realizing that he actually hadn't brought a clock.

"Yea we do. It's right in the middle, in the back." Eugene pointed to his night stand which had a digital clock showing the time of 4:57 p.m.

"Damn, got that little ass clock. I couldn't see that shit behind Mack."

The room started to laugh only to have Mack say, "Well maybe you should've stood up. We all see you vertically challenged."

The room exploded in more laughter while Corey defended his position. "I'll have you guys know that 5'7" is the average height for a male in America."

"That may be true, but for African-American men – you know those walking around this campus? I don't think that's the average my nig," Daryl said, while Eugene and Mack cried laughing on each other.

Kevin turned his head, trying hard not to laugh, while Sly laughed just from the shock of the jokes being thrown. As their debate carried on, there was another knock at the door. The fellas all looked at each other and Corey reached over and opened the door. There stood a smaller-framed white guy. Sly looked at the visitor, shocked, while the others looked annoyed.

"Hey fellas, the meeting at the field is in less than an hour. I'd suggest that you all make your way out to prevent being tardy."

"Ok, ok, Gary, we're wrapping up now," Kevin said calmly.

Gary nodded and bowed while closing the door.

"There are white people here?" Sly asked, confused.

"Duh nigga," Eugene responded sarcastically.

"Have you ever been somewhere where there weren't any white people? C'mon think about it," Corey added as the room laughed.

"I mean, I didn't know man. They never show that on shows and movies when it comes to this stuff," Sly said, defending his position.

"They are really hyping it bro. There are like 12 white people on the whole campus. I accidentally counted. Long story, but in short, Gary's cool," Kevin responded, summing up the racial diversity on campus for Sly.

"So y'all basically know everybody here already?" Sly asked, feeling behind before classes even began.

"I mean, we were here all summer, so most of our class and some upperclassmen, made out ok," Eugene said and everybody agreed.

"But you know us, so you'll be straight," Daryl said, reassuring Sly.

"Yea, so long as you don't say no dumb shit like you just did, or I'm cooking you," Corey quipped, and everybody laughed.

About a half hour later, the group headed over to the field. "That still trips me the fuck out," Kevin said as he walked on the far left of the group, pointing to the cemetery.

"Wanna see a dead body?" Mack asked, quoting a movie as everybody laughed.

Some of the guys from Roberts Hall were walking ahead and Daryl called out, "Man, that nigga Melo wack though," as the groups got closer.

Melo yelled back, "Funny, that's the same sound it made when my balls hit your girl in her eyes."

There was a brief pause in the group before an eruption of laughter.

"I ain't got no girl, bih," Daryl said, laughing off the joke.

"That's not what Tootie was saying after this summer," yelled Melo.

Everybody looked at Daryl, awaiting a response, while slowing down their walk.

"C'mon man, chill, chill," and everyone laughed again.

When they arrived at the stadium, there was a group of upperclassmen in the middle of the field. There were also a couple at the entrance of the stadium directing and guiding the freshmen into a particular section. Once in place, the group on the field approached the stands with a shorter, loud young woman in the front.

"Good evening, Essence of Excellence 5. I'm Kori Alexander Norren, president of the Leadership Initiative Team and of the class of Divine Destiny 7. Seniors make some noise."

As her New York shined through at the end, the students within the group exploded with excitement, the likes of which Sly hadn't seen while on the campus. After the group settled down, she continued,

"I know a good amount of you all were here during the summer, so we're going to try to break you up so you all can meet your other classmates as well." As Kori started to call out groups, she switched between letters of the alphabet, high school mascots, and random favorite sports teams, dwindling down the number of students left in the stands. Sly remained in the stands by himself before noticing that Brandon was still sitting behind him. "If you're from the state of Virginia and still over here, go with Cally," Kori called out. Sly got up and made his way down the stadium steps and heard footsteps behind him. When he reached the field, he sidestepped and paused to see Brandon, New York fitted and all, standing beside him. The two walked towards the small, bubbly girl waving to the approaching group. On the way, Sly saw Kori looking at Brandon.

"Is she looking this way?" Brandon asked.

Trying his best to maintain his cool composure, Sly barely parted his lips to respond, "Yea."

They kept walking and Brandon straightened up as they could hear Kori calling out another group.

"Yea I was about to say, I didn't think you were from Virginia," Sly said as Brandon smiled.

"Nah B, I'm from the BX, but I fuck with VA so far. But I'mma keep it a buck with you my G. You see that lil' cute chick that's 'bout to be our group leader? That's me," he said, as he moved his head back and forth to see in between the people in front of him.

Sly looked at the girl as they got closer and saw that she was probably an even five feet and cute as could be.

He turned back to Brandon, shrugged and laughed, "Whatever I can do to help man." He nudged Brandon as they approached the outskirts of the group.

"Oh my gosh!! Welcome to Fulton-Harley everyone. My name is Cally from Cali. I'm from L. A. and I'm a sophomore, Biology major. Do we have any bio majors in the group?" She paused her exhilarated rant for some much-deserved feedback. After the pause, she resumed, "No worries, what about S.T.E.M?" The group looked around in anticipation. "Oh, y'all are green, and not in a good way." As she laughed, some of the group joined in. Sly, along with a select group of remaining students, looked completely lost. Sly then looked at Brandon, who was dazed staring at Cally, just smiling or blowing kisses when she looked in his direction. Sly turned back to look at Cally only to see her winking back at Brandon. In Sly's head, he's thought, *Man, I have no idea what's going on here.*

"Ok, let me break it down for you all. Is anyone going to study Computer Science, Engineering, Physics, or Math?" Cally asked slowly.

Sly raised his hand and looked around to see that the same people who looked lost earlier also had their hands raised.

"Ok, cool, this is a great place to learn in that space and they have great internship and career connections as well. All y'all make sure you get to know your dean. They are going to be very important to you making it out of here. If you can, find another big brother or big sister in your major so that you can know what you're getting into. Lastly, I'm going to give you my number. This is to be used in emergencies only. I can take you all to Walmart, but this isn't going to be an everyday thing. There are like…" She paused for a moment to do a quick count. "There are nine of y'all, so not all the time, but I got y'all." She provided the group with her phone number adding, "You can just put me in your phone as 'Cally from Cali'." As she looked around the group to make sure everybody had it, she confirmed, "So does everybody have it now?  Go ahead and send me a text with your name in it. We're going to also go around the circle and introduce ourselves."

The group spread into a circle, back to the point where Brandon and Sly didn't have to move. Cally looked around the group, then panned back to Brandon, "You two have been in the back the whole time. Let's start with y'all."

Without any hesitation, Brandon began, "My name is Brandon Dunn, a Political Science major," he said boldly.

"And what part of Virginia are you from?" Cally asked with a cute smirk, waiting for a response.

The whole group's attention turned back and forth between the two before settling on Brandon. But right before they turned to him, Sly leaned back, and Brandon blurted out, "Richmond, Henrico, actually."

Cally looked at both Brandon and Sly with a raised eyebrow before calmly projecting, "Ok, next. What about you sir? Would you also happen to be from Henrico?" Cally asked in a joking manner while still looking between Sly and Brandon.

"Nope," Sly replied confidently. "Sly Jones, from Church Hill," he exclaimed proudly, as he looked around the group, recognizing one guy from a neighboring county of Henrico.

Cally looked hard at Sly, then around the group. The guy looked at Sly in a way, only to help Sly and Brandon out.

"Yea, I recognize him from around Richmond. You played for Denali, right?"

Knowing that was a truth they both knew and taking into account this Californian probably didn't know Richmond, Sly replied without hesitation, "Yea."

Sly nodded to his newfound homie, as Cally shook her head laughing. The rest of the group looked at each other confused.

"This is why you all gotta tell the truth. The reason I was assigned to this group was because my roommate last year was from Richmond."

Sly, Brandon, and the guy who had co-signed for them mouths dropped as the rest of the group laughed.

"So guys, I know that Denali is in Henrico County. My roommate went to Denali. So Sly, if that is your name," she said jokingly, "you probably know her. Her name is Jade. I also know that there's no way in hell he's from Henrico, or Richmond, with that heavy ass New York accent," she said about Brandon, trying to contain her laughter. Sly looked shocked. He remembered Jade from one of his classes as a junior in high school. They had been close in class. She would give him advice (to no avail) on trying to talk to girls in his class. He came out of his slight day dream to hear Cally still giggling before she asked, "So do y'all wanna try this again?"

Everybody shared a laugh before the whole group introduced (or reintroduced) themselves. After the last introduction, she pivoted her attention back to Brandon. "So, how did you end up over here?" she asked with both hands on her hips, smirking at Brandon to the point where no one in the group knew how mad she really was.

"To talk to you," Brandon said calmly and smoothly, as only a New Yorker could do. Cally had a look of shock across her face, as did the rest of the group. Sly looked at Brandon in awe.

"Well, aight den. But don't think I'm 'bout to just talk to you since you have my number. Ok Brandon?" She drew out his name and stared at him. He just smiled back and waved.

"Told you," Brandon whispered as he nudged Sly and smiled, never looking away from Cally.

"Bro, you a wild dude," Sly said laughing.

"So you all are dismissed for the evening. Make sure you're in your dorm by 11 p.m. Have a good night."

As the new group chattered amongst themselves while heading towards the exit, they heard Cally yell from behind, "And gentlemen, walk the ladies to their dorms please and thank you."

The guys threw up their hands in affirmation as they walked off the field along with the other groups that were being dismissed. After walking back from the opposite side of campus, Brandon led every conversation with and without the ladies there. As they approached Roberts Hall, the two dapped up, split and headed back into their respective dorms.

The remainder of the week was more of the same. Sly would prep for the events in Armstrong Hall hours prior to avoid being late. After checking the flyer on the way to Armstrong on Thursday, he realized that the itinerary listed the events for Friday would be announced. As he walked out of the dorm towards the only event listed for the day, he ran into Kevin who was coming from the cafeteria.

"You about to head to Armstrong Hall already? Bruh, you bout to be like 30 minutes early."

Sly hesitated before responding, "Shit, man you see them putting those people on stage. I don't want no parts of that," Sly said and they both laughed.

"What did they have good for lunch?" Sly asked with a piqued interest since his stomach was growling.

"Rotisserie chicken, rice, pizza, and fries," Kevin said in a monotone voice to express his disdain with the food options.

"Those the same things they served yesterday?"

Kevin turned to Sly and responded, "Yep, they serve those same things every day. Sunday through Saturday. The fried chicken from yesterday was the only thing we had to look forward to during the summer."

Sly grimaced at the thought of eating the same thing for days at a time. He then wondered if his parents knew this was a thing and had provided all of the variety to somehow prepare him for the lack thereof. "Damn ok, well I'm going after the event in Armstrong since there isn't a reason to rush over there."

Kevin laughed as the two dapped up and Kevin proceeded to his room. Sly headed on out of the dorm towards Armstrong Hall.

While walking towards Armstrong Hall, he took in the scenery for the first time on his own. As he passed Roberts Hall, he acknowledged a couple of fellas coming to the front of the dorm from the basketball courts. Sly continued past the dorms and opted to walk along the waterfront to the backside of Armstrong Hall. As he looked over the bay, he stopped and smiled for a moment, taking in the natural beauty of the campus before continuing his stroll. When he faced the front again, he could see a large white house. It looked completely vacant, but Sly remembered his tour guide from Next Class Up saying that the President of the University lived there. Attempting to be discreet, Sly tried to peek through the exposed windows before walking behind the privacy hedge. As he continued past the house, he glanced at his weekender to check the time. "Dag, still another fifteen minutes," Sly said aloud before looking around to make sure no one saw him talking to himself. He then walked between the women's dorm where the cafeteria was and Armstrong Hall. Some students were coming from the building, but they didn't look like they would be attending the event in Armstrong Hall. Sly assumed they were upperclassmen and turned the corner so that he could walk up the steps to get into Armstrong. Sly pulled back the door, entered, and looked around to see if he was the first person in attendance. As he walked past the double doors that lead to the ground floor seats, he saw no one. Relieved, he went up the stairs to the place he and his friends had been sitting in the previous events and looked down at the empty stage. Taking advantage of this moment of simple peace and quiet, he put his head down in his hands. Realizing he had grown too comfortable in the silence, he picked his head up and looked around to make sure he was still alone, then placed his head back in his hands again. "They said I gotta make the best of it. And I'm not going back to Richmond," he said softly while staring at the empty stage again. He glanced down at his watch again, but before he could read the time, he heard the students coming in through the bottom and all the chatter that came along with them.

Sly sat back in his seat and people started to come up to the balcony, as the bottom floor was filling up. Eugene and Kevin, along with a few others, came through the threshold from the steps, and Sly threw his hand up to signal where he was.

"Nigga, did you come straight here after I saw you?" Kevin asked, confused as to why anyone would be at the event so early.

"Basically, can't risk having to be down on that stage."

The group laughed, but just as suddenly as the laughter started, it paused when Daryl asked, "Where's Brandon and Fin?"

Everyone looked around, and they were nowhere to be seen, or in this case, heard. As the group continued to search the room, Fin appeared at the top of the steps and rushed down to the group to explain, "Yo, they almost didn't let me in. I got here at 12:59."

"So where's Brandon?" Kevin asked.

Just as he completed his sentence and sat down, Ms. King walked onto the stage as she had done the previous three days, with the students that were locked out when the clock struck 1 p.m. Fin pointed, "There he is!" with a little laugh. "I told him to come the way I went, but he ain't wanna listen," Fin continued as the rest of the group joined in the laughter. The group on stage started to sing and Brandon, who had drifted to the back of the group, was not interested in participating at all. As the group finished their song and hustled off the stage, Ms. King grabbed the microphone again reminding students, "I can see that some of you are still struggling with the first principle of Fulton-Harley. 'To be early,'" she paused to allow the class to respond, "is to be on time, and to be on time," Ms. King continued, "is to be late," the freshman class responded. Ms. King concluded with, "And being late is unacceptable. That's right. Now let's keep that in mind moving forward with the year. I want to be the first to congratulate you for unofficially completing your orientation. At 1 p.m. tomorrow, you all will have your coronation and will be properly introduced to the rest of the student body. Gentlemen, you all will need to wear a black suit with a white shirt. The tie color can be whatever you choose. Ladies, you all will need to wear a white dress with white shoes. Your accessories can be any color of your choosing. Each gentleman in here will be tasked with escorting two young ladies to the arena before the administration will give you all your grand entrance to Fulton-Harley. Afterwards, there will be a block party thrown in your honor." Ms. King paused as there was an uproar of excitement, only to interject with, "And your curfew will still be in effect tomorrow, meaning that you all will need to be back in your dorm by one in the morning. Do I make myself clear?" The freshman class responded with a murmur, "Yes ma'am." Ms. King pointed section by section to dismiss the auditorium. Sly sat back in his seat as the rest of the group talked amongst themselves about the party, waiting for Ms. King to point their way. Once she did, Sly popped up and beelined for the door, barely waiting for anyone.

"Yo Sly, you good?" Kevin asked, coming to the front of the group.

Sly never turned around, but responded jokingly, "Yea man, I'm good." Sly shrugged and gave a reassuring dap to Kevin. "Just don't do parties like that is all," Sly continued lowering his voice with Kevin.

"Well you know you don't have to go. You can always go back to the dorm, but I think this is going to be different than anything else that you've been to," Kevin reassured Sly.

"I'm not sure man. You've been to one party, you've been to them all," Sly proclaimed, and Kevin shook his head along with others who had heard Sly's comments.

"Nah brother, a FHU party is different from anything you've been to before," Daryl confirmed, wrapping his arm around Sly.

"That's literally the exact thing he just said," Sly responded, looking at Daryl but pointing at Kevin.

"He ain't wrong my boy," Daryl continued. Sly looked at Kevin as he just laughed and shrugged.

"You just gotta be receptive to it," Daryl said, hugging Sly as he stared off into space. "Because at these parties, that's the only time you're treated like a person and not a freshman." Daryl finished his thought as he smiled, still staring off into the abyss.

Sly moved Daryl's arm and looked at his dazed friend. "I guess that can be a good thing," Sly said as the group walked back towards the male side of the campus.

"Shit, fuck all that. It's still hot outside, and after the coronation, we 'bout to see what our class really working with. Tell'em pull out them sundresses and shorts," Melo exclaimed, as the rest of the fellas laughed and dapped each other up at the thought. The group split and all the guys went into their respective dorms.

As Friday's sunrise peeked through the window, Sly rolled over and pulled the cover over his head. In a rare occurrence, Eugene sprung out of bed and looked at Sly.

"Why you not up already?" Eugene asked with a big smile.

"Why are you up so early?" Sly asked, looking at the clock that read 6:34 a.m. He looked back at Eugene even more perplexed.

"It's Friday man. That's enough reason to be up. Plus I have PT this morning."

Sly just stared at Eugene as he finished getting dressed and sat down to tie his shoes. He looked back at the clock again before doing a double take between the clock and his roommate before Eugene stood up.

"What's PT?" Sly asked in a groggy voice, wiping the crust from his eyes.

"It's a workout I have to do in order for the military to pay this expensive ass tuition. Gotta get up man and get at it," Eugene pleaded to his high school friend as he walked out of the door. Sly was completely stunned that for the first time since being at Fulton-Harley, Eugene beat him out of bed and out of the room. Sly rolled around the bed a couple of times before gathering the momentum to get up.

After a sluggish morning of a trudged journey to the cafeteria, Sly returned to his room with only an hour to get ready for the coronation. When he walked through the door, he saw that Eugene had the ironing board out in the middle of the room.

"Need to press your shirt?" Eugene asked as Sly walked through the door.

"Yea," Sly responded, looking around the room to try to put together his suit.

Sly went into his closet and pulled out his only black suit, as well as a white collared shirt. He looked through the four ties his father had provided and chose the one that was black and red for the school's colors. As Eugene took his clothes off the ironing board, Sly placed his shirt on the board. Before Sly could start to press his shirt, there was a knock at the door. As Sly reached for the door, there was a yell from the other side, "Aye, I'mma need that iron bo'."

Sly opened the door and dapped up Mack as he walked in. "You can get it after me," Sly said as he started to press his shirt.

"Come on Easy. Come take this L real quick before we go become Fulton-Harley gentlemen."

Mack tossed the second controller on the bed as he turned on the PlayStation and TV. Sly finished his shirt and started to put it on when there was another knock at the door. Kevin walked in and right up to the ironing board, "Anybody using this?" Before Mack could even turn around, Kevin had placed his shirt down and started to use the iron.

"Aye bo', I got after you. Don't let nobody use the iron after you," Mack said, pointing to Kevin as he nodded to acknowledge his request. Mack and Eugene were waiting for the selection screen to come up when Mack exclaimed, "And you can't play with Vick today."

"He in the game, ain't he?" Eugene calmly responded.

"Yea, but..." Mack began his explanation.

"Well, until you beat me while I play with him, it's house rules, which means he's gon' run wild on that ass. Good luck," Eugene finished sarcastically, and selected the Falcons. As the first kick-off ensued, Kevin finished pressing his shirt, placed the iron on the board, and tapped Mack. Just then, there was another knock at the door. Sly walked towards the door as Mack began using the iron.

"Aye, can I use that after you?" Daryl asked, as he dapped up Sly walking through the door.

"Yea, you got next," Mack responded.

"Word, I'mma just play for you now then," Daryl said with a smile and picked up the controller.

"Don't lose the game bro," Mack admonished Daryl.

The NC native looked up at him and turned back to the screen before explaining, "Boy, you can't beat me on Madden. Relax, I got this."

Mack watched as Daryl forced a three and out on Eugene's first possession. Amazed, Daryl commented, "And aren't you on the football team?" Everyone in the room laughed.

Mack looked at the screen then back at Daryl, "You got lucky. I'm on the sticks, and I play offensive line bo'. Not worried about no defensive schemes. I'm only worried about pancakes," he said heartily, as he rubbed his stomach.

"Oh, we can tell," Eugene said laughing before adding, "But don't worry, Mack. Daryl can't really beat me either."

Everyone in the room laughed again and they continued to get ready.

There was another knock at the door. Everyone looked around at each other wondering who it could be since everyone was pretty much there. Finally, Eugene suggested, "It's probably Corey." Sly opened the door to see a face paler than anticipated.

"Hey, you guys. Mr. Parnell is expecting everyone downstairs within the next three minutes. We have to leave promptly at 12:30."

"Alright Gary, we'll be down shortly."

The slender fellow shuffled away from the door as he nodded his head. Sly turned to the rest of the room confused, "Who is that?"

"Nigga, are you deaf? Gary," Daryl responded, laughing as Sly gave his friend the side eye.

"I mean, who is he to us?"

"Another FHU student. Bio major, I think," Eugene added sarcastically.

"Yea, and I think he's a Florida native. A junior in classification, I believe as well," Kevin added, trying to contain his laughter.

"Ok, ok, but y'all know what I mean," Sly said laughing and taking his ribbing in stride.

"He's this floor's R.A. bro. He makes sure we all together and not doing nothing crazy. That's how he gets paid," Eugene explained to his puzzled friend. Sly, still looking around the room, heard Daryl add as he panned the other way, "And yes, he's here on minority scholarship." The whole room burst out in laughter before collecting themselves and heading downstairs to the dorm lobby. "Nah, nah, I just thought he looked a lil' old to be a freshman," Sly quickly added.

As the group made their way into the stairwell, they walked down to about the second floor where the crowd had backed up to hear Mr. Parnell address the dorm.

"Fellas in the stairwell, can y'all hear me ok?" His voice bellowed through the vertical shaft and Mack responded first and the loudest with, "Yea, speak up a lil' if you can though." Mack looked up at his fellow teammates who nodded in appreciation.

Mr. Parnell gathered himself for a moment before his voice rang throughout the halls and stairwell of Jackson Hall, "Aight, look fellas. Today, you all are officially Fulton-Harley students. Not only students, but advocates. You have a legacy to uphold and a promise to yourself and your loved ones that you'll allow this place to change you for the best. That journey starts today. Congratulations gentlemen."

The RAs at the front of the line arranged everyone in two lines and all the gentlemen of Jackson Hall made their way out of the dorm. As the group marched towards the middle of campus, they took a sharp left turn towards Roberts Hall. As the group passed the other freshman male dorms, they looped around to the basketball court, where there was the only female dorm on the male side of campus. As they walked through the narrow passage between the male and female dorms, Sly saw the sign on the right side of the door of the dorm, 'Bay Hall'. Sly remembered that he had seen women coming in and out of the dorm and never paid much attention to it. But suddenly, he could remember every time he had tripped on the court, or did something goofy. His palms became clammy and even as they walked into the air conditioned lobby of the female dorm, he could feel his underarms start to sweat just so slightly.

Eugene nudged Sly, "Aye bro, you good?" he whispered as the two waited for who they would be paired up with.

"Mmhmm," Sly responded, not trying to say too much, but also frantically frisking his body for his handkerchief before wiping his forehead and placing both hands in his pockets.

"What are you nervous about, man? Relax. You're just being a gentleman, you're not dating these girls. Relax bro, relax," Eugene said calmly.

Sly took a deep breath and nodded in appreciation of the reassurance. As the women came down, each gentleman took two women, one on each arm, and walked them out of the dorm. As the line grew shorter and shorter, Sly looked at Eugene for reassurance again before he left with his two assigned ladies. Sly stepped up and two women, both of whom were taller than him in their heels, took an arm and off they went out of the dorm.

As the three stepped in sync outside, Sly tried not to be awkward. The young lady on his right spoke first, "Hey, I'm Denise." Sly looked at her and smiled, as the other chimed in, "And I'm Trina."

"Hi, my name is Sly," he said above a slight whisper. "Are you guys roommates?" he added to the conversation, easing his shoulders.

"Yes, and God yes, please relax your shoulders. You're making me tense," Denise answered while laughing.

Sly tried to laugh off his awkwardness. "Ok, ok, where are y'all from?" he asked as they hopped the curb passing the cemetery.

"I'm from Mobile, Alabama," Trina responded with a southern accent thicker than cold grits and a sweet smile.

Sly turned his head to look at Denise, who then looked Sly in the eyes and said, "Houston, Texas. Where we do everything big," she said, as she paused dead in step and gave a slight twerk while her roommate boosted her.

"Ok, ok, I heard that," Sly responded, smiling and laughing with his new friends.

"What about you Sly? Where are you from?" Trina inquired.

"Richmond, just up the street," he said jokingly and pointed towards the highway as they passed the Student Center.

"Oh you're a local?" Denise asked, turning her nose up before laughing and adding, "My big sister said to watch out for locals."

"Hold up, ain't nothing local about a Richmond guy being in the seven five. I'm definitely not from bad news," Sly bantered, slightly offended by the accusation. "Nothing against Vick or A.I. I'm just not a beach boy," Sly added in respect to two of his favorite athletes.

"Ok, ok. As long as you not from here cuz I heard those same terrible thangs as well," Trina added.

Sly looked at her again, shaking his head to reassure her. "It's not that bad. But your accent is amazing."

"Isn't it?" Denise added as the Alabama sweetheart's cheeks turned rose.

"Not everybody like my accent y'all," Trina said humbly, as she bowed her head.

"They're stupid. That shit's dope. Feels like home when you talk, even though I don't have anybody in my family….. that I can think of…" Sly paused for a moment to think. "Nope, that sounds like you. But maybe it's because my family's from Georgia."

"I got family in Georgia too," both girls responded simultaneously before all three of them burst into laughter.

Sly opened the door for the ladies and they made their way into the arena. All three looked around as they followed their fellow classmates. They could hear the choir getting louder as they approached the actual arena floor.

"We don't have to go upstairs, do we?" Denise whispered as they went through one set of doors. "Because I don't know if my ankles can take it after that hike."

Sly and Trina tried to contain their laughter as Trina complimented her roommate. "Girl, you strutting in those thangs."

The three enjoyed a laugh as they made their way to their row. Sly released his arms, allowing Denise and Trina to walk into the row before him. As the rest of the class poured into the main floor of the arena, Sly took a second to look around. After scanning the crowd, he was able to find his parents and sister whom he waved to. Ria stood up and waved with both hands to her son. Alonzo nodded as Mina waved, both seated. Sly sat back in his seat trying to look naturally comfortable though his palms were sweating again. He squirmed to get his hands in his pockets, accidentally bumping Denise's elbow, "Hey, you good?" she quickly asked in a whisper. "Mmhmm," Sly responded with a nervous smile. Their exchange was interrupted by the ovation that Ms. King had received when she walked to the podium.

"Good morning. On this great morning we take the time to properly welcome in our Essence of Excellence 5, Fulton-Harley's Class of 2010." She stepped back from the microphone to join in applauding the freshman class. Sly looked around at the ovation and then back to his family who were all standing now. "You've made it through orientation and have only scratched the surface of the greatness you all will become here. Although you'll have your own trials and tribulations, you now have a family away from your own that will make sure that you're put in a position to win. That you're nurtured in both mind and spirit to become the best Fulton-Harlian you can become. Your administrators, professors, and fellow students will help this beautiful place become your home. No place can replace your hometown, but this can feel like a second home for you all." Ms. King stepped away from the microphone as Dr. Frances approached, and the ovation continued. As he reached the podium, gripping it on each side, he gazed into the crowd. "Welcome and congratulations Essence of Excellence 5," he said with a thunderous voice that was only matched by an eruption from the parents. "You all have proven to be diligent, intelligent, kind, and loving Fulton-Harlians. I'm personally very proud of each and every one of you and can't wait to see all of the great accomplishments that you share with our campus and the world. You all will be exposed to all different cultures here while also sharing your own. Embrace it, for it may be the only space where you're with like-minded individuals who are also striving to accomplish the same goals you are. Live in that moment and take advantage of it." Dr. Frances paused for a moment looking into the sea of freshmen, as if he could look them individually in the eyes. "Because the world outside of this campus may not be so ready and willing to work with you all. So utilize, uplift, and encourage each other to be the best, because at the end of the day, we want you all to go into the world and flourish. So that in some years, you all can come back and share the knowledge you've gained with freshmen who will be sitting in the very seat you're in. Parents, grandparents, upperclassmen, and friends of the newest class, please help me properly introduce Essence of Excellence 5." Dr. Frances finished with his powerful voice as the arena erupted into a frenzy type of cheer. Sly, along with the rest of the freshman class, looked around in awe of what they were witnessing. Sly smiled, relaxed his shoulders and wondered why he had been so nervous just a short time ago. As the ushers came down the line to dismiss the students, the students on each row stood to their feet, and Sly slid out in front of Denise and Trina before re-extending his arms. Both ladies latched on and they all followed the line of students outside.

When Sly and the ladies reached the door, he propped it open, and Trina and Denise walked through. He followed behind and held the door on the outside for a few more students before allowing other gentlemen to take over the duty. He turned back around to try and locate Denise and Trina, but could only find Trina who appeared to be talking to her parents. Sly turned back around and searched the crowd until he saw his father walking by. Sly waved down his dad as he walked over to his family. Ria gave her son a huge hug as he embraced her back.

"Hey punk," Mina said, trying not to show she missed him too much. Sly then hugged his baby sister before dapping up his father.

"How's it feel to officially be a Fulton-Harlian Buccaneer?" Alonzo asked his son with a big smile.

"I mean it's cool, I guess. I'm not playing right now so that feels weird," Sly replied with his honest thoughts.

"It won't be weird for long," his dad said reassuringly, but Sly looked at him with a side eye, before dismissing the undermining comment.

"How have you liked it so far?" Mina asked, intrigued by college life from stories their aunts would tell them.

Sly shrugged at his sister as he responded, "You know Auntie KJ and Auntie Jill were in school at a different time."

The two laughed for a moment before Sly's mother interjected, "So are you eating enough?"

Sly paused for a moment to think about the cafeteria before responding, "I mean, it's not like when I went to RMC for camp when I was small, but the food is decent," Sly said, shrugging again.

"Well, what do you like about the school so far?" Alonzo asked.

Again, Sly shrugged his shoulders, "I mean, it's just school, and it's just the freshman here so far. I don't know. There's supposed to be a party tonight. Maybe that will be interesting," Sly responded with less than zero enthusiasm.

"Well remember, you get out of something what you put in. If you want to sit in your dorm room all day every day, but you don't have a good college experience, that's on you, not the school."

Sly looked at his mom as she mimicked the shrug he had done with each answer. He smiled and laughed as he hugged his mother. "So you gonna go to the party?" she asked.

"Yeah, I guess," Sly replied reluctantly with a smile.

"Alright, sounds good. You need anything? You still have enough snacks and water in the room?" Ria asked as she held tight to her only son.

"I'm good, Ma. I'm ok y'all, and I'll make the best of it. I promise," Sly responded before letting go of his mother to hug his sister, and, lastly, to shake his father's hand.

"Aight man. We'll talk to you later," Alonzo yelled back, and Sly's family headed back into the parking lot to their car.

Sly watched his family walk away as he turned back around to find Denise and Trina again. Once he did a lap or two around the remaining crowd, he started his trek back to Jackson Hall. While making his way into the Student Center, he heard someone yelling behind him.

"Damn Jones, straighten out ya feet," Brandon yelled, as Melo and Fin just laughed.

Sly turned around laughing, "Man, I been pigeon-toed for as long as I can remember. It hurts to try to straighten my feet," Sly responded, trying to awkwardly walk by the group with both feet straight. Fin and Brandon laughed to the point they had to stop walking.

Then Melo walked up to Sly nodding his head, "I get it man. I'm slew footed like shit, and that shit hurts my knees if I try to walk any other way. Gotta own that walk though. Pimp it out." Melo went on showing his patented pimp stroll from Detroit.

"Nigga, don't do that," Fin advised Sly, while in the middle of laughter. All of them laughed together going past the graveyard.

"Nigga, if you gon' pull a walk like that, you might as well bury your chances at some pussy over there," Brandon said, pointing to the burial site.

They all laughed even harder. Then all of a sudden Melo straightened his face and said, "But you niggas don't have no hoes tho..."

Everyone paused for a moment. Sly looked back and forth between the NY and Detroit natives, not sure what was going to happen.

"Nigga, you's a lie," Brandon responded and the group broke out into even more laughter.

"You right, you right." They all laughed. Soon, they approached Jackson Hall and Sly dapped everybody up before heading up to his room.

When Sly reached his room, he placed his key in the door to only have someone open it from the inside. "Took you long enough to get back," Eugene said as he looked up for a moment from the game he and Strong were playing. Sly paused for a moment to notice that Mack and Eugene were already back in their basketball shorts and t-shirts.

"How did y'all get back so fast?" Sly asked, puzzled.

"The girls I escorted over, both of their families were there, so I just headed back," Eugene responded nonchalantly.

"Oh, I just didn't go," Mack said after E's response.

Sly and Eugene both looked at Mack as if he had three heads.

"Uhhh, how did you manage to do that?" Sly asked, truly curious.

"It's Friday man, walk through day, the day before game day. They weren't going to force us to do something that wasn't absolutely necessary the day before the game."

Amazed at the perks that the football players were receiving, Sly reminisced back to high school before reminding himself that it's the same thing. Sly rummaged through his drawers and picked out a pair of shorts. There was a knock at the door, and without pausing the game Eugene yelled, "It's open."

Kevin came through the door and swung it closed only for it to be caught by Daryl, "Damn nigga, you ain't see me?" he asked sarcastically as he looked behind him to see Corey coming in the room as well, so as to not do the same to him.

Kevin looked at Daryl with a confused face, shrugged and exclaimed, "Obviously not. Otherwise, I would've left it open."

"Ohhhhh, you gon' take that bo'?" Mack said, pausing the game to hype up the situation.

"He only hyped it because he getting cooked on these sticks," Eugene said, taking a jab at Mack and trying to diffuse the situation all at once.

Everybody looked at the score on the screen. "Damn Mack, and you playing with the Panthers losing like that. Disrespectful," Daryl said, looking at the screen and then at Mack shaking his head.

"Man shut up, I've beat him before. We were just using random teams."

"I was about to ask why is Eugene playing with the Dolphins?" Sly chimed in, only to have Eugene look over at the group and shrug.

"I got next," Daryl quickly claimed.

"And I got after him," Corey said quickly.

"Well now that that's settled, what's the deal with this party? It starts at eight?" Daryl surveyed the group before adding, "Even the parties during the summer started at nine."

Sly looked around trying to gauge the reactions, having nothing else to go off of.

"I don't know, but I know the rest of the student body is back for the most part, so the shit should be jumpin' for real," Mack responded.

"How you know that?" Corey asked.

"My big brothers on the football team keep me in the loop. Not much that happens on our campus without the football players being aware of it. Just the way it is," Mack said as nonchalantly as possible.

"So what's that mean?" Sly asked, lost to what was actually being discussed.

"Means that it's gonna be a real college party, not just girls our age," Kevin said with a bit of eagerness.

"Easy there, young fella," Corey joked and they all laughed.

"Bruh, I went to an all-boys high school. I don't think you understand how big this is for me," Kevin responded enthusiastically. All the guys laughed some more.

"Well, you'll have your pick tonight," Mack said confidently to Kevin.

"Skip, weren't you messing with that girl during the summer though?" Eugene asked and everyone's attention went to Kevin.

"Yea, but she ended up leaving after the Bridge. I still talk to her on Facebook though."

"Oh, so it's open season huh?" Daryl said with a devious grin.

Kevin returned the gesture with a sinister smile of his own while replying in a deep voice, "Yessss. Yessss." The room broke out in laughter as Kevin drove the point home while tapping his fingertips together. The laughter became even more hysterical.

As the laughter died down and they all began to watch the game again, Daryl said in a much lower volume, "Aye Mack, your boys could get us something to drink?"

Eugene paused the game and looked at Mack, as did the rest of the room. "What you trying to get?" Mack asked, looking at Eugene and pointing at the screen for him to unpause the game.

"Shit anything for real, but Henny if you can get it," Daryl replied, excited to not just be shot down.

"Word. After this game I'll hit my boy and see if I can get you right."

"That's a bet, good looking my G," Daryl responded then added, "Shit it's 'bout to be a hell of a night fellas. Hope y'all ready."

Just as he hopped up, Eugene pointed to the screen, "And......that's a dub. Next!"

"Perfect timing, now we can all do what we're supposed to be doing. Eugene can lose to me and Mack can get the alcohol, and who said things don't always work out the way they're supposed to," Daryl exclaimed as he grabbed the controller from Mack before it was placed in the chair and took his seat.

Mack chucked the deuces but before heading out the room pointed at Daryl and said, "And answer your phone and bring a backpack. You'll more than likely have to come get it."

"You sounding real confident today for someone who has never, and I repeat, never beaten me with their hometown team," Eugene said confidently.

"Least I got a hometown team. Sorry ass Richmond," Daryl cracked back.

"I'm a Falcons fan, and they can't beat the Falcons," Eugene said proudly.

"Nigga you a Vick fan. You ain't fooling nobody. Y'all Virginia niggas swear by Vick and A.I. on everything," Daryl said, trying to discount Eugene's fandom.

"You got anybody from your state better in those respective sports?" Sly chimed in.

"Nigga we got Jordan," Daryl replied with the cockiest response.

"I thought Jordan was from New York," Corey quipped.

"Yea I thought so too," Sly said, nodding along with Corey.

"And we know you ain't got nothing close to Vick so...." said Eugene, trying to end the argument and prove his point.

"My nigga Julius Peppers? Julius Peppers isn't as good a player as Michael Vick?" Daryl looked around the room as the group all shook their heads trying not to burst into laughter.

"Nigga, are you serious right now?" Eugene asked, taken aback, as the whole room exploded.

"Bruh, y'all gon' play the game or what?" Corey asked and took Daryl's spot on Eugene's bed.

"I get riding for your state, but at some point man, you start looking like a Cowboys fan," Eugene said while side-eyeing Sly.

"Ayyyyyyy, friendly fire nigga," Sly replied, throwing his hands up.

They all laughed as Eugene tapped his chest, "My bad, Jones, my bad."

After a few hours and rounds of games, Sly looked out the window to see the sun almost completely hidden behind the architecture of the building that sat across from the dorm. The group could hear the volume and number of voices increasing every half hour or so outside the hallway in the door.

"Aye, what time is it?"

The group looked around for the clock and then Corey announced, "It's 7."

"Shit, aight. Well I guess we'll finish this last game and then get ready," Kevin said as he selected a play.

"Nigga is it gon' take you a whole hour to get ready?" Sly asked, confused.

"It might. Gotta make sure the fit right and everything," Kevin said, as he and Daryl dapped each other up.

"True," adds Corey.

Sly shrugged, chalking it up to different approaches.

"And this nigga Mack still hasn't called me yet," Daryl shouted.

He placed his phone on top of the Playstation and selected his play. Once the cadence of the quarterback started, Daryl's phone lit up and vibrated on the console.

"Shit, that's him now. Here," Daryl stood up and handed the controller to Corey before stepping over the cords and heading towards the door.

"Aight y'all. I'll see y'all in a little bit," Daryl yelled before quickly exiting the room.

As the game wound down, Kevin and Corey dapped up Eugene and Sly and headed out.

"So...what's this party gonna be like man?" Sly asked after hearing the door close.

"It'll be cool. They had something like it during the summer, but like they were saying earlier it was just the people here for the Bridge. So this one should be kinda crazy."

Sly looked at his friend with a bit of concern.

"Look, it's gonna be cool. Just stick by me and you'll be fine," Eugene said, reassuring Sly while nodding.

"So what do you wear? Because it's hot. I was just gonna wear basketball shorts and a t-shirt," Sly asked, thinking his selection was a solid one.

"I mean, you can wear that. But you could also get dressed too," Eugene said, hinting at the latter and nodding at the closet behind Sly's desk.

Sly slowly approached his collection of clothes, shuffling through them as if something would magically appear that he thought would make him stand out. After what felt like an eternity, he shrugged, pulled out some cargo shorts and a short sleeved collared shirt. He threw it on his bed as he tried to find his shoes.

"Ok, see that's what I'm talking about. But you gon' press that shirt though, right?" Eugene asked, hopeful. Sly laughed under his breath as he nodded.

"You got cologne?" Eugene inquired.

"Yea, but I never really wear the stuff. My dad gets me some every year for Christmas, and I got it here, but that's not really me."

Eugene shrugged then added, "When we got here in the summer, the upperclassmen that spoke to us said that all men should have at least one cologne that they can wear for events."

He opened the drawer on his nightstand to showcase his collection. Sly then pulled out a small leather shower bag, opened it, and revealed all that had been gifted to him. The two continued the conversation before settling on sharing the collection for the year and what to wear for the night.

Sly was putting his shoes on when there was a knock at the door.

"Aye, open the door bruh."

Before Sly could manage to get up with his untied shoes, Eugene beat him to it, still buttoning his shirt. He turned the doorknob, and Daryl busted in the door, "My nigga!!! My nigga, have you had an Incredible Hulk before?" he asked, frantically, glaring at his dormmates.

Sly shook his head cautiously, thinking that he knew who the Incredible Hulk was, but wasn't sure what having an Incredible Hulk was. He looked at Eugene, who cooly replied, "Yea, with the Henny and the Hypnotiq. So…..that's what you got?" Daryl and Sly looked at Eugene with surprise. He shrugged, adding, "Y'all know I was hanging around those same football players, right?" Sly nodded, forgetting that Eugene had mentioned that he was going to walk on during the summer while he was Fulton-Harley.

"Ohhhh, that's where you would go randomly," Daryl asked with disbelief, and Eugene replied, "I would leave at the same time Mack would leave. Where did you think I was going?" Eugene asked back confused.

Daryl simply replied with a shoulder shrug, "HmmmMm."

They all laughed and the rest of the group began to pour back into the room. By the time Corey got to the room, the water bottle he had gotten from Mack was almost empty. Corey looked at the bottle and saw there was maybe a quarter left, "Aye, let me get a swig of that."

"Aye bruh, keep your voice down," Daryl replied, reaching for the bottle. Kevin passed it across to Corey who was in front of the door.

"Aye, where's Mack?" Eugene asked, as if he was the chaperone of the group.

"He's still with the other football players. I think he's gonna go from there. Don't matter now anyway. That shit dead, right Corey?" Daryl said, pointing at Corey as he flung the empty water bottle into the wastebasket.

"Well shit, y'all ready to roll?" Sly asked, and the group headed out the door.

On the walk over to the event, the guys heard the DJ already playing. They also saw the groups of guys and females pouring out of the residential side of the campus. As they talked amongst themselves of their individual goals for the night, Sly slowed down just enough not to draw notice to the palms of his hands beginning to moist. He put his hands in his pockets and tried to continue in the conversation.

"So, what you doing tonight Sly?" Kevin asked.

Sly answered, "Shit man, I'm just trying to stay out the way. I got a girl at Howard so I'm not doing nothing."

"My nigga, why?" Corey asked with genuine confusion, as Daryl nodded and added, "Ummmm, yea that's dumb. Nothing against her, I'm sure she's a lovely young lady. But after being here for the summer, you, my boy, have set yourself up for failure. You're about to walk into a party with some of the most beautiful black women in the world. All I can say to you, my friend, is good luck and Godspeed."

The group burst out laughing hysterically as they passed the Natural Sciences building. "Damn, that nigga said setup for failure. That's SUFF!" Kevin added, coining the term, as the rest of the group continued laughing. Sly laughed along, although becoming exponentially more nervous after Daryl's comments.

"Sly, did you drink?" Eugene asked, looking at his friend.

"No, why?" Sly responded nervously.

"Because you starting to sweat, man," Eugene said, a little less calm than normal.

Sly pulled his hand towel from his back pocket and wiped his head before draping it over his head.

"I told you it was hot," Sly replied.

"Y'all Virginia niggas stay with a hand towel," Kevin said laughing.

Sly responded quickly and sharply, "Nigga, it's hot."

All of them burst out laughing again just before reaching the Student Center.

As they approached the party, the group broke apart and went their separate ways to  speak with different people. Sly followed Eugene deeper into the party. He looked around and saw a flood of people doing a mix of everything. There were students that were on campus and were just passing through the party to see a few friends. He saw students doing dances he had only seen in music videos. It was also the first time Sly saw Greek organizations perform strolls, which were organized types of line dances, from what he could tell. He couldn't help but smile at the sight.  What he had seen during the Next Class Up was true, and it was a place where the students loved to be. As they made their way through the crowd, Eugene introduced Sly to football players, upperclassmen, and different women. After Eugene and Sly made their rounds, Eugene pointed to a pillar. "We gon' go post up over there." Sly followed his friend and they stood next to the post as they looked over the party. Sly looked down for a moment, and when he looked back up, he noticed that Eugene had walked off with a girl. After watching Eugene disappear into the crowd, he pondered how long he wanted to stay and what he should do at this point. Looking back at the ground momentarily, he picked his head back up and started walking back towards the dorms. As he passed the party's outskirts with newcomers and others who had

had enough, he looked back, disappointed that he couldn't find more enjoyment out of his first college party.

As he walked back, passing the Natural Sciences Building and the cemetery, Sly looked up into the starlit sky pointing out the Little Dipper, Big Dipper, and Orion's Belt in his head. When he looked back down from the sky, he saw a girl walking along ahead of him. He sped up to catch up to her and asked, "Hey, can I walk you back?" The young lady smiled at Sly and cheekily replied, "I think that you have to. That's pretty much the rules." The two laughed for a second before Sly replied, "Touché, touché. I'm Sly." The tall, mahogany-skinned, athletic girl responded, "I'm Jodi." The two shook hands and continued past an old military building that was serving as the campus' ROTC headquarters.

"So, which dorm do you stay in? Or I mean, which way are we going?" Sly stumbled over his words, trying not to appear one way or another.

"Oh, I stay in Tillson Hall," Jodi said laughing before adding, "But I was headed to the waterfront."

"Oh, so should I not go then?" Sly asked, suggesting that maybe she wanted to be alone.

"You really didn't pay attention in orientation, did you?" she replied laughing before continuing, "It's dark which means I should be escorted around campus. You don't have to. I won't tell but you should definitely know that going forward," she politely reminded her fellow Fultonite.

"You're right, you're right. I'm with you," Sly responded as the two made their way past the church before approaching a bench facing the water way bordering the university.

As the two sat down, Jodi started a conversation, "So what brought you here?"

Sly, not expecting the question, replied hesitantly, "Well, football didn't pan out like I thought it would...and I had only applied to one other school...and I didn't get in there...and I wasn't staying at home to go to community college, so I'm here. What about you?"

"Kinda the same deal. I only applied for one other school, but I wasn't staying home to go to Rutgers, and this was my bail out," Jodi responded while leaning back on the bench.

"Oh, so you're from Jersey?" Sly asked, piecing together her origins from her quick story.

"Yea, you football guys love Rutgers," she said jokingly and Sly replied, "I mean, they cool, but love is a strong word."

The two laughed some more before Sly asked, "You like it so far?"

"I can kinda take it or leave it, but at this point, I'm here, so I can't do much more than take it."

The two laughed again.

"I don't know. Honestly, it's gonna be weird being in school and not playing football. Also, I went to school with the same people for most of my life, and I think I suck at making new friends," Sly responded, shocked at his own evaluation of himself.

"Yea I feel that, but you made a friend tonight, so it's not all a wash."

The two laughed again.

"I appreciate that. I hope it's not all parties though. I really hope they have other stuff. I suck at parties," Sly said, looking at Jodi before pointing over his shoulder back at the Student Center.

"Yea, you've been to one party, you've been to them all. Shit's lame after a while," Jodi said flatly, as they both stared out into the water.

After a moment, the couple heard the DJ make an announcement about the freshman curfew. "So should we go ahead and head your way?" Sly asked as he pointed towards the women's side of campus. Jodi nodded as the two left the waterfront and continued their conversation to the door of Tillson Hall.

"It was really nice to meet you and talk with you, Sly Jones," Jodi turned and said to Sly.

"The pleasure was all mine, Ms. Jodi Valentine," he said and extended his hand to shake hers.

Jodi shook his hand briefly before extending her arms for a hug. Sly embraced the young woman for a moment, before opening the door for her and a few of her dormmates. As he casually walked away from the door, he heard the Tillson dorm director holler out of her window to the couples who were sitting in front of the dorm, "Gentlemen, it is 12:57. You have approximately three minutes to get into your respective dorms before you are out by 5." It was at that moment that Sly, along with the rest of the gentlemen, went from a standstill or casual stroll to a full out sprint to the other side of the campus.

As Sly passed through the threshold of the dorm, he noticed that the director had a bright red digital clock for all the incoming freshmen who were trying to make curfew. Sly looked around the lobby as there were others who had just made it there before him and were still trying to catch their breath.

"I'm gon' give a couple extra minutes to the big boys, but that's it," Mr. P said, looking out the door at a couple of others who weren't willing to run. "Once I shut this door though, that's it," Mr. P yelled out as the clock glared 12:59. The last few started their trot to come in. Sly headed upstairs to avoid all the congestion in the lobby. When he approached the room, he could hear even more voices than usual inside. He walked in to see the regular suspects

145

impersonating different people they had encountered at the party. Sly went in and sat on his bed as Daryl told a story about an upperclass girl who had said she would sign him out the following weekend, and how Kevin had two girls get mad at him because they both liked him, but he didn't know it about either one. Sly laid back and laughed at the stories being told, until Eugene looked at Sly's relaxed smile and asked, "Uh uh, you? Where the hell did you go? What did you get into?" Eugene asked, as everyone turned and looked at Sly.

"Well, I was standing there with you 'til you walked off. Then I walked to the waterfront and walked this girl back to her dorm. That's why I am just now getting back," Sly replied calmly.

"Nah," continued Eugene, "because I left and came back to where we were standing, and you were gone. That was at like 11:30. You went and sat on the waterfront with a chick for an hour and a half?"

"Oooooooo," Corey added, as everyone in the room hyped the situation.

Calmly, Sly reminded his friends, "If we see a woman walking alone at night, we're supposed to escort her to her destination and make sure she's safe. That's what I did."

"You right," Kevin nodded in agreement before adding, "but you went on a whole ass date my nigga." The room erupted in laughter, as Sly's face went from confused to worried to embarrassed.

## Scene 9
# First Day of School

Sly walked back in the room around 1 pm. Eugene was sitting on his bed with the controller in his hand. "How was your first day?" he asked, never looking away from the game. "It was school nigga. What you want me to say?" Sly said while yawning before face planting on the bed and passing out.

*Disclaimer for Dummies: It's not written anywhere that college will make you a better person, get you a higher paying job, or help you find the love of your life. College is simply a place that gives you an opportunity to do all these things while trying to grow yourself as a person. Not to say you can't do those things outside of college; just given my experience, it's not as easy and you won't have as many people to talk to who can relate to what you're going through. You must first know what works best for you though. If you weren't a huge fan of school, maybe you could focus on finding a passion instead of school. If you're not a morning person, don't sign up for 8 am classes every day. In short, you should strive to know yourself and then choose the path that you think is going to be best for you.*

*Scene 10*
# The Second Day of Classes

After feeling exhausted from just one day of classes in the same building, Sly was feeling more optimistic about being able to get outside in between classes. He admittedly didn't know where his other classes were located though, but he figured with the people he'd met so far, he would run into them or someone who could help him out. After finishing his morning routine – getting dressed and putting on his backpack and headphones – he prepared to head back to the building where he started each day, the Technology and Science Building, or T-Sci as Sly had heard other students refer to it.

As he left the dorm, he ran into Kevin who was also headed to his first class of the day. "Yo, wait up," Sly yelled in as soft of a voice as he could not to awaken people who were still asleep above the entrance to the dorm. While lowering his headphones, Kevin turned around and dapped up Sly as the two headed to class.

"What class you got?" Sly asked, noticing that of all the people that Sly had met that had been there during the summer, Kevin was the only person he'd seen in the morning.

"Got an Accounting class, you?"

Sly cringed after hearing Kevin's response and then replied back confidently, "Pre-Calc. Shit, should be a breeze. I already took it in high school."

"Why not test out of it then?" Kevin looked at Sly confused.

"One, I didn't know that was an option, and two, I mean I got a B in it in high school. This should be a good way to pad my GPA right?" Kevin nodded, noting the point Sly was making.

"Where is your Accounting class?" Sly asked.

"It's in the Black building on the other side of the Student Center."

"Like black as in color or Black as in name?"

Kevin stopped walking, as Sly kept walking but slowed down, then looked back at Kevin. "What?" Kevin laughed. "Bro, there are no black brick buildings on campus. It's the name of the building. The Black business building."

"Come on man, you gotta admit that's kinda ironic. In a good way though," Sly pleaded his case as both guys approached T-Sci.

"Actually, I think my second class of the day is in the Black building," Sly commented as the two dapped up before parting ways.

"Word, I think I have to come through here before my next class. I'll text you and we can meet."

"That's what's up."

Sly walked into the building's atrium and went down the corridor on the right side. He then turned into a classroom that had roughly nine students already in seats and a trickle of students coming in behind him. Sly sat towards the middle of the rows of seats, but offset from the middle of the whiteboard to the left of the instructor's desk. As more and more students filed into the classroom, he noticed that he hadn't seen the instructor yet. He looked up at the wall clock, and then checked his phone, noticing that both were reading 9 a.m. The rest of the class began to mummer about what happens if the teacher doesn't show. There was a voice in the back of the class that echoed out. "Look, he's gotta be fifteen minutes late, then we can bounce. But until then, can y'all chill out please?" Sly looked back to see who was talking. The guy who explained how it all works seemed super laid back.

"Aye man," Sly leaned over the seat behind him, "how you know that?"

"That's like the unwritten rule. I got some homies back home that go to University of Minnesota that have the same rule. It's just a courtesy rule."

"I can get that," Sly responded. "I'm Sly by the way."

"Wale."

The two did an extended dap across multiple desks just before the instructor walked into the room. He was a middle-aged man who appeared to have descended from the Middle East.

"Good morning class, welcome to Math 201 or Pre-Calculus. My name is Mr. Majtah." Sly just looked at his professor. He knew what he was saying but was still having a hard time making out his exact words. Sly leaned back in his chair and looked around at the rest of the class to see if anyone else was having a hard time understanding the professor.

"Ok, hmmm, now we're going to, hmm, balance this problem. Can any of you all, hmm, provide the answer to me?"

Sly couldn't focus on anything but the professor's accent. He looked at the board for a moment, trying to regain his concentration and attempted to solve the problem in his notebook. He worked out the problem the best he could, sensing a quiet pause in the room.

"Hm, ok. Who can come to board and show work?" Mr. Majta asked the class.

Before Sly could finish his work, his concentration was broken again. Sly hunched over and paid close attention as a short girl approached the board. As Sly checked his work against her work, he realized that he was on the right track. Feeling a bit more relaxed, he sat back in his seat. After the young lady finished working through the problem, the professor looked over the work on the board, with a couple of people in the class stating that they came up with the same answer.

The professor paused, "No, your work no right. Your answer right, but your work no right."

Confused, the whole class looked around at each other with a few exceptions. Mr. Majtah erased the lady's work before writing out the steps himself. Sly followed his work until he hit a particular step. It was clear that Mr. Majtah was using a different method than Sly had been taught while in high school, but he figured since the answer was right, he didn't have much to worry about. After that math problem, Mr. Majtah wrapped up and dismissed the class. Sly packed up his notebook and books before heading back out towards the Student Center.

As Sly walked out of the building, he realized that he had come out right in front of the cemetery. He turned left to gather his bearings to where he was before heading towards the Student Center. As he walked, he put his head down and his headphones up searching his MP3 player for a song. Sly had never been outgoing per say and was never the first to speak. His logic was, "I got these big headphones so no one will try to start a conversation. Even if they do, I can pretend I don't hear them," a conversation he had with himself. He selected a song and could hear the Biggie sample, along with Wayne's shout-outs. When he raised his head, Sly locked eyes with a caramel-skinned young woman, about 5'4", with a nice athletic build and one of the most beautiful smiles and dimples. For a moment, Sly could only see her, even though the two were passing on one of the busier areas of campus. As he walked by her, Sly's thoughts were racing. He pictured a million different scenarios that they could interact with one another. As the two became parallel, and with all the ambitious thoughts he had, he accidentally let one thought slip through. "Wow," he uttered, never breaking eye contact with the young lady, seeming almost star struck. As the blushing young lady walked past, Sly smiled. He turned his head back around, only to see Kevin laughing.

With a smirk of confidence, Sly asked, "What's so funny?"

"You know you said that shit out loud right?"

Confused, Sly asked, "What you mean?"

"When you just stared that girl down and then said 'wow' out loud."

"Nah, I didn't say it out loud..." then he stopped his sentence. "Was it that bad?"

Kevin laughed harder, "Nah man, it won't that loud, but it was loud enough for me to hear it about 10 feet away, so it is what it is. At least she was fine."

Both guys laughed as they headed towards the Student Center.

"You about to go to the Student Center?" Sly asked Kevin, already angling to walk around it.

"Yea man, it's always something going on in there. That's one of the best parts of the campus."

"Nah, I'm good on that. It always seems like it's so many people there. Just not trying to walk through that."

"That's how you meet the people here though man. That's where everyone always is," Kevin pleaded to Sly as the two dapped up and Kevin headed in.

"Aye, I'm going to the café after I get out of class. I'll meet you there," Sly shouted before the door closed.

"Bet," Kevin responded.

Sly walked in between the Student Center and the football stadium, looking at the offices. They were built into the walls of the stadium. As he stared at the offices, he saw a girl just as pretty as the girl he had just humiliated himself over.

"Don't say anything this time," he whispered to himself. He sped up his walk, finally reaching the Black business building. He pulled out his printed schedule and walked in the initial door to the building, noticing that this building had two sides as well.

"Are all of their academic buildings like this?" Sly wondered out loud.

"Pretty much" what appeared to be an upperclassman answered as he breezed past Sly, confusing the freshman even further. Sly looked both ways before heading right and finding the room number that matched the number on his schedule. When he walked in the room, there was African-American

History written out on the board. With a sigh of relief, he took his seat.

Sly settled into a spot near the right wall of the classroom, just trying to find some space to himself. He appreciated the ability to see everyone in the class in one glance and believed that the many gangster movies he watched prior to getting to college contributed to his stance. As he gazed around the classroom, he recited lyrics from "You Can Do It Too" while waiting for the rest of the class to file in. He noticed that one of the people who had walked in went to the front of the classroom. He was a shorter guy with long dreadlocks that hung almost to his waist and glasses that looked like they belonged at the bottom of soda bottles. As the last of the students filled the classroom, the gentleman in the front projected, "Good, glorious morning scholars. My name is Dr. Wayne Wright. You can call me Dr. W, Doc, or Dr. Wright. Just make sure you add the doctor. I worked really hard for that." The instructor laughed as the rest of the class was unsure whether the professor was serious or not. "Geez, is it too early for some of y'all to take a joke?" More of the class laughed as Dr. Wright exclaimed, "That's what I like to hear. I'll be your African-American Studies teacher for this semester," he announced, while going to the head of each row of seats, handing each student a stack of syllabi. "On this historical site, we'll hold our celebrations here on the plantation to show the fruits of our labor." The classroom went from cheerful to utter confusion within moments. The young students looked around at one another, whispering amongst themselves until one student towards the back raised his hand. "Yes sir, state your name and your question," Dr. Wright pronounced as he pointed at the young man. "John, from Cleveland, and, uhhh, are you allowed to say that here......to us? That just seems wrong." Half of the class started laughing while the other portion of students looked to Dr. Wright for a legitimate answer. As Dr. Wright looked around the room, he took a deep breath, "How many of you are freshmen in this class?" The majority of students in the room raised their hands with the exception of two or three students. "Ok, I know where your line of thinking is, but let me correct that for you. Fulton-Harley was founded in 1864, and when it was first established, there was one schoolhouse, and the rest of the land was just farmland. There was more than a fair share of students coming here being a farm hand during the day and getting their education by candlelight. For their graduations, there would be huge parties thrown on the plantation for all the students in their class. I'd like to think that when we have tests in our classes, we're keeping that tradition alive by honoring the hard work it took to get to this point and all the hard work you've put into learning your craft. That is why we celebrate on the plantation." Dr. Wright finished his explanation as some of the students clapped. While the professor continued to go over the syllabus that was handed out, Sly was still thinking about the information he had just divulged in his rant. *Was that a true story? Does he say that to all his classes? Do any of the other teachers use that phrase?* Sly tried to focus back on Dr. Wright as all of the thoughts swirled around in his head. As Dr. Wright finished wrapping up the details of the syllabus and laying out the timeline for the class, he opened the floor to the class for questions. "Does anyone have any questions about the information on the syllabus or about anything we covered today?" He looked around the class as the students looked around at each other. "Ok, ok. I'll see you all in a couple of days. Go ahead and read that first chapter and be prepared to discuss the chapter by next class. You all can go ahead and leave." Dr. Wright dismissed the class and all the students started packing up their bags and heading towards the door. Sly sluggishly moved his belongings back into his book bag but hurried when he saw Dr. Wright was about to leave the room. "Hey Dr. Wright, is that saying unique to just you?" Sly asked after thinking about the phrase the whole duration of the class. "As far as I know, but if more professors said it, maybe it wouldn't carry the stigma it does." As Sly fixed his lips to ask a follow-up question, Dr. Wright responded before he could get it out, "And no, I didn't make that story up. That's a legitimate story about the campus. You do understand you are in an African-American History course. It's kinda my job to know these kinds of things." Sly shook his head in understanding, "Yes sir." He left the classroom and headed back towards the Student Center.

Sly walked towards, and then around, the Student Center as he reflected on the first two days of his college experience. As he searched for the perfect song to listen to during his reflections, he noticed that there was a large group of people walking towards the Black building, but he couldn't tell what for. When the large group of students, all dressed in black suits, hurried past Sly, he wondered what kind of event the students were going to. Not interested enough to follow, Sly turned back around and continued walking towards the café, where he arrived just as lunch was beginning. He put his headphones up and the horns from the "Death of Autotune" beat echoed in his ears. Sly tuned everything out as he normally would do back home. This time, just a little longer to walk across campus.

## Scene 11
# "Aye Cuz!!"

After the week came to an end, Sly was excited and relieved that he had made it through his first week of classes. He had already spoken with his mom and had scheduled a ride out of Fulton-Harley for the weekend. He'd be back home in time to see his high school team play. They were already showing to be better than the team he had been a part of. He hopped out of bed at the sound of his alarm. Eugene threw a pillow over at Sly, "You got class today?" Eugene asked without opening his eyes. "Yup, but I'm all done by eleven. That's slight work," Sly answered excitedly. "Mmhmm," Eugene responded before he went back to snoring.

Sly proceeded to go through the routine he had developed for the classes he was taking. With no assigned seats, Sly made sure to get to class early each day to ensure he got the same seat every class. As he sat through his second class for the day, he received a text from his cousin on his dad's side of the family. *Aye cuz, what time you done with class?* read the text message. Sly opened his phone under his desk and replied. After a few minutes, he received another buzz, *Word, I'm going to come to the Student Center in a lil' bit*. Excited to have another person in the area that he knew, Sly informed his cousin that he wouldn't be out of class until 11. With everything going on around him, combined with everything happening around campus, Sly was finding it impossible to focus on anything the professor was saying. "Mr. Jones, you with us?" his professor asked, as he caught Sly daydreaming. "Yes sir," Sly quickly snapped out of it. "Ok, good. Can you tell me what we were discussing?" Sly, thrown off by the question, realized that he had been put on the spot. "No sir," Sly responded feeling embarrassed. "Please pay attention, Mr. Jones. Remember, this education isn't free. Even if you're on scholarship, someone is paying for you to be here. Remember that." The professor locked eyes with Sly for a moment before spreading the message to the class. Sly nodded his head in understanding, all while looking at the clock for class to end. As the clock wound down, and the professor set to release the class, he paused for a moment. "Before I let you all go, I want to say this. Like I said earlier, whether you're a scholarship athlete, on an academic scholarship, or not, someone is paying for you to be here. I know this may be your first weekend to do whatever you'd like, but I'd like to say to make good and smart decisions and make sure that you always remember why you came to Fulton-Harley." Sly mumbled under his breath, "Because I didn't get into Virginia Tech." The professor dismissed the class.

Sly slipped his headphones back up as he passed the threshold for the classroom door. He showed a peace sign with his hands towards the teacher, never looking away from the exit of the classroom. *Blowin' dro on 24's, that's just how my niggas roll*, Sly mouthed as he walked out of the T-Sci building. He paused for a moment, as he felt his phone buzz again.

"Aye, where you at?" Sly's cousin asked as he answered the phone.

"Uhhh just getting out of class, you?"

"Bet. I'm already here on your campus in y'all lil' student union and y'all got some thangs in here boy. Hmm."

Sly, who had come out of the building facing Jackson Hall, stopped and looked around. He gathered himself to make sure he could take the quickest route to the Student Center. He looped around the T-Sci building and entered the Student Center from the backside.

"Where you at?" Sly asked again.

He walked past the bowling alley into the main area of the Student Center.

"I think I'm in the student union. It's just a bunch of light skin girls in here wearing green and yellow. You gon' have to come to me, cuz I'm not moving," Dre laughed and Sly laughed along, heading towards the Student Center.

Sly approached the area where the students were congregated. As he browsed the area, he spotted his cousin leaning against one of the pillars in front of the restaurants that were in the union. As he stood posted, Sly noticed him glancing over his shoulder at a group of women wearing green and yellow like he had mentioned.

Dre opened his arms as Sly approached, "My nigga Jones. What's going on man?" The two dapped up as Sly responded, "Not much man. You know me, trying to stay out the way."

The two stepped back as Sly continued, "Boy you fresh out here, ain't you?" Dre was wearing a pair of Jordans with a pair of 501s and a Levi's t-shirt.

"Nah bruh, this is something slight," he replied casually as he looked around while continuing the conversation.

"So, how you like it so far?" Dre paused his gaze for just a moment to look at Sly, anticipating his response.

Sly paused for a moment and reflected over the first week before modestly responding, "I mean, it's cool, but it's not Tech." Sly shrugged, still feeling slighted by the admissions process.

Dre nodded his head as he went back to looking around, "I mean, I feel you, I do. But my nigga...." He paused for a moment to look at his cousin before waving his hand around the center inviting Sly to look for himself, "Like, fuck Tech." They both laughed as they dapped up again. "So what's the move for the weekend? I know y'all got some wild shit going on," Dre asked intrigued, letting his imagination run wild.

Sly shrugged, "Man, I don't know bruh. I ain't even gon' be here this weekend."

"Nigga where you going?" Dre promptly asked with utter confusion.

"Back home."

Dre looked at his cousin dumbfounded. "Why would you do that to yourself?" he asked with genuine concern.

Sly shrugged again, "Parties really ain't my thing, man, and I don't wanna sit in that dorm room all weekend."

Dre nodded, "Nah I get that, and shiiiiddd probably for the best, because Duchess would have your head if she heard anything," Dre said laughing about his high school classmate.

"You know she from the Bronx, right?"

"Nah cuz, I didn't know *my girl* was from the Bronx," Sly replied sarcastically as the two laughed.

Just as their conversation started again, a short, light-skinned, curly-haired girl approached where they were standing. As the young lady emerged from behind Sly, Dre stopped mid-sentence, complimenting the girl, "I really wanted those Jordan's too, but they only made them for women. They look amazing on you," he flirted while nodding at her shoes, followed with a wink. The young woman smiled, blushing as she turned and walked away.

Sly did a double take, looking behind him then looking at his cousin, "Bruh, how did you see her and where did she come from?"

Without pausing, Dre calmly replied, "Man, my court vision is crazy."

Both of them laughed, but as the young lady approached again, Dre collected himself before proclaiming, "Hmmm and you got them curls out here poppin' today, huh? You just know you cute, huh?" as he looked the girl directly in the eyes.

She blushed even harder than before as she headed back towards her group of friends. Discreetly pointing over her shoulder, the girls at the table tried not to make it so obvious that they were looking back. Without moving, Sly mumbled to his cousin, "Looks like you might have a small fan club."

"Maybe, but I guess we gon' see, right?" Dre replied as the two chuckled.

They noticed the same girl walking by for a third time. And without hesitation, Dre coolly expressed, "And I see you coordinated the colors in the Baby Phat with the Jordans. I see you boo."

The girl smiled, showing her teeth and even giving a small laugh. Sly looked at his cousin with a huge, child-like grin, "You bullshittin', just bag the joint," he commented as his cousin gestured to slow down.

As the young lady prepared to walk past for a fourth time, Dre promptly changed his tone, "Aye shawty. You done walked past here four times, and I've complimented you every time, all while you smiling and giggling. Now, I could be wrong, but you appear to be feelin' a nigga. So you gon' give me your number or what?"

Sly's face dropped to the floor as he stared at his cousin for the explanation he had told him to wait for. Once again, the girl was all giggles and laughs, "You're so funny!" she continued laughing as Dre handed her his phone. She promptly entered her number, gave him a hug and waved to the two before returning to her friends. Doubling back, she said while blushing, "Oh, what's your name?" Dre nodded as he faced her, "My family calls me Dutch." He wrapped his arm around Sly's neck. The young lady smirked as she waved and walked off.

As Dre stepped back to his post, Sly looked befuddled at his cousin.

"Uhhhh, what the fuck just happened?" he asked with all seriousness.

"It is what I said it was," he said with a shrug and a smirk. Then he continued, "But like I was saying before man, what's going on tonight?" he asked, still eager to make the same impression on other women.

"And what about Dutch? Like, you not wrong... and that is your last name, but I've never heard anyone call you that," Sly said to his cousin, only slightly less confused.

"Look here, Jack. Every person doesn't need to meet the same person. Some people get Andre, others might get Dre. I might give you Dutch, but a nigga better hope to high hell he never gotta see Von," Dre answered with a straight face.

"Uhhh, okkk, hmmm, well.....Like I said man, I'm going home, but I can definitely plug you in with some people bro," Sly responded as he looked around the Student Center.

He spotted Melo, DJ, Dennis, and Danny standing at the top of the steps near the railing. Sly signaled to his cousin to follow him through the crowd as the two made their way up the stairs to the clearing. Once in front of the whole staircase, Sly noticed that every person that Eugene had introduced him to were all sitting on the last step or standing on the clearing between the first and second floor. As they climbed the steps, Sly looked back and said to his cousin, "This is perfect. Everybody I know is up here. And you remember Eugene, right?"

"Yea, that's bruh that played football with you right?" Dre asked, hyped to have another Richmonder in the area.

Sly introduced Dre to the group and Dre dapped up the few closest to him and threw up the peace sign to the others. They stood at the top of the steps, taking in the grandeurs of Fulton-Harley. As the fraternities and sororities strolled, the middle of the Student Center looked more like a club than an educational building.

"Who's ready to turn up for the weekend? If you done with yo' first week of class, make some noise. The freshman, E of E 5, make it live," the guy on the microphone announced, and the Student Center erupted in cheers, with the freshmen making their presence felt.

"Ok, ok, I see y'all. Let's see if y'all 'bout something. Let's go DJ Mile High."

As the DJ dropped a couple of bombs through the speaker, the crowd anticipated the next song before finally hearing, "Yea buddy, rolling like a big shot, Chevy tuned up like a Nascar pitstop...." Instantly, the student body sang along, as strolls and dances became more intense and elaborate.

"Yea, we turning up tonight. The summer afterparty tonight. Get your tickets. We'll be selling them all of tonight and up until five tomorrow. It's gonna be bananas, but not like them over there, in a better way, but we good ice. We good," the DJ said, while laughing and pointing at the group of men wearing black and gold giving him a hard time.

Sly looked at Dre, pointing down to the DJ while saying, "Well, there ya go," he said jokingly. The group talked amongst themselves while also looking among the greatness that was Student Center Fridays.

## Scene 12
# Where's Daryl?

The morning sun peeked through the cracked blinds as Sly glanced at the clock and turned it off before the alarm sounded. He figured he'd spare Eugene this Friday. He got up, grabbed his things for the shower, and left the room, making as little noise as possible. As he made his way to the bathroom, he noticed that there was barely any movement around eight in the morning on Fridays, which he enjoyed. No one in the bathroom. He could take a long shower to wake up before walking to the cafe for breakfast. Upon returning from his shower, he proceeded to get dressed, and heard his half asleep roommate mutter, "So what did we learn about scheduling?" Eugene laughed himself slightly awake.

"Take yo ass back to sleep. Plus, I don't mind being up in the morning if I know ahead of time," Sly said, slipping on his hoodie before putting on his backpack.

"I see you took all them damn books out your backpack though..." Eugene continued and rolled back over.

"Ok, yea this campus is too big to be walking around with those books all the time. After doing that for a little bit, I was good on it," Sly said laughing while heading for the door.

As he grabbed the knob, Eugene suddenly asked suggestively, "Aye, you staying here this weekend, right?"

Sly looked back shrugging with a slight shake of the head, "Hadn't really planned on it, why?" Sly paused before leaving the room.

Eugene sat up to speak to Sly. "Look man, you said you were gonna make the best of being here, but literally the best part of being here is the weekend and you're purposely missing it. I can't tell you what to do, but I don't think you should miss this week. Have you already called your parents?"

"No, not yet. I usually call them after my class," Sly responded, after hearing his friend out, still not completely convinced.

"How about this – don't call them until after Student Center Friday. If I can't convince you to stay by then, and they can't come get you, I'll find you a ride home," Eugene argued persuasively.

Sly paused for a moment, figuring he had nothing to lose, and responded, "Ok, that's a deal, but if I wanna go home, you gon' make it happen."

Sly stepped back towards the foot of Eugene's bed and the two dapped up. Then Sly headed back towards the door. He opened it and said, "But that's a tall task, my boy," letting the door gently slam behind him.

After breakfast, Sly made his way to his only class of the day. As he walked through the heart of the campus, he noticed the subtle changing of the colors of the leaves. He zipped his hoodie all the way up and the few leaves that lined the sidewalk crunched beneath his feet. Sly mumbled different lyrics as he made his way past the Arts building, looking both ways before crossing the street, while slowly, but melodically, bopping across the way. He walked into the T-Sci building and held the door for a couple of young ladies while looking over at the front gate of the campus in the process. He paused to notice a security officer escorting what appeared to be a parent and a student around campus. Sly couldn't make out who it was so he shrugged his shoulders and headed into the building. He assumed that it was someone important on campus for them to have a security detail. As he hustled down the hallway to make it into class, he took his seat and pondered who the VIP was.

Class ended as quickly as it began, while Mr. Newman concluded with, "Remember, next Wednesday, our test on Object-Oriented Programming. Remember to study over the weekend. We'll have a session for us to review on Monday, so bring your questions. Class dismissed." Those closest to the door rushed out as others took their time packing up their things. Sly put his book back in his bag, along with his notebook, and pulled up his headphones. He headed for the door and nodded to Mr. Newman who waved him over to his desk. As Sly approached, he saw that the professor was pulling print out of code to the front. "Your code works, Mr. Jones, but it's not efficient," pointing to the block. "You have the loop twice within itself. The second loop isn't written properly, so I must penalize you for it. Make sure you double check your work to be sure it looks right, not just to make sure it works right. Those things matter later down the line." The professor highlighted the mistake, taking fifteen points off the total, which landed Sly a 'B' for the assignment. Sly looked at the paper as Mr. Newman wrote out the grade, transferring it to the computer and dismissing Sly, all in one gesture.

Sly left class, disappointed in himself. He tried to perk up, remembering that it was Friday and that he could go home if he wanted to. As he made his way out of T-Sci towards the Student Center, Sly recited more lyrics. He took a brief moment to peek into the ballroom because he could see something being moved. He entered through one of the side doors of the Student Center, and could see that they were just rearranging the chairs, but there was no stage. He walked past, throwing deuces to those he made eye contact with, continuing towards the bowling alley. To his surprise, there was no one actively bowling, even though the lights were on. As he approached the double doors, he heard the DJ starting to scratch, even over his own headphones. He removed his own soundtrack and heard more clearly, "Chillin' in the club in my B-boy stance, my hoodie on with my gat in my pants, and I'm fresh to deaf, I'm fresh to deaf……" Sly snapped out of his own personal headspace and took a quick look around to see if anyone caught his awkward moment before approaching the crowd of Student Center Friday.

He made his way through the crowd and up the stairs to greet the fellas. As Sly finished his rounds of dapping people up and hugging the few females that the guys had introduced him to, he took in one of his favorite sites on campus. As he looked upon the crowd below, he saw Eugene coming up the steps, saying what up to their group.

"I know you love this scene, so why not experience this all weekend?" Eugene asked as he reached Sly, nudging him slightly off his spot.

"There's nothing even happening this…." Sly started before the hype man interrupted, "Ayyyy, y'all know what it is. It's time for the pajama party. This Saturday in Opal Gymnasium. It'll be five dollars at the door.  You must show your Fulton-Harley ID to get into this party. Gotta bring your IDs," the hype man repeated.

The music continued as Sly looked at Eugene, mouth gaped open with nothing to say.

"Uh huh, looks like your plans are set for the weekend sir," Eugene said as he stood beside his friend. He took in one last view briefly before heading up the second flight of stairs to talk to some other football players. Sly stood there pondering if he wanted to still keep up his end of the bargain by staying for the weekend. He stood and gazed, thinking for a bit while interacting with some of the fellas before going up the second flight and leaving through the back exit where he entered. He put his headphones back up and decided on the scenic route back to Jackson while further pondering his decision.

He walked back to the front of T-Sci, crossing the street and the security guard booth in the process. He mumbled to himself, "Last time I checked, I was the man on these streets. They call me residue. I leave blow on these beats." As the guard looked out of the doorless post, he tipped his cap to Sly. Sly paused and nodded to return the gesture, rounding the corner to walk out of the front gate of the campus. Heading towards the back gate, Sly continued, "Now tell me I ain't real, this AR that I'm holdin' got a gangsta grill." He continued walking , taking his time to really look at his campus, unlike he did on his tour. He noticed the architecture of the older buildings,  the only houses that were next to campus. He passed the gate and headed back towards the back of campus. As he walked past the honors dorms, he admired their grandeur, slowing his pace. He then turned back towards the direction he was walking and saw Jade and Cally.

He called out, "What's up Jade? Hey Cally," unaware of his elevated volume with his headphones up. As he approached the two, Jade reached out and pulled down Sly's headphones.

"Nigga, you loud as shit. What's up though? How you liking Fulton-Harley so far?"

"My bad," Sly apologized before shrugging, changing his course to follow them and continue the conversation, "I'm still on the fence about it. I don't want to go back home, but I do go home every weekend."

Both women looked at Sly like he had suddenly grown a second head. "What?" Sly asked, noticing the looks.

"Boy, how can you have an opinion, if you haven't been here for a weekend?" Jade asked with a serious tone.

Cally added, "She's got a point, ya know. You have to give it an honest chance, and this might be the best weekend to do that. Them Ques know how to party."

"But that's just the thing, I'm not really a party person," Sly responded.

Jade wrapped her arm around Sly, shaking her head. "You're thinking like a party back home, well…..home for you is Richmond though. This is not going to be like that. Plus you're cute, so you got that going for ya. You'll do fine," she said while shaking Sly.

As the two walked towards the café, Cally added, "Yea, any preconceived notions that you had about parties before you got here, you can get rid of. You'll have a good time love, I promise," she said reassuringly and pinched Sly's cheek.

The two ladies walked up the stairs to the café as Sly made his way towards the waterfront. He placed his headphones back upright, shuffling through his MP3 player before selecting a song. As he looked out at the water, Sly squinted from the glare, only gaining relief with the passing of different vessels. He slowed his walk that could almost be mistaken as a slumber, just in a state of endless possibilities. He neared the end of the street in front of the waterfront and started back towards the intersection that led out of campus. He crossed the street with an increased pace back towards Jackson Hall. Once at the door, he raced upstairs, and barged into his room. Eugene and Mack paused their game and looked at Sly in amazement and confusion.

"I'm gonna stay this weekend!" Sly said with a firm, excited declaration.

"……..Ohhhkay. Ummmm, can we finish the game?" Mack asked with pure confusion, as Eugene laughed, smiling at Sly while saying, "Yea."

The next day, the dorm seemed eerily quiet. The group mostly stayed in Sly and Eugene's room, growing to as many as seven people at one time, with Corey's roommate coming to hang out as well. Some would leave to get random snacks or take naps, and there was the trip to the café, running into the fellas from Roberts. They also noted how quiet it had been throughout the day and how some guys in the dorm had made plans to hoop that afternoon, but it fell through. As Sly, Eugene, Kevin, and Daryl made their way back to the dorm, they spotted Mack coming between the cemetery and the field.

"Aye boy, we back on them sticks 'til the party, right?" he shouted as he approached the door and the group walked in.

They paused, holding the door as Eugene responded, "Come on in here and take this L."

Mack hustled as he came in the door with a rowdy response, "Man, fuck all that. You not about to beat me right now."

At that very moment, Mr. P popped out, staring Mack in the face. "Watch your mouth young man. I mean that," he said sternly as Mack nodded.

The group hurried upstairs, laughing as Mack mumbled under his breath to Eugene, "I still meant that shit."

The group laughed harder as they passed the second floor threshold.

Sly opened the door to the room and everyone walked in. Sly texted Corey to let him know that they were back at the room. Eugene turned on the Playstation and threw Mack a controller. As the tv came on and the game console's chime sounded, there was a knock on the door.

Sly opened the door and Corey walked in, "I got next."

"You got last," Kevin responded as everybody laughed.

"Yea nigga! What the fuck? You don't think we wanna play?" Sly chimed in.

"Yea, but y'all gone all lose anyway. You might as well let me play," Corey responded confidently with a laugh.

The group booed him, all while joining in the laughter. They continued gaming until the sunlight completely faded. Sitting back on his bed, Sly looked out the window, suddenly leaning forward looking at the clock. The clock read 8:47.

"Uhhh fellas, what time does that party start?"

"I think it starts at 9, don't it?" Daryl responded without looking away from the play on the screen.

"So should we not be getting ready to head over there?" Sly asked, puzzled.

"What would we be getting ready for? It's pajamas. Either wear pajamas or wear some basketball shorts and a beater," Corey said as he shrugged and leaned back in Sly's desk chair, nearly losing his balance. Sly sat back, realizing the point that was made, and continued to watch the play on the screen.

"But what about all the stuff y'all did before the block party?" he popped up again and asked.

"Chill, you hot right now. That was first weekend stuff. Why you asking all these questions? You sipping tonight?" Mack asked as he looked at Sly.

Sly sat back again, shrugging out the game noise to hear the hustle and bustle outside their door again. The group in the room might have been set, but it was a mad scramble in Jackson for everyone who was looking for liquid courage for the party. As the guys finished the final game, Kevin and Corey raced out yelling simultaneously, "I'll meet y'all downstairs," and they bolted down the hall towards the side hallway. Daryl casually walked to his room, returning shortly with a Fruitopia bottle full of his new favorite drink, Incredible Hulk.

"Nigga, where did you get a Fruitopia bottle from?" Sly asked, genuinely concerned.

"It's not Fruitopia," Daryl replied quickly.

"Duh nigga," Eugene responded as they all laughed.

They made their way down the stairs and Daryl tucked the bottle in the left pocket of his pajama pants. He got in the middle of the group for better coverage as they crossed the lobby and exited the dorm.

As they cleared the view of the door, Daryl pulled the bottle out of his pocket and took a huge swig before offering it to the group. Eugene grabbed the bottle and took a sip. As he passed it to Mack, he took a small swig compared to his size. "K Skip?" he gestured to Kevin with the bottle. Kevin grabbed the bottle next and took a little swig before offering it to Sly who refused. Kevin handed the bottle back to Daryl and the rotation proceeded until it got to Mack for the second time, who killed the rest of the bottle. He then tossed the bottle in the trashcan at the intersection in front of the cemetery and the group made their way across the street. As Sly looked around, he could see different groups of people still heading over to the gymnasium. As they passed the T-Sci building, Sly asked, "Are we gonna walk through the Student Center?" The group looked at each other and Daryl answered boldly, "I mean, shit, we can." Collectively, they shrugged, and Eugene pulled one door back and Daryl the other, and they all walked in.

As they made their way into the Student Center atrium, it was eerily quiet. Daryl turned the corner first and looked around exclaiming, "Man, this shit boring. Ain't nothing going on in here.

That's why I only come in here on Fridays." The group laughed and cut over towards a side door and headed back outside. As they exited the Student Center, only a couple hundred feet from the gym, they saw a small line forming outside the party. They walked with anticipation to the steps of the gym. Sly walked behind the group, still looking around and behind at the trail of people he noticed heading to the function. When they approached the entry to the gym, they walked through the first door of the breezeway, where there were cops and metal detectors. The fellas removed all contents from their pockets and held their hands above their heads as they went through different detectors and doors to enter the gym.

As they walked in, there was a big, tall Que standing behind a table with two women seated in front of him. "Five dollars," he said as he looked over the group, even Mack. Everyone took out their money and handed it to one of the women. They approached the opening to the end of the two tables to the left. Sly, still looking around and down the hallways, had never seen any kind of party like this before. He looked ahead of the group into the pitch dark that was the gym. He spotted a few track lights around the perimeter of the gym, but as they entered fully, he could barely make out figures. As the group sunk deeper into the party, Sly wandered with Kevin, dancing with women as he was presented with opportunities. With each dance, Sly grew slightly more comfortable with his surroundings. After a few songs, Sly went to the bathroom to catch his breath and grab a drink of water. Upon re-entering the gym, he ran into Brandon and Melo, and the three of them paraded around the party. After a few more songs, Sly and his friends ran into Jade and her friends. Sly and Jade took turns introducing their friends, as Brandon stared at Cally, interrupting, "No introduction needed." He reached for her hand and spun her around. The introductions came to a brief pause as the group heard through the speakers, "Cash Money Records, taking over for the 9-9 and da 2000...." As shirts were grabbed and hands were put on the floor, there was a flurry of twerking throughout the gym. Every woman was eager to prove that she was, in fact, working with some ass.

As the party carried on, Sly walked to the edge of the party, gassed and drenched in sweat. Now that his eyes had adjusted, he could see more clearly and take it all in. He looked to the side and saw people making out and getting lap dances on the floor. He paused for a moment before walking back into the large crowd, looking for his next dancing partner or homie. In what seemed like no time, DJ Mile High announced on the microphone, "Freshmen, y'all got five minutes to get back to your dorm before y'all...." and the crowd responded with, "Out by five!!" Just as the upperclassmen finished their statement, there was a pouring of freshmen towards the lobby of the gymnasium. Sly headed towards the door spotting Kevin and Eugene. They briefly traded stories, looking behind them to take in the sight once more before Kevin interjected, "Hey, y'all seen Daryl?" Sly and Eugene looked behind as Kevin looked in front of the group. Together, they circled the party. They ran around the perimeter, trying to scope out to see where their lost friend was. As they carefully weaved through the party, meeting on the other side and throwing up signs of no luck, the DJ announced again, "Some of y'all fast asses need to be put out, three minutes." There was a smaller group now light jogging towards the exit. After a moment, Sly and the fellas sprinted out of the gym, jumping down the stairs and dashing towards Jackson Hall.

As they approached the dormitory, they could see the clock: "12:58," Sly said, gasping as they continued running. They reached the front door of the dorm with less than a minute to spare, panting in the lobby with all of those freshman guys trying to catch one more twerk. They made their way upstairs and Kevin followed, still worried and confused as to where Daryl could be. Initially, they were headed to Sly and Eugene's room, but stopped by Daryl's room first in hopes that his roommate had at least seen him. Cole answered the door, still pretty wide awake for someone who didn't go to the party. "What's good fellas?" he asked while opening the door. The group nodded in unison as they panned their view to see Daryl, who was sitting perfectly upright, with a bottle of water between his legs, both hands firmly grasping the bottle. Eugene asked the question that the group was wondering, "How long has he been here? And did he come back alone?" Cole shrugged, "He was leant on the door when he got here, but he didn't fall so maybe he got here on his own. He been here though, for like fifteen minutes." They all looked at their drunk friend, sleeping in the most awkward position, and just laughed. "Aight, Cole. Thanks man," Sly said and the other two echoed the sentiment. They walked back over to the door of Eugene and Sly's room and opened it. Instantly, Mack busted in. The group compared their stories and experiences until about 2:30 a.m. before Kevin and Mack decided to return to their rooms. Sly continued talking to Eugene before drifting off to sleep.

## Scene 13
# The Head Discussion

Even after a couple of weeks, the topic of conversation continued to be the pajama party that everyone seemed to have had good memories of. The group had been told the tales of Homecoming, but that was still a couple of weeks away. As Sly sat in his room with the usual suspects, Eugene hopped up after he had lost on the sticks and posed the question: "Anyone trying to go to Fin's room? I gotta get a cut."

"For what?" Daryl asked as he checked in the mirror.

"You know I gotta be right for the ROTC gig. Whatever they say I gotta do for them to continue cutting that check to Fulton-Harley, I'm doing my nigga."

"Respect," Sly chimed in.

As he stood up, Daryl followed suit. "I'll roll with you. I got a presentation that I gotta be dressed for. Might as well get a line too."

The two left the room and headed downstairs while the rest of the group remained in Sly's room.

The pair made their way out of Jackson Hall, headed towards Roberts. On the way, Quentin and Isaiah came out of the honors dorm that was between the two buildings. Daryl yelled out to them, "QG, Zae, what up?"

The two boys paused, allowing the Jackson residents to catch up before greeting them. "Not much. Bout to hit the café, then maybe hoop 'round 4. What y'all about to do?" Quentin asked, as Daryl responded, "Bout to go see Fin."

"We'll probably meet y'all out on the court," Eugene answered before the group exchanged daps and Daryl and Eugene continued into Roberts Hall.

Upon entry, Mr. Gooden was sitting in the lower level of the lobby with some other students. They overheard him talking about having too many people in the room at one time and causing too much noise during the quiet hours. The two walked into the open office and signed their names. Trying to avoid detection, they decided to go up the stairs instead of waiting in front of the elevator, knowing that it would ding, once it reached the first floor. As they made their way up to the third floor, they exited the stairwell, checking around for RAs before making their way to Fin and Brandon's room. When they approached the door, the pair could hear an argument about Jordan, LeBron, and Kobe getting heated. They knocked on the door and could hear Fin trying to say as quietly as possible, "Shut the fuck up!"

There was a pause before he opened the door to Daryl and Eugene and exclaimed, "Ahhhh, it's just these niggas."

Everybody laughed and the two came in dapping up Melo, Nino, Wale, Lincoln, Jalil, and Harold.

"Shit, where the hell y'all niggas been? I thought y'all left after the summer. I'm pretty sure I saw you leave LK," Daryl said, looking at Jalil and Harold.

"I did leave, but I came back," Harold responded.

Jalil pleaded their case, "Architecture has been kicking our ass man, from day one."

Harold nodded in solidarity.

"I can respect it," Eugene responded empathetically. The rest of the group agreed.

There was a brief pause in the conversation before Melo stated, "Well, we know that at the end of the day, you'll be out here creating structures that will be looked at as masterpieces of their time and forever. But let's talk about the here and now, fellas. Who done got their dick wet?"

The room exploded with laughter as Fin tried to calm the room. He paused on Nino's cut,

"Ayyy, chill out Melo. You gon' make Fin cut me for real," Nino shouted across the room, still laughing.

Melo, with a straight face, continued, "Y'all acting real cute, come on now."

"I mean, it is this one joint in Mildred Hall that got some fire head," Daryl commented as the room fell silent, waiting for him to elaborate.

"So I heard."

The group groaned in defeat and disappointment.

"Ol' heard it through the grapevine lookin' boy," Jalil shouted out. Everybody laughed.

Melo circled back, "How y'all like your head though?"

"Nigga, you being serious? Asking that in a room full of niggas?" Wale asked, still laughing.

"I mean, y'all my niggas. If I know a joint give head like you like, I can try to throw you the lob," Melo commented back calmly.

"But how would you know what a girl's head is like without getting the head yourself first?" Harold asked with a serious tone and without hesitation.

Melo responded, "By asking Daryl."

The room's laughter could be heard echoing through the hall of the third floor.

"But for real though, how y'all like your head. Me personally, she gotta have good saliva glands."

The room erupted in laughter again.

"I mean, a lot of spit does make it better, but did you have to say it like that? She gotta have good saliva glands, da fuck outta here," Brandon said, trying to slow his laughter.

"Aye shorty, what those saliva glands talkin' 'bout?" Fin chimed in on the comment.

"Hands, no hands?"

"Hands," Eugene quickly commented.

"Nah, just give me the mouth. That's where you see the talent," Lincoln said in rebuttal.

The rest of the room gave their opinion on the matter before Melo asked another follow-up question, "Standing up, sitting down, or laying down?"

The room, fully engaged in the conversation now, went around answering the question. Lincoln looked at Melo and interrupted Daryl's argument on why standing to receive head was the best, "Hold up, you been on a roll asking these questions but you haven't answered like the last two. So Melo, which is the best?"

"You know you can't put me on the spot, right? I'm the one curating this shit, but you got it. The best to me is sitting on the edge of the bed so that you're able to lay back but your feet are still on the floor."

The room nodded in acceptance of his answer. The group anticipated the next question and Melo blurted out, "Y'all ever had a joint lick your ass while she was giving you head?"

The room paused, everyone trying to accurately understand what Melo had just asked.

"Nigga what?" Brandon shouted, and everyone in the room hysterically laughed at the question.

"I'm assuming that you've had this happen since you asked us. But my question to you is....how? How did this happen?" Eugene asked with a look of pure concern and horror.

Melo recounted the experience with the young lady in detail to the gentlemen as they hung on to his every word. As he concluded his story, he finished with, "So long story short, I mean yea..... that's what happened."

"Aye yo. You wildin' my guy," Nino commented, as the guys laughed again.

Melo shrugged in response to the room.

"You kissed her after that, didn't you?" Brandon asked as the room grew quiet, in anticipation of his answer.

"I mean, she was licking on me..." Melo answered, shrugging with a smirk.

The room filled with mixed reactions, mostly laughter.

"You a nasty nigga, Melo," Nino said while keeping his laughter light.

# Scene 14
## 'Dry' Campus

After the first two months of school, Sly was finally starting to come around to being at Fulton-Harley. He was still trying to figure out how to navigate having so much free time on his hands, but he wasn't fazed by it as much as he had previously thought he would be. With his rhythm to the schedule he had put in place, he thought he could keep in pretty good shape to walk-on in the Spring and keep his grades up. As he returned to Jackson Hall after his 1:30 class, he walked through the doorway and heard the dorm director shout out into the lobby, "Meeting this evening at 7. Mandatory attendance." This was the most upset Sly had heard Mr. P since being at Fulton-Harley.

As he raced up the stairs, the dorm seemed very somber. The fourth floor was unusually quieter than normal. Sly burst in the room to see Eugene sitting at his desk, as Mack played the PlayStation.

"Y'all heard about the meeting?" Sly asked as the two looked and nodded their heads, not breaking the silence permeating throughout the building.

"So....y'all gon' tell me what happened?" Sly asked as the concern grew in his voice.

"Supposedly, a few of the New Orleans niggas got drunk earlier today and was walking around campus. The campus police put them in the car, but then these niggas jumped out the cop car, and ran into our dorm. Ran into the dorm my nigga," Eugene explained to his roommate.

Sly stood by the door, baffled. As he processed the information he had just received, he put his thoughts together, "Wait, it's only like 3, and this already happened? And who was it?"

Mack and Eugene shrugged their shoulders. "But I do know they some New Orleans niggas from y'all floor," Mack said, pointing back and forth between Sly and Eugene.

Sly looked at Eugene who again shrugged, as he thought to himself who could've been involved in such an activity in the middle of a Thursday. Since Sly was done for the day, he pondered the thought and sat back on his bed. Daryl, Kevin, Corey and his roommate, Nate, came into the room talking about the meeting. They all wanted to know if Eugene or Sly knew who the culprits were. Around 5 or so, the group that was in the room went to the café for dinner. While they sat eating their meals, they could hear rumblings amongst the students about their dorm. The rumor mill was hard at work, as the fellas seldom spoke, listening to what was being said around them.

"What do y'all think is gonna happen?" Daryl asked with a quiet tone.

"I mean, it is a meeting for the whole dorm. I don't think anything is gonna happen," Kevin said calmly.

They waited until Eugene finished his plate before placing their trays on the belt, clearing the utensils in the process. Sly made his way to the door, holding it for Corey who was coming out behind him. Sly squinted his eyes as he walked out, looking directly at the sun as it was setting behind the female side of campus. He turned around and caught up with the group before looking up at the sky, enjoying the colors and the smell of the water. They made their way over the few vents on campus that had steam coming out.

"What do y'all think this is for?" Nate asked, as he walked past, placing his hand over the steam.

"I heard that certain buildings on campus are steam powered," Kevin said.

"But why would they make some of the buildings steam powered and not all, especially when the campus is beside a body of water?" Sly asked, puzzled by the logic.

Kevin looked back at Sly and shrugged his shoulders while answering, "Mmmmhm, someone told me that, so that's what I'm telling y'all since you asked." The group laughed as they walked past the backside of the on-campus church.

"Y'all trying to go to the Student Center until the meeting? I think they got an event in there tonight," Nate asked.

"Pretty sure that event starts at 7. So why you trying to go to the Student Center?" Eugene asked, looking for the point in Nate's suggestion.

"I don't know, just to see," Nate continued, still looking down the street towards the building as the group walked towards Jackson Hall.

"Well, you're always free to go," Corey said to his roommate. Nate paused for a moment before doing a quick double take and catching up with the group. They made their way inside and back upstairs. On their way back to the room, Cory and Nate were met by Mack at the door.

They sat in their usual spots as they turned on the game system, while everyone constantly checked the clock. With each passing minute, approaching the hour, the group heard the dorm grow quieter and quieter. As the clock expired on the game, everyone looked at the real clock and it read 6:56. Eugene turned off the console and they filed out of the room into the stairwell. No one said a word. They joined the rest of their dormmates, making their way down the stairs. The RAs stood in the office, some snickering while others turned their noses up at the freshmen walking out of the building. The Jackson Hall residents made their way across the street to the large lawn that laid between their dormitory and the Architecture building. As they crossed the street, Mr. P stood to the side, as if he was counting the young men as they were crossing to ensure that they were all there. As the flow of people slowed to a trickle, Mr. P yelled back to the building, "Ok, go ahead and check." While everyone looked in the open door across the street, the freshmen watched as all the RAs headed to their respective floors to check for any students that may have still been in their rooms. The group stood relatively quiet, with little side conversations going on here and there, anticipating the start of the meeting. As each resident stood waiting, still staring at the door, the RAs reappeared and gave a thumbs up. With that gesture, Mr. P moved in front of the middle of the group and the residents made a semi-circle around him and the RA staff.

"Gentlemen, I wanted us to meet this evening to discuss the events of today. As some of you may have heard, a small group of your fellow dormmates thought it would be a good idea to get drunk in the middle of the day and go for a walk around campus. Gentlemen, this is a dry campus, on top of the fact that none of you who reside in Jackson Hall are of legal drinking age. You all are in a privileged position, being able to attend Fulton-

Harley University. You can take advantage of all the tools, resources, and connections that being at this University affords most of you. Now you fellas are old enough to know right from wrong, but I don't think you all are at a mature enough stage for you to understand the gravity of the issue that you all created." He paused briefly to glance around the group, shaking his head in disappointment. "But.....I too was once in your shoes, fellas. I get it, chasing skirts, getting you a lil' taste here and there. But y'all can't do it in the dorm. Not my dorm. So here's what's going to happen. I spoke with Dr. Frances about the situation, pleading with him to not take any kind of action against the gentlemen who committed the offense or the dormitory." The group murmured amongst themselves as the mention of the school's President made the situation a lot more serious. "After pleading with him and providing an alternate solution, there will be no administrative action taken this evening in the wake of the events that happened today." Without being too excited, the group let out a sigh of relief. "But," Mr. P continued, "I'm going to give you all ten minutes. Ten minutes to bring down all the alcohol and anything else you all have up in your rooms that should not be there. We'll have tables set up in the lobby for everyone to bring everything down and place it there. After the allotted time has expired, the RAs and myself will thoroughly go through each floor inspecting you all's rooms. If there is anything in your room that is forbidden on campus, you'll be expelled and ordered off campus by 5 tomorrow afternoon. There will be no listening to your story or second chances. This is your second chance. Do I make myself clear, gentlemen?" Mr. P finished his speech as he gazed into the eyes of his dorm residents. "Yes sir," the group responded before a couple of students rushed back into the door, leading the group back into their dorm and up to their rooms. As the group walked back into the building, Sly looked around, wondering what would be exposed as he looked to his right at the large foldable tables Mr. P had referenced in the lobby across from the office. As everyone made their way back to their rooms, Sly and Eugene headed up to their room on the fourth floor. Sly opened the door and Eugene went over to his side of the room. Sly plopped down on the bed and laid back, "Shit, do I have to go back downstairs if we don't have anything in here?"

After a moment with no answer, Sly sat up to see Eugene pulling a couple of water bottles out of his desk drawer. "Easy?" Sly asked, surprised as he stared at his friend in shock.

"Don't be like that. Just because your first drink was some flat ass Coke and some warm SoCo. I wouldn't wanna drink either after that."

The two laughed, as Sly thought back to the graduation party that Eugene was referring to. "I mean you know I don't care bro, but I didn't think you would have it in here is all," Sly said, trying to get his cool points back.

"You know me Jones, I like to be prepared. It's hot trying to get something the night of a party. I just get it and hold it for when it's needed," Eugene said, explaining his logic.

Sly nodded in understanding, while shrugging, "I mean, I guess that's good logic."

The two laughed again and Sly noticed that one of the bottles was basically full of Vodka.

"Are you about to take all of them downstairs?" Sly asked, now intrigued by the situation.

"I mean, yeah. You heard what he said, right?" Eugene answered.

"Look at this bottle. It's the same as the water bottles you already have. Just keep that one. Take a couple of water bottles out of the pack, put that one in there so it looks like you haven't reached it yet and then place the actual water bottles back in front of it," Sly whispered to his roommate as the RAs and dorm director were patrolling the hallways.

Eugene looked at his pack of water, then to his roommate before pointing to his temple and saying to his high school friend, "Check you out with the million-dollar idea."

Eugene took some of the waters out of the pack before sticking the alcohol filled bottle towards the back of the packaging. The two examined the package of water for what seemed like eternity before heading downstairs with the bottles that Eugene had stored. As they made their way down the stairs, Mack was coming from upstairs with a large Hawaiian Punch bottle that was about half full. Sly pointed at Mack as they started down the stairs.

"Jungle juice," Mack responded before looking around and taking a small sip then placing the cap back on. As they soberly walked down the winding stairwell, they saw others coming down with every kind of liquid container possible. As they continued down to the lobby, Sly looked into the lobby where Mr. P had directed students to bring down their alcohol and whatever else. Sly spotted a laundry detergent container, a few Hawaiian Punch bottles, similar to Mack's, a couple of thermoses, Gatorade bottles, and tons of water bottles filled with Vodka, White Rum, or Gin. Each table looked like students were trying to organize the liquor that was being turned in. All the darker liquors were on the front tables as all the lighter or clear liquids were placed on the tables closest to the back wall. As students dropped off their stashes, Mr. P instructed everyone to go back upstairs to their respective rooms. Sly waited outside of the room as Eugene and Mack came back out, then the three made their way back upstairs. As they approached the fourth floor, Mack asked Eugene, "Y'all gon' be on the game after this?" Eugene responded "yea" and Mack dapped up the roommates before heading up to his floor for the room inspections. Sly opened the door of their room as the pair waited for the dorm director to make his way up to their floor.

The floor was relatively quiet compared to its normal noise level. Every room was quietly waiting and listening for what was going to happen next. With slow, hard steps, resembling those of a giant, Mr. P reached the fourth floor.

"Fourth floor of Jackson Hall, go ahead and come out to your doors."

Sly and Eugene opened their door as the rest of their floormates did the same.

"Gentlemen, this is your last opportunity to be forthright and turn in any kind of liquor or contraband and not face any penalties. If you are caught with anything, and I mean anything, by anyone, not just me – but anywhere on campus – you will face expulsion. Do I make myself crystal clear?"

The floor replied in unison, "Yes sir."

Mr. Parnell went down the right side of the hallway, with Daryl and Cole's room being the first room to the right. The two nodded at Daryl, as the RA and dorm director invaded their room. After a few moments of everyone staring at their door, unable to see what was happening inside, Mr. Parnell came out and announced, "I hope you all have your rooms clean too. We may have to start implementing room checks cause some of y'all need help cleaning."

Murmured chatter filled the hallway until finally, someone with a deep southern accent blurted out, "Not on this floor. We keep our stuff clean."

Mr. P shook his head, "Listen gentlemen. If I implement something like that, it won't be for just one floor. It will be for the whole dorm. If you don't want that to happen, y'all need to help those who need it. Just like you don't want to have mandatory room checks, I don't want to walk around this dormitory and have to smell y'all's body odor. I told the lower floors and I'll tell the fifth floor when I go up there next," Mr. P concluded.

He continued to make his way down the hall, thoroughly inspecting each room. As he came back up the hallway towards Sly and Eugene, the door of their floormates closed behind them with each inspection. As Mr. P and Gary went into the room, looking under the beds and in the closets, Sly and Eugene sat on their beds while their room was searched. Mr. Parnell gazed over at Eugene's side of the room, seeming to look directly at the pack of water on the floor.

"Looks to be all clear here. Y'all fellas have a good night," Mr. P said as he and Gary hurried out on to the next room.

Eugene turned on the game console and Sly sat in the second chair as they selected their teams for Madden. Slowly, different members of their friend group came back upstairs to their room. The squad sat in relative silence, listening to the sounds outside the door, before Corey asked in a whisper, "Does anyone still have anything?" Without a word, Daryl, Eugene and Mack all looked at Corey shaking their heads in confirmation. The room then erupted with laughter.

## Scene 15
# First Night off Curfew

As the leaves turned colors and fell from the trees, Fall semester at Fulton-Harley was in full swing. Sly headed down to the lobby and heard Mr. Parnell yelling, "Happy Homecoming!" as he made his way down. Sly threw up a peace sign with a smile and continued towards the door. He thought to himself, *It's Monday, and it's not like homecoming at Denali, where each day was themed. At least, I hadn't heard anything about it or seen any flyers about it.* Sly continued about his daily routine and went to the café for breakfast before heading to his first class of the day. Making his way from the café towards his class, he passed a couple of guys walking towards him yelling in different directions, "Norva tickets. Get ya Norva tickets." Sly walked past the gentlemen, wondering what they could possibly be yelling about before 8 am. As he made his way into the T-Sci building, he spotted different colored flyers hanging around the atrium. Sly walked towards his classroom but slowed down momentarily to read what was on the brightly colored paper. As he read down the list of events, he glanced back to the top to read, "Fulton-Harley Homecoming 2006", and realized that what he had experienced in high school was not going to compare to his first college homecoming experience.

Sly went into his classroom and noticed that there were fewer people in attendance than there had been at any other point. He surveyed the room then headed to his self-assigned seat. The professor walked in and shuffled up to the board and his desk. "Good morning class, and happy homecoming week to you. As a gesture of school spirit, I'll be canceling class for Friday." Those in attendance looked around in concern, as the professor continued,

"But we will be having our midterm exam next Wednesday, ok?" Through mixed reactions, the sparse class responded, "Yes sir." The professor proceeded with his lesson for the day for the few students in attendance, who were obviously having a hard time concentrating. A couple of moments before the end of the class, Mr. Majtah looked at the clock, and then back at the class. He shook his head and announced, "Class dismissed." The students almost sprinted out of the classroom, in a rush to get through each class to engage in all the activities that came with homecoming season.

Sly stopped by the Student Center before his last class of the day and paid closer attention to the Homecoming flyers as he passed them. From what he could tell, it appeared that the first event of Homecoming week was going to be a comedy show. Sly looked at the flyer, assuming that it was like the football games and that he would be able to attend just by flashing his student ID, until he further noticed the prices at the bottom of the flyer. "I don't have thirty bucks for that," Sly said aloud, but to himself, and he put his headphones back on his ears. Before walking off, he looked at the flyer again to see if there would be anything else he might be interested in going to with a lower price point. Without an immediate solution, Sly headed out of the Student Center and on to Dr. Wright's class.

As he entered the Business building, Sly noticed that it was somewhat busier on that side of campus than normal. Tables were being set up in particular spots in the halls of the building like they might host vendors later in the week. As he made his way into the classroom, Dr. Wright spoke to the students coming in, "Good glorious morning students, and happy homecoming week." As the room filled and Dr. Wright made his way from the door to the front of the classroom, the chatter in the room became quieter. "Is anyone going to the comedy show tonight?" he asked the question to the class as a couple of students raised their hands in response. "It's gonna be a good show. I heard we got Mo'Nique." The chatter picked back up before Dr. Wright spoke again, "Ok, ok. Well, just to make sure we're all on the same page, I will not be canceling any classes this week. We only meet today and Wednesday, and none of the events for Homecoming happen during our class time. I'll be in attendance and I'll expect the same of you all. Is that crystal?" Dr. Wright said, as he looked around the room receiving a less than enthusiastic, "Yes sir." Dr. Wright proceeded with teaching his normal class, while half the class paid attention and the others were already making plans for the rest of the week. As the class carried on then concluded, Dr. Wright remarked to the class, "Remember to study for our celebration on the plantation in between your Homecoming fun. Let's remember why we're here, people," he exclaimed as the students poured out of his classroom.

Sly exited the Business building, feeling slighted by his professor, even though he himself didn't have any plans for Homecoming. As he headed back towards the residential side of campus, he elected to go back through the Student Center. The Student Center was packed to the point it looked like a Student Center Friday. Sly had never seen the building this active so early in the week. DJ Mile High was on the stage. He faced the student body with his hype man beside him and asked, "Who's ready for FHHC 0-6?!?!" As the Student Center echoed with cheers, Sly looked around while trying to avoid getting sucked into the middle of the Student Center. As he continued to shuffle his way through the crowd, he looked up on the steps to see the usual suspects, all posted near the platform or just below it, sitting on the steps.

Finally, Sly made his way up the steps and spoke to his classmates while cracking jokes on the way up. He dapped up Melo and Danny before greeting the rest of the squad.

"Aye, y'all going to the comedy show?" he asked the two gentlemen, as they all looked down at the madness that the Student Center had become during Homecoming.

"I hadn't planned on it," Melo said nonchalantly as Danny added, "Yea, naw. Not for thirty dollars. And I really like Mo'Nique too."

Sly shrugged at the answers and Danny quipped back, "Nah, I can't do thirty for some jokes. I can sit in the room with y'all niggas for some jokes for free."

All three of them laughed as they watched the sororities stroll to "Knuck If You Buck".

"They really be out here being mad disrespectful to each other," Danny commented as he pointed to the ladies making gestures towards another sorority.

"Shit, they can disrespect me any damn time. Those girls fine as shit, boy. That red do something to a nigga," Melo commented and they laughed again.

Sly dapped up the two before heading back out of the Student Center early to beat the rush of people who would soon follow. He headed back towards Jackson, passing Corey and Nate in the process.

"Yo, you not gonna stay in the Student Center? I heard the shit was turnt," Nate asked as the two approached Sly.

Sly shrugged. "It was cool, but there's a lot of shit going on in there," Sly said, pointing behind him to the Student Center.

"That's what I like to hear," Corey replied, rubbing his hands together.

"Ok Birdman," Sly quipped, and he and Nate shared a laugh at Corey's expense.

"You gon' be at the courts later?" Corey asked before dapping Sly again.

"Probably. Why, you gon' be out there?" Sly asked.

He couldn't ever recall seeing Corey on the basketball court.

"Hell nah, man. Football field or on the track, I can't be touched. But y'all draw a little crowd sometimes hoopin'. So, I gotta make sure I'm in the vicinity."

Corey's answer clearly showed his confidence and knowledge of self.

Laughing, Sly responded, "Ok, that's word. We'll make sure to put on a show and give you plenty to talk about."

Sly strolled past the Architecture building, beelining for the front door of Jackson Hall. As he approached, he noticed that the last few residents that had come out of the door were wearing huge grins on their faces. Curious, Sly entered the dorm in a somewhat cautious manner. Crossing through the lobby, he heard Mr. P's voice yell out of the office, "There's no curfew this week for Homecoming. If you're going to go somewhere over the weekend, you'll still need to sign out, but there won't be any curfew this week." Sly slowed his pace to make sure that he heard the dorm director correctly. After passing the door, Sly paused for another brief moment and listened to make sure that he heard the entirety of the message before racing upstairs.

He burst in the room, panting and out of breath. Before Sly could get the words formulated, Eugene said, "Nigga we know, no curfew. Don't matter though. Not like niggas got anywhere to go," he continued without ever looking up from the game. Sly felt belittled for his excitement, but realized that his friend had a point. Still, he refused to accept defeat.

"I mean, you could make a move," Sly suggested, not giving up on the idea of the endless possibilities that college life could offer.

"And go where? With what car? And do what? On a Monday. And if I do bag something, where are we going? Not like we have visitation here. We might as well be in prison," Mack ended his rant, throwing his hands up in the air.

"I feel like that's a tad bit extreme. Prison, my nig?" Sly proclaimed, trying to reason with Mack as he continued, "I get it's not much to do, but just being able to go out and take a walk or some shit is the exact reason why it's not like prison though," Sly added to affirm his logic.

"Nigga, I was speaking figuratively. Of course, it's not like prison. But locking down the dorm so you can't come and go as you please feels closer to prison than school," Mack further explained, sticking to his guns.

"Well shit, I hope I have to never compare the two, cuz I know prison is trash," Sly said as all three of them laughed.

They gamed for a while longer, then everyone filed out of Sly and Eugene's room, as the sunlight dwindled. Shortly before the group returned from the café, the sun was basically all but gone.

"Y'all going to the comedy show?" Eugene posed the question to everyone in the room. Everyone shook their heads, and Daryl added, "Nah, I'm good on that, but what's the first night off move?"

The group looked at each other, before Kevin spoke, "I mean, you got 'em. You tell us?"

Everyone laughed, as Daryl commented back, "I have no such thing sir. But please, speak it into existence."

"I mean, it is a Monday. How much stuff could possibly be going on?" Sly asked, only to be met with criticism for his lack of ambition.

"But the possibilities, man. That's what college is all about, possibilities," Mack said as he dapped up Daryl, as they both understood what was at stake.

"I'm pretty sure college is about an education, but I could be wrong," Corey retorted as the group laughed.

"You know what I mean, man. You could sit in your room and get your degree, but did you really experience college if you take that route?" Mack pleaded his case.

"I think that's more on a person-by-person basis, as well as the school. I don't think it's possible to just sit in the dorm here. And if you do, it'll be a true testament to will power," Kevin added to the conversation.

"I hear all that. But again, fellas, what's the move for tonight?" Daryl persisted with his question.

"There are no moves for freshmen guys. The freshmen girls are gonna get signed out by the upperclassmen trying to fuck them. Unless you find an older chick on campus who doesn't live on campus, you'll be on a dummy mission," Eugene explained, summing up that there was little to no hope for him or his friends.

As the group gamed and more time passed, Kevin looked back at the clock that read 10:49 p.m. He turned his attention back to the game while announcing to the rest of the group, "Aye, ten minutes before the curfew." Everyone glanced at the clock. Sly grabbed his hoodie and headphones before heading towards the door.

"Uh oh, looks like someone has a move," Eugene quipped as the rest of the group egged him on.

"Come on Easy. You know Duchess would have my head if I did some shit like that. Not going out to make no noise. Just going to take a walk," Sly explained as Daryl commented on his excuse.

"Take a walk?? Is that what we calling it nowadays? Let us know how your 'walk' went when you return."

Laughing with the rest of the group, Sly responded, "I'll return with a full report," before he closed the door and headed down the steps.

When he reached the bottom floor, there was a small pack of guys huddled around the door, waiting for the clock to strike 11. Sly made his way through the crowd of what he perceived to be even bigger goody-two-shoes than he was. He walked out the front door, flipped up his headphones and escaped into the darkness towards the cemetery.

As Sly made his way past the Architecture building and turned towards the Student Center, he looked around and noticed that there was no one out taking advantage of the extra time the Freshman class had been granted. He went from quietly reciting the lyrics to himself to belting them out loud, putting on his own little concert. "The red dogs trippin' and these niggas still snitchin'. The ol' lady cross the street still bitchin'. It's three in the morning, take yo ol' ass to sleep. Third time she done called the police this week. Lookin' at my Frank Muller it's about that time....." Sly recited with confidence and happiness as he repeated the words from one of his favorite rappers. As he continued rapping, passing by the converted high school that now housed the school's Thespian courses, there was a tap on his shoulder from behind. In a moment of embarrassment, Sly turned around, cheeks flushed. He turned to see who had caught him in the act.

"You were into it, weren't you?" Jodie asked, laughing, as Sly just stared at her, stunned. "Oh, don't be so dramatic," she added while nudging Sly who still hadn't spoken.

"Man, you caught me off guard like shit. Where are you coming from?" Sly asked, trying to gather his thoughts while giving Jodie a hug.

"They told us yesterday that we would be off curfew for the week for Homecoming, so I was in the library trying to make sure I got everything done before Thursday. That way, I can do whatever I want this weekend," Jodie explained to Sly as they walked back towards the residential side of campus.

"That makes a lot of sense, and I'm glad to hear you're out here trying to make the best of the situation. Sounds like your dorm director was trying to set y'all up for success. Also sounds like you've grown to kinda like Fulton-Harley, but I could be wrong," Sly commented after hearing the excitement in Jodie's voice.

She shrugged while giving a little giggle then responded, "It's more so the people. I'm still not a fan of the administration or the state of Virginia," Jodie stated firmly, to which Sly responded, "No one is a fan of Virginia. Just happened to be where my parents were when I was born, and they never decided to leave," Sly said, feeding into the statement Jodie made. They both laughed.

"You just headed back to Tillson?" Sly asked while passing the Journalism building and crossing over to the women's side of campus.

"Yea, where else would I be going?" Jodie asked with a somewhat serious tone.

Sly noticed the change and responded with a shrug, "Girl, you grown. I don't know what you got going on."

"Boy bye. I'm not out here trying to be labeled a hoe within the first three months of school. And you know that's what they gon' say about the girls that are already signed out and have been signing out since school started," Jodie continued with her logic, as Sly tried to understand it all.

"Wait, so you've seen girls getting signed out since we been here?" Jodie, with a straight face, nodded to Sly, before adding, "Yea I don't know if they already knew people here or what, but the girls in the dorm can be mean, for no real reason. Just like the people are the reason I'm staying, the people are also the reason I'm not the biggest fan of this school. But I guess the good outweighs the bad," Jodie finished explaining. Sly nodded, understanding the logic behind the lesser of two evils.

They made their way to the front of Tillson Hall, and Jodie reached her arms around Sly's neck for a hug before he held the door open for her and a couple of her dormmates to walk through. Sly headed back to the male side of campus, shortly before receiving a phone call from Duchess.

"Where are you at?" she asked frantically.

"Walking back to my dorm, what's up?" Sly responded, not sure of where the conversation was going.

"Oh, because one of my classmates from high school said they just saw you walk a girl back to their dorm. So who is she?" Duchess asked with an assumption on the tip of her tongue.

"Her name is Jodie, from New Jersey, and she didn't want to be here either. I walked her back to the dorm because that's a rule here Duchess, I had to. I'm not doing anything though. I promise," Sly tried to explain to his girlfriend who wanted no parts of his explanation.

"Whatever Sly, whatever," Duchess said angrily through the phone.

Sly responded reassuringly, "Hey, even though I'm not there with you and you're not here with me, we're still together always, ok?"

There was a slight pause on the other end of the line before Duchess responded, "Ok, Sly, I'm trusting you."

## Scene 16
# FHU Homecoming

Fully embracing the lazy college student persona, Sly rolled around in the bed to no alarm around nine in the morning, still resisting the urge to open his eyes.

"Nigga get up, it's Homecoming," Eugene yelled and threw a pillow at his roommate.

"But the game doesn't start 'til three and that's when my parents said they'd be here," Sly said as he turned over, trying to decide whether to get up or not.

"Well, you saw what the week was like leading up to this. You think that the game is the only thing going on today?" Eugene asked as he stared at the back of Sly's head.

"Ok, ok, you made your point. I'm getting up," Sly said reluctantly as he got out of bed and looked for his toiletries.

Upon returning from the bathroom, Sly noticed that Eugene was already dressed in his tracksuit and about to head out. Before he spoke, Sly paused and mentioned, "I almost forget that you're on the football team sometimes." Eugene looked at Sly, who paused before adding, "What? Whenever we were in high school, we both played. Now I'm not playing. I just have to remind myself that I'm not playing and that you are. Just weird is all."

"You gon' get a chance to correct it next semester," Eugene responded before dapping his friend and heading to the gym to prep for the game.

Sly headed to breakfast, per usual, and while there he ran into Daryl and Melo.

"Aye, y'all hype about Homecoming?" Sly asked as he slid down in the seat next to Melo and across from Daryl.

"I mean, the week is pretty much over. The only thing left today is the game and then there is some kind of party tonight," Daryl responded.

Sly asked in response, "Is the party on campus?"

Daryl and Melo both shrugged their shoulders as they continued their conversation about all the events throughout the week and the final one later that night.

"Well some way, shape, or form, I'm sure we'll find out more information about that party tonight and can figure that shit out," Daryl exclaimed as the other two agreed.

All three of them grabbed their trays and emptied them into the proper receptacle before heading for the exit.

As they made their way out towards the Student Center, they encountered a small group of guys huddled out front. "Norva tickets, get your Norva tickets. Twenty a pop," one guy yelled as he swiveled his head back and forth. Sly and the fellas walked past the guys, "That's like the second or third time I've seen them this week. What's a Norva?" Sly asked as the other two shrugged while the two groups crossed paths. One guy out of the group asked, "What party y'all hitting tonight fellas?" As the three freshmen shrugged, the guy followed up with, "Y'all should check us out," as he handed each of them a flyer. The group of party promoters passed, continuing their advertisement.

The three friends started walking again as Daryl asked, "Where's Norfolk?"

"On the other side of the tunnel," Sly responded quickly. They looked at each other stumped while continuing towards the Student Center.

"Maybe Dre is going," Melo said as they turned the corner of the backside of T-Sci.

When they entered the Student Center, they could already hear music being played, along with a slowly growing crowd. The three made their way to their usual place on the steps and waited for the others to trickle in. As the fellas slowly showed up, one here, a couple there, a group or so lastly, they finally filled the landing. Overlooking all that was Homecoming Saturday, Sly received a text on his phone, 'Be there in 30', from his sister. He slipped his phone back in his pocket after responding and heard Will, another one of the fellas, ask, "Aye, y'all trying to go down to the tailgate?" in his North Carolinian accent. "I'm game," Sly said walking down the steps. Melo and Daryl went too, as well as a few others, but the majority of the group stayed.

As the four of them went towards the back exit, they branched off from the others that had come down and opted for the closest exit. They waded through waves of people, vendor tables, and exhibitions before making it to the exit of the Student Center. Once outside, they were hit with the aroma of several stalls preparing different types of cuisines, like fried foods and desserts. They greeted some of their classmates, resisting the urge to stop at any of the food vendors. Melo, feeling incredibly tempted, commented while walking away, "Shiiiittttt, I might have to come back and get me a funnel cake though." They all laughed and made their way across the street. The group formed a type of line as they walked through the narrow walkway between the gymnasium and the tennis courts, greeting fellow Harlians the whole way. As they reached the end of the path, they gazed upon the ocean of black and red, showcasing all the love amongst the different classes, fraternities and sororities, and the welcoming of outsiders as well. It was a true testament to what the school meant to so many people. They made their way into the crowd, giving daps, handshakes, and hugs to everyone they came across and was introduced to. As they walked further into the parking lot, they ran into Will's roommate.

"Ayyye, what up folk? What y'all on mane?"

"What up wit it fool?"

The two dapped up as Will turned around. "Aye, this my roommate, Hurse."

Sly dapped the guy up as he appeared to already know Daryl and Melo. Will slipped a flask half way out of his pocket as the group circled around.

"We just need to get some cups," he commented as he looked back over towards the tents.

Daryl walked over, accompanied by Hurse, who started joking alongside Daryl as soon as the two were beside each other. They waited for a moment before the two came back offering up the cups to the group.

"I'm good, my parents 'bout to pull up in a minute," Sly said, refusing the cup.

"Where you from?" Hurse asked quickly.

"Richmond," Sly responded, just as quickly.

"Ohhhh shit. You a lil' local," Hurse said, laughing with the group.

"Nah, it's close, but it's not local," Sly responded firmly with a smile followed with, "Where you from?"

"Shawty, I'm from da A, but my folks stay out in Memphis," Hurse answered proudly.

"Man, I went to Memphis once and loved that shit," Sly replied excitedly, as Hurse responded again even more proudly. "Man, yea Memphis be turnt, just like Atlanta."

The two dapped again before Will distributed the alcohol amongst the cups.

"I'm 'bout to head over to meet my parents, fellas," Sly stated before he dapped up the group and made his way towards the back parking lot of the stadium.

While passing by the arena, he spotted Kevin and Brandon. He waved them down, and as they walked closer, he shouted, "I'm going to get some food with my parents if y'all want some." The two quickly went over with Sly as he made his way to the further parking lot on the campus. Sly called his sister and she guided him over to their truck. "Heyyyyyy, how have you been enjoying your first college Homecoming?" Ria asked, excited to hear her son's answer. Sly shrugged, "It's been cool. These are my friends, Brandon and Kevin." The two guys shook Sly's parents' hands as well as his little sister. "So, where are you guys from?" Sly's father asked after a brief pause. "DC," Kevin responded, followed by, "The Bronx," Brandon opted to state his borough, instead of the state. "Oh, those are cool and big cities. That must have been interesting," Mina commented. "Yea, something like that," Kevin said with a laugh as Brandon nodded, chuckling along. Alonzo had already set up the grill after asking the question, throwing hamburgers and hot dogs on it afterwards. The group of guys continued the conversation with Sly's mom and sister about their experiences thus far in their college careers. "You guys eat cheeseburgers?" Alonzo asked from the back of the truck. "Yes sir!" Kevin and Brandon responded in unison. "Ok, good. You know Sly doesn't eat cheese, except on pizza." Brandon and Kevin looked at Sly, trying not to laugh with Brandon saying under his breath, "What kinda weird shit is that, bro?" And with that comment, all three laughed, with Sly pausing to say, "It's because of the mold, man. Don't make it weird." All of them laughed again, as Alonzo came back to the front of the truck with a serving tray full of hotdogs, hamburgers, and cheeseburgers. The three boys ate until their hearts' content. Encouraged by Sly's parents, they continued the conversation about their ambitions and future endeavors.

Sly stood up and brushed off his shirt, then placed his paper plate in his seat before stretching. As his arms came back down, he offered to take his friends' and family's plates over to the closet trash can.

"So what have you done so far for Homecoming week?" Alonzo asked, interested in Sly's response.

"Nothing really. We got off curfew, shockingly. That's about it."

"Why is it shocking?" his father asked firmly.

"No reason, just all the rules is all," Sly responded nervously.

"So you haven't done anything all week?" Ria asked as Mina stared in her brother's face before letting out a long, "Lammmmeeeee."

Alonzo pulled out his wallet and handed his son forty dollars. "Go do something tonight. I know there has to be a party or something. Go to it."

Sly looked at the money in his hand, then at his parents, before looking over to his sister who had joined the chant of Kevin and Brandon, "Do it, do it, do it, do it."

"Don't be lame," Mina screamed over his friends.

"Yea, there is a party tonight and there are guys walking around selling tickets. Ok, I'll go," Sly promised his parents, knowing he had no real way to get to the party.

As Sly and his two friends walked away from Sly's parents, waving them farewell, Brandon asked Sly, "So which Homecoming party are you going to?"

"There's more than one?" Sly asked, puzzled by the idea.

"Yea nigga, the only party can't be in Norfolk. Wherever the fuck that is," Brandon answered quickly, to which Sly responded just as quickly, "It's across the tunnel."

"Dre?" Kevin asked, looking at both Brandon and Sly.

They all shrugged, confirming that none of them had seen him all day. As they made their way back into the thick of the tailgate, they were greeted by more fellow Harlians. They walked back towards the Student Center, this time on the opposite side of the tennis courts, and Sly noticed they could clearly hear the roar of the crowd at the game.

"We must be winning," Brandon said.

"We've won every game this year. That's why I didn't go to the game today because Homecoming is usually a scheduled blowout," Sly said as they walked past one of the entrances of the stadium.

When they approached the Student Center, they saw Dre coming out.

"Just the man we were looking for," Kevin said as Sly and Brandon nodded.

"I ain't do shit," Dre exclaimed, as he started to walk away from the fellas while they laughed.

"Nah, nigga we were gon' ask what party you going to tonight?" Sly asked as the group co-signed the question.

"Ah, shit, well I was gonna fuck with that Norva. What y'all doing?" he asked, relieved.

"Shit, probably the Norva if we can ride wit' you," Sly said in a type of question.

"Shit, that's a bet."

"Word, now I just gotta find one of them niggas selling a ticket," Sly said as he turned around surveying the crowd back towards the tailgate.

"Wait, my nigga, you really didn't do anything this week?" Brandon asked, after being away from Sly's parents for at least an hour or two.

"Nah, didn't really want to. Well, I take that back. I did want to go to the concert but I didn't have the bread."

"But Mack snuck us in that joint," Kevin said as he dapped up Dre in remembrance.

"Hell yea, that Jeezy and Wayne show was nuts. You really fell asleep?" Dre asked Sly, as he nodded his head in disappointment.

"Damn, Grandpa. Yea nigga, you gotta get out tonight," he added on.

"Well shit, let me go find one of these motherfuckers and buy a ticket then, damn," Sly commented as he walked away from the group in search of one of the party promoters he had seen earlier.

# Scene 17
## The Norva

Sly walked around the tailgate for about another hour or so with no sign of the shouting promoters anywhere before he gave up and went back towards the dorm. He walked on the outside of the Student Center, passing the vendors in front of the stadium. He made his way past T-Sci and the Natural Sciences buildings, opting to walk all the way to the corner in front of the church. When he reached the corner, he heard from behind him to the left, "Norva tickets, get your Norva tickets before prices go up." Sly picked his head up and made a beeline for the group of party promoters. "Aye, let me get one of those tickets, man," Sly said. The guy looked at him and said, "twenty dollars." Sly put his hand in his pocket, being very sure to only pull out one of the bills that his father had given him. As he handed the guy the money, another handed Sly a ticket, "Party starts at ten." Sly responded, "Word," while thinking in his head, *damn, that's late*. He walked back over to the tailgate to see that the game was wrapping up and people were exiting the stadium. He headed back towards the Student Center to see if anything was going on or if he would run into someone out of the group.

After getting to the Student Center, he met with Kevin, Daryl, and Corey, and they walked back to Jackson Hall. Along the stroll, Corey, leaning over from the side, asked the group, "What party y'all going to tonight?" There was a slight hesitation before the rest of them answered in a staggered fashion, "The Norva."

"Isn't that across the water? I know y'all ain't got no whip so how y'all getting over there?" Corey asked, confused.

"Damn nigga, we can't have other means of transportation?" Daryl asked, stunned by his friend's assumption.

"I mean really. It's a valid question," Corey stated after Daryl's remark.

Sly and Kevin just chuckled and shrugged their shoulders as they made their way past the Architecture building.

"The way they've been pushing these tickets on campus, I know it's gonna be crazy," Sly said, trying to boost himself up for the party.

"Yea and it's not gonna be on campus, so it's 'bout to be majority upperclassmen," Kevin added again as he reminisced on the pajama party as the group made their way into the dorm.

They headed upstairs towards Sly's room when they noticed the hustle of Jackson Hall go into overdrive. As Sly opened the door to an empty room, Corey commented, "Dag, I don't think I've ever been in y'all room and y'all won't both here." He plopped down in the seat in front of the gaming console.

"You think Eugene'll get mad if I play the system?" Daryl asked as Kevin picked up the other controller.

"I'm sure he not gon' mind. Just don't mess with his franchise," Sly said as he laid back on his bed.

"So.....what y'all wearing to the party?" Corey posed another question to the group.

Sly looked at the other two, sitting up in the process, then back to Corey with a question of his own, "What you mean? I just bought my ticket. Dude didn't say anything about a dress code."

Corey laughed, as the other two joined in.

"Bruh, this is a college party, with grown women. You can't just go in there any kinda way. Gotta have some swag to ya," Corey said confidently as he rocked back in the seat.

"I guess..." Sly said nonchalantly as he sat back. He proceeded behind Corey, forcing him to sit upright in the chair as he checked the closet behind him. "So what is the dress code?" Sly asked, now hoping that he would have something that he could wear.

As Sly listened to his friends describe outfits they had in mind, he searched endlessly through his closet, hoping he could find something that went together. With each detail his friends mentioned, he selected pieces that he thought would look nice together.

"What time y'all getting ready?" Sly asked eagerly.

"Chill out man. Literally, the game ended like an hour ago. We got at least another three hours before niggas start moving to get there," Daryl said calmly before celebrating a touchdown at Kevin's expense.

They continued playing as Eugene and Mack made their way back into the room.

"Nice win today fellas," Kevin said as Mack quickly responded, "Y'all niggas was not in that game."

The whole room laughed at Mack calling their bluff.

"I went in for a minute, but y'all were blowing them niggas out so I just left," Sly said in support of the football team.

"But y'all been blowing everybody out. I'm not 'bout to sit and watch that when there are all these fine women walking around. Y'all get into a good close game and I'll come watch then," Kevin said as the rest of the room laughed and nodded in solidarity.

"Y'all boys already know what y'all wearing tonight?" Sly asked, hoping he wasn't in the boat alone.

"Oh course, you know I'mma be fresh," Eugene responded without even looking at his inquiring roommate.

"Shiiiitttt, you know, I might even have to pull out the Jesus piece to do a lil' flexin'. Ain't nothing but something to do," Mack added, setting in a touch of panic for Sly as he was the only one without a solidified outfit.

Sly changed seats between those playing the game as he frantically looked through his closet once more. He decided on an outfit, taking the suit jacket, pants, and shirt out of the closet to hang on the door of the stand alone. After doing such, he took his regular seat towards the head of his bed. The games passed with each hour, with the normal shit talking as the time flew by. Sly selected his play midway through the third quarter as he turned towards the clock in the room, waiting for Daryl to set up his defense. Right before the ball was snapped, there was a knock on the door. Eugene got up and opened the door.

"What up niggas?" Dre shouted with excitement as he strutted through the door in a yellow and powder blue suit with a matching hat.

He looked around the room at the freshmen still sitting in their loungewear, not even attempting to get ready yet. "Uhhhh, is y'all niggas still trying to go? Y'all look like y'all content being in a room full of sweaty guys all night."

The rest of the group looked around at each other, then back to Dre as they got up talking shit as each of them left the room. On their way out, Kevin and Corey both asked if they could ride with Dre.

"Y'all two make it a full car. That's five, and I'm not packing no more than that in that car."

Hearing the conversation, Sly became nervous because he realized that he had not yet asked his cousin for a spot in his car.

"Aye cuz, uhhhh, I heard what you said, but you got space for one more?" Sly asked nervously.

"I had already included you in that headcount. You don't remember asking me earlier? Melo gon' be our other person," Dre responded without hesitation. "Now hurry up and get dressed nigga, cuz if I miss some twerks because of you, we fightin'," Dre finished before picking up the player one stick and going back to the Madden game menu.

Sly gathered his things and made his way to the bathroom as the rest of the dorm prepared for their first college weekend without a curfew. Sly slid sideways up the steps as there was a group of football players coming down from the fifth floor, all in different phases of getting dressed. As he spotted Mack bringing up the rear, Mack said, "If Daryl is looking for me, tell him I'll be in room 218." Sly acknowledged Mack's statement, "Aight." Sly finally entered the bathroom at the top of the landing between the floors. While showering, Sly heard all the sounds throughout the dorm echoing in the doorless bathroom. After showering, he stepped out of his shower shoes, back into his slides, and headed towards his room. When he entered the room, Eugene, who was still in the room when he left, had already made it back and was half dressed.

"Damn nigga, you moving slow as shit," Dre commented.

Sly noticed the difference in preparation speed, but quickly responded, "I didn't know it was a competition. Plus, when have you ever been one to get to a party on time? I learned that fashionably late shit from you."

Dre paused for a moment to ensure the touchdown on the play call before responding, "This, my good sir, is different. Of course we can be late to a party where we are the only age group there. But here, we gon' be small fish in a big ocean. Gotta get there early and remind them often."

Dre's presentation almost sounded like he was trying to prepare the group for an epic battle.

"Ok, ok, I guess that makes sense," Eugene commented as he put his sweater over his outfit.

"Ok E, I see you went all in on the Earth tones, huh?" Dre said while staring at Eugene's fit.

At that very moment, Mack busted in the door and immediately commented on Eugene's outfit, "Aey bo', when you start working for UPS?"

Dre and Sly tried to keep a straight face before all of them burst out in laughter.

"You one to talk, looking like you robbed a husky pimp."

Mack tipped his hat as the room continued to roll around in laughter.

As Mack came further into the room, he asked Dre to quit the game he was playing. Within seconds, Daryl and Kevin also came into the room.

"Nigga, you expectin' a package?" Kevin joked as the rest of them laughed.

"Nah, nah, nah, I got a package for some Norva hoes though," Eugene replied with a nonchalant demeanor.

The whole room reacted with "ohhhhs", hyping Eugene up, "Ok, Mr. Camp, I hear you. Pimpin' since been pimpin', since been pimpin'," Dre commented as the laughter continued.

"Aye, Sly, Kev, y'all ready? Y'all heard from Corey yet?"

"Nah, he the only one that ain't came back up yet," Sly answered, as he looked around the room again.

"Aight, well someone text him and tell him to start walking towards the parking lot over behind y'all arena."

"Ok, but damn, why you park all the way over there? They were letting people on campus all day from what I saw," Kevin commented, while Sly added, "Yea, my parents were able to come on campus after the tailgate without an issue for a sec before leaving."

As they made their way down the steps, Dre paused and looked back at both of them and rebutted with, "I would've loved to have pulled up in front of your dorm, but do I look like someone's parent?" Then he added, "But I am trying to have someone call me daddy tonight, hello!"

The trio broke out in laughter as they reached the bottom of the stairwell and entered the lobby. They were greeted by Mr. P who had been wearing a Kool-Aid smile the whole week. They left out of the dorm and as soon as the door closed behind them, Kevin said sneakily, "Looks like Mr. P got some cheeks coming through tonight as well."

"Shit, everybody trying to get lucky tonight, with the exception of Sly," Dre said jokingly, and nudged his cousin in his ribs.

"Yea, yea, yea, that just means I'm the best wing man you got," Sly quipped confidently as he dusted off his shoulders.

As they turned the corner, headed to the main street on campus, they saw Melo coming from Roberts Hall.

"What's good, you filthy animals. Y'all ready to turn up?" Melo asked as he took a swig out of the water bottle he was carrying.

221

"Shit, hell yea. Let me tap that," Kevin said as Melo approached the stopped group. He passed the bottle to Kevin who took a little and then passed it to Dre who proceeded to do the same. As he handed the bottle back to Melo, the group continued towards the Student Center when they heard someone call out from behind, "Aye, wait….wait up." As they turned around, Corey was coming up, trying to tuck his shirt in his pants in the process. They elected to walk around the building, as it was a rather warm day for it to be as late as it was in October. They walked through where, earlier in the day, there were several tables and hundreds of people, only now replaced by these five freshmen. Back down the paved sidewalk that was crowded only hours earlier, they commented on the (still relevant) pajama party as they passed the gymnasium. "Only a couple hundred more feet to go fellas. We almost there," Dre said only half-jokingly. They continued to make their way through the still, somewhat full parking lot, covered with cars and plastic cups. They passed the fountain, and Sly noticed that there was a light shining in the middle where the water was spurting. He surprisingly also realized that he hadn't been walking the entire campus after all on his walks. "Aye, I really don't think they thought the light in the middle all the way through," Melo said, as he pointed out the light in the middle was red. The rest of the group laughed hysterically at his explanation. "Y'all gon' keep bullshittin', or we gon' get in the car so we can get to this party?"

As they made their way into the back lot on campus, they saw Dre's car parked off to the right. "Sooooo…….all these spots were free and you parked all the way over there?" Corey asked, looking at Dre with a smile. "I ain't even supposed to be over here, and you ain't gon' pay for the towing so……" Dre responded with the same rude delivery. As they made their way to the car, they spotted a couple of cars taking the road they had just crossed to get to the highway on the backside of the campus.

When they finally made it to the car, Melo shouted out, "Shotgun!" and it was followed by, "Window!" "Window!" ".....Shit," Corey said last as he looked at Sly and Kevin who smirked. Sly took the seat behind Melo, "I know how far Richmond niggas like to lean back when they drive. You can have the seat behind Dre, Kevin," Sly said laughing as he got in the car. Kevin opened the back door, looking at Corey who was trying to negotiate his way out of the middle seat. "So look right, if I can get you like two drinks in the party, you gon' let me take the window?" Without a word, Kevin smirked, shaking his head no as he placed his hand on Corey's back pushing him into the car. Dre turned the key in the ignition, ejected a CD, then flipped through a small CD book to pick another one. Finally, he pulled off and Melo and Dre let down their windows to let the cool, October, ocean breeze pass through the car.

As they pulled out of the parking lot and onto the backroad headed towards the on ramp, they steadily made their way over the speed bumps in place to prevent people from zooming by the nearby hospital. When the car approached the top of the hill, where the group could see the light and the on ramp, they were met with brake lights that didn't appear to be moving at all.

"Hot damn, look at this damn traffic," Melo exclaimed, while the guys in the back tried to make the best of their vantage points.

"Yea man, that's why I hate driving in the 7-5. The damn tunnels always have traffic," Dre explained.

He shook his head and tapped the gas to creep forward as the light changed, getting onto the on ramp which was also backed up.

"Aye Kev, grab me that water bottle back there, Jack," Dre hollered to the back of the car as he lit a Black & Mild.

Kevin felt around on the floor before finding the bottle and passing it to the front. Sly took notice of the brown liquid as they slowly passed under one of the street lights on the highway.

"Y'all be on that Brandy?" Dre asked as he offered the bottle to the car.

Melo grabbed the bottle, took a swig, and then replaced the cap before saying, "Shidddd, you know I'm with whatever dawg. Trying to just see some hoes man. Where da hoes at?"

The car laughed as Corey grabbed the bottle next. After he took a sip, he passed it to Kevin before echoing Melo, "We headed to them now, nigga damn. Patience, young grasshopper."

The laughter continued as the bottle continued to be passed around. Once again, Sly refused to drink.

"Aye nigga, why you not drinking?" Dre asked his cousin, looking at him through the rear view.

"You know I don't drink," Sly responded quickly, thinking that his family member would just drop it.

"But we 'bout to go to your first Homecoming. You don't wanna have a little?" Dre persisted as Corey swirled the remaining quarter bottle in Sly's face.

"Nah man, I'm good. I don't like the way it tastes," Sly refused again, and he snatched the bottle from Corey before handing it back to Melo.

"Oh, you a 'I need a chaser' boy. Oh aight," Dre teased as the rest of the car laughed.

Sly looked at his cousin before joining in the laughter, "Nah, just not for me," he said calmly.

"I can dig it," Dre replied, tipping his cap.

As the car drove out the other side of the tunnel, the traffic seemed to loosen up a bit, allowing them to come up to the speed limit.

"Looks like we gon' have a good time after all, boys," Dre commented, as he attempted to spark the cigar.

"You smacked nigga, roll up the window," Melo said laughing.

Dre looked over as he rolled up the window. He cracked a smile, blew out the smoke, then responded, "Not yet, but I'm hoping to get there, and then proceed to slap some cheeks, hello." He rolled the window back down as everyone in the car broke into laughter. Dre pointed to the sign that said their exit was two miles away. The car filled with anticipation as Melo turned up the music when they approached the off ramp. Dre slowed down as he came into the city. He carefully made his way through a green light while looking around. "The dude I work with said that this place is right beside the mall," he said.

"What mall is this?" Kevin asked, as the guys who were not from Virginia looked around like tourists.

"That's MacArthur. Pretty dope mall for real. Got like three floors in that bitch. Maybe four."

Sly had only been in the mall a few times, but that was enough to make an honest review. The car came to another light, only pausing momentarily before making a right turn and continuing down the street. Everyone looked for a sign or a large group of people. They passed a few blocks before Dre said, while looking around, "Yo, where the fuck is this place?" As he turned right again, there was a massive group of people walking towards a corner.

"Found it," Sly responded jokingly as the rest of the group laughed.

"Aight, now we gotta find parking." Dre sped off in the direction of a parking deck that was a block up before seeing a space off to the left and making a questionable turn in the middle of the street to get to it.

"I'm pretty sure that was illegal," Corey said jokingly, as everyone laughed.

"Well, won't nobody here to give me a ticket for it, so I guess it didn't happen," Dre said smoothly, finishing his cigar and popping the trunk to get his jacket, all in the same motion.

"Aight, before we get over there, everybody got their ID? Everybody got their ticket?"

All the gentlemen checked their pockets for the necessary items for entry. Lastly, they straightened their ties and jackets, and finished the remains of the bottle before walking towards the street where they had seen the crowd.

As they approached the street, they could hear the growing crowd, which was an indication that this would be a party like none of them had seen before. They picked up the pace of their walk, but not enough to dampen their cool. As they reached the corner, there were what appeared to be several different groups of women crossing the street with caution in their heel selections for the evening. Dre hurried over to one young woman who was having a hard time walking and put her arm over his shoulder, "Oh, thank you. Such a gentleman. And so dapper," the girl said, smiling and winking at Dre, as he placed his arm around her waist.

"Well, you know, that's just what us Richmond and Hampton gentlemen do," he said, nodding to the group to engage and returning the wink to the young lady who was grinning ear to ear at this point.

"Oh, you all are Hampton men? Oh we got some good ones here ladies," the woman gracefully said to her friends who appeared to be sizing up the gentlemen.

"So where y'all go to school?" Melo asked, somewhat breaking the trance the women appeared to be under.

"Oh, we attend FAMU," one of the girls said.

"Where's that?" Kevin asked.

"Florida," Corey answered in tandem with another one of the girls in the group.

"So how did y'all hear about this?" Sly asked, seriously curious.

"Well, I'm from Norfolk, and a lot of my friends went to either Norfolk State or ODU, and I still get a lot of stuff about what's going on, so we came up."

Sly looked at the group of ladies, stunned they had traveled so far for a party. As the larger group made their way into the line, the line monitor for the party came down and gave directions. "I need a straight line, people. It's really simple. A straight line. No one's getting in until I get a straight line," he said. As people slowly moved back, allowing a straight line to form, the large man continued, "If you have any kind of bottle or lighter, go ahead and throw it away. You cannot bring any kind of container or lighter into the venue." The man strolled up and down the line repeating the phrases. Sly and the fellas continued their conversation with the ladies they had just met while the monitor continued, "Make sure you have your ticket and your ID out when you get to the door. You must be eighteen to enter the party. If you are under eighteen, you will be denied entry to the party." Everybody continued conversing, as Kevin fell eerily silent. He nudged Dre, who turned around from the young lady with a slightly glossed look.

"Aye…..uhhhh, I'm not eighteen yet," Kevin said as low as he could, considering their environment.

"Oh shit, well damn nigga. Well come back and pick us up around two." Dre tossed Kevin the keys, then turned around and went back to talking with the young lady.

Kevin nudged him once more, "Uhhh….. I don't know how to drive."

Dre looked at Kevin with a dumbfounded face, "Nigggggaaaaa. Hot dammit let's go."

The pair hopped out of line as Dre yelled back, "I'll be back fellas, and Steffany, I'll be right back."

The pair sprinted out of line and back up the block just as a light rain began to fall.

With the sudden addition of moisture in the air, the line quickly bent to the very whim of the coordinator. Everyone quickly shuffled forward and the remaining fellas went under the marquee sign of the venue. Sly approached the gated off part of the line clutching his wallet while handing the bouncer his ticket and identification as he looked around. The bouncer looked down at Sly, shining his flashlight between the ID and Sly's face. After a thorough inspection of both, the man looked back up at Sly and uttered, "Hands please." Sly placed his hands out, not sure of what the request was for. The large man pulled out a permanent black marker and wrote two large 'X's on the backs of Sly's hands. Sly looked at the man stunned, and without another word, he waved Sly through as he handed him back the ticket and ID. Sly took a couple steps before turning around to wait for Corey and Melo to come through. As they stepped on the other side, Melo fixed his collar and looked back at the security. "See, he ain't have to do all that." They laughed and handed their tickets to the ladies at the door who scanned them and handed them back individually. The three made their way through the breezeway into the venue and saw the DJ on stage. There was a large, open room with a circular overlay that looked down on the middle of the dancefloor. The group slowly walked in, Sly in the front, just looking around, noticing different things throughout their gaze. All of a sudden, Melo shouted, "Aye yo, what up doe, cuz?" Sly and Corey looked around to see who Melo was talking to. Out of the crowd emerged a slim guy who was roughly the same height as Melo.

"Oh shit, what up Melo? How you likin' this Homecoming shit so far?"

"This shit sweet, for real, I ain't gonna lie. Shit cold," Melo commented, giving Fulton-Harley its just due.

"But, check right, these are the homies, Sly and Corey," he continued introducing his friends to his cousin Tyrone.

"That's word. Well y'all family now, so if you drinking, let me know something."

They all dapped each other up and headed towards the closest bar. Sly stared onto the dance floor, watching the crowd grow while checking back towards the door every so often.

As they approached the already crowded bar, Tyrone pointed to the steps past the bar and shouted, "There's another bar upstairs." The group went upstairs where there wasn't as much congestion. As they walked towards the bar, Sly split off and stood at the railing to look down at the growing population on the dance floor. As he watched, he felt Melo brush up against him. He leaned forward, peering into the crowd. "This shit icy dawg. Look at this man." The two took in the experience as Corey approached, trying to drink as much of the drink he had been handed before he reached the railing. As all three looked around, Sly looked back and noticed Tyrone head back downstairs. He turned back around as they continued admiring the crowd, waving and pointing to the other freshmen who had found a way to indulge in the experience. Moments passed and the trio went back down to the main floor of the party.

Just as their feet landed on the last few steps, Sly noticed Fin and Lincoln walking in. He tapped the other fellas and they all went to greet their friends. "How's it been so far?" Lincoln asked the group as he looked around the venue. "It's been cool. We just got here ourselves for real, and people still getting here. My cousin Ty is here so if y'all need a drink just find him," Melo responded as their circle opened, so that they all could see the dance floor. As they surveyed the layout of the party, each person split and went towards what, or rather who, they had been gazing at. Melo and Corey headed in the same direction towards one group of girls. Before they reached the girls, they devised a plan on who would talk to who before Melo interjected into the young ladies' dance circle. Fin went towards a group of freshmen women who had also somehow made the trip across the water. Lincoln went directly to the bar and searched for Ty or any upperclassmen he knew so that he could get a drink. Sly spotted Jade and her group of friends and made his way over towards them. As he looped around the edge of the dance floor, he kept an eye on where he was going while still looking around the whole party, simply amazed at the size of the event. He made it over to their group but noticed a guy had approached Jade. Sly paused for a moment, trying not to intervene, and heard Isis yell, "Awwww, look at Sly in his suit." Using the opportunity to duck out of the moment, Jade looked over at Sly with a wink before telling the guy, "Oh sorry, looks like my date just showed up. Where have you been?" She looked at Sly as everyone waited for his response. Sly paused momentarily, processing everything before blurting out, "You know tunnel traffic is crazy. How you doin' sweets?" as he winked back at Jade. The guy looked at Jade, cut his eyes at Sly, then walked away. Jade exhaled as she smiled at Sly, "I owe you one, my nigga. Check you out. You went and got fresh and shit. Okay, okay."

"Yea, I can put a lil' something together, but this shit is crazy really," Sly said looking around for a moment before he continued, "We were in line and met some people from FAMU."

"Yea that's typical," Cally chimed in.

"Yea, we done already spoke to different guys from Howard, West Virginia, Virginia Union, North Carolina A&T, and I think we talked to someone from Texas, too," Tina's other friend, Rosalyn, mentioned.

"Yea, Ros, don't forget the guys from NYU," Jade mentioned nudging her friend, and they all laughed.

"Damn, that's crazy. How do they do that for just a weekend?" Sly asked, just trying to consume all the information.

"It's Homecoming season, and this is just what happens," Isis said bluntly as the others nodded in confirmation.

"Where the rest of your friends at?" Jade asked, then added before Sly could respond, "I think this is the first time that I've seen you at a party alone."

Sly shrugged then waved his hands around above his head and said, "Most of them are just scattered."

"I did see, what's his name, uhhhhh..." Jade started as she looked to her friends for assistance.

They looked at her with a loss for words, before she started again, "Melo, I think that's his name, yea Melo."

Sly nodded, "Yea, we rode here together."

"With who?" Ros shot back, as they all waited for an answer.

"My cousin down here at school too. We rode with him," Sly said calmly as he realized that he was in rare space.

"Oh, so you just got everything working for you, huh? Got someone with a car so you can get around. Got some upperclassmen chicks to give you the game. You just got it all figured out, huh?" Jade said jokingly, and the whole group laughed.

Sly smirked and shrugged off the obvious advantages that he had over other freshmen. "I'm just a regular guy. I don't know what you're talking about."

"Yea, yea, yea. Look, don't get yourself in no trouble with that Howard girl, aight?" Jade said as the two hugged, followed by departing hugs for each group member before they walked away.

Sly stood in the vacant spot for a moment and looked around for his next destination. He spotted Fin and Melo talking to some girls from campus and went in that direction. As he waded through the crowd, Sly felt a pull on his arm from the opposite direction of where he was headed. When he turned around, it was one of the FAMU girls from the line outside. "Hey cutie!" The young lady grabbed Sly by the hand and guided him behind her before she started dancing. As the two danced, the other girls in the group recognized Sly and instantly started hyping their friend. The DJ mixed in the next song, and the young lady stopped dancing, then gave Sly a huge hug and kiss on the cheek. While still looking at his dance partner, Sly heard one of the other girls ask, "So where's your cousin?"

Sly looked up to see the girl Steffany, then looked past her and made eye contact with Dre who had just come in the building. "Oh, you know. He's around," Sly said casually as Dre came behind the girl with a bright yellow dress and wrapped his arms around her waist.

"Ya miss me?" he asked as he gazed into the young lady's eyes.

"Maybe a little. But you think you slick. You probably been running around this whole party ducking me. You probably don't even remember my name," she responded, cutting her eyes at Dre through her grin.

"Now Steffany, I had to go back across the water to make sure that my guy wasn't stranded and came back just to see you. You really gonna do me like that?"

"You know it's a cold world cuz," Sly chimed in to help his cousin's case. Though Sly agreed to be his cousin's wingman, in that moment, he was just trying not to stare too hard at the girl who had pulled him over.

Steffany had a type of puzzled look on her face as she added, "So you Fulton-Harley guys really are gentlemen. I'll be damned."

Everyone laughed as the two exchanged numbers. "What y'all doing after this?" Steffany asked, intrigued even more from the chivalrous feeling she was receiving.

"Well, we ain't got nothing planned, so if you trying to do something, just let me know and me and the fellas will roll through," Dre responded, not breaking eye contact.

Sly looked at the girl that he had danced with once more and she blew him a kiss and waved, as he and Dre walked away.

"Nigga......this shit wild," Sly said as he put his arm around his cousin and they made their way to the outskirts of the party towards the bar.

"You ain't never lied. Man it's some thangs in here. My Lord."

They looked around before Sly mentioned, "You know she stopped me like twice while you weren't here. Thought you had just dipped on her, I guess."

"Well I mean, she is here from Florida, so I'm not the one who's gonna be dippin', but ya know, whatever," Dre commented as he dapped up Tyrone. He got a drink and knocked it back in just a couple quick gulps.

"What happened with Skip?" Sly continued, curious as to how his cousin managed to make it back to the party so fast.

"Shiiddddd, I did 'bout 90 the whole way there and back, and it was pouring. I'm surprised I didn't hydroplane somewhere," Dre said as he laughed and shrugged off the pure insanity of his statement. Then he continued, "Man, I didn't think about it, but Kev never needed a license being up there in DC, so he never had a need to go get one. And he said they don't have it in school like we did. But shit was smooth, couldn't miss this shit," Dre finished.

He turned his head and intensely followed a young woman with his eyes who was approaching the bar. The two marveled for a moment or so before they went into the middle of the dance floor. There, they linked with other friends from the group and enjoyed dancing and mingling with all of the other party goers.

As the party wound down, the DJ started playing slow jams. Sly recognized the first song and the trend at the recent party he attended at Fulton-Harley. As he nervously looked around, Sly felt a tap on his shoulder. He turned around and noticed a much shorter girl standing in front of him with her hand extended to him. Sly took the young lady's hand as she stepped closer to him and placed both of Sly's hands around her waist. The two danced as Sly looked at the girl, wondering if the two had maybe crossed paths on campus. As the song began to change, the woman looked up and gazed into Sly's eyes and said, "I've seen you on campus. I'm pretty sure your friend likes my cousin, but I thought you were cute and wanted to introduce myself. I'm Heidi." Sly stood in shock by the beautiful, dark chocolate woman's confession. He attempted to piece his thoughts together before responding. Just as he parted his lips to respond, he noticed her cousin she referenced standing behind her. She waved while she talked to Melo. Stuttering over his words, but still trying to seem outwardly cool, Sly said, "Oh for real? Well damn. Thank you, gorgeous. My name's Sly. How come I haven't seen you on campus?" The two shook hands and walked towards the side of the dance floor to continue their conversation.

"I'm a nursing major, so most, if not all, of my classes are in the nursing building, so I'm rarely anywhere else on campus."

Sly nodded in understanding and continued with his questions. "Oh word, I can get that. Where are you from?"

"We're from Orlando," Heidi pointed back to her cousin again, "And what about you?" she asked, while tucking her hair behind her ear and flashing a smile.

"I'm from Richmond. So according to everyone from out of state, I'm a local, but Richmond is not like the seven five."

"I get it. People think that Florida is all the same, but it's different pockets in the state that do things differently," Heidi said, making the same distinction for her city.

"Well y'all do have 'Florida Man' headlines though," Sly said jokingly, and Heidi joined in confirming, "You not wrong, Sly, you not wrong."

The two laughed for a moment, flirting a little and looking into each other's eyes. Heidi interrupted her cousin's conversation with Melo to introduce Sly to.

"Y'all just rude, huh? Sly, I know you ain't know, but Heidi, you saw me talking to your cousin. The audacity," Melo said as he turned his nose up in a joking manner before everyone joined in on the laughter.

"Rhonda, this is Sly. He's from Richmond."

"Nice to meet you, Sly. Is that short for something?" Rhonda asked.

Sly responded quickly, "Yea," and hoped that it wouldn't lead to the obvious follow-up question.

Rhonda stared at Sly as she waited for the response, "So what is it?"

Sly paused again before looking around the group and venue, "I'd really rather not say."

"Come on, it can't be that bad," Heidi egged Sly on to make nice with her cousin.

"Allister," Sly said under his breath, trying to whisper as low as possible in the party.

"I'm sorry, I couldn't really hear you. What was that?" Rhonda asked.

Sly repeated his given name, only a little louder.

"That's not that bad. Is it a family name?" Rhonda asked. Then her cousin chimed in, "I think it's a cute family name. It is a family name, right?" Heidi smiled at Sly and he nodded at her.

Melo and Sly continued talking to the young ladies then Sly realized that the music had stopped playing in the background. While Melo was in mid-sentence, Dre placed his hands firmly on Melo's shoulders as he popped his head out to the side, "Well, hello ladies. I hate to have to pull these gentlemen away, but we have to make some moves to get back," Dre said, pulling Melo away and signaling to Sly to follow behind. Before he left, Sly typed his phone number in Heidi's phone then handed it back to her. The two groups went their separate ways as Sly checked his phone to see a text message from a phone number saying that it was Heidi. He smiled as Dre and Melo walked in front of him. He put his phone away and caught up to the fellas. As soon as he reached them, someone yelled, "Aye, wait up." They paused and looked back to see Corey running out of the venue trying to correct his tie. "No need for that big fella, an undone tie at this point in the night means you had a good time," Dre commented as Corey caught up. The four stood outside for a moment and spoke with the FAMU women again before leaving the party and making their way back to the car. As they walked in the general direction of where Dre had originally parked, they reached the top of the street and Melo, Sly, and Corey continued off to the right. Dre, on the other hand, made a sharp left turn and snickered to the fellas, "Oh y'all think I'm still parked over there? Y'all supposed to be the smart ones. Y'all know that spot was gone as soon as I pulled out." The three gentlemen looked at each other and laughed, realizing

Dre made a valid point, then changed course and followed him to the car's new destination.

## Scene 18
# Finals

Sly rolled over as his alarm blared, somehow louder than usual. He sat up in his bed and allowed his legs to swing off the side. He then turned off the alarm as he watched Eugene toss around while also trying to peer out of the frosted windows. Sly proceeded to pick out his outfit and get dressed for the day, having opted to shower the night before due to the freezing cold morning temperature. As he got dressed, Eugene rolled over, "You really going to class today?"

"Yea, why wouldn't I?" Sly asked, confused.

"You know they just gonna go over everything you've covered in the class. That's what a final is. It's the final exam to prove you know what the course is about," Eugene said as bluntly as possible.

"I mean, duh nigga. But if they're gonna tell me what I need to know, especially for their exam, I think that could be useful," Sly responded, questioning where his roommate was going with his point.

"Don't listen to me. I haven't had a class on Friday since I been here, and I refuse to participate in that nonsense."

The two laughed as Sly put his shoes on. Then Sly opened the door and closed it slowly behind him as Eugene made himself comfortable and drifted back off to sleep. As Sly made his way down into the empty lobby, he felt the cold draft through the crack at the bottom of the door. He zipped up his jacket before opening the door and heading towards class.

Students trickled into the classroom and Sly slipped in amongst the few as Mr. Majtah moved towards the front of the room. Sly took his regular seat then unpacked his notebook and pencil, with his final feeble attempt to make out what his professor was saying. He frantically jotted down everything he thought he heard the professor say. He peered over the professor's shoulder and copied the examples from the board. Confused and frustrated with how the class had gone thus far, he figured, *I've done this before. Shit, I got a 'B' in this same damn class less than a year ago.* He took a deep breath and refocused on the task at hand as he filled up page after page with notes. As the professor wrapped up the class, he paused for a moment to gather himself to make sure he was well heard and received. "I would like to bring to you all's attention that the final exam is a significant part of your final grade, thirty percent. This isn't something to be taken lightly and some of you are already in a space where you may need to retake the course. I urge you to study as much as you can and partner with some of your more successful peers." He scanned the room and made brief eye contact with Sly before he dismissed the class. Sly stood up slowly, never taking his eyes off his professor. He was thrown off by the uneasy look he was given, but the glare was never returned as Mr. Majtah made his way out of the classroom with the other students.

As Sly exited T-Sci disoriented, he realized that he had come out near the Administration Building. Looking around at the same herd of students making their way to class, he went down the steps and headed towards the Student Center. As he approached, he felt the soft touch of a snowflake land on his nose before opening the door. Sly quickly brushed his nose then rubbed his hands together, happy to be back inside. He passed the ballroom and rounded the corner toward the bowling alley before stopping at the water fountain for a quick sip. As he entered the atrium of the Student Center, he saw a couple of students sitting at the bar tables in the middle. Aside from them and the staff running the restaurants, the Student Center seemed weirdly empty. Sly walked through the section where there would normally be a lot of different people seated and noticed that it, too, was empty. Puzzled by where everyone was, Sly continued through the vacant Student Center and out through the back doors.

From the short walk inside, it appeared that the wind and weather had picked up. Sly pulled his hood back up as the snowflakes had already increased in size. He walked into the wind, staying on the pavement to avoid the already soaked grass. He looked up to see the door just a few feet away before he scampered over to it and hurried inside. He shook his head to shake off the snow before taking down his hood and walking away from the door. He dreaded the walk across campus back to his dorm, but continued on with the rest of his day, nevertheless. He made his way through the hallways of the Business building and noticed that everything seemed to be business as usual. Sly arrived at Dr. Wright's class and took his normal seat. Everyone was either settling in or making their way to their seat as well. Sly looked up at the clock just before grabbing his History notebook from his book bag.

"Good morning family and welcome to our closing preparation for our final celebration on the plantation," Dr. Wright said with equal parts energy and enthusiasm. Sly looked around to see if anyone in the class shared their professor's spirit. "As we discussed in the last class, your final exam will be cumulative. Everything that we've covered in class and that you all have already been tested on can be on the exam. But because you're all such great students, we're going to go over exactly what's on the exam. Are you all ready?" he asked and everyone perked up and grabbed their writing utensil of choice. Dr. Wright proceeded to outline to the class what would be on the exam and the individual topics that the class should study meticulously. Sly tried his best to write down everything that Dr. Wright was saying plus all the bullet points on the board. As his hand started to cramp, Sly paused, thinking of an alternative for note-taking. He took out his textbook out and bent the corners of pages of relative information. Dr. Wright concluded class, gazed at his students then uttered, "It has been an honor and privilege to educate you in your first semester at Fulton-Harley and I'll forever be grateful for you all. I know that you all will go on to do great things and will inspire others to do the same." He waved and dismissed the class, as some students moved to the front of the class to speak with him further. One girl yelled, "We love you too, Dr. Wright," on her way out of the classroom. Sly made brief eye contact with his professor, exchanged head nods, and headed out of the class to avoid the crowd at Dr. Wright's desk.

When Sly walked out of the building, he looked up expecting more snowflakes. Instead, he was met with bright sunshine. Confused, he squinted his eyes and pulled down his hood as he walked towards the café. As he made his way through the deserted campus, he pulled his headphones up and scrolled through the songs until he settled on one. He passed the building that held his English class and looked around mumbling, "Never in a million years did I imagine I'd get my thrills, listening to the squeals of the PJ wheels…." He continued rapping along as he watched one or two students enter before him at a time. He jogged up the steps and noticed a piece of paper taped on the inside of the door, just as he reached for the handle. He read it quickly before opening the door for the group of ladies that were walking up behind him. They walked in, he followed behind, and they all submitted their tickets for lunch. Sly pointed back to the sign as he asked the café worker, "So y'all gon' open again at nine and stay open until eleven?" She handed him back a half ticket and said, "Yes, baby. We do that for finals every semester so that those who are staying up late can come get a snack. That way, y'all don't have to order no pizza or any foolishness like that. We'll have it all right here for you." Sly smiled as he thanked the lady and proceeded to enter the line to grab a meal.

After lunch, he walked out of the café, unzipped his hoodie, and noticed the slight spike in humidity. He flipped his headphones back up and headed back towards Jackson Hall. In true Sly fashion, he put his head back down and started mumbling again, "I like my beat down low, down low, down low, down low. I like my top laid back, laid back…." Sly strolled along, almost looking for people, but not straying from his normal route before he finally reached the dorm. He entered his room and Mack and Daryl were there playing the system, while Eugene sat at his computer. "Do y'all not have finals?" Sly questioned. Without looking away from the screen, and in tandem, they responded, "Only two" and "Kinda". Sly dismissed the first answer and looked directly at Mack and asked, "How do you 'kinda' have finals?" Sly pulled out his desk chair. "It's like this bo'. I got finals, but there's just a proctor, not the actual professor. So, I'm gonna have someone take my test for me and then my last one is online, and I'mma do that joint upstairs with my book beside me. Annnddddd………touchdown, " Mack said proudly. Sly shrugged at Mack's response, who seemingly had college all figured out. Realizing his situation didn't compare, Sly pulled out his Pre-Calculus book and placed his laptop on his desk to begin studying.

"You about to study right now?" Daryl asked, still glued to the game.

Sly looked at him, and then the others, before turning his attention back to Daryl, thoroughly confused. He answered, "Uh yea. Is there a reason I shouldn't be?"

Laser focused on the play at hand, Daryl gave a delayed response, "I mean, I heard the library is where it's at during finals time."

Now Sly was really confused. "What do you mean?" he asked, only half paying attention, as he opened his book and entered his password on his computer.

"I mean, there will be the pretty and smart ones in the library, my guy. Everybody needs a little break when the mind gets tired," he said. He smirked for a split second and looked over at Sly who couldn't do anything but laugh.

"Bro, I think you got the wrong idea about the library. You gon' cause them girls to fail."

"So long as I pass," Daryl said without hesitation. The room laughed, even causing a pause in the game.

"That's savage bro," Eugene commented and Daryl gave him a Jordan-like shrug.

As the day turned to evening, the four became six, as Kevin and Corey came into the room. Sly pushed back from his desk noticing it was dark outside and chose to finally participate in the room's conversation. As the conversation moved from topic to topic, Corey picked up the brush on Eugene's nightstand and brushed his freshly cut hair. As he looked in the small mirror that was beside the bed, Eugene peeked through Kevin and Daryl for a direct view of Corey and asked, "Uhh, when did I say that you could use my brush? What? You trying to get your waves like me, huh?"

The room laughed as Corey shrugged it off, "Shit, you might wanna get like me little tike. This fresh cut ain't for no fresh man, you feel me."

There was a slight pause before Kevin blurted out, "Nigga what?"

The whole room burst into laughter.

"I'm going to see an upperclassman chick, man. Y'all chill out," Corey quickly retorted to clean up his mis-timed joke.

Mack looked closely at Corey and examined him before saying quietly, "Corey, your head like a whole ass cube bo'. That shit clear as shit with this low cut."

Kevin and Daryl paused the game and everyone in the room took their time looking closely at Corey's head. He looked back at each one of them irritated. After maybe a moment, the room erupted in uncontrollable laughter.

"Oh my God, bruh," Kevin said, rolling out his seat.

"That's your name from now on, Cube," Daryl quipped in between breaths as they all continued laughing.

All the while, Corey stood there with a straight face.

"Cheer up Cube. At least you got the upperclassmen," Sly chimed in and the room exploded in laughter once again.

The friends continued gaming before Mack sprung up and asked, "Aye, what time the café close again?"

"Eleven," Sly answered, remembering the details on the flyer.

"The café is open?" Kevin asked, confused, while looking at the clock.

"Man, you and Eugene need to get out on Fridays, Skip," Mack said as both just shrugged their shoulders.

Eugene responded, "Kinda late for that now."

They laughed as Mack got up. "Well shit, it's only gonna be open for another hour. I'm about to head that way."

Everyone in the room followed behind. Sly hesitated for a moment, before eventually got up, grabbed his keys and locked the door behind him.

After trekking across campus, they arrived at an over-capacity café that had people still coming and going. The fellas slowly climbed the steps and waded through the crowds of people just hanging out and those trying to get inside. Finally, they reached the ticket lady who was only checking student IDs. "Aight now baby, we got hot dogs, hamburgers, fries, and pizza. You don't need a ticket. Just go on and get what you want," she said. They walked past the lady and into the line where the food was being served. Sly noticed that only this one line was open, which was probably the reason for the backup. They all grabbed trays as they methodically waited for their turn to be served. Sly pointed to the pepperoni pizza before holding up two fingers and then pointed to the fries. After he received both plates, he placed them on his tray one at a time. Next, he picked up two cups and filled them both with drinks before following Daryl over to the clearing where people were getting up from their seats. The rest of the group had already claimed the seats. While the group ate their meals, Sly looked around, trying to gauge the room. He noticed some students who appeared to not have a care in the world, or as he had coined, 'The Mack Effect'. Then he noticed the polar-opposite end of the spectrum, those who seemed to be stressed to the point of exhaustion and defeat, agonizing over the exams to come. Sly felt conflicted. He had only one class that he was worried about, but he reassured himself that he had taken Pre-Calculus before. There was no way that he wouldn't pass the class.

As the fellas left the café, the group ran into Danny, Lincoln, and Dennis.

"This shit packed like a bitch," Lincoln said as he dapped up the group when the two intersected. Everyone nodded and looked up towards the door.

"Was it worth it?" Dennis asked.

"It wasn't anything special, just some hot dogs, hamburgers, fries and pizza. Normal shit," Kevin answered.

They continued to all dap each other before the three headed inside. Sly and the rest of the group slowly made their way back towards Jackson Hall before Daryl posed the question, "Who trying to go to the library?"

"Right now?" Sly asked, befuddled.

"Yea, right now. Why not?" he asked, reassuringly.

"Ummm, maybe because we don't have any books. Da fuck, my nigga?" Kevin said, and everyone laughed as they still trudged towards Jackson.

"As long as I pass, Skip, my boy, as long as I pass. I can't take the test for them," Daryl said, and the group laughed just as hard as they had before.

"Daryl out here to ruin lives," Corey explained as the group continued to laugh.

"Quiet Cube. If she can entertain me and get good grades, I know she's a keeper," Daryl came back. He received nods of approval with that logic.

"I really can't argue that logic," Corey said and everyone laughed again.

As the group entered the dorm and went up to Eugene and Sly's room, Daryl posed the query to the group again, "Last chance. I am going to go grab a bookbag, but I'm still going to the library."

"Ahhhh," Corey blurted out as everyone laughed.

"Shiidddd, I'll go. I don't have my first final 'til Tuesday. Let me go down and grab my bag," Kevin announced and left the room.

Daryl looked each of his friends in the eye with a suggesting shrug out the door.

"Fuck it, I'll roll. I mean tomorrow is Saturday. I'll be right back," Corey said, as he dapped up Daryl and headed out the room.

"Thank you. Anyone else?" he asked, looking at Eugene, Mack, and Sly.

"You do realize it's quarter to midnight right? Who you expectin' to see in there?" Sly asked Daryl.

"Like I said earlier, women that can entertain me while also maintaining their work. I know I'm going to ace my finals. Otherwise, I wouldn't be out at all," he calmly and eloquently explained.

"Yeaaaah, you really can't argue that logic," Mack said, echoing Daryl's comments.

The two that had left returned ready to go. Daryl gestured to the room, "Last chance fellas, any takers?"

"Y'all go 'head. I'm sure we'll hear about it," Eugene responded, and the three left the room.

## Scene 19
# Christmas Break

As the days dwindled down to Christmas, the temperature in the city steadily decreased to increase the Christmas spirit with thoughts of a Winter wonderland. Despite being born in the month, Sly despised the colder months of the year, touching the window and shaking his head. He retreated back to the living room where the family was in the dimly lit room watching TV. Just as Sly took his place and got comfy, his mom asked, "Have you received your grades yet?"

Sly looked at Ria puzzled, before he responded, "Oh, uhhhh, no I haven't seen them, but they should be posted."

"Anything we should be worried about," Alonzo bellowed, never breaking eye contact with the TV.

"Nah…. I don't think so," Sly answered, really unsure as he tried to recall every answer he bubbled and wrote down during finals week.

He tapped his foot nervously, as he knew he had received mostly good marks during the semester but wasn't sure how it had all been calculated. As his parents went up the stairs, Sly attempted to stay seated and calm as he anxiously rubbed his hands on his pajama pants. He popped up and paced back and forth in front of the steps as he recounted each bad grade he had received over the past four months. His heart raced as he entered their room and took a seat where he could see his parents, but not the computer screen. He sat and watched as they used the same portal to check Sly's grades that they used to pay his tuition. As his parents navigated the site, Sly labored to keep his heart rate down. Each silent moment built more and more anticipation.

"Uh, Sly, come here and explain this," Alonzo said sternly as he pointed at the screen, all the while glaring at Sly.

Sly cautiously approached his parents as he watched the joyous expression leave their faces. He stepped in between them and glanced at the screen to see his father pointing to a 'D'. Sly shuffled back in confusion, quickly trying to defend himself, "I know this stuff. I know I know this stuff. I couldn't understand the professor. I took this same class last year at Denali and got a B+ in it."

Sly pleaded his case as his heart rate and inflection in his voice spiked. Noticing her son became more and more frantic, Ria placed her hand on Sly's shoulder, "We know you can do better, because we've seen you do better. You did finish the semester with a 3.3 GPA, so overall good, but you've never brought home a 'D' Sly. Are you sure you aren't too distracted at Fulton-Harley?"

Sly took a moment to contemplate the question posed to him. As he reflected on his first semester, beginning in classrooms, those reflections quickly shifted to a reel of party memories flashing through his brain. Before getting stuck in that space, he quickly answered his mom, "Distracted? By what?" Sly said, trying to reassure his parents.

"Son, I've watched you play football for over ten years. I've never seen your head more on a swivel than at Homecoming," Alonzo said as Sly's mom laughed and he blushed a tad.

"I was just looking around. It was a new experience for me," Sly said, trying to justify his wandering eyes.

"Look Sly, we were young at one point too, so we get it. All we ask is that you remember what you went to school for," Alonzo added, and Sly nodded, acknowledging his shortcomings. He promised his parents that he would do better in the upcoming semester. "You better. School is too damn expensive for you to be bringing home 'D's," Alonzo said as they walked out of the room. The three approached the steps when Mina came out of her room and asked, "What's for dinner?" They briefly paused before starting down the steps and their mother answered, "Well Mina, we're trying to figure that out now." The four went downstairs to enjoy a meal together, taking advantage of the fact that their family was whole for the time being.

Sly popped up out of his sleep and looked around before realizing the day then laid back down. He heard his sister shuffling around in her bed in the next room. "Mina, you up?" Sly whispered to his sibling, as he got up and approached her door. He heard his sister's feet hit the floor in the silent house before she responded, "I've been awake for a while. I was just waiting on you," Mina said calmly as she stood in the doorway to her room. They went downstairs, being mindful to avoid the third step that creaked. When they reached downstairs and turned the corner, Sly's walk slowed as he appreciated the Christmas décor and smell of fresh pine as he wasn't home for the lead up. He watched his little sister bounce around from gift to gift, peeking at the base of the tree to see the latest version of Mortal Kombat. Sly picked up the game case, ripped off the plastic wrapping to grab the booklet inside, then placed the game back under the tree. He skimmed the book to see which new characters had been added. Mina showed her big brother the gift she had been asking for all year while complying to Sly's request for the remote. As soon as the remote touched his hand, Sly turned on the TV and cable box simultaneously. He then typed in the channel number as he waited for the picture to come to the screen. As the sound of the marching bands blared through the speakers, Sly quickly tried to turn it down before he placed the remote on the arm of the chair, confident the picture would be up soon. A few moments later, Sly and Mina heard their parents shuffling upstairs before making their way down.

"Merry Christmas, Merry Christmas!!!!" Ria shouted as both of her children ran over to give their mother a big hug.

"Merry Christmas, Ma," Sly said, squeezing his mother.

"Yea, Merry Christmas, and thank you," Mina said with a quick hug before darting back underneath the tree. Sly's mom headed into the kitchen as Alonzo followed and grabbed a coffee mug out of one of the cabinets above the stove.

Before she got started on breakfast, Ria asked her son, "What time were you going over to Duchess'?"

Sly shrugged as he answered, "I guess I should go ahead and get ready to go now, so I can head back to this side of town at a reasonable time, right?"

His mother nodded to the sentiment, never turning away from the mixture she was stirring. Then she responded, "That's right, because everyone is gonna get here around five, so I need you back before four, just in case I need some things at the last minute."

"You mean everyone is *supposed* to get here around five," Sly said, as the family all laughed.

"Yea, ok. You better be here before four, understood?" Ria asked with a straight face in between the laughs, while still mixing the pancake batter.

"Yes ma'am," Sly responded promptly.

Mina and her brother continued watching the Christmas parade, anticipating breakfast, and allowing their inner child to shine through. After seeing a special performance in the parade, Sly ran upstairs to change his clothes before he heard his father's voice echo through the house, "Food's ready!" Sly raced downstairs and joined everyone who was already sitting around the kitchen table. Sly pulled out his seat as his mom placed the last serving dish filled with corned beef hash on the table. The family all bowed their heads and Ria prayed, "God, bless this food. Bless this house. Bless our family, as our children strive and overcome obstacles to achieve great grades. We thank you for allowing us to celebrate another Christmas together, and we're praying for many more. In Jesus' name, we pray…" They all proclaimed, "Amen," and passed the dishes around. After a filling meal, Sly headed towards the door before Mina stopped him, "Hey, give this to Duchess' little sister." Sly paused as his sister handed him a small box. "I know she'll love this," Mina said smiling as she hugged her big brother. Sly kissed his little sister on the forehead and waved bye to his parents before walking out the door.

Upon his arrival, Sly tugged and pulled to get the three boxes out of his back seat. He could hear the screen door of the house swing open and slam shut. Before he could turn his head, he heard, "Carrottttt!!!!" and felt Duchess jump on his back, kissing his cheeks while they shared a laugh. He stood up as she dismounted him, only to be picked right back up and swung around with a big hug from her boyfriend. They gazed into each other's eyes for a moment and smiled before sharing a kiss. Ms. Dawkins stood in the doorway of the house and watched her daughter enjoy a moment of happiness before shouting out into the yard, "This is a nice Hallmark moment, but you all need to come in the house. It's cold out here." Sly and Duchess looked back towards the house, smiling uncontrollably, then picked up the presents and headed towards the house.

As the couple made their way inside, Sly hugged Ms. Dawkins and Shanice, Duchess' sister, before grabbing the smallest box off the top and handing it to her. "And this one's for you. It's from my little sister." Shanice looked up at him with a huge smile and screamed, "Thank you Sly and Mina!!!!" As she took the small package and ran down the hall, Sly turned his attention to Ms. Dawkins, "And for you, ma'am," Sly declared as he handed Duchess' mother a wrapped box. "Why thank you, Sly. You didn't have to." He smiled and shrugged at Ms. Dawkins. Lastly, he turned to face his love. He started patting his pockets. The calm look was gradually replaced by one of panic and confusion, as Sly frantically continued to check his pockets, making Duchess nervous in the process. "Stop playing Sly. You really lost my gift?" Sly looked up at her after a couple of minutes with a smile as he pulled a small gift box out of his front right pocket. "You play too much," she yelled with a smile, punching her boyfriend in the arm. Sly pulled her close and kissed her on the forehead. She stood in front of him and unwrapped the gift with equal eagerness of her sister. Duchess opened the box and pulled out a thin gold chain with a cross hanging on the end. She held it up for her mother to see before asking, "Is this real?" Her mother and sister laughed as her mom added, "Don't be out here trying to turn my baby neck green."

"It's real," Sly said calmly as they all shared a laugh.

"How did you afford this?" Duchess asked, mesmerized by the brand new jewelry.

Sly shrugged again, ignoring his girlfriend's question and replacing it with another, "Do you like it?"

"I love it, Carrot!" Duchess affirmed softly. She threw her arms around her boyfriend's neck and squeezed him tightly before giving him a kiss on the lips.

"Ewwwwww sissy!!" Shanice screamed as she laughed and pointed at her big sister.

The four of them all sat together for a moment before Ms. Dawkins went into the kitchen. Duchess and Sly sat on the couch while Shanice continued playing with all of her Christmas presents. Duchess leaned her head on Sly's shoulder as they sat, hand in hand, watching her little sister and the television simultaneously. After a moment or two, Duchess whispered to Sly, "I'm worried about next semester, Carrot."

Sly leaned his head on top of hers and responded, "Worried about what, baby?"

"Us," Duchess said, sitting up to look her now concerned boyfriend in the eyes.

"What are you worried about?" Sly asked with a genuine concern for preserving his girlfriend's peace of mind. He genuinely wanted to understand so that he could put her at ease.

"You guys will be off curfew this whole semester and you want to walk on the football team."

Not seeing her point, Sly stared, waiting for more before responding after a small pause. "Ok, but what does that have to do with us?" Sly asked, not making the connection.

"You're gonna have all kinds of women in your face. My friend from high school told me about how the guys are at Fulton-Harley."

Duchess stared her boyfriend down, only to receive a massive hug and kiss on the forehead.

"Ok, first, I don't know your friend or what experiences she's having. Can't speak to that. Second, I'm not just going outside since we're off curfew. I did it once, and there was literally nothing happening or to do, so I don't do that. And lastly, baby,

I'll be a walk-on, not a scholarship athlete. Most people won't even know I'm on the team. You really don't have anything to worry about."

Duchess side-eyed her boyfriend, who now had his head on her chest looking into her eyes.

"I'm trusting you, Sly. Please don't make me regret it," Duchess said softly as she rubbed his head.

"I won't, I promise," he responded in an equally mellow tone before the two exchanged a kiss.

After about an hour or so, Duchess got up and went to her room. At that moment, Ms. Dawkins leaned her head out of the kitchen and signaled for Sly to come talk to her. Sly got up, walked towards the kitchen, and glanced down the hall for Duchess before sitting at the kitchen table next to Ms. Dawkins. "Sly, you know I like you, right?" Ms. Dawkins said, looking firmly at the young man. "Yes ma'am," Sly responded to her query, wiping his hands on his jeans. "Ok, well my daughter feels a hundred times stronger than I do. You understand where I'm coming from Sly?" He slowly nodded in confirmation as the two locked eyes. "She's worried you don't feel the same way about her but her personality won't allow her to show concern. You have to look after her even though you all won't be together, you understand?" Ms. Dawkins continued and Sly nodded along with her, agreeing on all fronts. Locked into the importance of the conversation, his concentration was broken when Duchess returned with a huge smile on her face and began playing with her little sister. Sly watched for a moment before looking back at Ms. Dawkins, who provided him with a nod of dismissal, then he left the table. Before he walked back into the living room, he stepped back into the kitchen towards Ms. Dawkins, "Ms.

Dawkins, I love Duchess. And I love y'all like family. I'd never do anything to hurt her or y'all." Sly looked at Ms. Dawkins and the two exchanged a hug before he walked back into the living room. After a few moments passed, Ms. Dawkins came to the edge of the kitchen to ask, "You going over your cousin's house after here?" Sly responded, "Yes ma'am," as he sat on the floor with Shanice, who gave him a tour of her new doll house. "Ok, well I'm going to give you something for your aunt and uncle. Make sure they get it, ok?" Sly turned his head and nodded as she placed the item on a chair next to the steps. Sly glanced at the clock and realized that the day was already halfway over. He rose to his feet and gave Shanice a hug before he headed into the kitchen to say goodbye to Ms. Dawkins. As the two embraced one another, she whispered in his ear, "Remember our conversation." Sly stepped back, looked Ms. Dawkins in the eyes and slowly nodded. As he turned away from her mother, Duchess came back up the stairs, "You're leaving already?" she asked with a pout, extending her arms in front of the stairs. Sly grabbed his girlfriend around the waist and picked her up. As they both smiled and looked into each other's eyes, Sly responded, "Baby, I gotta go see the rest of the fam. But we got another week at home. I'll be back over here, you know that." The two shared another kiss then the couple headed down the stairs towards the door. "I love you baby," Sly whispered to Duchess before he kissed her on her forehead. "I love you too, Carrot," she muttered in his ear as the two embraced one final time. Sly popped open the screen door and hopped down the steps to make it to his car in a couple of bounds. He honked his horn and waved out his window to the family standing on their porch, then pulled away.

Sly woke up in a dark room and wiped the crust out of his eyes. As he stumbled out of his room, he saw the bright red setting sun through the window behind the chandelier. It made several small prisms throughout the upstairs hallway. Sly descended the stairs and heard the TV announcer making a call, "He fakes a pass and takes the shot. Bang!!!" Sly moseyed towards the loveseat, crossing his father's face. He plopped down on the seat and listened as his father barked, "Aye, don't just fall on that couch. That's why the shit's uneven now." Sly sat back up and glanced into the kitchen to find the time. The two of them sat and watched the game, creating their own commentary. Ria came downstairs and asked, "Why are y'all always sitting in the dark?" She hit the dimmer, which only added a slight glow to the room. They both turned around and looked at Ria, before hearing Mina streak down the hallway to crash onto the other couch, "What did I miss?"

"The Redskins suckin', per usual. That's why I switched the game," their father replied as Sly burst into laughter.

"Oh, your boys ain't much better."

"But we are better," Sly quickly snapped back with amplified laughter.

Just then, his phone buzzed with a text. He leaned over, making his pocket available for entry. As he looked at his phone, his mom called from the kitchen, "I'm surprised you're not running out of the house across town."

Sly looked over at his mother before he remarked, "Nah, not tonight Ma. I'm about to go meet some of the fellas at Reggie's to shoot pool."

"Oh, how's he been? And his parents?" Ria asked about one of Sly's longest friends.

Sly stood up and stretched as he responded, "I'm sure they're doing well, and they'll more than likely be up when I get there. I'll tell them y'all said hi."

He ran up the stairs and returned in a hoodie before heading out through the garage.

Sly turned down his radio as he slowed into Reggie's neighborhood. He noticed the cars of a couple of former teammates outside as he parked across the street. As he approached the house, Sly could hear his friends in the pool room and hesitated a bit before electing to go to the front door. He hopped the steps, made it to the door and rang the doorbell. "Reg, there's somebody at the door," he heard Reggie's mom yell from upstairs. There was a brief pause before the door swung open. "Yo, what up man?" The two young men dapped up then walked into the house. "Ma, it's Sly!" Reggie yelled as they made their way into the living room. "Hey, Mrs. Applewhite!" Sly replied, yelling up to the second floor. "How ya momma doing? And ya baby sister?" she asked as the two guys made their way into the kitchen. "They're good. Mina will be in high school next year," Sly responded as Reggie handed him a soda from the fridge. They turned around to head into the garage and heard Reggie's dad coming down the steps. "Jones, how ya been man?" Sly dapped up Mr. Applewhite and responded, "I'm good, Coach G. Y'all been ok with all of us gone?" Sly joked with his former coach. "Dag, she's that old already?" Mrs. Applewhite yelled down. Coach G walked his son and Sly back into the garage where Eugene, Lenny, and Sam were already shooting pool. "Damn, I remember when you all were that age," Coach G said as he looked around the room of young men he had coached since they were old enough to play organized sports. "And now we out here runnin' things," Lenny said as all the fellas laughed. "Aight, aight now," Coach G responded, chuckling at the fact that his players were right.

Coach G wished his old squad a good night, and the players did the same. Sly went around the room and dapped up his friends.

"Jones, how you like FHU? Eugene said y'all had some joints out there," Lenny said while lining up his shot.

Sly shrugged with his answer, "It's aight, who got next?"

As Lenny and Sam exchanged shots, "I got next, and nah don't tell that lie. Sly love it at FHU," Eugene added and all the fellas laughed together.

"It's cool but I'm not ballin' yet so meh," Sly said and shrugged his shoulders before continuing, "I could take it or leave it at this point. I ain't sold yet," Sly pleaded his case.

"Shit, for forty stacks a year, you better find something to love about it," Eugene chimed in.

"And I already know 'Zo already told you that," Lenny added as laughter continued to fill the room.

"Nah, you right though," Sly responded as the laughter continued.

"Aye, y'all started y'all season yet, Sam?" Reggie asked, as he took the pool cue from him.

"Man, the season was already in swing when I got to campus. And they were talking about red shirting me."

"That's shitty," Sly added.

"Hell yea, and you supposed to be pitching, right?" Lenny asked.

"Yea, but I may end up playing short if I wanna get on the field," Sam said while shaking his head.

"That's better than nothing. They already told me I wasn't playing this year when I got to campus," Lenny said calmly, as all of his friends stopped and looked at him.

"You's a lie. How they not put yo' big ass on the field?" Eugene called out, as everyone burst into laughter.

"Nah, we got this 6'7" dude doing work. He already league bound, so I just been trying to pick his brain and do his workouts."

"Let me find out the military school putting out NFL prospects. Shit, I might have to transfer," Sly responded, saluting Lenny in the process, as everyone laughed.

"What about you Reg? How was your first season?" Sam asked, and they all awaited the answer.

"The playbook is like an actual book, bound and everything. And the game just moves faster. That's really the only difference."

"That's a really toned down answer," Eugene said, mocking Reggie.

"I mean, it really ain't that different y'all."

The room laughed before Sam rang in, "Yea, that's because you were doing all that wild shit before we graduated."

The room erupted in laughter again, as Reggie just smirked and smiled. "Y'all keep it down down there," Mrs. Applewhite yelled down.

"Yes ma'am," the young men responded in unison, as they had done millions of times before.

## Scene 20
# Welcome to Fulton-Harley Football

The Jones family pulled back in front of Jackson Hall. Sly didn't even wait for the car to come to a complete stop before he jumped out.

"In a rush?" Ria asked her eager son.

"This is a different approach from you," Alonzo chimed in as they all exited the car to see Sly off.

"Yea, this is it. Walk on this semester and become a Buccaneer," Sly said confidently as he hugged each one of his family members.

"Aight now. Just remember what you're here for," Alonzo reiterated to his son, only to have him respond, "Yea, football. Aight, y'all let me know when y'all make it home safe." They all laughed as they hopped back into the car, and Sly headed back into Jackson Hall.

Sly scaled the staircase, slightly winded by the additional stairs that weren't accounted for at his parents' house. When he walked into his room, the whole gang was back, playing Madden and talking shit as if the semester had never ended.

"Look who liked Fulton-Harley so much they came back for a second semester," Daryl shouted as the rest of the room laughed at Sly's expense.

"Y'all know why I came back," Sly responded with a confidence in his voice that was new to the room.

"Oh, you walking on too?" Corey asked, snickering.

"Yea, why?" Sly asked.

Corey burst into laughter, "I've seen you on the court. You're too slow to play college football."

The rest of the fellas looked at Sly for his response, "But I've seen you on the court too, and you lack the coordination to be a DB. And I mean, do I really have to say it?"

"Say what?" Kevin asked, prompting Sly for his response.

"He's short!!!" Sly yelled, as everyone in the room laughed harder.

"Corey, what you like, a solid three inches from being a midget?" Everyone in the room laughed uncontrollably, as Corey stared at Sly and the latter just shrugged.

"You brought this on yourself, but you'll get a chance to prove your point."

"Oh, I know," Corey responded quickly and eagerly.

The following day, Fulton-Harley began its Spring semester of classes. Sly woke up early with his same routine from the previous semester. Eugene rolled over annoyed, "You got another eight o'clock class?"

"Yea, why not? I already got the rhythm of this schedule, so adding the football stuff should be easy," Sly responded with his newfound confidence.

"Hmmmmm, if you say so," Eugene mumbled and rolled back over.

Sly left the room, went down the stairs, and made it out the dorm with virtually no traffic, compared to the first semester. He hurried over to the café for breakfast before rushing to the opposite end of campus for his first class of the day. Sly shuffled amongst the herd of students waiting until the last minute to arrive. When he finally reached the classroom, which was on the backside of the Business building, Sly slid into the classroom to see it filled, with one lone vacant seat right in front of the professor. Sly rushed over to take his seat as the professor waited for him to sit before going to the front of the classroom. "Good morning class. This is Psychology 103. My name is Dr. Payne. Please check to make sure you're in the right class." Sly looked around the room and noticed a couple of students get up and exit the room after checking their schedules. After the last student left, Dr. Payne continued laying out the class rules, "Going forward, when the clock hits eight, I'll be closing and locking the door. You can miss a total of three classes. After that, your grade will be an automatic fail." The professor paused at the onset of murmurs around the classroom. "Are there any questions?" she asked as the voices continued without a hand raised. Dr. Payne proceeded to hand out the syllabi and began teaching the class.

Following what felt like the longest fifty minutes of Sly's life, Dr. Payne dismissed the class. "And I'll expect you all to have the book by Friday's class!" she yelled as the students hurried out. Sly headed towards the Student Center, enjoying the scarcity of people moving around campus in the earlier hours of the day. While passing through, he noticed a flyer on the activity board about the football walk-on interest meeting, set for five that afternoon. He took his headphones down and carefully read the location before placing his headphones back over his ears, chanting, "We ready…We ready!!!" as he passed the bowling alley. Sly exited the Student Center and hopped along. He was so excited for the chance to compete on a division one stage.

Sly coasted through his classes and really struggled to focus on any topic as he replayed different drills and plays in his head throughout each class lecture. He finally arrived at his last class of the day and took a look around at the stadium-style seating for the course. He grabbed a seat off to the side, and as the room filled, a lady who appeared middle-aged and of Middle Eastern descent, came to the front of the classroom. "Good afternoon class. My name is Dr. Kushmir, but you all can call me Dr. K." The class collectively greeted the professor after her introduction and she proceeded to hand out syllabi to be passed around. As she instructed everyone to open their Biology book, she continued to discuss how the class would cover the various topics. As Sly turned to face his professor, he struggled to keep his eyes open as her voice drifted in and out. Ultimately, Sly lost his fight to the afternoon itis and was abruptly awakened by the clashing of a book closing in his ears. When he opened his eyes, half of his class had already packed up and left. He looked back towards the front of the room, where the professor had locked eyes with him. "You are Mr. Jones, yes?" Completely embarrassed, "Yes ma'am. I'm sorry for falling asleep," Sly quickly apologizes to his professor who responded with a laugh. "It's no problem, Mr. Jones. It is your grade after all. I get that you all are super busy and have a lot of different experiences going on. I would advise you against sleeping through exams and quizzes though. Just don't go to sleep in the front of the class. It's distracting to the other students. If you can take a seat on either side and at least three rows up, I'll continue to count you as here." Surprised by the professor's sense of humor, "Yes ma'am," Sly answered quickly and hurried out of the classroom. As he walked out of the building facing the cemetery, he glanced around before heading back to Jackson Hall before his much anticipated meeting. As he rushed into his room, he was surprised to discover he was the only one there. He put his book bag down and thought of how to best utilize the room he currently had to himself for the first time since being at school. Decidedly, Sly changed his clothes and turned on the PlayStation. As the loading screen flashed across the tv screen, Sly tapped on the button relentlessly, in an attempt to speed the process. He could hear more and more voices in the hallway and he desperately wanted to take advantage of this moment alone before the guys rolled in. Just as his game kicked off, Mack, Eugene, and Corey all walked into the room. Mack went around the front of the tv and exclaimed, "Go ahead and back out so I can play bo'." Sly backed out the game and handed Mack the second controller in the process. "I got next," Corey shouted. "We gon' have to leave after this," Sly said as he pointed to the clock in the back of the room. Mack and Sly played while the room was relatively silent. Suddenly, Mack addressed the tension.

"Y'all boys nervous?"

"Nah, never that," Corey said, sticking his chest out.

Sly waited for the following play to end before he responded, "I mean yeah, a little. It's like a childhood dream bro."

"Nah, I feel you. That's how you know you gon' go hard," Mack said before adding, "……And that's a touchdown."

"Hot dammit," Sly shouted as he tossed the controller on Eugene's bed.

They all laughed before heading out of the room and to the meeting.

The four made their way out of the dorm and towards the T-Sci building. As they entered the building, they veered right, all the way to the end of the hall where there was a stadium-style classroom. The fellas shuffled over to their seats. Sly and the boys dapped up and gave pounds to other players, acknowledging all the guys he had met on the court or ran routes with out on Trenton Lawn. As the locker room banter continued, an older black gentleman came to the front of the room. "Ok now fellas, let's focus down." With just those few strong words, the room fell completely silent within moments. "Alright, good evening gentlemen. My name is Coach Samuel Nottingham. You'll hear players and staff refer to me as Coach Sno. Behind me, you all see my coaching staff. I will not always be available to you all. Get familiar with the gentlemen standing behind me. More specifically, your position coach." He paused for a moment and made sure that his instructions were received by every young man in the room. "This coming Saturday, at ten in the morning, we'll be holding a combine of sorts for you all. Each walk-on will run their forty yard dash, agility drills and skill specific drills, while being coached up throughout. Following Saturday's drills, we'll be starting Spring conditioning Monday morning. Conditioning will occur every day during the week and will start promptly at five each morning." Coach Sno paused again as some murmurs started to fill the room. Suddenly, one potential player left out of the room. "And that gentlemen, is the exact reason we do this, on top of preparing for the season. This isn't for everyone. Those who are late to conditioning will be required to complete additional conditioning. This will be team conditioning. Your coach may ask you all to do something additional as well. After a few weeks of conditioning, we'll hand out equipment and start Spring practices. You will not be given equipment if you miss more than two days of conditioning. There are absolutely no exceptions to this rule. Am I understood?" Coach Sno paused for another moment and received a mix of "Yes sir" and "Yes Coach." He paused again and scanned the room before he continued, "Also, once we start practice, we will be implementing a lifting routine for you all as well. Each of you will be required to lift either before or after practice. Your last obligation will be Study Hall. You all are students first and are not eligible to play without the proper grade point average. Our strength coach will put you on a proper workout for your position. After three weeks of conditioning and two months of practice, we'll have our Spring game. If you all impress my coaches and me to that point, you may get your opportunity, and I would implore you to seize every chance you get. I know a lot of you may have been highly successful in high school, but I want to let you know that means nothing here. You will have to outwork those beside you to get any and every opportunity you're afforded. Do I make myself clear?" And with zero hesitation, the classroom responded as a whole, "Yes sir." Coach Sno took one last look around before he announced, "Welcome to Fulton-Harley Football, gentlemen."

## Scene 21
# Athlete or Scholar?

Time was flying by. A couple of weeks had passed and Sly, with the exception of one missed day of conditioning, had been the ideal teammate. But for every stride he made towards achieving his dream, he quickly realized that the life of a college student-athlete would be far different than what he had become accustomed to.

Sly rushed out of conditioning, jumped down the steps of the gym, then sprinted back towards Jackson Hall. He reached the dorm and bounded up the stairs to grab his things for the shower. After a quick, but thorough wash off, he raced back down the stairs, and let his adrenaline carry him all the way to Dr. Payne's class. He snuck into the room and grabbed his seat in the first row and Dr. Payne closed the door behind him. "Nice of you to join us in such a timely manner, Mr. Jones." Out of breath, "Sorry Dr. Payne, but I'm here and on time," Sly said energetically as he adjusted in his seat. The professor watched Sly get settled into his seat as she walked over to the light. She flipped the wall switch and allowed the overhead projector to light the room. As Dr. Payne approached the head of the classroom, Sly felt his eyelids become heavier by the second. He squirmed around in his seat, fighting, as he dipped in and out of consciousness. He continued to fidget, until he decided to just place his head in his hands for a moment. In what seemed like only a wink, Sly opened his eyes and saw the students that were seated behind him exiting the classroom. Puzzled, he looked around, eventually locking eyes with his professor, who stared at her pupil with utter disappointment. Sly gathered his things in an attempt to escape the angry gaze of his professor. As he slung his backpack over his shoulder and headed towards the door, he heard, "Uhhhh….. Mr. Jones, can you come here for a moment?" Sly turned and shuffled over to his professor's desk with his head hung. "Mr. Jones, are you having issues sleeping at night? Or are you not getting enough rest?" Confused by the question, Sly attempted to respond with no doubt, "No, I feel well rested." She confirmed, "Well I know you are now, sir. You just slept through my class. But this is the third time you've fallen asleep in here. Participation is a large part of this class and you can't participate if you're snoring. Understood?" she questioned Sly while scrolling on her laptop. "You're already at a 'C' right now, and that's without your participation. Typically the participation percentage helps most students, but it is currently hurting your grade. I need you to understand that you need to participate and stay awake if you want to make it out of this class and on that field," Dr. Payne said without looking up. Now twice as confused, Sly looked at his professor with a befuddled look before slowly making his way towards the exit. "This isn't my first Spring semester, Mr. Jones. You'll have a decision to make in the end. Remember, your education is an investment and what you're pursuing is a dream. You should treat them both accordingly." Sly paused in an attempt to fully understand his professor's message before he exited the classroom. Sly left the Business building and walked back towards the Student Center as the words of his professor lingered in his head. He opened the door to the Student Center and heard a voice behind him shout, "Ay Jones, hold that." Sly looked back to see Hurse walking up behind him. Sly dapped up his new teammate and they walked into the Student Center together.

"Hey Hurse, hey Jones," a group of freshmen women called out. Sly waved as Jason peeled off to go and talk to the group of young women. Sly quickly turned his head when he heard the crackling of the speaker which usually indicated it was connected.

Once that noise subsided, Mile High started scratching the records to kick off his morning set. Per usual, Sly made his way to the spot at the top of the stairs and listened to the set while watching the lower level slowly fill. Sly watched as the DJ and his hypeman promoted the party for the weekend, "That's right, tomorrow night we'll be at the Legion. Come out and turn up with us. Aye, Mile High, show them people what it is." Mile High proceeded to do a couple of scratches before the Student Center heard the drop, "Mouse drop the track, that'll make you bounce it back, Cuz I'm on." There was a rush to the atrium as the song started. Sly smiled at what had become one of his favorite sites on campus. He continued watching his student peers and dapped up his friends and fellow classmates who came to the top of the steps or passed through. As the group grew with more and more people, Sly moved towards the banister, more off to the side, while the rest of the group looked over the crowd and plotted out their weekend.

"We at the Legion this weekend?" Melo asked as he looked at the group around him.

"Nigga, hell yea," Daryl responded emphatically as the two dapped up.

"That shit 'bout to pop. We in there," Daryl continued, as he looked down on the crowd and signaled to a young lady who was looking up at the group.

Sly listened to his friends talk about the event and allowed their excitement to energize him.

"Nigga, you awake?" Kevin asked as he nudged Sly.

"Yea bro. I'll be straight since we made it to the weekend," he answered his friend while he leaned on the railing and looked down at the restaurants on the first floor.

"Between you and Corey, I don't know who looks worse. That conditioning got y'all niggas hurt," Wale said while laughing with Kevin.

Sly looked over at Corey who was sitting next to the handrail. Even with all the music and commotion, he, too, struggled to keep his eyes open in the middle of the day. Fin nudged Corey as he passed him to get to the landing on the steps, "You good my nigga? Looks like you got a dope nod."

Corey looked up for a moment then put his head back down and simply responded with a middle finger.

"No bullshit though. It's only like this because we start at five in the morning, every morning. But that's supposed to stop in the next couple weeks or so," Sly said as he yawned and stood to his feet.

The group sat at the top of the stairs, listened to the music, and conversed with passing classmates. Sly leaned back against the railing he had been sitting near, then he heard a voice call out, "Sly, you gon' come and shoot a little bit. You been missing since the semester started." It was Rhonda coming up the stairs, asking about shooting pool. As she saw his face, she twisted hers up to let him know she was expecting a response.

"Yea, I'mma come up there for a lil bit," Sly said as he walked up the remaining steps with her.

"You know I walked on. That's why I haven't been up here," Sly tried to explain, as they cleared the steps and started down the hallway towards the game room.

"Oh, so you big time now?" Rhonda teased, as Sly held the door and followed her in the room.

"Oh shit, look who's back. You here to get those L's you've been duckin'?" Wes called out, as he aimed his shot. Him and Sly dapped up after he stood back up.

"You know he went out there with the brutes because his touch game not like that," Maxine chimed in.

"Damn, I only been gone for like a month and now everybody better than me all of a sudden?" Sly asked, laughing as he smiled hard. He then dapped up and hugged his game room family.

"We been better than you. Better act like you know, bro," Greg said as a few joined in the laughter. He circled the table to scan for his next shot.

"Damn, well let me get next and I'll show you I still got it," said Sly.

"You got it," Wes said proudly, as he buried the eight ball in the side pocket. "But it ain't lookin' good for ya slick," he continued and tossed Sly the rack.

Sly carefully racked the balls, placing the one ball in the front, and the eight ball in the middle, then rolled the rack a little before freeing the triangle. As Sly was pulling away the rack, Wes shot the break, causing a loud crash, as the different colors raced around the table. Wes continued to shoot, sinking his first three shots. When he missed the fourth, Sly stood silent at the corner of the table and glanced across the table for the best opportunity. He scanned again before setting up for his first shot. He lined up the shot slowly and made sure to strike the ball firmly and flush. Clack!! Clack!! Clack!! Sly continued circling the table after knocking in four balls with only three shots.

"Oh he locked in," Greg yelled out, as Sly lined up and knocked down another shot. "Y'all going to the party tomorrow?" Greg asked the group as he continued to watch.

"Is there something else going on?" Rhonda asked and the group shifted their focus back to Greg, waiting for a response, as he casually shrugged.

"Sounds like if you wanna party, you're going to the Legion," Wes responded right before he took his next shot and watched the ball hit the lip of the pocket and roll away.

"You going?" Sly asked, while immediately setting up a shot for the same pocket.

"Nah, I left the Legion in my sophomore year. Y'all have fun though," Wes answered without looking up from the table, as he watched Sly sink the shot.

"Damn, Sly on a mission," Maxine said laughing as Sly lined up his last ball before the eight ball.

He glanced around at the group before taking a closer look at the table then tapped the pool cue on the far opposite corner pocket. Sly lined up his last shot, hit the cue ball with a back spin, and kept the ball from following the eight ball into the pocket.

"Ok, ok. I see you retained your skills and even got a lil' sharper while you were at home," Wes said as he and Sly dapped up.

"The student becomes the teacher," Sly said jokingly as he bowed.

"Boy, hell nah. You wouldn't beat me again," Wes said laughing.

"And I guess we'll never know because I got next," Greg called and picked up the pool cue that was leaning on the wall then approached the table. Sly, still holding his cue, looked around for a moment before he noticed another student looking for a cue and handed it to him.

"You gon' have to play Wes. I gotta run to get lunch before my lift session and practice," Sly said as he relinquished his spot on the table.

"Oh yea, you did say you were doing that," Maxine confirmed then Rhonda asked, "You like it?"

Without hesitation, Sly blurted, "It's college football. What's not to love? And I know I can out work anyone on that field. I'll be out there next year. Watch!" With his confidence spiked, Sly waved bye to everyone as he left the game room with a huge smile.

In a rush, Sly ran to the café to get something small to eat, then ran back across campus to the football field. He walked in the walk-on locker room full of energy, "What up squad?" Sly dapped up a few of his new teammates and headed to his locker.

"Aye, y'all going to that Legion party tomorrow?" Jason asked the room of gentlemen as they strapped their pads on.

"Hurse, where else would niggas be going? Not like it's any other parties going on this weekend. At least not the size of this one anyway," Jimmy blurted out with a few co-signing murmurs in the background.

"I mean, you right Stick, but I was talking 'bout a kickback type deal," Jason responded right before Gene yelled, "I don't care where the party is. As long as I'm coming to these practices, I ain't paying for shit!" All the fellas joined in a laugh as they headed out onto the field.

As the walk-on group hustled onto the field, Sly slowed down for just a second to soak In the fact that he was living a dream. He pulled down his helmet and left the back buckles unclasped as he hopped into one of the stretching lines. While the captains called out the stretches, Sly noticed that the coaches had just come out and they walked down the rows of players.

The wide receiver coach went down Sly's row, "Jones, you ready to work today?"

"Yes sir," Sly yelled confidently with his mouthpiece in and he dapped up his passing coach.

After the stretches concluded, Coach Sno called a huddle. "Alright fellas, we'll be working on special teams today. We'll do some position work early, then we'll move into special teams and end practice with some go live. Let's get to it gentlemen," Coach Sno said, then he left the huddle.

"Aight fellas, let's put in this work. Hit your marks and keep it tight. We all know the goal is to have a great season next year and that starts here, right now. Let's go fellas, Bucs on three, Bucs on three! One, two, three…Bucs!!!!" The team yelled and disbursed directly after. In the midst of the scatter, Sly went over to Coach Springer and his fellow wide receivers followed suit.

"Ok fellas, let's partner up. We gotta be able to block effectively fellas. Blocking effectively allows us to more effectively run the ball. If we can run the ball effectively, then that opens up the passing game. Gotta be able to block before you can catch a ball."

Once everyone was lined up, he pointed to one side, "You all are on offense, defense comes downhill," Coach Springer yelled as he blew his whistle.

The defensive side walked towards the other players' line and were met with quick hands to the chest plate of their shoulder pads. They continued a few times then switched sides, allowing all the players to get practice. After substantial reps for all, Coach Springer directed his receivers to form a line in front of him. Simulating a snap, the first in line ran towards him, who was about fifteen yards out, and lobbed it above the player's head, who high-pointed the ball before securing it. As he passed the coach, he waited as he threw the next pass to the player behind him before flipping the ball up to the coach. Sly peeked from the middle of the line and waited for his turn. Coach Springer adjusted the ball for each player, throwing low to some and high to others. Finally, it was Sly's turn. He lined up and took off and Coach Springer floated a pass well above his head. Sly took a step, leaped into the air, and reached as high as he could with one hand, grabbing the pass in the process. As he came back down, he tucked the ball away before flipping it back to Coach Springer. The line went through completely twice and was working on a third before the horn blew to move into the special teams portion of the practice.

The walk-ons from the receivers line hustled over to the punt formation and split into two groups to become gunners. One after another, the young men lined up against a different cornerback, walk-on or otherwise. Sly sprinted to his spot and got set before the ball was snapped. He looked in towards the ball and saw the upback wave his hand between the long snapper and the punter. Sly twitched off the line, causing the lunging corner to miss his jam, and he reached for Sly's passing jersey. Sly sprinted down the field as the cornerback trailed him, both of them slowing as the return man called for a fair catch right as Jones pulled up in front of him. Sly turned around and headed towards the sidelines so the next group of players could go on.

"Ahhhhhh, hell nah Benson. You gon' let this walk-on embarrass you like that? Shit, I should just give your spot to him," Coach Damon, the defensive backs coach, screamed at his corner.

"Line the fuck back up and don't let it happen again."

Then he paused, "Fuck that. Jones, do that shit again. I got some junkyard dogs in my unit," Coach Springer yelled behind him, as both coaches stood beside each other waiting for the next snap. Sly faked, trying to release outside, then stepped across Benson's face. There was a clash of the pads which locked the two up as they sprinted down the field tussling. Sly attempted to shed the block, only to have Benson use his momentum against him, and shoved him past the returner right as the whistle blew.

The two jogged back as Benson mumbled, "You ain't gotta go so hard."

Sly slowed down for a moment to become even with his teammate, then responded, "If I don't, I won't make it, so it looks like you gon' get some work every time we line up. I'm trying to make it. Fuck everything else."

Benson looked at the walk-on and stuck out his hand, "Respect."

The two dapped up and returned to the end of their respective lines. A punt before Sly was set to go again. Coach Sno called everyone over to the center of the field to end practice. "Aight gentlemen, good practice all in all today. Good day's work that we'll build upon tomorrow. Dugger go ahead and break them out…… .Before I go, I've heard about this party this weekend. It would behoove you to be on your best behavior," Coach Sno said before he and the rest of the coaches walked off.

The morning sun beamed through the cracked blinds and there was a continuous banging on the door. Sly rolled out of his bed and shuffled over to the steady thumping. He opened the door without even looking to see who it was, then fell back into the mess of sheets he had created.

"Y'all niggas in here dead to the world, huh?" Kevin said laughing as he is followed in by Daryl.

"We were up at five in the morning running at the beginning of the semester. We catching up on sleep. But we gon' be awake when it matters," Eugene said as he rolled over and adjusted his pillow.

"Eugene, Mr. All American, y'all chose that struggle," Daryl said laughing as he pointed at both roommates.

Mack burst into the room, "What y'all still doing in bed?" he asked Sly and Eugene, then dapped up the others on the game.

"Damn Mack, why so loud?" Sly complained and pulled the comforter over his head.

"What the fuck I'mma whisper for now? You're clearly awake. Y'all missing all this Spring action," and he pointed out the window.

"Bro, it's ten o'clock on a Saturday on a college campus. Please relax. Plus, it's Virginia. It'll be in the thirties this morning, get up to about seventy-five this afternoon, just to drop down to the forties when the sun goes down. Shit, a whole ass trap," Sly said as Eugene and Mack laughed along.

Kevin added, "Yea, y'all weather bi-polar as shit."

As the laughter continued, Corey came in the room, dragging his feet in a zombie-like state.

"Damn homie, you good?" Eugene asked his teammate.

"Yea bro, I'm just tired and sore as shit. The lifting schedule is killing me because I still have to go when we have conditioning."

"Damn bro, you might need to go back to bed," Sly said, as he sat up. The rest of the group laughed then Corey dropped into a computer desk chair.

The group lounged around for most of the Saturday, with different people making an appearance. Some even came over from Roberts Hall. Sly peered out the window as the day of lounging came to an end and the sun tucked itself behind the Architecture building. He then shuffled through the chairs of people in the room to reach the door. He cracked it open and looked down the hall to see how active the dorm was. He dapped up a couple of dormmates who walked by.

"Stick, you going to the party tonight?" The tall and lanky fellow poked his head back out his door before he got a chance to close it.

"Oh, fa sho' dawg. Do a lil' some'n some'n, ya feel me?" Stick responded while doing a little jig in his doorway.

"Ha, that's word. Tell Toro we gon' get him a twerk tonight," Sly said jokingly.

"I don't dance!" a voice yelled out behind Jimmy as he and Sly laughed.

"You ain't gotta dance. You just gotta stay upright. I bet if that lil' cute chick from St. Louis tried to dance with you……." Sly tried pleading the case before Toro cut him off, "That's different and y'all would just be witnessing the making of a baby."

Sly and Stick laughed as Toro joined the conversation fully after his statement.

"You a wild boy, man. I'll catch y'all out there tonight," Sly joked briefly before shutting his door. Some of the guys in the room went back to their room in an attempt to get ready. Sly laid out his outfit on his bed then gathered his things to go shower. As soon as Sly returned from his shower, the room was filled with the usual suspects, pre-gaming and gaming all the same, with water bottles already in rotation.

"Aye, what time do the shuttles start running?" Corey asked as he took a swig from a bottle and passed it to his roommate.

"I think nine or nine-thirty maybe," Sly answered as he laid across his bed, then glanced back over his shoulder out the window to see if there were any big groups leaving.

"Well shit, when we gon' head that way?" Nate asked with anticipation.

"Easy there, young whippersnapper. We gon' leave outta here shortly," Corey said jokingly to his roommate.

"Y'all niggas just alike…. Thirsty as hell. No wonder they put y'all together," Daryl joked as the rest of the room laughed.

"Niggas parched," Mack added and Kevin countered, "The dehydrated duo."

The jokes continued to rain down until Corey spoke up, "Bet I'm the only nigga that come back with a number tonight."

He looked at each guy in the room while the others then looked at each other, trying to determine whether or not Corey was serious.

There was a small pause before Sly responded, "Shittt, I'll take that action. And you can't tell the chick it's a bet. I don't care how desperate you get. You banking on these chicks wanting a 'my size' boyfriend."

The room exploded with laughter before the others chimed in, wanting a piece of the bet as well.

"Y'all gon' really let me take all y'all money? Nah, I ain't gon' do that to y'all," Corey said jokingly as the laughter continued.

"That's because we were about to clear your bank account," Eugene said only half-joking as he opened the door. The guys finished one water bottle and Mack tucked the remaining one in his back pocket. The fellas walked through the lobby and waved to Mr. P. He sat in his office with the door open to see his residents off into the night. Mack pulled the bottle from his pocket when they cleared the view of the dorm. He passed it around all while snickering as he remembered different jokes from the week.

The group walked past T-Sci before angling towards the closest external street to campus. When they passed one of the Administrative buildings, they saw a wave of young women headed in the same direction behind them. Sly looked both ways, as his friends just walked into the street.

"It's past nine on a Saturday, and the party isn't even on our campus. Come on here wit'cho scary ass," Daryl slurred as the rest of the group laughed.

After they crossed the street, the group headed towards the shuttles and Mack split, heading into Bay Place.

"Aye, I'mma meet y'all there. I'm 'bout to ride with some of the guys."

"Aight, we'll see you there," Kevin responded as the rest of the group pressed on towards the shuttle. The group crossed the thoroughfare between the apartment complex and the shopping center next to it. They then hustled over to the Burger King, according to the directions given by DJ Mile High, only to witness the shuttle already pulling into traffic.

"Damn man, we missed it," Sly said as he watched the bus at the light pull off.

"That shit will literally be back in like twenty minutes. The Legion is right around the corner," Kevin said as he peeked around the corner they had come from and saw more groups headed in their direction to catch the next shuttle.

"See, this is actually perfect. You can set your first twerk up with this group so when you get in the party, you hit the ground running," Corey chimed in optimistically as he walked over towards Kevin and greeted the group of young women in the process.

Sly tapped Daryl as he leaned on the column in front of the bookstore entrance.

"You good?" Sly asked his slightly inebriated friend, who turned with a kool-aid smile, "I'm golden, my guy. Golden, like the golden gun from Goldeneye."

Sly looked at his tipsy friend, then paused before responding with a laugh, "Ok, golden boy. I hear you. Just don't get lost this time."

They both laughed as the group waiting for the shuttle grew. The next shuttle arrived a short time after. As it parked, there was a surge in the group as everyone pushed to make it on this shuttle. The fellas boarded the bus, still fully engaged in all the conversations that had been happening prior to the bus' arrival. The driver attempted to pull away from the curb, as undergraduates continued to pile into each other's laps. Sly sat on the edge of a seat as the bus pulled out of the parking lot. He looked around the bus and suddenly made eye contact with one of the ladies leaning on the bus' back door. He smiled at the young woman and pointed at his seat. She smiled back and shuffled towards Sly. As he stood up, she placed her hand on his shoulder to sit him back down then sat on his lap. "Hey I'm Shanell. What's your name?" Completely thrown off by the turn of events, Sly responded slowly, "My friends and my mom, when she's not mad, call me Sly." She half-heartedly laughed as the two shared a brief moment before the bus came to an abrupt stop. Sly peeked out the window to see that they were already at the party. The students got off the bus with more excitement than when they had loaded. The last of the party goers hopped off and the shuttle pulled off towards campus to pick up more students. The group stood there as the security officers started to yell out directions for entry to the party. "Fellas to the line on my left. Ladies, you all will be in the line on my right. No food, no drinks, no lighters, no weapons. If you got It in your pocket, better throw it away or go put it in your car now. Otherwise, you won't be coming in here." The group dispersed, ladies and gentlemen going to their respective sides. Sly walked towards the end of the line followed behind Kevin and Daryl, then he realized that Eugene and Corey were still waiting where they'd all been dropped off. Sly walked back to his teammates, wondering what they were waiting for. Before he could ask his question, Eugene blurted out, "We're waiting for the football team," apparently, in response to one of the bouncers. Nevertheless, Sly was grateful to at least understand what was happening. Sly and Corey stood there and looked around while Eugene never looked up from his phone. As the line shrank and time passed, Sly fidgeted until he saw a white truck speed into the parking lot along with three other cars. The cars all parked beside each other, and as they watched, they saw Mack hop out of the white truck. "What's good bo's?" he yelled out while giving Eugene a dap that could've popped his arm out of place. Corey joked, "Oh you big turnt." And without missing a beat, Mack turned to Corey, "Like a motherfuckin' knob, nigga!!!" The group laughed as they lagged behind the older football players who were dapping up the bouncers. Sly stood off to the side and watched the greetings. Then Eugene grabbed him and placed him in line in front of him as they all walked in. After they passed the bouncers and security guards, there were two folding tables with women sitting behind them. Sly walked up to one of the ladies who was taking the money for the party. "Five dollars." Sly paused for a moment, trying to figure out why he thought the price was something different. He reached into his pocket and pulled out the only cash he was carrying. Sly placed the crumbled five dollar bill in the outstretched hand of the woman before the bouncer opened the door to the entrance of the party. The music blared out of the dimly lit room through the crack in the door as Sly slipped in. He waited for Eugene and Corey as he scanned the party, already seeing Daryl and Kevin in the mix. Sly proceeded to walk around the party with his friends, dance and enjoy his time. While taking in the party scene, he looked towards the back and saw all the football players he had walked in with, plus more. Sly wondered if they had always been back there or if this was something he had just noticed since he now knew who they were. He continued floating through the party and then wondered if he had earned the right to stand with the football team. After a little time, Sly causally made his way to the back of the party and dapped up all the receivers and some other position players he knew. As he posted amongst his teammates, surveying the party from a different perspective, he noticed Benson and a couple of corners head back towards the team. They made their way past the receivers with the normal teammate taunting for their positions.

Benson was walking past before he noticed Sly and extended his hand. The two dapped up and as Benson pulled him in, he said just over the music, "Keep working, but know that shit that happened yesterday is never gon' happen again." He stepped back to see a smiling Sly who responded with a shrug, "Yea, guess we gon' see about that one, huh?" Benson laughed as they dapped up again and he tapped his fellow corner, "I like this guy. No back down in him." Sly stood tall in his new sense of belonging as he watched the party through the eyes of a football player. Standing next to the team, Sly fidgeted with his hands, trying to look the part. As he watched the party, he noticed that there was a steady stream of women making their way to the back of the party. He also observed the different looks he receives from his classmates as he stood amongst his teammates. He noticed a girl from one of his classes walking by, and she did a quick double take, making sure it was the right person in the dark room.

"Sly?" the young woman questioned as she approached him.

"Hey Winnie," Sly said as he waved to his classmate.

She surveyed the group as she approached him. "When did you join the football team? You've never made mention of it in class."

Sly shrugged and leaned over in Winnie's ear, "Not quite there yet."

"Sure looks like you are to me," she said as she took a step back and looked Sly up and down. She then grabbed his shirt and pulled him close, away from the group. After a couple of songs, Sly went back to his spot amongst his freshmen players and listened to them joke about how he had disappeared into the crowd.

"Honestly, I ain't think you were coming back," Stick said laughing.

"Shiiiidddd, I seen her wrap her leg around you. You know what she wanted," Hurse added as they had a laugh, still scoping out the party.

Sly chopped it up with his teammates and continued to have various similar experiences throughout the night. Some women explained they thought it was a prank, while others were shocked he hadn't mentioned it prior. Sly was just happy to feel a part of the team and was enjoying the perks that came along with it. As the party wound down and the students headed towards the exits, Sly was bumped on the back of his shoulder. He turned around with a slight scowl before noticing it was Benson. "Not bad, right?" He asked the freshman with a straight face. Sly tried to play it cool, then answered with a huge grin, "Man, hell yea." They both laughed and dapped up once again, while heading toward the exit in the group of students.

## Scene 22
## Study Hall

As practice wrapped up, Sly heard individual murmurs between players and coaches as they huddled around Coach Sno while he closed out the practice. "Alright gentlemen, that's a good day of work. Clap it up. Alright. If you're sore, go see Tommy in the training room, and don't be in there messing around. Get in, get your treatment, and get out. Freshmen, you all will have Study Hall after every practice. You'll be required to stay in Study Hall for an hour and a half. That gives you more than ample time to tackle the homework you've been given. You all are not to leave the Study Hall until the time has expired. If it starts at six thirty and you all have to be there an hour and a half, what time do you leave Study Hall?" Coach Sno asked the group as they answered collectively, "Eight!" Coach Sno smirked, "See, that's how y'all got here. Being smart. Also, upperclassmen, we've spoken before as well. You all are also required to attend Study Hall until further notice. Is that understood?" Some of them let out a hardy, "Yes sir!" and others responded with mixed reactions. "Ok fellas, great practice. Grizz, break 'em down and get 'em off my field," Coach Sno instructed his captain as he and the other coaches headed back into the football offices. "Aight fellas, good day of practice. Let's come out tomorrow with the same effort and energy so we can build the team out. Bucs on three, Bucs on three. One, two, three....Bucs!!!" The team yelled loudly as they dispersed into the locker rooms.

Sly fell into a spot in the line as the players filed into the walk-on locker room. "Damn man, this Study Hall shit sounds a lot like curfew," Gene said as he unbuckled his shoulder pads and slang them to the ground.

"It's nowhere near that bad," QB responded as both sides of the argument could be heard throughout the locker room.

"Shiid, I'ono 'bout y'all, but eight is the literal beginning of the night," Hurse stared and shrugged while the majority of the locker room cheered and laughed. After a small pause, he added, "Oh, and we off curfew. They done fucked up now," Hurse laughed as he walked through the locker room dapping up everyone. The group continued to laugh and joke as they filed out of the locker room. Sly hurried off to grab a book he would need for his first Study Hall.

Upon his exit, Sly sprinted up to the room and returned to the lobby with the same velocity. "Uhhh uhhh, no sir. Runnin' through here like you've lost your mind? Back to the steps, Mr. Jones, and act like you got some sense," Mr. P yelled out of the office. Sly's head turned before he nodded and walked back to the steps and then slowly walked out of the dorm. "Thank you!!" he heard Mr. P yell out before the door closed. When he stepped out the door, he saw an old Lincoln Town Car rolling by blasting, "Is you rollin'? Is you rollin'? Bitch, I might be. Bitch I might be." The car slowed as it passed Sly before turning into a parking spot in front of Roberts Hall.

Sly watched for a moment, then headed towards the car as he saw Hurse and one of the basketball players exit the car in the middle of an argument. "Nah, nah nah. Ya bullshittin' Hurse. Virginia is definitely in the South. Richmond was the capital of the Confederacy. Tell'em Jones!"

Sly walked over and dapped up Hurse and the basketball player who was towering over them both.

"As much as you hate to hear it Hurse, Flip got a point. We were the capital of the South," Jones said, siding with his fellow Virginian to Hurse's disliking.

"Y'all don't know. That's just that biased ass education y'all got up here," he explained as all of them laughed.

Sly glanced down at his phone before extending his hand to the gentlemen. "You know we gotta be at Study Hall in twenty minutes, right?" Sly asked Hurse as he started to walk off.

"Oh shawty, that's plenty of time. But you might wanna start joggin' so yo slow ass get there on time," Hurse mocked as they laughed.

Sly slowly backed away and yelled back, "which makes the fact that you can't guard me that much sadder."

They all laughed, even those passing by, and he turned and headed towards the football office.

As he walked through the doors of the office, he was greeted by one of the students who helped recruit players. "Hey Jones." Sly picked his head up as he walked through the door, "Hey Sandy, you good?" She nodded as he approached her desk. "That's good to hear. Have a good night." She waved as he walked past her desk, making a left into the hallway.

Sly walked down the dark hall towards the only open door, where he could hear his teammates and coaches. He turned into the door to see about thirty guys, some on computers, and a few had open textbooks in front of them. The majority of them were cracking jokes and talking amongst themselves. Sly scanned the room, looking for an open seat, and noticed the offensive line coach sitting at the head of the room. As he looked back and forth, he threw his hand up to Corey and Eugene as he went and sat down. As he pulled out his textbook and one of his notebooks, he scanned the room once more as he placed his things on the desk top, cracking open the textbook to a spot where he had previously left his pencil. The book fell open and Sly took out the pencil, glancing down at the page. He flipped open his notebook and turned past the pages of poetry and doodles to reach a blank one. As he glanced over his book, he began listening to the conversations around him, as he loosely tried to do his work. His focus dwindled as he heard different topics being discussed around him. Sly started a new poem, trying to ease the clutter between his ears. He scribbled down his thoughts, checking over his shoulders from time to time, then he heard a voice behind him. "Jones, you wanna watch this video?" one of the players yelled out, pointing at the laptop. Sly shrugged, closed his notebook and stood up, shuffling behind the chairs before reaching the steps. As he lazily made his way towards the group, he noticed some of his peers looked shocked, while others moved closer to the screen, or others covered their eyes or turned away.

"Bruh, what are y'all...."

"Shhhhhh!!!!" Multiple teammates hushed Sly, while one pointed to the title of the video.

Sly's eyes widened as he realized what he was watching. Although the video was playing through headphones, the gunshots rang throughout the Study Hall. The coach at the front of the room looked up from his notebook for a moment, causing the young men to quiet down momentarily. Sly watched the screen closely as he had heard about the videos, but thought they had been taken down from all media outlets. He watched as several individuals ran across the screen only to be followed by two guys wearing trench coats and walking at a Vorhees pace. The scene cut and shots rang out throughout the headphones. "Aight now, y'all break that shit up!" the coach barked as he pointed at the group. Sly headed back towards his seat, as did all that had gathered around the computer. He sat down and attempted to finish his piece he had started before getting up. As he looked around, trying to refocus, he noticed the kicker in the far front corner of the room. Before he could figure out why he was so isolated, the alarm rang. Sly looked up at the clock and saw the glaring eight thirty. He heard all the other players rush out of the room. Within thirty seconds, the room was cleared with the exception of a few guys. Sly put the last of his stuff in his bookbag and headed towards the door. He got there at the same time as the kicker.

"What's up, Ty?" Sly said as the two dapped up.

"Ain't shit fo' real, already got my work done. Bout ta go back to the room and chill," Tysean answered as he grabbed the door for them to exit the building.

"Did y'all have to do Study Hall first semester?" Sly asked as the two walked back towards the dorms, and Ty nodded.

Sly paused for a second before asking another question, "Bro, it be loud as shit in there. How do you focus the whole time?"

"Headphones help..." he joked as they both laughed before he continued, "For real man, I just understand this shit temporary. Me and Remy went to a powerhouse school in Florida. Every year, we'd have all these scholarship players come home. There would always be at least one who would be physically fucked up beyond football. See that shit enough times and your mindset about it will eventually change. I know I could be a receiver here, but I'm thinking after college. Not like these niggas with league dreams. No offense, if that's your thing."

Sly gave Tysean a slight side eye before stating, "That might be the realest thing I've ever heard about football from an actual player."

Tysean nodded as he replied, "We all love the game, that's why we play. But risking your well-being and future, I can't get with it."

The two laughed as they dapped up again and Ty exited the stairwell on the second floor. Sly allowed his conversation with Ty to sink in, re-evaluating his approach to football and school as he opened the door to the usual suspects.

# Scene 23
# Organizational Fair

Class dismissed and as Sly loaded his materials back into his book bag, he struggled internally on whether he wanted Chick-Fil-A or not. As he approached the door, he felt the heat from outside radiating from the door and the skylight above. He took down his headphones, pulled his hoodie off and tied it around his waist, then pulled his headphones back up and walked through the double doors. Once outside, he paused for a moment and looked around before he decided on the chicken sandwich meal. As he reached the corner between the T-Sci building and one of the Administration buildings, Sly saw a crowd around the entrance of the Student Center, where the ballroom was located. Initially, he began to walk towards the front door, in an effort to avoid the crowd, but his curiosity got the best of him. He approached the crowd cautiously and waded through to get inside. On the other side of the threshold was a sign on the double doors of the ballroom, "Organizational Fair, March 24th, 2007, 11 am-2 pm," Sly read in his head before standing on his tippy toes to scan the room. As he glanced, he remembered Mrs. Reeves who reminded him to think about life after football. Against his better judgement, he took a deep breath and headed into the crowd.

Sly walked in with his head on a swivel, trying to remember other hobbies he had that didn't involve a sport. As he perused each table, he took a step back to look at the people, the information on the table, then spoke before moving on to the next. As he drifted towards the right side of the room first, he passed a couple of sorority tables and a table that appeared to be for the band. He headed towards the back of the room in the corner, and as he turned, he saw Heidi wave to him from across the room before fully turning the corner. Mesmerized by her allure, Sly accidentally walked into the person in front of him.

"Damn homie, you good?" the guy asked as he turned towards Sly.

"Yea, my bad man. I was distracted," Sly said, never looking at the guy, but instead, still focused on Heidi.

"Shiddd, it's a lotta distractions out this bitch. Name's Richard, but call me J.R.," the gentleman said and  extended his hand towards Sly.

"Nice to meet you bruh. And yea, in all honesty, I don't know how any of us are getting any work done," Sly joked as both of them laughed.

"Shit man, let me try to find something in here," Sly said, as he looked around again and started to walk away.

"Well, we are looking for male vocals in the chorus. And it's filled with distractions," J.R. mentioned as the two laughed again.

"Man, I couldn't carry a note if it had handles. But I'll definitely come to check out a concert."

The two dapped up as Sly continued to make his way around the fair. Soon, he noticed a comic book club along the back wall of the ballroom as he made his way down the right aisle. His excitement spiked, only to be followed by a wave of doubts about his perception. Sly slowed down to observe the table, taking in the rare copies, memorabilia, and action figures. He continued his stroll and looked back at the table as he stumbled into another. Sly looked up and realized that he had accidentally walked into one of the fraternity tables. Well aware of the rule that freshmen couldn't pledge, Sly looked at the tables casually. He continued from table to table, answering any and all conversational questions that were thrown to him from various members. As he evaluated each table, as well as the interactions within each group, Sly heard a man shout out, "So what are you looking to pledge?"

Somewhat thrown off by the question, Sly responded honestly, "I'm not sure. I don't really know anything about any of y'all. My grandpa's friends were all Kappas, and they came to church looking like retired pimps. And my pop's best friend is an Alpha."

"So what do you know about Omega men?" the gentleman continued with his line of questions, stepping to the front of the table.

"I know y'all got a lot of athletes like Shaq and MJ. Y'all the dogs, right?" Sly asked nonchalantly and shrugged.

"Yes……yes we are," the fraternity member answered, trying not to correct the freshman.

"Well I'll holla at y'all," Sly said before dapping up the gentleman to make his way to the other side of the room.

Sly continued to browse  the different tables, looking left and right as he walked down the aisle. He paused when he came across a table where all their representatives were wearing suits. Sly looked down at the banner they had draped over the table, *Young Democrats Coalition*. Before Sly could raise his head back up, he heard a voice shout out with enthusiasm,

"What's good bro? You interested? Of course you are. We are not voting Republican over here."

Face to face, the tall light-skinned fellow, with a blue blazer and his red power tie, extended his hand towards Sly, who proceeded to shake it.

"I mean.... I guess you're right, but this is an all-black school. Did y'all really need a group?" Sly asked.

"Great question. We actually deal with getting the community out to vote and help with the overall effort. By the way, my name's Duncan."

"Oh ok, word. My name's Sly."

The two dapped up and Sly wrote down his contact information on the sign-up sheet. Sly walked away from the table with a feeling of accomplishment and pride knowing he would be able to lend a helping hand to those who wanted to see the world be better. Riding that high, Sly looked at the other tables, hoping that he would find another space he could lend a helping hand. As he looked around, he spotted the Student Recruitment Board and noticed the first guy he saw speak at Next Class Up was at the table. Sly waded through the growing crowd in the ballroom to approach the table.

Xander extended his hand to Sly, "Hey man, how ya doing? Interested in showing our school off to potential students?"

"Yea, actually, I came over because I remember seeing you on the box. It seems like it could be fun," Sly said to the upperclassman.

"It is. We work with the Admissions Office and we need a few more men to show the school. As you can see, we're highly outnumbered. Not that I'm complaining, it's just a fact," Xander said, pointing over his shoulder at the nine other student recruiters, all of whom were women.

Sly glanced over his shoulder before responding, "Ok, I get that. Not trying to get myself into any more trouble, but it sounds cool."

"Bet. Take this sheet. We're going to have an interest meeting next week. Tell ya boys to come too," Xander pleaded to Sly.

"Yea, I'll tell'em but don't get ya hopes up."

They both laughed as they dapped up. Then Sly walked towards the double doors and looked back into the ballroom for a final scan before leaving.

Sly left out of the ballroom and then the Student Center through the same doors he had initially come in through. As he headed back towards the café, he noticed a few of his classmates and sped up to walk with them.

"Ms. Simmons, Ms. Thomas, Ms. Gaines, how you ladies doing today?"

"Hey Sly. Where you coming from?" Melissa asked as Sly sped past them, turned around, and shuffled backwards to keep the conversation going.

"The org fair. There's a lot more clubs here than I had at my high school," Sly said with excitement as he shared the different handouts with the ladies.

"Well, I would hope they have more to offer than your high school, because if they didn't, that'd just be sad," Alita said laughing as they passed the different pamphlets around.

"Where you about to go, Jones?" Jasmine asked, as she handed him back the information.

"Shoot, I'm headed to go get something to eat. That's the only reason I come to this side of campus," Sly replied, and they all shared a laugh.

"Sir, I've definitely seen you in front of our dorm at seven in the evening," Melissa said, pointing at Sly as she laughed.

With no hesitation, he responded, "To be a gentleman, or on wingman duties. Nothing more," Sly said, as he raised a scout's honor.

"Yea, ok Jones, whatever story you want to tell. But you don't strike me as a Scout."

They all burst into laughter as Sly tried to defend himself, "I'm not out here making no trouble. At least not on purpose."

Their laughter continued as they walked inside of the café together.

As they walked in, they noticed the crowded seats being shuffled about as different groups rotated in and out of the room. Each of them went and grabbed their meals then sat at a table where the ladies had found some of their other New Yorker classmates.

"Aye Jones, what's good B?"

"Shit, I can't call it, Hawk. I ain't seen you since the football meeting. Where you been?"

"I been in class, my nigga. I wanted to go out there 'til this nigga said five in the morning. Uh uh, not me nigga. But I won't just gon' walk out the meeting like that dummy did."

They both laughed as they dapped up.

"Don't let all that heavy lifting throw off the lil' shot you got, Jones. Don't wanna get exposed when you done on the field and come back to the court."

Sly heard the remark and turned to look down the table. "Yea I said it," Patrick leaned forward laughing.

"I'm still gon' be able to lock up Pills. Don't make me make an example out of you."

The two laughed, exchanging a pound behind the seats before Nino added, "Yea, but now you gotta go shoot a thousand shots just to get your lil' shot back. I've walked past that weight room while y'all were in there. Look like y'all been eating fucking dumbbells and shit. You were not that swoll when I met you, pause."

"Ayo, my guy, what you sayin'? Like you wildin' my nigga with that statement," one of the other New Yorkers further down the table blurted out before the whole table broke into laughter.

The conversation continued, changing to the topic of northern versus southern states, with Sly as the only representation for the latter.

"Like, y'all don't have art schools down here. Like none," Alyssa chimed in.

"Well, we have specialty schools where you can study art," Sly responded, only to be met with a rebuttal of, "But you all don't have a high school dedicated to just the Arts. Like, I went to a high school in Brooklyn that was an art school, and I studied opera."

Sly looked at the girl as if she had grown a second head. "Wait, so you have an opera vocal range?" Sly asked, confused.

"Yeah, been had it since like eighth grade," Alyssa assured the table nonchalantly as everyone tuned in.

"What? I'm calling bullshit. I heard yo ass talk since we got here and I ain't heard nothing that makes me believe that," Hawk interjected.

Alyssa looked down the table, "Y'all really don't believe me?"

With looks of doubt and slight confusion, everyone stared at Alyssa to confirm her thoughts. She shook her head as she looked up and down the table.

"Can you take this up there for me, please?" Alyssa asked Alita before she stood up from the table.

She headed back towards the entry of the café where the last surge of students were pouring through the doors. She stopped and gathered herself in front of the railing, so that she was front and center before the whole lunch room. She paused for a moment, making sure that everyone from the table was watching. "Aye, what she about to…." Pills started to ask before Alyssa hit an opera note that echoed through the lunch room, and she held the note for four seconds. Just as abruptly as it started, she finished, running out of the side door to escape the ovation. Sly, with his mouth gaped open in awe, turned to the rest of the table who all had similar reactions plastered on their faces.

## Scene 24
# Why'd You Tell Her?

Sly turned on his side as he watched his friends play Madden and debate various sports and hip-hop topics. He glanced outside to see the glow of the setting sun as it slowly hid behind the horizon. Stuck in a daydream, Sly's trance was broken by Corey asking the group a question, "Anybody know about any moves tonight?"

"Nigga, we sitting in here with you. If we knew something, we'd be doing something," Daryl answered, annoyed.

The rest of the room shrugged as they glossed over the question, returning to the debate of Michael, Lebron, and Kobe.

"Did they mention anything at twelve to two today? I didn't get a chance to go. Maybe there is something going on off campus," Corey persisted with his line of questioning, maintaining his pursuit of a good time.

"Bro, let it go. It's a dead Friday," Kevin said, laughing as Daryl reached into the pack of water under Eugene's bed and threw it towards Corey.

"Here nigga, cuz you clearly parched."

The room erupted in laughter, as Corey continued to plead his case.

"Ok, ok, but you and Kevin don't do anything but school. Me, Sly, Eugene, and Mack got jammed schedules and can't cake like you niggas do around the clock. Y'all just lucky I won't around to be another option," Corey responded confidently.

Eugene and Sly chuckled and shrugged, agreeing with Corey's sentiment until the end of his rant. Then there was a small pause followed by more laughter.

Just then, Sly received a message and announced to the room, "Aye, Dre said he just parked in Africa, and he's walking this way."

"Word," Eugene nodded, acknowledging his roommate's announcement.

The conversation continued as Sly received another message. Dre simultaneously knocked and walked in the room, "What's good, niggas? Where the bad bitches y'all keep stashed away on campus?"

Everybody laughed as he went around the room dapping up each person.

"How are you always able to get up here?" Daryl asked, confused by Dre's constant presence.

"Ya know half y'all class think I go here. Shiddd, I might as well be a Buccaneer. Argh bih, where's that booty?" Dre responded to Daryl in a pirate pose and an eye closed as the rest of the room cracked up.

"Aye, Heidi just texted me about a party in Bay Place."

The whole room instantly fell silent as they all turned and looked at Sly before Mack spoke up, "Heidi who?"

"Whoodie whooo?" Dre yelped after Mack's question.

"Yo, but how did you end up with Heidi's number?"

Sly shrugged and replied, "She was at the student recruitment meeting I was trying to get y'all to go to. Did y'all know it's like eight or nine chicks, for every one dude here?" Sly proudly stated the fact that he remembered from the meeting.

"Wait, does that take into consideration chicks that are fuckin' other chicks?" Corey asked, with a serious tone.

"I'm going to say that the Admissions Office probably isn't keeping track of that," Sly answered while the others pondered on the numbers.

"Yea, that seems high. It's gotta actually be like four or five," Eugene chimed in after some quick math.

"Wait, so y'all think half the chicks on campus are gay?" Kevin questioned his friends.

"I mean, I think this is purely from a numbers perspective, but that does seem high," Sly said about the stat.

Dre interjected, "Y'all just being greedy with the pretty bitches, huh, motherfuckas."

The room burst into laughter again.

As the laughter died down, Daryl asked Sly, "So what's the deal with this party?"

Sly shrugged his shoulders, providing his friends with all the details he was given. "I don't know. She gave me the apartment number, said it was a party, and to come thru," Sly explained to his friends, who digested every detail.

"Bro, she just wants you to go," Corey said calmly.

"But you wouldn't just invite one person to a party if you knew that person was always with a group, right?" Sly asked, confused.

"You would if it ain't your party," Dre said with a grin and a shrug.

"Even I can tell she just wants you to come, and I ain't even really been paying attention for real," Mack commented without looking away from the play happening on the screen.

Sly shrugged off his friends' assumptions, "Nah, y'all wildin'. She knows I have a girlfriend and I haven't been to any event you guys weren't at."

"Did YOU tell her you have a girlfriend?" Eugene asked promptly.

"No, but I did tell Rhonda because she asked about me," Sly said confidently.

"And do you think she invited you to get all of us to come out?" Daryl asked rapidly.

"I mean, if she only had one of our numbers, yea."

Sly's friends bombarded him with questions as he denied what seemed so blatant to them.

"Y'all will see when we get there. It'll be a dope party, and I'll play the back like normal."

"Yea, yea, yea, whatever nigga. You not foolin' nobody in this room," Dre said, laughing as the water bottle made its way around the room before the group headed down the stairs.

As they made their way down the stairwell, Daryl yelled, "Aye, if this is a suff, we fighting, Sly."

"Can't be a suff since we weren't doing anything anyway. Don't put your failure on me," Sly said jokingly, as they approached the Biology building.

"Aye, I'm 'bout to walk past my car real quick. I have a lil' something in the trunk if y'all wanna swig."

The whole group veered right, doubling back around the cemetery. As they walked and talked, Sly noticed a fog roll in over the cemetery.

"I don't think I'll ever get used to this shit."

"Stop being scary, Sly. I don't even notice them dead people anymore," Kevin said, reassuring his friend.

"Only dead people I'm worried about are the ones I can fit in my pocket," Daryl said as the group only half-jokingly agreed with the sentiment.

They passed the burial grounds and noticed that the back gate had been pried open a little.

As they made their way around the gate and towards Dre's car, he hit his key fob, causing the lights to flash under the streetlight where he was parked. The group walked to the back of the vehicle. Sly stood off to the side as his friends took turns swigging the bottle. Sly stared into the darkness until he saw a set of headlights. He gently tapped the side of the car and everyone looked up. Eugene took a final swig before closing the bottle and tossing it into some clothes in the trunk. The group walked towards the street, as the campus police car slowed in front of the guys. They stopped at the edge of the sidewalk and waited for the car to continue so that they could return to campus. The car paused for a moment, never rolling down the window, before drifting off through the back gate of campus. It was obvious that he wanted to stop the young men but didn't have a reason to the naked eye. As they crossed the street, continuing their conversation, Sly slowed his walk to make sure the officer wasn't doubling back. The group veered onto campus, cutting past Opal Gym, as they walked into the clearing between the academic buildings. They made their way past the statue of Fulton-Harley's most famed alumni. "If this nigga could see us now..." Daryl joked only to have Corey answer, "He'd either be super disappointed or trying to catch a twerk. There would be no in between." The group laughed as they continued past the library and crossed the street into Bay Place. "Aye, what's the apartment number?" Eugene asked as they stepped on the curb. Sly opened the phone and responded, "79B. Y'all know where that is?" Sly looked up with a face of confusion, as he looked from sign to sign in the dimly lit complex. The group wandered through the main street of the complex, calling out numbers as they became smaller. "This way," Corey called out as they approached the building. Sly waited for someone to go up the stairs first as he stared at his phone. Once he looked up, he saw the rest of the group staring at him before hearing his cousin, "Well nigga, this yo invite. Lead the way." Sly looked around at his friends then put the phone back in his pocket and headed up the stairs. As they reached the landing between the first and third floor, Sly looked from one door to another before eyeing the correct door right beside him. He moved to the left side of the doorway, allowing everyone up on the landing. Just then, there were two other women who were coming up the other flight of stairs. "Good evening ladies, how y'all doin' tonight?" Daryl blurted out, and the two girls smiled and waved before entering the apartment across the landing. Sly thought they were a good distraction to try to move to the back of the group. "Uh nigga, what are you doing? If you don't get yo ass up here and knock on this door," Dre said and grabbed his cousin, nearly using him as a door knocker only seconds after taking a swig from his water bottle. Sly paused for a moment then knocked on the door. They could hear someone yelling, "Who the fuck could that be?" Sly looked back at the group as they all gave him a look while shaking their heads collectively. A tall, dark-skinned guy opened the door and looked down on the group of freshmen before asking, "Who the fuck are y'all?" With all eyes squarely on Sly, he began to stumble over his words. "Uhhhh, I mean, I was told that, well, that there was a party here. Heidi……Heidi told me to come he….." Just as he was finishing his sentence, a hand reached across the threshold grabbing Sly by his collar and pulling him into the party. The man in the doorway, along with Sly's friends, watched as he was pulled in. Once inside, Sly followed the hand to reveal a smiling Heidi standing less than a foot in front of him. "I'm glad you came," she said softly and they exchanged hugs and smiles. He then turned back to see the upperclassman shut the door on his friends and he heard Daryl yell, "This nigga suffed us!" Sly felt his hands get clammy as he heard his friends head down the stairs away from the apartment. Sly scanned the room for any other familiar face. As he panned from right to left, he started to feel a slight panic, until he reached the left side of the room. There, he spotted his high school friends, Jade and Rosalyn, chilling on the couch with a couple of their home girls. Sly nodded at the women, and they smirked back as they began watching their little brother. Sly relaxed his shoulders as his focus shifted back to Heidi.

"So you know that invite was just for you, right?" Heidi asked and laughed while both of them stood beside the wall.

"Well, I kinda see that now," Sly said calmly, trying harder to not seem so oblivious.

Heidi giggled and continued, "You want something to drink?"

Sly shook his head as he continued to look around. As he scanned the room, Heidi could feel his body tense up. She reached up and tilted his head down, then whispered in his ear, "Relax."

Just as she said it, Sly felt a sense of calm and immediately dropped his shoulders and gazed into her big, brown grinning eyes. He pulled her closer and for the next five songs, there was barely any room between them. The two danced on the wall as if there was no one else in the room. As they continued, with Heidi's body pressed against his, Sly sang the different R&B lyrics in her ear. She continued winding her body on Sly's as the songs changed. Eventually, Heidi turned around, faced her dance partner, and they gazed into each other's eyes with their foreheads pressed against each other's. As they stalled in the moment, Heidi moved her arms around Sly's neck, and he gently placed his left hand on the small of her back, then pulled her closer. The two continued singing the lyrics to mirror each other's ears, creating a vacuum where it was only the two of them. Their eyes locked once more before they moved towards each other for a kiss. Time stood still, if only for a moment, as they embraced each other. The passion of the kiss overflowed as Heidi held each side of Sly's face and he gripped her ass, giving small pulse squeezes as they made out. Moments passed and they were both still fully engaged. As the song slowed down, and eventually changed, Sly's eyes shot open. He looked at Heidi, with her eyes still closed, as they were still engaged in their kiss. Sly released and backed against the wall, scanning the room before glancing in the direction of his high school friends. As he looked in Jade and Ros' direction, he could see Jade shaking her head. Sly looked at Heidi again, who was now looking back at him confused. He opened the door and dashed out.

Sly ran through the apartment complex, across the academic side of campus, and raced to his dorm. He sprinted up to his room and burst through the door to see everyone back in the room playing Madden like they had been there all night.

"What the fuck, Kramer?" Dre belted out, followed by Daryl's, "Nigga, why are you here?"

Finally, the questioning ended with the most obvious from Kevin, "Nigga you ok? And why you so sweaty?"

Sly looked around the room at his friends before sharing his truth.

"While I was at the party..." He paused for a moment to catch his breath before adding, "And I kissed Heidi."

His friends all looked at each other puzzled, then Eugene asked, "Ok, so what happened after that?"

"That's it," Sly said in between breaths before blurting out, "I have to tell Duchess."

Everybody in the room stopped and stared. They even paused the Madden game. His friends looked around at each other before Kevin advised, "I don't think that's a good idea, bro."

"Yea, nah nigga, you trippin'. Don't Cheddar Bob yaself," Daryl laughed and the room laughed along then quickly died down when they noticed Sly wasn't laughing.

"But I gotta be honest. That's what I'm supposed to do as her boyfriend, right?" Sly asked, pleading his case.

"I mean, yea, in theory, but now it's done. If you like Duchess, you better keep your mouth closed," his cousin advised, still sipping from his water bottle.

"But she made me promise to be honest," Sly continued.

"She probably made you promise some other things too, but that's neither here nor there, partna. This ain't the way to tell her," Mack chimed in, as Sly weighed the opinions of all of his friends.

Sly sat on his bed for a moment, taking in everything his friends had said. Their conversation carried on as Sly sat with his thoughts. He pondered the conversation a bit longer before popping off his bed and announcing to the room, "I'm gonna tell her." He ran out of the room. Once he was in the hall, he walked to the end and made a right. He sat on the sill of the window as he fidgeted with his phone. Kevin peeked around the corner and asked, "You sure you wanna tell her bro? Once you do, you can't take it back." Sly's eyes started to water and he responded without ever looking back at Kevin. "Yea man, I kinda feel like I have to." Sly waited at the window with his back turned, listening for the sound of his room door closing. After he heard the door shut, combined with the subtle silence that filled the halls, Sly dialed Duchess' number.

As the phone rang, Sly's hands became drenched, so he switched the phone back and forth between them, wiping each hand simultaneously on his shorts. There was a brief pause and click before Sly heard his girlfriend's voice, "Hey Carrot!" Duchess exclaimed when she answered the phone. Sly attempted to match her energy with his shaking voice, "Hey Duchess." He paused for a moment to gather his courage before hearing Duchess' demeanor change through the call, "Sly, what's wrong?"

"You know I love you, right?" Sly stumbled through the question. There was another pause where each party was waiting for something different. Hesitating, in an attempt to find the right words, Sly started his story. "I went to this party, and....." Sly paused, not wanting to tell his girlfriend the shameful truth. "I kissed this girl at the party. I know it was wrong and that's why I wanted to call and tell you. I'm so sorry Duchess, I really am," Sly said, sobbing into the phone. There was silence on the other end of the line for a moment, and as Sly listened closer, he could hear Duchess crying. "I'm so sorry, baby. I really am. I...." Sly tried to continue before hearing the click. He looked down at his phone, through his tears, to see the short call time blinking before his phone went back to the dial screen. Sly stared blankly at the phone as he attempted to figure out a solution to the problem he had created. A moment or two passed while Sly reflected, then he called his parents.

Alonzo answered the phone, "Hey son, how's your Friday night going?" he asked, only to hear his son upset on the other end of the line. "What happened, man?" Alonzo listened to his son plead his case, while also trying to convince him that everything would work out in the end.

"I mean, it wasn't on purpose Dad, and I was honest," Sly repeated, confused as to what he had missed.

"I know Sly, I know. But you can't do anything at this moment. Personally, I don't think you should've told her, but that's just me."

A bit confused by his father's logic, Sly responded, "Uh ok, ummmm, is Mom still up? Can I talk to her?"

There was shuffling around on the phone as Alonzo handed the phone to Sly's mother. "Hi Sly, what happened?"

Sly proceeded to explain his actions and line of logic to his listening mother. There was a small pause after he was done, before she started, ".....Yea, I'm going to have to agree with your dad, you shouldn't have told her."

"Y'all know that makes no sense, right. That goes against the whole bit of being honest that y'all raised me on," Sly pointed out to his parents.

"It does, but at least that way she wouldn't be upset," Ria explained to her flustered son.

"So.....lie?"

"Not so much lie as omit certain parts of the truth at certain times," Sly's mom tried to explain.

Sly looked at his phone more puzzled than ever. He told his parents good night and hung up the phone. Unsatisfied with his parents' advice, he then proceeded to dial Ms. Dawkins. The phone rang and he felt his hands become sweaty all over again. As the phone rang for a third time, Sly figured he had called too late before hearing Duchess' mother's voice, "Good evening Sly, how are you?"

"I'm ok, Ms. Dawkins. Can I ask you a question?"

"What happened, Sly?" Ms. Dawkins asked with concern in her voice.

Sly proceeded to explain what had transpired only a couple hours earlier, apologizing in between each sentence. Ms. Dawkins listened to Sly carefully, acknowledging his apologies in the process.

"Ok, Sly, it's ok. And you called Duchess afterwards and told her what happened?"

"Yes ma'am," Sly responded, waiting to be scolded, berated, or corrected.

"Well Sly, I know you didn't mean to hurt her and I appreciate you being honest. But in reality, you shouldn't have told her."

Sly pulled the phone away from his face and looked at it in sheer shock before responding, "......I, ummm, I'm sorry, what?"

And without any delay, Ms. Dawkins continued, "Yea, you shouldn't have told her. You just gave her something negative to think of every time she thinks of you."

Confused and feeling himself become more flustered, Sly responded, "Uhhhh ok, thanks Ms. Dawkins. Can I give you a call tomorrow?"

"Sure thing Sly. Have a good night."

Sly disconnected the call before looking at his phone in disbelief. He attempted to call Duchess back but received no answer. Tapping the phone on his temple, he pulled it away and dialed his grandma's house phone. Sly stared out of the window into the night sky as he listened to the phone ring. His aunt answered the phone as the fourth ring concluded.

"Hey shorty. What you up to?"

"Hey Auntie," Sly answered his aunt unenthusiastically, who appeared to be fully awake, despite the late night hour. As his aunt adjusted her voice, she asked her nephew what had happened to put him in such an unpleasant head space. Sly proceeded to explain to his aunt, in more detail, what had transpired that night. She listened intently, waiting for the conclusion. There was a brief pause after Sly finished his explanation before he heard his aunt ask, "So.....why'd you tell her?"

"Y'all have preached honesty to me my whole life, so I did what I thought was the right thing. I don't understand how it's wrong now," Sly spewed, finally allowing some of his frustrations to show.

"Hold up shorty. Watch your tone. You were right to be honest, but you were wrong with your action. It was a young, dumb mistake. You'll be ok."

Not comforted by his aunt's words, Sly sighed into the phone before asking, "Is Grandma still awake?"

Sly placed the ear of the phone against his forehead as he faintly heard the shuffling of the phone changing hands.

"Hello." Sly heard his grandmother's voice and instantly relaxed his shoulders a bit.

"Hey Grandma. How are you?"

"I'm doing alright. How about yourself dear?"

"Not so good Grandma," Sly slurred through the oncoming tears.

Sly proceeded to repeat the story, and after he completed the narrative, he waited for his Grandma's words to confirm that he wasn't a bad person.

"Well, Sly, you were honest, which was the right thing to do..." Sly silently celebrated being right for a moment before she continued, "But you broke that little girl's heart, Sly."

Sly listened as tears filled his eyes from his Grandma's disapproval. "I know you didn't mean to, but you did. And when you do something like this, you need to think about how you're going to fix the problem as well. So before you even part your lips to create this issue, you need to ask yourself, 'Do I care enough to fix it?'"

"But I'm trying to fix it, Grandma!" Sly pleaded to his wisest relative.

"Your efforts are lost amongst your actions, which make your words hollow until you can do something about it. Do you understand?" Sly nodded his head as he stared at the floor, then remembered they were on the phone, "Yes ma'am."

"You gon' be ok. Ok Sly?" His grandma tried her hardest to comfort one of her older grandchildren.

"I mean, I don't really have a choice. I created this problem," Sly mumbled through his sniffles.

"You're going to be ok. Just remember that when you are about someone, you all are a unit, even if she's not there with you."

"Yes ma'am," Sly responded again, always minding his manners when speaking to her.

"You'll be alright, ok. Love you, Sly."

"Love you too, Grandma."

The two disconnected the call and Sly sat for a while in the hall, staring out the window into the darkness that hung over the Trenton Lawn, except for the dim lights coming from the dorm rooms. As he sat on the window's ledge, he let his head rest against the window, watching a small wet spot form on his shorts. Sitting for what seemed like ages, he heard a door open. "Aye man, you good?" Sly heard Eugene ask from their hall. Furiously wiping his eyes, without turning around, Sly replied in a lowered voice, "Yea, I'm good." He pulled himself back upright and dragged himself around the corner, where Eugene placed his arm around Sly before they walked back into their room.

## Scene 25
# Mildred Hall Panty Raid

The following week, Sly found himself going through the motions. Class, practice, eat, sleep, repeat. The guilt had been steadily eating him alive, taking large bites upon each unanswered call. He moped around the campus, then back to his room for further sulking, without actually speaking. Headphones up, head down to avoid eye contact and any chance of making the same mistake again. Sly walked into his room to see his friends, but in atypical fashion, he just walked past and crashed face down on his bed.

All of his friends looked at him, and there was a brief pause before Daryl exclaimed, "You can't be sad for the rest of your life, bro. It was a kiss, she'll get over it."

Sly peeked at his friend from the corner of his eye, but never responded.

"Daryl's right, ya know. And he ain't right too often," Mack chimed in, as Daryl looked at Mack offended.

"Fuck all that bro. If you want it to work out, it will," Kevin said to the motionless Sly.

"Nah, y'all all wrong. He just needs another girl," Eugene proclaimed, waiting for his roommate to say something.

Sly rolled over to his back and scanned the room before answering, "But that's not what I want though."

"Not yet, because you feel guilty, but that'll pass. What you did wasn't that bad in the grand scheme of things. Not like you fucked her," Daryl explained as the rest of the room stared at him for his rationale.

"You ain't have to say it so aggressive," Kevin said and the room started laughing.

"Facts are facts, my guy. Regardless of how I say it," Daryl said, justifying his tone and selected verbiage, while adding, "Damn, you let my words get your panties in a bunch?"

The room laughed and Sly joined in with a small chuckle.

"Ahhhh, there he is," Eugene announced while laughing.

"Oh, ok we got it then. We just gotta keep callin' Skip pussy," Corey chimed in as everyone laughed.

"Aight, aight. I'm good for real y'all. Leave Skip alone," Sly commented as he faced the group to see everyone still laughing.

The conversation and laughter continued, but was soon halted by a knock at the door. Eugene rose from his bed as the banter went to a whisper. He opened the door to reveal a heavyset, light-skinned guy from the third floor. The two dapped up after a quick discussion and the young man left without coming in or speaking to anyone else in the room. Eugene closed the door and turned around to all eyes on him.

"Uhhh, nigga, what the fuck was that?" Sly asked, puzzled by his roommate's secretive actions.

"Nigga, you about to be on line or something?" Mack asked before Kevin added, "No bullshit. Super secretive."

Everyone laughed as Eugene looked back into the fairly empty hallway then closed the door. He faced the room and lowered his voice before he began, "Y'all know Tremayne?"

"Besides Songz nigga, no. But I'm assuming who you were talking to," Corey blurted out, only to be met with a side eye.

"We obviously don't know this nigga, but continue," Daryl said, cutting off Eugene as the laughter started again.

"Ok, well the nigga stays on the third floor. They've been planning a panty raid and he was telling me that it's a go for tonight."

The group all looked at each other in a moment of confusion, lost on whether or not they should be excited. As the consensus was being reached around the room, Daryl shouted out in as low of a voice as he could, "Fuck it, I'm game."

The rest of the group laughed.

"Wait, wouldn't we get in trouble for something like this?" Sly asked his friends.

"Nah, I've heard the older players mention this. It's like a Fulton-Harley tradition," Mack replied before adding, "But y'all gon' have to go without me. Got another mission to go on."

The room laughed as everyone gave Mack his props.

"So how does this work? Is it like the movies, and what's the dorm that we would raid?" Sly asked, curious about living out something he saw in all the top college movies.

"I'm pretty sure we're going to the dorm to take their panties, Sly," Kevin answered his friend with the basics and they all laughed.

"When you put it like that, it sounds less fun and more sad," Sly said, while they all continued their laughter.

"Do the guys in Roberts know this is happening too?" Corey asked, and Eugene nodded in confirmation.

"So wait, there are six female freshman dorms. We wouldn't raid all of them, right?" Kevin asked the group and looked back at Eugene for the answer.

"No, we're only going into Mildred Hall."

"That shit is a maze," Daryl commented as the group turned their attention to him.

"Uhhhh, nigga, how would you know this?" Corey asked the question that everyone was thinking.

With a Jordan-esque shrug, Daryl responded confidently, "You know, I see what I see, and I be where I be."

"And now this nigga Shakespeare," Corey threw his hands up as the room burst into harder laughter from their exchange.

"So when is this supposed to happen? Wanna make sure I'm in my room, so when y'all come running back, I can see it from my window," Mack asked as everyone, again, looked back to Eugene.

He cracked the door and checked the hallway again before closing the door and responding, "We're supposed to get to the café at midnight and go from there."

"So we going?" Sly asked.

After some chatter on the matter, the group agreed that they would meet at the room at a quarter to midnight and would walk over together that night.

After finishing his last class and grabbing a bite to eat, Sly returned to his room and crashed onto his bed to enjoy the temporary silence in his room. He felt himself drifting off until he heard a knock at the door. As he rolled over to answer the door, it opened and Eugene, along with Kevin, Daryl, and Corey barged into the room. "Get yo ass up nigga!" Corey shouted as he plopped down at Sly's desk. Without moving any other part of his body, Sly slowly raised his right arm and, with one quick flick, produced his middle finger to the audience. He heard their laughter along with the beep of the PlayStation turning on. Drowning out the banter, Sly drifted off for a bit before waking up to the door slamming. His body jerked as he whipped around, trying his best not to fall off the bed. Sly looked around the room before glancing outside to catch the absolute last moments of dusk. "You good bro? You look lost like shit," Kevin asked, as Sly attempted to wake up. Sly reached for the ceiling while rotating his head back and forth, "Yea I'm straight. What time is it?" Without a word, Kevin pointed to the digital clock beside the bed. Sly read the time, hopped out of bed, then stood on his tippy toes and reached up.

"Aye Easy, what time is all this supposed to happen again?" Eugene paused the game to address everyone in the room at once.

"We gon' leave here probably around eleven forty and we'll walk over to Mildred Hall. We supposed to go up a stairwell over by the café, but that's the plan right now."

"Shit, we got time for real. So everybody can get an L burner before we leave," Corey said, after scoring the final touchdown. He twisted his hand to make an L and stamped it on Eugene's chest before yelling out, "Next!!" Eugene got up from the seat as Daryl sat down and picked up the controller.

"And you not gon' be yellin' next like that. You got lucky," Eugene retorted, as he took a seat on his bed.

"A last second field goal is lucky, shit. You, my good man, got dubbed. That's what some of us refer to as skill," Corey responded, defending his antics.

"Not out here catching dubbingtons, oh no!" Daryl said as the room laughed.

The fellas continued gaming late into the evening. Having lost track of time, Sly glanced back at the clock.

"Aye, do we have to do anything besides show up?" he asked.

"I guess it would be wise to wear all black," Eugene responded.

Everyone else turned to look at the clock then announced they were going to change and come back. Sly rummaged through his drawers to find a black hoodie and some charcoal sweatpants. Then both he and Eugene waited patiently for their friends to return. Several moments passed before Corey walked back into the room and following shortly behind was Kevin and Daryl. The friends fell back into their respective spots as Corey unpaused the game that he and Daryl were in the middle of. The fellas continued their night, as Eugene answered a phone call. The room fell silent as the guys attempted to listen in on the conversation. Eugene listened to the person on the phone before releasing a small sigh along with, "Ok," then hanging up the phone.

"What was that about?" Daryl asked.

"That was one of the guys that set it up. Apparently, the female dorm was tipped off so they're calling it off."

After an initial reaction of disappointment, Sly then blurted out, "Well at least we knew before leaving," quickly taking off the sweatpants he had placed over his pajamas.

"How do you think they found out?" Corey asked and they went around the room giving their theories on how their plan was foiled.

Sly looked at the clock again and asked his friends what they were about to do.

"Ain't shit to do at this point. I'm going downstairs and going to bed," Kevin announced, then he opened the door, raised a peace sign, and closed the door behind him.

"Damn man, I was looking forward to the debauchery," Daryl said laughing, dapping up the remainder of the fellas in the room before exiting himself.

Corey dapped up the roommates and headed out as well.

"Damn, oh well. Guess there really won't be any college movie pranks being pulled. That's kinda sad, but I guess that does make sense," Sly said to his roommate and he got up to cut the lights off in the room.

Bang! Bang! Bang! Eugene and Sly both sprung out of bed. Sly rubbed his eyes repeatedly as Eugene sluggishly approached the door. When Sly finally got his eyes to focus, he could see that the time was quarter after two as he heard Gary's voice at the door, "Mandatory meeting downstairs on the Trenton Lawn. Mr. P said if everyone isn't downstairs, the whole dorm is going back on curfew." Sly put his sweatpants back on before he and Eugene exited their room. As they shuffled down the stairs amongst the zombie-like crowd, they made their way across the street onto the large lawn in front of the Architecture building. Mr. P stood off to the side with his arms folded, patiently waiting for the parade to end. Sly stood amongst his friends and dormmates, waiting for the meeting to begin. While waiting, he looked around and saw a few students coming from the direction of Bay Place. Sly continued to pan the group before hearing Mr. P start the meeting.

"Gentlemen, you all should be ashamed of yourselves. For any of you who were involved in tonight's activities, we will find out and there will be harsh consequences." The group looked around at each other as Mr. P continued, "For any of you that don't know what I'm referring to, some of your dormmates thought it would be a good idea to try to steal some of the young ladies' underwear in the middle of the night." Daryl mumbled under his breath, "Well when you put it that way," as Sly and Kevin tried not to let out a chuckle. "Not only did you all threaten the security of these young ladies, but the glass door at Bay Hall was shattered in this botched attempt. Lastly, those who were caught in the act, please step forward. And don't make me point you out." There were low murmurs as the crowd moved and a small group of individuals, including Tremayne, stepped in front of the group between the mass and the dorm director. As they went forward, the light chatter turned to laughter and finger pointing. With the smell of baby powder wafting in the air, the culprits looked more like they had experienced a hellish makeover. "Take a good look at these gentlemen. These boys were pelted with baby oil, baby powder, and everything else as they attempted to leave the dorm they weren't supposed to be in in the first place. I hope you all feel as embarrassed as you all look. This is completely unacceptable." There was a moment of silence before someone yelled from the back, "They got y'all out here looking like powdered donuts." The dorm laughed as Mr. P tried to downplay the joke, "Ayyyy, that's not what we are here for. This is no laughing matter, fellas. You all are adults now and the kiddish pranks have real consequences. You all laugh, but these fellas in front of you have probably experienced their last night as a Fulton-Harley student." Mr. P paused for a moment just to allow his message to sink in. "That's a sad reality. For those who might have forgotten why you're here, let this moment serve as the only reminder you'll need. Please remember why you're here. Do I make myself clear?" There was a collective, "Yes sir," before all of the residents of Jackson Hall headed back into the dorm.

## Scene 26
# The Rumor Mill

Coming out of his morning class, Sly felt full of energy as he jumped down the steps to the sidewalk. As the sunshine intensified, he headed towards the Student Center. He walked along the back hall, headed towards the atrium where he could hear disgruntled yelling over his headphones. Sly went to grab a chicken biscuit while raising one side of his headphones so he could hear both the cashier and the argument. As he approached the register, he could hear one girl yell, "I should've known yo hoe ass did that shit!" Sly and the cashier made similar faces at each other as she pointed to the total, not to disrupt the conversation they were listening to. "Oh yeah? Well if you were doing all that you say you do, he wouldn't have come looking for me." The statement was met with a brief but chilling silence, causing everyone to freeze. "Them sound like fightin' words. I'm out," Sly said jokingly to the cashier as they shared a laugh and a fist bump after Sly bagged his food. Sly headed out of the Student Center and back towards the T-Sci building remembering he had left something in his previous classroom. On his way to the classroom, he thought about the fact that that had been the first argument that he had seen on campus, outside of a party. Without knowing anything about the situation, besides what he heard, Sly figured it was a one off and continued about his day. After leaving T-Sci, he trailed back towards Jackson Hall. Along the way, he noticed that the smiles and laughter between folks on campus had been replaced by stare downs and mean mugs. Normally, he would only look up when his path was impeded, but

Sly was genuinely curious as to what caused the change on his campus. As he approached his dorm, he heard someone yell out, "What's all that shit you was poppin' online, huh?" Sly looked over his shoulder and saw a guy pushed another on Trenton Lawn. Sly watched for a moment, as the yelling and shoving escalated, then other dormmates stepped in to cool down the situation. Sly shook his head as he let the door close behind him and headed up the stairs.

Sly reached his room and walked in to see Eugene, Kevin, and Corey hovered around the computer. "What are y'all doing?" Sly asked, confused by all the unusual behaviors he'd witnessed up to that point.

"We looking at Scholar Sip."

"You lookin' at what?" Sly responded to Kevin's answer as none of them looked away from the screen.

Sly made his way back to Eugene's desk after sitting his book bag on his bed. As they huddled around the screen, each pointing at different entries, "So what is this?" Sly asked, confused about what he was seeing.

"From what I can tell, it's like an anonymous Twitter feed for our campus where people are just airing out dirty laundry," Corey responded. Then he asked, "How does a girl get the name Flip Cup?"

"How does anyone get the name Flip Cup?" Eugene asked before they all started laughing.

"Have you all seen your names on there yet?" Sly asked his friends and they all shook their heads in denial as they continued to scroll.

"Not yet, anyway," Eugene added after a little delay.

The group, hovering over the computer screen, was joined by Mack and Daryl, who also read the hilarious and harsh comments. "This shit is outta hand, and I got class," Sly said as he stood up to stretch. "Me too," Kevin said, rising to his feet as Daryl nudged him out of the space so he could take his seat. "Nigga, don't you have class too?" Kevin asked Corey as he and Sly stood in the door. "Oh, you right. We gon' have some fun with this shit later though," Corey exclaimed and the trio exited the room.

As they left Jackson Hall and made their way towards the Student Center, there was an eerie silence on campus for it to be such a gorgeous day. Even the footsteps seemed muted, with the absence of students engaging with one another. They entered the Student Center and the silence followed into the relatively empty building. That was very strange given that it was closer to noon. They passed through and heard the occasional ding at the cash register, looking at one another, but careful not to break the silence that surrounded them. As they exited the building towards the academic side of campus, Corey whispered, "Ok, but y'all thought that was weird too, right?" Sly and Kevin both nodded as the three made their way into the Business building. They went their separate ways, with Sly making his way to the largest classroom in the building for his Ethics class. There sat Eugene, three rows back with an open seat beside him, tapping on it. Sly took the seat, then looked at Eugene in astonishment, "When I left, I assumed you weren't coming. How'd you get here so fast?" he whispered as the professor started her lecture. "It wasn't fast, just faster than you. And you know we have to come to a certain amount of classes and I think I missed all I can….. I think," Eugene answered quietly. "You here to ask her if you got any more?" Sly quickly gathered and his roommate responded with the same urgency, "Yup." They laughed under their breath as the lecture continued.

The professor was finishing her lecture and wrapping up the class when she reminded her students, "Remember, our test is next

Friday. I don't care how nice it is outside, you still need to come to class to take the test. There will be no exceptions. Is that understood?" There was a unified, "Yes ma'am" and class was dismissed. As the rustling of book bags opening and notebooks being put away amplified as the students cleared the classroom, Sly heard his roommate ask, "What you about to do?" Sly looked down at his phone, although he knew what time class ended, and slowly responded, "Well, we got practice in two hours, but I'm not just sitting in the Student Center. Maybe going back to the room?" Shrugging his shoulders while giving his explanation, Sly stood up and put his book bag on. "That's word. I'll see you at practice then," Eugene responded and the two dapped up as Sly left the classroom ahead of Eugene.

Upon leaving the Business building, Sly heard a call behind him, "Jones!" He paused for a moment and moved his headphones above his ears to listen for another call before he noticed Corey walking towards him. "Was that you?" Sly asked, as his friend approached with an upbeat pace. Corey nodded his head as he continued crunching on a bag of chips. They entered the Student Center and noticed that the noise anomaly was still occurring. In the process of passing through the building, the pair ran into Danny and Fin who were picking up Chick-Fil-A for lunch.

"What's good fellas?" Sly greeted the gentlemen and the four exchanged daps.

"Ain't shit. Been looking at Scholar Sips. That shit entertaining as shit," Danny said laughing.

"Yea, it's already been like three fights in Roberts today. We ain't had a fight in the dorm all year until now," Fin added as he chuckled.

"We been watching, but I might troll a bit. I know a couple niggas don't like each other. I may just help them resolve their issues...with their fists...with each other," Danny said jokingly as they tried to contain their laughter.

"Shit, I'm game," Corey exclaimed and the four headed back towards the dorms.

As they approached Roberts Hall, they saw Mr. Gooden standing outside the front door. "What's your business here, gentlemen?" he asked, sternly pointing at Sly and Corey, as he waved Danny and Fin pass.

"They're with us, Mr. Gooden," Danny responded, just for Mr. Gooden to give his rebuttal. "I'm sure they are, but due to the rumor mill site, non-residents are not permitted in the dorm at the moment. This is more of a safety measure than anything else."

Corey and Sly looked at Mr. Gooden confused, even though they both knew what he was referring to. After a slight pause, Fin spoke up, "C'mon Mr. Gooden. They were coming to me to get a cut for their presentation. You know how professors can be if we're not properly put together."

Mr. Gooden stared intensely at the four gentlemen, panning back and forth before he quietly bellowed, "Go ahead and check-in at the office. I'll have you all's names and student IDs. Don't make any trouble in my dorm and I won't make any trouble for you, understand?"

"Yes sir," Sly and Corey responded as everyone made their way back into the building. They hurried into the dorm lobby, provided their student IDs, and made their way back into the lobby to follow Danny and Fin upstairs.

They approached Fin's door and could hear the chatting from behind it. Fin opened the door and the group walked in and were met with joking mixed responses.

"Uh oh, here come these Jackson Hall niggas causing problems," Melo said laughing as he dapped up Sly and Corey.

"Nah, nah, we ain't here to cause no problems," Sly announced, only to be followed by Corey with, "Not with y'all anyway."

Everyone laughed as the focus shifted over to Wale who was sitting in front of Fin's computer.

"Clank likes to have his booty ate," Wale read, as the whole room went silent then Corey responded, "Nigga, what?"

"Yea, that's what it said. 'Clank likes to have his booty ate,'" Wale repeated, trying to keep a straight face.

The room exploded with laughter, then Sly paused for a moment, "Wait, like Clank the football player?"

Everyone stopped, looked at Sly then burst into laughter again.

"With a name like Clank, this really shouldn't be a surprise," Melo said, causing the laughter to spike, before Brandon fell on the floor.

"Bro, stop. Read another one, read another one."

Wale continued scrolling down the site before blurting out, "Awww, that's just sad and disgusting."

"What?" Danny asked.

"Carmen likes to get shitted on, two girls, one cup style," Wale read, as some of the guys became visibly sick from the comment.

"Like, how do you even discover you like some shit like that?" Sly asked, confused by that statement.

"Alcohol and Taco Bell," Melo exclaimed from his seat and the room erupted in more laughter.

Sly looked over at Melo who shrugged, then paused before stating, "I'm scared to ask any other questions."

The laughter echoed in the room as they anticipated the next comment.

"Logan has webbed feet," Wale read, then everyone in the room looked around.

"Logan with the walk?" Fin asked, as everyone looked around at each other and shrugged their shoulders.

"Oh shit," Wale said as he stopped scrolling and turned around. "Corey acts big, but really is a bitch."

The room suddenly went quiet and they all turned their attention to Corey who was approaching the computer.

"Aye bro, you got a whole ass enemy out here," Melo said, as Wale slid over so that Corey could see the post.

"Who do you think would say something like that?" Sly asked, as Corey ignored the question.

"There are plenty of Coreys on this campus. They probably not talking about me, and if they were, they didn't come say it to me so..." Corey said, as his voice trailed off and he shrugged.

Wale attempted to start scrolling again, but Corey insisted on him keeping the post visible.

"Bro, it's not handwriting, and there's no name. You can't stare at it and figure out who it is," Wale claimed as he moved Corey's hand from the laptop and continued scrolling.

There was a small lull before Wale read, "'Sly plays innocent, but he's a dog.' Damn nigga, who heart you break?"

The room laughed and turned to look at Sly as he looked puzzled at the computer screen, thinking who could've written the message.

"Awww shit, I'm running into everything now. Brandon ate my ass.'"

Everyone in the room turned and looked at Melo who gave a nonchalant shrug, never moving, leading everyone to burst into laughter.

"You a nasty motherfucka, B," Brandon said as the room's laughter continued.

There was a knock at the door and the group paused for just a moment as Brandon welcomed Lincoln, Will, LK, and Jalil in the already packed room. Wale continued reading from the site with the additional commentary. In the midst of the laughter, Sly checked his phone, "Oh shit!!" he showed the phone to Corey who was still visibly upset before going around the room and dapping everyone in a hurry. They raced down the stairs, into the office to grab their IDs, then sprinted out of the dorm towards the field.

With everything going on at Fulton-Harley, football practice proved to be the one consistent thing on campus. As practice was concluding, Sly caught up with Benson, "Aye bro, what's the deal with this Scholar Sip site?"

The two dapped up as Benson laughed, "Damn, that shit up again?"

"What you mean again?" Sly asked as Corey and Stick came over to listen.

"Yea, they block that site every year, and every year there is some kind of proxy or something and then it's available again. Y'all on there?" Benson asked as all three freshmen gave different responses. He laughed more before adding, "Don't claim anonymous problems. If it ain't brought to you, dead that shit," Benson said while pointing to his temple before dapping up all three freshmen again and heading into the main locker room. They made their way back into the walk-on locker room and discussed the free game they had been granted. As they entered the locker room, the ongoing conversation blended as Scholar Sip had taken over Fulton-Harley completely. Taking longer than normal, the young men slowly cleared out the locker room and took turns sharing the wildest thing they had seen on the site. Sly changed back into his sweats to head back towards Jackson Hall then he left with Corey and Stick. The three gentlemen walked back towards their dorm, splitting from those who were headed directly to the café for dinner.

"I don't know how niggas just go to the café after practice," Corey said, shaking his head.

"Shiiiid, I do. Be hungrier than a mothafucka after practice, for real," Stick answered as all three laughed and walked into the dorm.

"Aye, I'm 'bout to stop by Kevin room. You coming?" Corey asked as he paused for a moment.

Sly thought about it for a second before shaking his head. "Y'all niggas gon' end up in my room anyway."

They laughed as Jimmy and Sly headed upstairs and Corey went down the side hall towards Kevin's room.

With all the different issues popping up on campus, the week flew by. There were several fights, public arguments, and private business aired out during the week. On Friday, Sly checked his school email account, revealing multiple unread messages. At the top, he read an email titled "Blocked Site". He then attempted to reach Scholar Sip, which had been blocked on every proxy that had been known on campus, receiving a 404 error. Sly chuckled to himself as he thought about all of the activities that had happened related to those posts. He heard the door creak open as Eugene came into the room followed by Kevin and Daryl. Eugene went to open his computer as Sly blurted out, "They took down Scholar Sip."

"Man what?" Daryl asked, surprised.

"Oh, I know," Eugene answered calmly.

"I mean, I get how that happened. It got really wild around here for the past week," Kevin chimed in. They proceeded to turn on the PlayStation and started up Madden. Corey and Mack came in a short time later. Sly looked around the room, noticing that things had pretty much gone back to normal before asking, "Corey, you ever find out who wrote that post?"

"Nope," he replied, never looking away from the screen.

Sly looked around again and then asked, "So is everybody gon' act like this week didn't happen on campus?"

"I mean, probably," Daryl answered ironically as the room laughed.

## Scene 27
# The High Five

Sly sat on his bed looking out the window, watching the sun play hide and seek with the limited skyline of the campus. The evenings were getting longer and warmer as the semester edged towards completion. He gazed at the passing students and future architects coming out of the buildings across the lawn and on the sidewalk.

"Uhhhh, if you done looking out the window like you Dawson's Creek, or some shit, it's your go," Daryl said sarcastically, attempting to hand off the controller.

Sly snapped out of his daydream, while taking the controller and the seat next to Kevin.

"Everybody getting that Titans work today," Kevin announced as they were on the team selection screen.

"Wait, you lost to him and he had the Titans?" pointing at Daryl and laughing.

"Yea, yea, yea, you bet not lose nigga," Daryl said snidely.

"Ok, ok, I can't help you Daryl, but Kevin here is talkin' crazy, but we got something for that," Sly laughed as he scrolled through the teams, thinking about matchups, before ultimately selecting his Cowboys.

"Oh, so we just playing garbage games today, huh?" Daryl asked jokingly as Eugene chimed in, "I mean, you were the first person to pick a team, and you chose the Panthers, so..."

Daryl looked at Eugene with a straight face before joining the rest of the room in laughter. There was a light knock on the door, and before Eugene could reach the door, there was a piece of paper slipped underneath it.

"What's it say?" Corey asked bluntly.

"We're having a floor meeting tonight at eight about our theme for the high five," Eugene said, looking over at Sly as he nodded.

"Ahhhh shit, that shit gon' be turnt. When is it?" Daryl asked with anticipation, causing his voice to crack.

The room laughed as Eugene looked at the paper again and stated, "There's no date on the paper so I'm guessing either this weekend or next."

Just then, Mack burst in the door, "Who ready to get wild on this high five shit?"

Daryl stood up and dapped up Mack. "My guy!"

"Y'all foolish as hell but I can relate," Sly said as the room laughed.

"Do y'all already know what y'all theme is gonna be upstairs?" Kevin asked.

Mack looked at the group with a devious grin before warning his friends, "Just don't let ya girl come to the fifth floor, cuz she never gon' wanna come down. We got the Karma Sutra poppin' off upstairs."

The group looked at Mack, puzzled, before Eugene stated, "Y'all niggas did not think that all the way through."

The group laughed and Mack paused for a second, looking at his friends with the same puzzled face.

"We definitely did. I'm trying to be in something tonight, by the end of the party at least. Y'all know what the Karma Sutra is about?"

"Duh nigga," Daryl responded, as the room laughed.

Sly hesitantly spoke up, "Uhhh, I... I don't know what that is."

"Oh shit, really? My bad Jones," Daryl said before adding, "Think of it like a bible for sex."

Sly looked at his friend with pure confusion before Eugene blurted out, "Bro, that was an awful description.

As the room laughed, Daryl defended his explanation, "It's an ancient text, like the bible, and the main topic is sex. Sex Bible. Explain to me how I'm wrong."

The argument went on for a moment, only to turn into the group cracking jokes on one another. After a few hours, Mack, Corey and Kevin returned to their respective floors. As the clock neared eight in the evening, there was another light knock on the door. Daryl, Eugene, and Sly came out into the hallway where they could see Gary patiently waiting for the rest of the floormates to come out.

"Good evening fellas. Hope your second semester has been going well. Despite y'all having a hard time following rules, Mr. P's words, not mine. But we're going to have a High Five party this weekend." There was a small celebration up and down the hall before Gary continued, "You all will be able to decorate the hall however you see fit. What theme would you all like?" With no noticeable pause from Gary's question, over half the floor residents blurted out, "Mardi Gras!!!" Gary looked around asking, "Does anyone else have any ideas?" A random voice towards the end of the hall shouted, "We gon' have beads?" And one of the New Orleans natives yelled back, "It ain't Mardi Gras without them." The floor cheered right before Gary calmed the crowd once more. "You all have a few days. The DJ for our floor will be DJ Mile High. Let's make this a great time fellas." The floor cheered before Gary dismissed the meeting and everyone went back into their rooms.

Over the next couple of days, the floor worked together to get supplies to decorate the hallway. Sly hadn't been in much of a party mood after his last party experience. He had been sticking to his routine of class, practice, and dorm. As Sly was leaving Calculus class, he heard one of the upperclassmen in his course call out, "Aye Jones, what dorm you stay in?"

"Jackson," he answered quickly as he gathered his things and rose from his seat.

"Ok, bet, bet, yea, ok. And what floor do you stay on?"

Sly slowed down and looked at the guy hesitantly before responding, "Fourth."

"Ahhhh, shit. Aight bro, but you got any homies on the first floor?"

Sly looked at his classmate with a blank stare before he headed towards the door, "You not gon' be able to get in bro. That's what they keep telling us."

"Everything has a price, young," the upperclassman said with a straight face, flashing a wad of cash as Sly was walking out the door.

Sly slowed his pace, letting the words sink in before he spun around and responded, "Let me see what I can do. But what's it worth to ya?" Sly asked as his classmate looked at him trying to figure out a price.

"I'll throw y'all a fifty ball to make it worth your while."

"Each," Sly stated firmly, looking at the upperclassman.

The older student looked at Sly who had walked back and was now standing over him to the side. The pause grew longer before the student finally agreed. Then Sly headed back towards the door, "Word, I'll holla at you once I've spoken to my man."

Sly chucked a peace sign over his head as he left the barely occupied room and headed to his next class. While attending class throughout the week, Sly noticed he was receiving a steady stream of similar questions and requests from most upperclassmen. As the party drew closer, Sly could feel the anticipation in the air around the campus. As he made his way through the Student Center that Friday, Sly heard the DJ from his one free ear, "Ayyye, we turning up in Jackson Hall this weekend. If you don't live in Jackson, sorry fellas, but you can't go. Me and Mile High gon' be in the spot though. Fourth floor, put those J's up." Sly kept watching as he formed a J with his thumb, index and middle finger, placing his hand high in the air, as a smile stretched across his face. Before the end of the DJ set, Sly headed back to the dorm to help finish with decorations.

Sly burst into his room with Corey, Mack, Daryl and Kevin looking up at him.

"Where's the fire nigga?" Daryl asked as they all laughed.

"Ha ha nigga. Where's Eugene?"

"He ran out to get something but he said he'd be right back," Kevin answered before Mack added, "Relax, we not taking anything except snacks."

They all laughed as Mack reached for a second pack of fruit snacks. Just as he grabbed it, Eugene walked back into the room.

"Uhhhh, what are you doing?" he asked, as Mack slowly grabbed the pack, never breaking eye contact with Eugene as the laughter intensified.

"Y'all crazy as hell. Did y'all know we gon' have DJ Mile High on our floor?" Sly cheered as he checked his snack stash under his desk.

"Duh nigga. He stayed on y'all floor two years ago," Corey responded quickly.

Sly looked at his teammate before asking the room, "Did anyone else already know this stuff?"

"I mean, I knew but I don't think it's like common knowledge really," Kevin answered.

Sly looked back and forth between the two before dismissing the information, internally acknowledging that he had missed a lot in the first semester and shrugged it off.

"So what's the move with the decorations? What are we supposed to be doin'?" Sly asked as he began realizing that he was somewhat hosting this party, making it kind of his first.

"The Nawleans niggas ain't gave no direction yet, so I guess we'll find out today or tomorrow," Eugene answered as he stared at the game.

Sly finally went and sat on his bed and called last in the process to ensure his spot on the sticks. After they wrapped up that last game, the fellas ended the night of gaming to discuss the possibilities of the next night.

Sly woke up the next morning with an eagerness he hadn't shown since his first day of conditioning. He sprung out of his bed and hopped over to his closet humming under his breath. As he rummaged through his closet and drawers, Eugene rolled over to look at the clock before barking at his roommate, "Nigga, stop!!" Sly turned around to see Eugene staring at him with a straight face before finishing, "It's 8 a.m. on a Saturday morning. Do you mind bruh?"

"My bad man. Moving with too much excitement," Sly responded, as he pulled his shirt over before slowly closing his wardrobe.

"Yea, I can see that," Eugene said, as he rolled back over and covered his head from the brightening sunrise.

Sly made his way downstairs and headed towards the door when he heard Mr. P from the office, "Good morning, Sly." Very chipper, Sly responded, "Morning, Mr. P!" while spinning and opening the door with his back in case Mr. P came out of the office. Sly paused for a moment and took in the sunshine before he started his hike to the café with thoughts of waffles and corned beef hash. He began to walk in that direction but as he approached the Chapel on campus, he saw a girl walk past with a Chick-Fil-A cup. Without hesitation, Sly made a ninety-degree turn and headed towards the Student Center. "Plus, I won't be able to get it tomorrow. Might as well get it now," Sly said to himself out loud, trying to justify his sudden change of heart. He looked around to make sure that no one had heard the conversation he was having with himself. Upon arriving at the Student Center, he walked up to the Chick-Fil-A area and grabbed two chicken biscuits before turning around and placing them right beside the cash register. The worker looked down before asking Sly, "Cash or FHU Bucks?" Sly pretended like he had to think about it for a second before he finally responded, "Bucks," which was the obvious answer for a broke college student. As the young lady pointed to the bag, he nodded his head before pulling his headphones back up. He walked into the atrium, first approaching one of the bar tables in the middle, before he ultimately skipped that option and headed up the stairs instead. He reached the landing and thought about going to the top, but opted to just sit at the landing and enjoy the view of the Student Center for a moment. He closely examined all over from where he sat in between bites, excited to see the building he spent so much time in a different light. After he finished the first biscuit, balled up the foil, and placed it in the bag, he took out the second sandwich. Sly then stood up and brushed his shirt off before heading up the last few steps. He walked down the hallway, passing the student gym before doubling back and walking down the other hallway past the dance studios and rooms. He nodded and waved to a few that were in the dance troupe practicing. He walked past the game room, peering in at the pool tables that had been neatly racked before the last student left for the night. Sly continued down the hallway until he reached the stairwell. He made his way down the stairs and opened the door to a burst of warmth and sunlight. He crossed the backside of the T-Sci building making his way to the sidewalk. He turned his headphones all the way up then took them off his ears and placed them around his neck. It seemed so rare to have the opportunity to take in the majesty of his campus during the second semester. Sly walked past his turn, drawn to the water as if a siren sang his name. While in his trance state, he walked past an upperclassmen dorm. Just as he was about to pass the entrance, a group of young ladies approached the glass door. Sly hopped the steps in a hurry, opened and held the door for the ladies, like a true Fulton-Harley gentleman. "Oh, thank you," the first woman said with a smile. "Yeah, thanks. I've never seen you before. You a freshman?" the second young lady bluntly asked. "Uhhhh, yea. I stay in Jackson," Sly said nervously. "Oh ok dope. We'll see you tonight then, cutie," the last girl said and she gazed into Sly's eyes as she walked past. "Oh ok, see you there," Sly said, shaking his head in disappointment and walked away.

He continued his stroll, passing the church on the lawn in front of the water. He sat on the bench closest to the water, separated from the others. He turned his music off and just stared at the water, taking subtle deep breaths. He thought about the party, and then he thought about Duchess, and he held his breath for just a second. He hadn't been to a party since Heidi had invited him out. He felt his chest tighten as he thought about that night. He stared deep into the water, trying to continue his meditation, but was too distracted by his racing mind. He scrolled through the songs on his MP3 player before a small smile flashed across his face, and he selected a song. "My block pumpin' and I'm trying to keep that ho pumpin'," he recited with enthusiasm, trying to put himself in a better mood, as he walked along the water. He'd been avoiding the area as a whole, since the waterfront is known throughout historically black colleges and universities as Lover's Lane. He rounded the area and headed for the basketball court, avoiding the corner that still had a little standing water from the previous day's showers. Sly clapped twice as he saw Melo, Dennis, and Brandon shooting around at the opposite end of the court.

"Let me get one," Sly yelled as he approached the group of guys. Dennis did a quick bounce of the ball before tossing it behind his back to Sly, who set and shot the ball. The ball hit the rim with a thud before rolling out, "Two for a dollar?" Sly yelled again, signaling Melo as he skipped the ball across the court to Sly in the corner. "There it goes," Sly cheered as the ball passed through twice, barely skimming the rim.

"So what's the deal with this party tonight?" Brandon asked as Dennis chimed in, "Y'all really not about to let no other guys in though? Somebody gon' try to get in there."

"Nah, I don't think so. And don't y'all have visitation?" Sly asked, laughing, only to hear Melo snap, "Yea, they can get lost with that three feet on the floor bullshit though."

All of them laughed as Dennis added again, "That shit gon' be crazy tonight though. Tyrone said that shit was crazy last year."

"Oh, that's word. Mile High gon' be the DJ on our floor," Sly said proudly.

"Oh yea, y'all shit fittin' ta be icy dawg," Melo added after hearing the additional tidbit.

"So what's y'all theme?" Brandon asked as all of them stood under the rim, flipping up layups and keeping the conversation going.

"We decided on Mardi Gras, but ain't shit been done yet, so I don't know for real. You know all them Nawleans niggas on my floor. They said we gon' do Mardi Gras and no one objected because they said they would take care of it. I ain't heard nothing about it since," Sly responded, flipping and spinning the ball off the backboard.

"That shit gon' be wild, B," Brandon said as he caught the rebound.

Sly shrugged, "We gon' see bro. I feel like everything has been overhyped since we've been here."

"But yet, you ain't transfer or nothing," Dennis said with a chuckle, never looking away from the rim.

The group laughed as Sly shrugged again. He dapped up his friends before walking towards the gap between Roberts Hall and the freshman male honors dorm.

Coming from the shadows of the building, Sly squinted and placed his hand over his eyes to allow them to adjust to the sunlight. He looked around as he continued his steady stroll, dapping up a couple more classmates before he made his way back into Jackson Hall. He walked into the dorm and glanced back and forth between the lobby and the office before he took off up the stairs. He hopped the last three steps, arriving on his floor to an empty hallway. He examined the walls, looking for any sign of decoration before entering his room.

"Ayyye, that's that bullshit," Sly could hear Mack yell before he could even get the door open.

Sly went into the room, checking the score before adding, "Damn Mack. You letting Corey do you like that?"

"Man, shut up," Daryl snapped back as Sly and Eugene laughed, while Sly went and flopped on his bed.

He peeped at the clock, plotting on lunch before asking, "Aye, where is everybody? It's been mad quiet all day."

"Bro, it's like noon and ain't shit really happening on campus until tonight," Corey answered without looking away from the screen.

"The quiet before the storm," Eugene said ominously as the room laughed.

"Easy, did the N.O. guys come by while I was gone and tell us what they gon' have us doing?" Sly asked as his anticipation spiked again.

Eugene made eye contact with his roommate and shook his head before looking back at his computer screen. Sly laid back and watched the game. Eugene checked his phone and cracked the door as Kevin walked in followed by Daryl. The loose members fell into place as they continued calling next and watching to see if anyone would get blown out.

The hours and games passed all the same. There was a knock on the door and they all looked at each other. Eugene opened the door. Stick stood in the doorway with two jugs of detergent in hand with a huge grin and chuckled, "Time to decorate!" The group looked back at the clock that read 7:23. The rest of the group ran back to their respective floors. Eugene took one jug of detergent, while raising and offering the second to Daryl. Daryl stepped forward to extend his arm and take the container. The three of them looked at the detergent then back to Jimmy before Sly asked, "So what we supposed to do with this, Stick?"

"Oh, right," Jimmy said, reaching in his back pocket to hand Sly and Daryl both paint brushes.

Daryl, Eugene, and Sly looked at their hands full of materials before Daryl asked the most essential question, "Uh….ok. So what are we supposed to do with this?"

"Paint whatever you want on your door with the detergent. When we put up the black lights, it'll make your door glow. We gon' put up the black lights and hand out beads right before nine."

The group looked back into the room to see they had about an hour before the start of the party.

Jimmy dapped up the fellas, "Eugene, there's only a little detergent in that one so y'all can kill it. Daryl, just knock on my door after you're done with it."

Daryl nodded before making his way down the hall with Jimmy before they went into their respective rooms. Eugene closed the door and flopped back into his seat at his desk. Sly sat on the corner of his desk as the pair pondered what should adorn their door. As Eugene called out different ideas, Sly stared down at the floor as he listened to his friend. Eugene's voice faded as Sly could feel his heart rate increase with each passing thought.

"Sly……Sly?" Eugene yelled as he waved his hand in front of Sly's face.

Noticing Eugene's hand, Sly raised his head. "My bad man. I just realized this will be my first party since I told Duchess about the last party."

Sly hung his head again with the weight of his mistakes weighing on his shoulders.

"Nah, we not doing this today. So you made a mistake. What's the saying on the field?"

"Play the play," the duo said in unison.

"Damn right. Now what's done is done, and you can't fix it right now. You haven't talked to her, have you?"

"No, she won't answer my calls," Sly answered unenthusiastically.

"So you can't fix it right now. You should at least try to enjoy yourself man," Eugene advised as he stood up. "Now let's turn up cuz this shit about to be crazy tonight," Eugene directed his roommate as he grabbed his shoulders in an attempt to shake some sense into him.

"Ok, ok...," Sly reluctantly agreed, as a small smirk crossed his face.

"Let's do the area code on the door," Sly picked from the suggestions that Eugene mentioned.

The two opened their door and saw the commotion of all their hallmates painting different graffiti on their doors and walls. Sly paused for a moment to walk over to the stairwell to look up as well as down. He could hear different music playing over top of one another as there were people running between floors in an attempt to put the finishing touches on their themes. Sly started to walk away before he did a quick double take to see DJ Mile High and a couple of his friends downstairs.

"Aye, Mile High downstairs. Somebody come help me get these speakers and shit," Sly yelled back into the hall as five guys from the floor followed him down to the lobby.

When they made it to the first floor, the freshmen all dapped up their DJ for the night.

"Y'all ready for tonight?" one of Miles' friends asked.

"Shiiidd, we was built for this. Y'all with us tonight, right?" one of the five responded as Miles nodded with a smile as he stuffed some equipment back into his backpack.

"Yea, it's gonna be packed on y'all floor," Miles warned.

"Shit, we ready," another one of the gentlemen said, as all the guys there echoed the sentiment while laughing.

The group of guys worked together to get the deck and two large speakers up the three flights of stairs. They reached their floor and Miles looked left and right, then pointed to his right, "Let's set up over there. I'm trying to stay out of the middle of the hallway."

"Nah, you can just set up in my room, and put the speakers in the hall," Quinton, the walk-on quarterback, barked as he was directing different aspects of the setup.

"Aight, let's get this right then," Sly pointed to the other end of the deck for Quinton to pick it up.

He continued with directions before Sly yelled out, "Aye, QB," still pointing to the deck.

"Oh, my bad Jones," Quinton said as he quickly grabbed the other end and placed it just inside the door's threshold.

The two dapped up as Sly slid back past the table. As the fourth floor crew finished switching out the neon lights, the flip was switched and the hall glowed with splattered detergent showcasing different sayings and representations of the tenants. Quinton then walked down the hall, handing fistfuls of beads to his floormates. When he reached the end of the hall, DJ Mile High scratched before the speakers blasted, "Crème de la crème, homie. Top shelf, ya know." The horns blared as the fellas dispersed, some going into their room to pass the time. Others opted to linger in the hallway with anticipation. Sly returned to his room where everyone, as usual, was huddled around the game.

"Why y'all not on y'all floors?" Sly asked, puzzled by the scene.

"Well, we don't have anything on my floor," Kevin answered slowly.

"Ok, Skip gets a pass. I always forget you on the first floor," Sly said as he looked over to Corey and Mack.

"Oh, we were done hours ago. That's why I'm still here on the sticks," Mack said laughing and pointing at Eugene.

Sly turned his attention to Corey. "Damn, a nigga can't floor jump a little?"

"Not now nigga," Sly said jokingly and they all laughed and the two dapped up.

Sly shuffled through the chairs in the middle of the floor and flopped on his bed. He rolled over to glance at the clock and noticed movement outside his window. Thrown off, he sat up and leaned all the way back to get a better look.

"Hey guys, uhhhh, that's a lot of people," Sly said, dumbfounded by the outpouring of women coming towards Jackson Hall.

The others rushed over to get a look. There were girls from their class, but also women coming from the direction of Bay Place and the parking lot in the back of campus. Sly laid back and took a deep breath, trying not to think too much about the hoard of women approaching his dorm.

"I got last," Sly said as he sat back up.

"Yea, let's see if we in here that long," Corey said laughing and the rest of the guys laughed too.

"Nah, he can play, but you gon' be playing by yourself," Daryl added as the group continued to laugh.

They passed around water bottles and Sly waived the offer. Once both bottles were empty, Eugene stood up, "So, uh, yea, let's get it."

Everybody laughed and followed suit. Sly, still on his bed, paused to see if there would be anyone staying on the game. But as they all made their way towards the door, Sly slowly got up and followed behind.

"C'mon man, it's gon' be a good time," Eugene said, as he grabbed his friend by the shoulders and shook him.

Sly smiled, "Aight, aight. Let's go."

They walked into the steadily filling hallway and closed their door behind them. Sly looked around for a minute as Eugene made his way through the crowd. Sly stood stiff, mouthing the lyrics as he nodded his head. He scanned the floor, from one end to another, before a short, light-skinned girl gently tugged the beads around Sly's neck down to her level.

"Are you looking for somebody?" she asked.

Sly shook his head, puzzled by the question. Without releasing the beads, she turned around, and began twerking Sly back into his door. As he gathered his footing, he danced along with his head on her neck. After the song, she took a step away, let go of the beads, and ran her finger along Sly's jawline. "See you later?" she asked as she gazed into Sly's eyes. "I ain't going nooooo where," Sly responded with a giant smile. She smiled and winked at Sly, then she disappeared into the crowd. "Ok, ok. So you good now?" Eugene asked, as he reached out to Sly, who slowly nodded with a grin, and they exchanged daps. They both headed into the middle of their hallway and got lost in the sea of people.

As the party raged on, the ever-changing crowd pointed from side to side as they yelled, "To the windoooooow, to the wall." There were a few scratches of the record before Mile High started the next song and someone screamed, "Fuck Daryl Abernathy." Sly looked around, making eye contact with Eugene, Corey and Kevin in the process. The group looked at each other, befuddled, and Sly stood on his tippy toes trying to find the source of the yelling. He then felt a small tap on his arm that was pressed against the door. Sly turned to see Daryl signaling to him to open the door. Sly unlocked the door, looking back to his friends. He waved his hand for the others to meet back in his room.

Daryl slipped in the room, followed by Sly who left the door unlocked for the others to come in. Eugene and Kevin followed, with Kevin checking to see if he could see who was yelling as he closed the door.

"Uhhh, Daryl. What the fuck was that?" Sly asked as the group burst into laughter atop the muffled music.

"Nah, not what. Who? Cuz she clearly hates you," Kevin said as the laughter continued.

"Aight, look. So remember that night we were all supposed to go to the library?"

Eugene and Sly looked confused as Kevin answered, "Yea, during finals last semester?"

"Yea, see. Some of us studied," Daryl said with a chuckle.

"That's the biggest 'F' I've ever seen someone take from studying," Eugene responded and the room made jokes about the scenario playing out.

"You can't just sit in here all night though," Sly pleaded with Daryl.

"Nigga, I won't doing that anyway. She knows I'm in Jackson but not which floor. Just leave y'all door unlocked so I can duck off if need be."

Sly and Eugene nodded at one another as they all headed towards the door to re-enter the party before Sly added, "Don't fuck no chick on my bed though."

Eugene added, "That goes double for me."

They all laughed as they opened the door, leaking back into the party one at a time. Sly twisted the doorknob a couple of times before closing the door shut.

Women continued to pour into the dormitory as the party continued. Sly walked past his door again, twisting the knob to make sure he hadn't been locked out. He leaned towards the door to hear the voices in his room over the music. Sly cracked the door, playing the role of a stranger in his own room. Five women were sitting throughout the room.

"Hello..." Sly said as he waved, walking past the women to grab his key.

"Oh, you're Eugene's roommate," the young lady said with a smirk.

"Is that a bad thing?" Sly asked with a face of concern and intrigue.

"Not at all, Mr. Jones," another one of the ladies responded and they all joined in on the laughter.

Sly looked at all the women as they indulged in their inside joke. "Ok...well y'all enjoy the rest of y'all night," he said, backing away from the group and placing his hand on the doorknob, without ever taking his eyes off of them.

"Oh, we will. Make sure you do the same... and we'll see you later."

Sly waved one last time as he closed the door. Slightly unbalanced, he stepped back into the party and looked back at his door, replaying the interaction in his head. He made his way towards the DJ booth before hearing again, "Fuck Daryl Abernathy." He then turned around to look back down the hall and saw his door open and close quickly. He laughed to himself as he leaned against the wall, surveying the party.

The floor shook with all the dancing, as people traveled up and down the stairwell to visit the different levels of the dorm. Sly stepped out of the hallway, looking up and down the flights of steps as he watched the crowd traverse the stairs. Throughout the last hour, Sly periodically popped into his room, only to be greeted by a new group of females each time. Some he knew, some knew Eugene, and others were complete strangers; but Sly greeted everyone with his big smile and southern hospitality. As he made his way towards his door again, he walked in and closed it behind him. As he turned, he could hear the cry again, "Fuck Daryl Abernathy." He poked his head back out and scanned the crowd. From one direction, he could see the young lady coming from the opposite way from before. Sly quickly turned his head and saw Daryl's door crack open and close in a blink. Sly laughed to himself as he went back out of his room for one last lap around the party.

As the party winded down, more and more doors opened, as the dancing and music became slower and more sensual. Sly ducked back into his room after a dance, peeking down the hall as he shut the door.

"Y'all threw a gooooood High Five," Jade blurted out as Sly jumped to see her whole friend group laughing.

"Yeah, it was definitely better than last year," Isis added, as Sly sat at his desk.

"That's what's up. That's what's up. I mean, we did kinda have a cheat code with Mile High," Sly responded as the girls all agreed.

"Y'all seen Eugene?"

The girls shook their heads and continued their conversation of highlights and gossip. Sly listened to the conversation, interjecting ever so often. After a song or two, Eugene opened the door holding hands with a young lady. Jade and her friends then stood up and headed for the door, greeting Eugene on their way out. Sly popped out his seat and extended his hand, "Hi. I'm Sly, Eugene's roommate." Eugene interjected, "Sly, Kadance. Kadance, Sly." The two had a quick handshake before Sly grabbed his phone from his nightstand. "You kids have fun," he said laughing and slowly closed the door behind him.

## Scene 28
## "Ahhh shit, wait...ok"

Sly walked back in his room and dapped up Daryl, Eugene, Kevin, and Mack before discarding his book bag after what felt like the longest Friday ever. His book bag clanked against the metal desk as he took one step to split the seats before collapsing onto his bed. The trash talk continued before Eugene peeked around Mack at the clock, popping up with a burst of energy.

"Damn nigga, you ok?" Daryl asked in between barbs he threw at Kevin as their game carried on.

Eugene cleared the papers from his desk, frantically removing any trash he came across. "Remember the flyers around the dorm? This is the first weekend of visitation."

The fellas looked at each other before Kevin paused the game and walked into the hallway.

"Ayye!!" Daryl yelled as if he had just snapped the ball, but before he could get it out, Kevin had returned.

"Damn, you right man. Shit starts in like three hours. Y'all whole floor smell like Febreeze and Axe nigga," Kevin said as the whole room laughed.

"Niggas will clean up when they have to," Sly added as the laughter continued.

"Glad to hear that Sly," Eugene said, cutting his eyes at Sly, while cutting his laughter short.

"Aye, look man. I'll do a little cleaning, but nigga, I wanna be in bed by one, so you gon' let me know, right?"

Eugene ignored the question as he fidgeted under his desk. Sly looked away, only to turn back around to see Eugene looking at him with a smirk, "I need you on this two man mission."

Sly looked around the room before asking his longest standing friend, "Why don't you throw that op to one of them? You know where I'm at with Duchess, man."

Daryl raised his hand, looking back and forth between Sly and Eugene.

"Yes Daryl," Sly answered as the room switched their focus.

"While I'll gladly take this, you need it waaaaayyyy more than me," he said as the room erupted in laughter.

Sly looked puzzled at his friends before there was a knock on the door. Eugene opened the door to reveal Dre standing in the doorway with a book bag.

"Ayyye, Dre how you feelin'?" Mack yelled as Dre walked in, shutting the door behind him.

Dre paused for a moment and opened his book bag to reveal two water bottles before he responded, "...Incredible..."

Everyone burst into laughter. He took a big swig of one of the bottles he had before putting it in rotation. Corey had come in shortly after Dre and intercepted the bottle from Kevin as he flopped on Eugene's bed.

"Uh uh, get up nigga," Eugene said, as Corey popped up and Eugene remade the bed.

"Oh, you about to have somebody here?" Corey asked nosily.

"Nah nigga, I'm just channeling my inner Martha Stewart for the fuck of it," Eugene responded sarcastically, and the room laughed.

"I mean, even more for the second part," Sly added as the laughter spiked.

As the fellas continued the conversation, Dre pulled out the other water bottle from his book bag, this one being just as dirty, brownish-green as the previous bottle. The bottle was set in the same rotation, fueling gaming, shit-talking, and jokes. Sly attempted to pick up his side of the room, as the group began to thin out as time dwindled down. With their room clear for just a few moments, Eugene went to close the door until he felt someone pressing against it. Mack leaned on the door, with Daryl and Dre leaning on his back until they all spilled back into the room.

"Aye, y'all still in here by yourself? Uh oh, did you S.U.F.F. yourself?"

"She headed over here now, so y'all boys got a good ten minutes before I'm kickin' y'all out," Eugene stated with authority as he flashed the message on his phone.

"Aight, aight," Mack said, backing away with the other two laughing.

Eugene closed the door again and looked back at Sly who had picked up the mini basketball off the nightstand. As he spun the ball on his finger, fidgeting about, Eugene asked, "Yo, you good?"

"Mmhmm," Sly hummed as the ball slid around in his hands when caught between shots.

"We just gon' watch a movie, nothing to worry about."

Sly side-eyed his roommate before stating his case, "I'm ok man. I just still haven't heard from…"

"Aht, aht, aht, not tonight," Eugene interrupted his roommate.

"So now she's Candyman?" Sly joked as the two laughed before Eugene interjected, "In this room, nigga yes. That shit's bad for you."

"Ok, ok, I'm good. What we 'bout to watch? You not 'bout to have me watching *The Notebook,* or no shit like that, are you?" Sly said only half laughing this time.

Eugene made a face before they both burst out laughing.

"Nah, I'm not gon' do that. It ain't that deep."

"How do you know?" Sly quickly quipped.

"Huh?" Eugene replied.

"What?" Sly sneakily blurted before the two fell out laughing all over the floor.

Eugene attempted to collect himself as he pointed at his phone and then at Sly, who was covering his mouth with both hands, trying to keep his laughter down. Eugene took a deep breath before answering the call, "Hey, y'all downstairs? I'm on the way."

Eugene disconnected the call and the two tried to wrangle in their laughter before Eugene left the room.

Eugene made his way down to the lobby, giving Kadance a hug on his arrival. She announced to Eugene and probably the first two floors based on her volume, "Eugene, this is my roomie, Whitney." The two shook hands just as Eugene opened the door to the dormitory office. The ladies walked in, with Eugene following, and they each handed their student IDs to the residential aid on duty. "What's your room number?" he asked, never looking up from his clipboard. "Four, oh, six," Eugene articulated for the gentleman. As the upperclassman placed the IDs in an index card holder, he looked up, "Aight, you know the rules. Check out at eleven." Eugene nodded as the trio exited the office and made their way into the stairwell. "How far up do we have to go?" Whitney asked, pausing to look up the middle of the stairs. "Well, we don't have to go all the way to the top," Eugene said jokingly. "Damn near," Whitney shot back with a smirk in a quiet, but playful voice. They made their way up the stairs, as the conversation and laughter continued.

Eugene opened the door, letting the ladies in first before he closed it behind him. Sly hopped off the bed, stumbling in the process, as he extended his hand while Eugene introduced him. Whitney chuckled as she tilted her head up and the two shook hands. "Nice to meet you..." Sly said, waiting for a response. "Whitney," she said with a grin as she used her index finger to tickle Sly's palm. "Yo, what the...." Sly stuttered, pulling his hand away in a hurry, but laughing off the awkwardness. "What's wrong with you?" Eugene asked with confusion. Sly paused, looking in between his roommate and Whitney before answering Eugene, "Nothing, I'm straight." He looked back down at Whitney who was trying to contain her laughter. "Well, y'all make yourselves comfortable," Eugene announced to the room, as Sly tried to get out of the way. "So what movie are we watching?" Kadance asked as she climbed onto Eugene's bed and crossed her legs. "Hmm, ma'am?" Eugene said with a subtle, but stern, tone. "Oh, right." The young lady quickly took her shoes off, then also took off her jacket and got under the covers. "Ok, so we got *The Wood,* we got popcorn, we got candy, and we got snacks," Eugene announced to the room as he pointed and held up the DVD case. "Oh you got...oh you got wood, huh?" a muffled voice yelled outside the door, as there were other voices laughing along. Eugene ignored the taunt and Sly hid his face behind Whitney as they both tried not to laugh. Eugene got up to turn off the lights in the room.

The movie started, and the four of them nestled in, sharing small conversations as the movie progressed. The mocking outside from the hall continued, with random voices blurting out various jokes and wise cracks based on the movie lines.

"Hey Eugene! Hey Eugene! Hey Eugene...I bet you won't touch her butt," a voice yelled from outside as the laughter grew louder and louder.

Eugene tried to ignore the teasing before Kadance insisted, "Your friends clearly have jokes tonight."

Eugene hopped up and Sly tried to muffle his laughter as Eugene approached the door. When he cracked the door, Mack, Daryl, and Dre stumbled in with the empty water bottle skidding across the floor.

"Ohhhh, y'all watching *The Wood*," Dre said, trying not to laugh.

"Y'all done got nice and comfortable in here. I see you sharing the snacks with them," Mack said with a slight chuckle, but with more of a straight face.

"What y'all niggas want," Eugene asked, annoyed with his friends.

"We can't come and check to make sure that you doing good? Oh, she must really like Eugene, she got the shoes and socks off," Daryl said as he looked by the edge of the bed.

Just then, Kadance pulled her feet back and the comforter back towards her, leaving a white streak across Eugene's dark blue sheets.

"What the fuck is that? Is that baby powder? I know that's not ash from your feet?" Dre blurted out as everyone in the room tried and failed at holding their laughter.

"Aye man, you gotta chill out," Sly said, trying to calm the situation.

"Nah bruh, that was a big ass white streak on them sheets. You saw it just like I did," Dre said soberly.

"Y'all niggas gotta go. Y'all fuckin' up the wave," Eugene said, annoyed as he pushed and hurried the fellas out of the room.

"Where the rest of your fine ass friends at?" Dre hollered as he, along with Mack and Daryl, are  pushed out the room.

Sly continued trying to hide his laughter, as they resumed watching the movie after missing a solid third of it.

## Scene 29
# Next Class Up (Again)

Sly made it back to his room after a long day. He walked in to see the usual suspects gaming and talking shit. Sly placed his book bag next to his desk before he started back out the door.

"Damn, where you in a rush to?" Kevin asked, before Eugene added, "He going to see Whitney."

Sly turned around stone-faced before responding, "First off, no rush. I just move quick. Second, Whitney cool, but remember, I still have a…."

"Aht, aht, aht. You don't have shit except for Whitney's number in your phone," Eugene cut off his roommate.

"That's because you insisted I ask for it, and she probably felt awkward giving it to me," Sly said to the room.

"But have you called her or texted her though?" Daryl asked as the room went silent, awaiting Sly's response.

He looked around the room and paused before answering, "I mean yea. That's rude not to, since she gave me her number, right?" Sly asked as everyone in the room started laughing.

"Whatever. Look, I'm about to go to this student recruitment team meeting. Y'all should come," Sly urged his friends and they all looked at him without moving.

"Nah, I think we straight," Mack said as they all laughed.

Sly shrugged before heading out the door and downstairs.

Sly reached the front door of Jackson Hall and looked to see if anyone else was walking in the same direction. He headed out, walking beside the Natural Sciences building before cutting between it and the T-Sci building. As he made his way towards the Administration building, where the meeting was being held, he could see women approaching the building. He searched the oncoming crowd to see if there were any guys in the group, with no luck. He walked towards the front of the Administration building and grabbed the door from a young lady, allowing her to walk in, as he held the door for the remainder of the people. After the flood of people were all inside, Sly walked in himself and checked behind him to make sure that there weren't any stragglers coming in behind.

He walked into the lobby of the building and noticed that everyone had gathered on the left side at a check-in desk for the tours. Sly looked over to the crowd of mostly women and saw Xander with a few other women in front facing the group. He threw up his hand and made his way towards the wall next to the door, while Xander did the same. "Thank you all for being on time. My name is Xander Reginald McGill and welcome to the first Next Class Up meeting!" There was a brief applause and cheer before one of the women stepped in.

"Glad to hear that enthusiasm. You'll need it. Hi, my name is Blanca Diamante, since we're doing whole names." She looked back at Xander and everyone laughed. "In the next couple of weeks, we'll be training you all on the routes for the event and providing you with the information you'll need to know in order to give a proper tour. But it will ultimately be up to you to study said information and be ready to present it to whatever prospective student or parent may come in a couple of weeks," she finished with a more serious tone, and the room fell silent.

There was a creaking door nearby and two women came from the back chatting. Xander stepped beside Blanca to introduce the women.

"Ok everybody, this is Dr. Denise Chandler and Ms. Alexandra King." The two ladies waved to the group of students. "Dr. Chandler is the Director of Admissions and Ms. King is the head of the Student Ambassador Team."

The lady on the right stepped towards the group. "Good evening, I'm Ms. Alexandra King, and as Xander alluded to, I'll be the one guiding those you see in front of you. We expect your best effort. For many of you, Next Class Up was your first experience, and more so, interaction with a Fulton-Harley student. Keep in mind that you very well may be the first representation of Fulton-Harley University and that should be considered as an honor. I can't wait to get to know each of you as you help us display what Fulton-Harley is all about."

The room applauded as the two women headed back to the back, seemingly resuming their previous conversation. The attention shifted back to the chairs of the group.

"After Next Class Up, you'll be extended an invitation to apply for membership onto the Student Ambassador Team. Hi everybody, my name is Millie Fontaine. I'm a senior so somebody will be taking my spot," she said waving her hands.

"Ok, Millie. We hear you!" Blanca said laughing and the group applauded again.

"So, our next meeting will be in this building on Thursday at 7 p.m. We'll see you all then," Xander said, dismissing the prospects.

Sly slid back towards the door and held it for the flood of people exiting the meeting.

Sly followed the majority of the crowd then branched off back towards the male side of campus as he saw a few others split from the group. The gentlemen acknowledged one another, albeit, non-verbally, as they went into their separate dormitories. Sly sprinted back up the steps to his room to see that the fellas hadn't moved since he had left.

"Nigga, why are you always running in here?" Eugene asked as Sly had not so gently ran into the door before entering.

"I thought it was unlocked," Sly pleaded.

"You do be coming in this bitch like Kramer though," Kevin said jokingly.

"Aye yo, pause my guy," Daryl said laughing as everyone joined.

"There were some bad joints there, won't it? That's why you ran back in here?" Eugene asked his roommate.

Sly smirked at him with a shrug before responding, "I mean. I told y'all you should go before I left. I don't know what more you want me to do."

He flopped on his bed and turned his attention to the game his friends were playing.

"I know y'all got another meeting. When is it?" Mack asked.

"You know yo ass ain't going out there," Sly said, trying to hold back his laughter, only to be encouraged by the laughter of others.

"Shiddd, I can show some joints around campus."

"Bruh, we giving these tours to high schoolers. You will go to jail," Sly said, and the whole room burst into laughter.

"Oh nah, bruh. I'll give the transfers tours," Mack responded, never skipping a beat.

The laughter escalated from Mack's calm and serious response.

"What?" he asked, genuinely confused by the laughter.

"Yea…That's not how that works. So y'all going with me to the next meeting?" Sly asked, trying to hide his enthusiasm, only to be met with a collection of answers all equaling to no.

Over the next couple of weeks Sly was ripping and running all throughout campus. From classes to football, from football to Student Ambassador Meetings. But despite having less free time, Sly appreciated every little opportunity he received in whatever space he was in. He took advantage of the environment that his Biology teacher had created, taking naps amid her class. As long as he maintained that A average, she would continue to allow him to sleep. As the week wound down, the ambassadors in training, as they were called, had one final meeting in the Convocation Center. Running from his dorm after hopping out of the shower, Sly sprinted into the building as the meeting began. "Nice for you to join us, Sly," Blanca said sarcastically, as the group gathered in front of the stage. "Thank you all for making it to our final meeting. Next Class Up will be tomorrow and we want to make sure that we have everything in place. First, you all will be outside lining the building, giving an energetic Fulton-Harley welcome to all arriving students and their families. At seven thirty, we'll bring everyone inside and you all will go to your assigned post where your sign and number are located. From there, you'll serve as ushers for the program. We will be doing a couple of the school chants during the program, so lots of energy and movement. Lastly, we'll be singing the Alma Mater with the choir to conclude the ceremony before the President dismisses us. At that point, you'll want to grab your paddle and place it high into the air in front of the section where you're standing. Those that will be on the floor, you'll be taking four rows with you. Those that will be on the second level, there will be two of you per section. One can take the upper and one can take the lower. You'll lead your group out of the building headed towards campus." Blanca paused for a breath as she pointed over top of the crowd to the doors behind them. "Even numbers will go around campus towards the front, passing the Fulton-Harley sign. The odd numbers will take the back road onto campus. Don't worry, the gate will be open. You all will loop around and the first few places you'll see are the football field, the cemetery, and Jackson Hall." Xander stepped forward to provide further instructions. "We're going to run through a couple of mock ceremonies so that you all can get the swing of how the program will flow and where y'all will need to be." The ambassadors and other volunteers went into the corridor, awaiting their signal to run through the practice. The building, though mostly empty, sounded as though it was hosting a championship game with all the screaming and energy that the students were bringing, pretending to hype up prospective students. Sly looked around, starting to second guess his decision, as they all cheered and screamed. The group then sang their Alma Mater, linking arms and kicking from right to left. As the song concluded, the group cheered again. "Good job, everyone. It looks like we're finally ready for Next Class Up tomorrow," Ms. King remarked as everyone came back towards the stage. "Now I want to remind everyone again that you all are to be here, dressed and ready to roll at six tomorrow morning." Her comment was met with a mixed reaction of more cheers and a collection of groans. Ms. King looked around at the group with a confused, "Hold on, hold on. I'm sorry, was that the first time you all were hearing that?" The murmurs quieted down quicker than they had started. "That's what I thought. Let me also make this clear, that this is not mandatory for anyone that's not already on the team. Meaning, you are not required to show up tomorrow morning, but you will disqualify yourself from being a part of the Student Ambassador Team going forward. Do I make myself clear?" With pouty faces, the students responded, "Yes AK," in unison. Then her tone switched back to something more cheerful, "Ok, my Fulton-Harley elites. We're going to be welcoming in our next class of great Buccaneers. Go get some sleep and we'll see you all bright and early tomorrow morning." The group cheered all throughout the Convocation Center as they disbursed through different exits. Sly took the exit in the back of the building, opting to take the back road past the cemetery back to Jackson Hall.

Sly arrived at his dorm, nodded to Mr. P and made his way into the stairwell and up to the fourth floor. As he twisted the knob to enter his room, the fellas were seated playing Madden. He turned to his wardrobe and took out the freshly pressed suit and hung it over the door.

"Awww, check this nigga out. You got a presentation tomorrow or something?" Corey asked as the room laughed.

"Y'all niggas know I'm giving tours tomorrow for Next Class Up," Sly commented as everyone continued laughing.

"Oh, that's right. Sly is about to be the golden boy of Fulton-Harley," Kevin said jokingly.

"I think you already got that title in the bag," Sly said, joking back as the room continued their laughter.

Sly continued to lay out everything he needed while the group shuffled around for turns on the game. After a few games and playing one himself, Sly climbed under the covers after he lost his game.

"You about to go to sleep already?" Daryl asked as he glanced back at Sly and the clock, respectively, before selecting his next play.

"Something like that. I gotta be at Convocation at six tomorrow morning."

"Nigga, what?" Mack asked, pausing the game as everyone turned around.

"Why y'all act like that? Didn't y'all come to Next Class Up?" Sly asked the room.

"Came on a scholarship visit," Mack quickly answered.

"It was too far for me to make that trip," Corey answered, as Sly scanned his other friends for answers.

"I came and it was dumb early when we got here," Kevin remembered.

"Thank you. The shit starts at eight in the morning. You know people coming early or could be coming from out of town. That's why we gotta be there so early," Sly explained while sitting up.

"Ok, ok, you got it bruh. Calm your nerves or you'll never get to sleep," Eugene joked as Sly laid back down with a smirk.

"I hate you niggas," Sly uttered and everyone in the room laughed.

The alarm beside Sly's bed went off. He rolled over and saw his clock showing 5:30, and seeing beyond it, Eugene's face of disgust.

"I mean, you can't say I didn't tell you," Sly expressed to his roommate.

"Doesn't mean I have to like it," Eugene said, as he rolled over.

Sly popped out of bed and rushed to shower before returning to the room and putting on his suit. After getting his shirt tucked in, he threw on his jacket, picked a tie and tied it as he left his room. Sly then rushed down the steps and ran into one of the other gentlemen who was suited and headed towards Convocation. Sly sped up to catch the young man walking in front of him. Sly grabbed the guy's jacket to assist him with getting his arm in the sleeve. "Thanks, Sly. I mean, I get wanting to start the event early, but would it have killed them to start at nine instead of eight?" The gentleman, who Sly then recognized as his pool buddy Greg, protested and they both laughed.

"Yea, you not wrong bro, but I guess they trying to take into account everyone coming in from outside the state," Sly argued on the other side of the debate.

"Well, they should've gotten here last night. That's gotta suck though. I remember coming last year from Arkansas and doing a turnaround trip, and I wouldn't wish that on nobody," Greg stated as Sly looked at him confused.

"I've been shooting pool with you this whole time and had no idea where you were from. You don't sound as country as Arkansas folks. Could've fooled me," Sly admitted, as they both laughed and walked past the cemetery.

They looked around and saw a small staggered line of volunteers and Student Ambassadors making their way to the Convocation Center. Once they reached the doors, Sly held the door for Greg and a couple of ladies who were trailing behind them before letting the next guy hold the door for the next few people who came into the building.

"Goooooddddddd Mooooorrrrrrnnnnnniiiiinnnnnnggggg!!!!!" Ms. King exclaimed from up on the stage. All the students, still in a very zombie-like state, attempted to respond and match her energy. "Uh uh, it's time to wake up y'all. Our first future students will be here soon. Xander, did you bring the radio to play music?" Without answering, Xander placed the boombox on the stage and plugged it in on the platform before connecting the device to his phone. As the music blared through the arena, the Student Ambassadors handed out juices and doughnuts to the volunteers. After about twenty minutes, Ms. King called everyone towards the stage so that they could go over the final details of their game plan. At the end of her spiel, the group said a prayer and she dismissed the students to their designated spots to welcome the prospective students. Still groggy, Sly and his group made their way out to the small bridge that crossed a moat, leading over to the Convocation Center from the farthest parking lot.

"Is it me or were we set up, because I feel like this is the biggest parking lot over here and most people are going to come past us?" one girl said as the group tried to wake themselves up in their own individual ways.

"We definitely got set up, but I'm here already. We are about to turn up," another girl said, already yelling.

"Shiiddd, what you been sippin' sis? I'm trying to get on your level," one of the few upperclassmen women who wasn't on the Ambassador team said.

The overly hyper girl pointed to a Gatorade bottle she had sticking out of her bag, "I mean, I don't know how else you could be up at six in the morning trying to hype up some teenagers. These lil' niggas don't care, so I'm 'bout to make this fun for me. I'm already out of class for the day and it's Friday. Fuck it, turn up."

The group, who had only recently known each other through preparing for the events, laughed as a few passed around the bottle until they saw the first student approach the crosswalk across the street. One of the girls finished the bottle before tossing it into one of the trash cans that were in the area.

"Wheeewwwwwwww!!! Welcome to Fulton-Harley!!!!!!" The girl who had provided the Gatorade bottle screamed, as the rest of the group cheered for the upcoming students. One of the few guys that were on the team was standing with the group and speaking to the guests through a megaphone. As the first person came across the bridge and closer to the Convocation Center, the gentleman asked through the megaphone, "Where you guys from?" The student seemed taken aback by the loud question, as did her father, but their mom, "We're from Prince George County, Maryland. My daughter would be a second-generation Fulton-Harley student," the girl's mother proudly proclaimed. "Oh ok, I see you out here, Legacy!!!" one person yelled out as the group made their way into the building. The group cheered as more and more students crossed each time. Sly even asked the guy if he could get a turn on the megaphone. The upperclassman handed Sly the device as another group came across the bridge.

"Ok, ok. Where y'all coming from this morning?"

"My house," one guy said shortly.

"Ok, ok, VA in the building. What about y'all?"

"We're from Nashville, Tennessee," one of the young ladies said as she and her mom stated their hometown together.

"That's what's up. Hope you brought some food with you. What about y'all in the back?"

"We came up from Florida."

"Oh ok, welcome, welcome. I can say you'll definitely get all four seasons here so I hope you brought a jacket," Sly commented, enjoying the banter from all of the students and their families.

As the flow of people dwindled to a couple of late comers here and there, a couple of the chairs of the Student Ambassador Team came outside to wrangle up the students who had been doing the greetings.

Sly's group, as well as the others, made their way inside and they scattered once indoors. Some grabbed another doughnut, others rushed to the bathroom, and a select few just made their way to their next location. Sly made his way up the stairs to the second level where he could see his section and the paddle he had placed under the seat prior to the students arriving. Sly stood next to the seat and looked around the arena, thinking about how fast the year had gone by and how he was in their shoes less than a year ago. He smiled as he reflected on all the things that had led up to that point before his daydream was interrupted.

"Good morning, soon-to-be Buccaneers and welcome to your future," Dr. Frances exclaimed as the arena exploded in cheers and applause. Sly scanned the crowd, realizing that the incoming class may be larger than his. As Dr. Frances concluded his speech, Dr. Xavier instructed the choir to stand. Noting the cue, Sly locked arms with the current students and volunteers as the Student Ambassadors, choir, the heads and directors on stage, and all of the alumni in the crowd sang the Alma Mater. The arena echoed with cheers, and after the song, Ms. King approached the microphone.

"At this time, we'd like for you to find the Student Ambassador at either the top or bottom of your section. They'll be holding a paddle with a number, and they'll be your tour guide to lead you all around campus."

As the groups made their way down the bleachers, Sly hurried over, grabbed his paddle and held it high above his head. He walked backwards, checking behind him every couple of steps as he could see his group take form in front of him. As they made their way down the stairs and out the double doors, Sly took a headcount to make sure he knew all the group members he was responsible for. He glanced up at his paddle number, feeling thankful he didn't have to explain the cemetery first. He gathered everyone together and began their stroll, heading towards the road before hanging a left and walking towards the front of campus.

"So to your left, there is our old gym that our men's and women's teams used to play in from the 1970s into the early 2000s. And the building we were just leaving is where they currently play," Sly finished.

"What about the volleyball team," one girl asked.

Sly looked at the girl with a face of shock for a split second, before thinking, "Uh, actually I think they still play in the older gym," Sly said, half sure of his answer.

"Oh ok," the young lady replied with a shoulder shrug.

Sly continues to walk backwards, realizing he was about fifty feet away from the closest box.

"So, where y'all from?" he posed the question to the group.

"New York," "Baltimore," "Tallahassee," "Houston," "St. Louis," the group sounded off with some students not responding.

"Oh ok, so we got a nice little mix. No west coast people?" Sly asked the group.

One person raised their hand in the back. "Oh word. Glad you could make it. What part of the west coast?" Sly asked.

"Portland," the young gentleman said quietly as the whole group turned around.

"Oh wow, that's dope man. You're the first person I've ever met from Portland. So welcome, man," Sly stretched out his hand as the two dapped up.

"Well, my name is Sly. I'm from Richmond, Virginia, and let me be the first student to formally welcome y'all to Fulton-Harley. I'm going to be stopping by these boxes for our Student Ambassadors to give y'all information about the school, but if y'all have any questions about the school in general, just ask and I'll try my best to get you an answer before the end of the tour."

The group gave Sly a small applause before they reached the first box.

As the tour continued through the academic side of campus, Sly pointed out different buildings that hadn't yet been covered by the students on the boxes and gave the prospects his experiences at those locations. They walked in between the Student Center and the football stadium as Sly expanded on his dreams to the group. He probed the students as to what they would like to study, whether they would attend Fulton-Harley or not. Most students shrugged with multiple answers, but one answered definitively, "Accounting."

Sly looked at the young man, "Can I ask why?" He was genuinely intrigued by the young man's answer.

"You're always near the money if you're in Accounting, and they always need someone to count it and make sure it's right," the young student said confidently and unfazed by the question.

"I can respect that man," Sly said as he dapped up the young man. Sly raised his head, overlooking the group, and out of the corner of his eye, saw Kevin about to head into the Student Center. Sly waved his hand, "Yurrppp. Yo Skip!" Sly called out, trying to get his friend's attention. Kevin threw his hands up and walked towards the group. "Everybody, this is my friend Kevin. He's one of the first people I met on campus."

"Hi," Kevin said as he faced the group.

"And this young man said he wants to major in Accounting, said that's where the money is," Sly explained to his friend.

"He's not wrong," Kevin said, and he, along with the prospective student and his parents, sat to talk for a moment.

The group continued walking towards the residential side of campus, as Sly peppered the group with different facts about spots they passed on campus. The groups started to walk past one another as the general routes went by the wayside. Sly led his group towards his dorm and spoke about all of his experiences, the good and the bad. As he pointed out the dorm and his room to the group, he heard someone yell out of one of the windows, "Don't come here. They don't treat us right. You'll be giving away your First Amendment and your money." Sly froze, unable to think of how to combat the negative comments he had just heard, while the group stared at him blankly. He racked his brain for a response, coming up blank, before one of the Student Ambassadors walked by with their group stating to both, "But here it is second semester, and they are still here. There will always be people at every school that think that the Administration isn't doing enough, but you have to also look at what those people are doing to change what they are complaining about." Sly mouthed 'thank you' to the Student Ambassador, as she winked at him and continued taking her group in the opposite direction.

After looping the residential side of campus, Sly led his tour group back to the Student Center to conclude the tour. He shook the hands of different prospective students and their parents as they all headed into the Student Center before disbursing. Sly made his way upstairs into the room they had been instructed to report to return the paddles. As he opened the door to the suite, he was greeted with cheers of other Student Ambassadors and volunteers alike as Xander welcomed them over the megaphone, "And how about a round of applause for Fulton-Harley's newest tour guides!" Sly pumped one fist, along with the two others that had just walked into the celebration. He placed his paddle in the bin and grabbed a plate of food from the caterers. Sly went and sat down with Greg, Wilbur, and Baron, the only other freshmen males who had actually seen the event through.

"How was it fellas?" Sly asked as he quickly said grace and looked around the table.

"It was cool. I had some Midwest people in my group. Shit seemed kinda random," Baron said before Wilbur added, "Same here, but none of them were from Chicago. That threw me off."

"I didn't have any Midwesterners. I did have a kid from Portland though. What about you, Greg?" Sly asked before Greg responded, "My whole group was from the tri-state area. I think I may actually have a New York accent now," he said laughing, as the rest of the group chimed in.

"I don't know Greg, your accent ain't heavy, but you definitely got a twang to you," Sly said as Baron agreed, "Yea, like, not quite a drawl, but almost."

They laughed again as they saw Xander approaching the table.

"How was it fellas?" he asked the group as they all gave remarks about their positive experiences.

"So y'all gon' be on the team next year, right?"

They all nodded and Sly responded, "I'm sure I was the last one to get the application in. Now we just gotta do the test and interview."

"Y'all will crush the interview, just need y'all to do well on the test, and you'll be in," Xander drove the point home with the younger guys.

"We got it in the bag, man. We'll be on the team next year," Greg stated confidently and they continued the conversation.

## Scene 30
# The Football Exit Interview

Sly sat on his bed and looked out the window with his newfound free time. After having such a busy schedule for the majority of the semester, he now had no idea what to do with all of his idle time. He peered out the window, looking at the campus as students prepared for the summer. When he looked back into his empty room, he skimmed the room for a moment, trying to jog his memory of something he needed to be doing. He looked back and forth for a minute, racking his brain, before he noticed his blazer and remembered. He grabbed his headphones and headed back outside.

He strolled out of the dorm and threw up a peace sign to those who were still on the lawn throwing and running routes. He slowed down his speed and took in what had come to be his favorite time of year on campus. He walked past the Natural Sciences building as he gazed over the cemetery which the groundskeepers had adorned with fresh flowers. He then continued to make his way to the football office. When he entered, one of the girls who helped with recruiting players was sitting at the front desk.

"Hey Sly, here to sign up for your exit interview?"

Sly nodded to the upperclassman woman as she handed him a sign-up sheet. He looked up and down the page, trying to determine which slot would best fit his schedule. He glanced over the names on the list before writing his name next to a slot for three the following afternoon. He started out of the office and saw Gene coming from the back of the building.

"Yo Toro, you just did your exit interview?" Sly asked, assuming Gene had already made the team.

"Yea, that's some bullshit!" he said, as he stormed out of the office without any kind of dap or anything.

Sly looked at the young lady behind the desk. She just looked and shrugged back at him.

"Has that been the sentiment with most of the meetings that you've seen?" he asked, as the girl looked around before answering, "It's been a mix. Some were good, and some were bad. I haven't been here that long, so I can honestly say I've seen it kinda split down the middle."

Sly nodded at the woman before heading out of the office. He looked around for Toro, but he could no longer see where he went. Sly headed back towards the dorm, thinking about Toro's reaction and taking it with a grain of salt, along with the statement from the young lady.

Upon reaching Jackson Hall, Sly ran back upstairs to his room, which had been filled with the usual suspects in just that short time.

"Aye, Easy, you already did your exit interview?" Sly asked his roommate.

Eugene shook his head, "Nah, I got mine tomorrow morning."

"What about you?" Sly continued with the questions, pointing to Mack.

"My exit interview is just a technicality. I'm on scholarship bro. Unless I do something to get stripped of that, I'm just going to sit and talk for a second."

Sly cut his eyes at Mack before shrugging his shoulders.

"What about you?" he asked Corey, and he shook his head too.

"Yea, mine isn't until tomorrow either."

"Damn, ok," Sly said as he shook his head, trying to get the bad thoughts out.

"I saw Toro after his interview and he was hella pissed," Sly mentioned to the group.

"Toro ain't make the team?" Corey asked as everybody looked to Sly for more information.

"I don't know if he did or not. He was just mad coming out the back office while I was signing up for my exit interview."

"Was Eve in the office?" Mack asked.

"Eveeee???" Sly asked, trying to rack his brain for the person that he was referring to.

"You know, the short, light-skinned chick with the big smile and bigger tits," Corey described, as everyone laughed.

"Ohhhh, that's her name? Yea she was there. She's the one that I signed up for my time with," Sly answered, surprised he had been interacting with this person and never knew her name.

"Oh word, bet," Mack said as he handed the sticks to Sly and headed towards the door.

"That boy on a mission," Eugene joked as Mack just smiled, looking back into the room before abruptly leaving.

"That would be wild if Toro doesn't make the team though," Eugene mentioned again as the conversation went on. They continued to game while discussing how politics could be at play, even at the college level.

The following morning, the conversation lingered in Sly's head as he prepared for class. He jetted out of the room, per usual, making a beeline for his first course of the day. Time flew by, as if he had shared his thoughts with the universe. His first class seemed to end as soon as he had gotten comfortable in his seat. As he was departing, his professor stopped him, "Sly, I see you're a lot more attentive this past week and congratulations on your group project. You all received an A."

"Thanks Dr. Payne, just focused down on what needed to get done. Thank you for working with me," Sly commented as he extended his hand for a shake.

"Are you sure it wasn't because you're not having to wake up so early for conditioning and practice?" Dr. Payne asked Sly with a straight face, causing Sly to second guess his grade before she cracked a smile. "I know you're going after what you want to pursue, but I'm proud that you didn't lose sight of the real reason you're at this school. Good job, Mr. Jones."

"Thanks, Dr. Payne," Sly said smiling, then he exited the classroom.

Sly rushed back across campus, sprinting up the stairs to his room. He had calculated about thirty minutes out to get back to the room, change and get to the football office on time. As he reached his room, he could hear the ruckus inside. He barged in and immediately took his suit out the closet and laid it across his bed.

"You breaking the suit out two times in two weeks. What are you running for, President, now or something?" Kevin joked as the rest of the group chimed in with laughs.

"Now didn't we have a whole ass conversation about this yesterday? I ain't doing this wit' you niggas!" Sly said frantically as he started getting dressed.

"Oh yea. Y'all Friday night lights niggas got hopes and dreams and shit," Daryl joked before adding, "Don't worry, you'll be sitting here with us soon enough. That goes for all of y'all, except Mack. He's getting paid to be here."

"Fuck you, I'm gon' make the team," Sly said, only half joking.

"Yea, aight nigga. Just don't cry when you don't," Daryl said, reassuring his friend.

As he finished getting dressed, Sly tucked an extra handkerchief into his interior suit pocket. "I'm 'bout to go get this good news nigga," Sly said, mocking Daryl as the two dapped up laughing before he left the room.

Sly made his way towards the football office, even slower than his walk to class had been. On the walk, he critiqued all of the mistakes that he had made in football over the past two months and who he knew for sure he had outworked. Going through the continuous checklist in his head, Sly looked up to see his reflection in the glass doors of the office. He walked in and saw another one of the ladies that helped with recruiting sitting behind the desk. Sly sat in one of the seats that was in the lobby while acknowledging the young lady with a head nod.

"Are you here for your exit interview?" the young lady asked.

Sly nodded to confirm.

"Jones at 10:30?"

Sly nodded once more.

The pair sat in silence as Sly fidgeted, trying to calm his nerves. He pulled out the handkerchief as one of the other ladies peeked out from behind, "Jones?" she called, scanning the room. Sly stood up and wiped his hands with his hankie before heading back towards the room.

As he entered the threshold of the office, he saw Coach Nottingham straightening up some papers on his desk before he stood up.

"Sly! How are you doing today, sir?"

"Doing well, doing well sir. How about yourself?" Sly replied back nervously, firmly gripping his handkerchief before extending his hand to the coach.

"Glad to hear it, Sly. Were you nervous coming in here today?" Coach Sno asked. Sly paused for a moment, thinking about all the ways he could answer the simple question.

"A little, but I trust the work I put in this Spring," Sly answered confidently, waiting for Coach Sno to take a seat so he could follow suit. The two sat down across from one another with a large oak desk in between.

"Mr. Jones, I must say I was impressed with your work ethic and how seriously you took all the workouts. I thoroughly enjoyed you out work some of our scholarship players. Give them something to consider when they take a play off that you're coming for their spot."

"Thank you, sir," Sly chimed in as Coach Sno continued, "You were always prompt and from what I could see from the report, you have one of the highest GPAs on the current team. Glad to see you're one of the ones that remember why you came to school. You should feel proud of what you were able to accomplish against the level of competition you were up against." Sly looked at the coach with a little speculation, as the coach continued, "Well, at the end of the day, we need to cut down the roster, because unfortunately, we're unable to keep everyone. And in this particular instance, we're not going to be able to take any of this year's walk-ons due to some circumstances out of my control. I'll be leaving Fulton-Harley and heading to Bethune-Cookman. The incoming coach has requested that we not take on any new players and has requested that anyone with walk-on status try out again next year."

Sly stared blankly at his coach as he tried to gather the words to articulate how he was feeling. Finally, he blurted out, "Again?! I'd have to walk on all over again?! There isn't any way for us to at least know if we would've made it?" Sly asked frantically as Coach Sno shook his head.

"Sly, you're a great player and I think you'd have a spot on the roster if you came out again, but unfortunately, I can't make that promise to you. Regardless of what you pursue, Mr. Jones, you should pursue it with the same tenacity that you approached this game with. You will shine if you take that same work ethic and approach. You have my word."

With his fist clenched and every imaginable thought running through his head, Sly stood up in sync with Coach Sno, wiping his hand on his slacks before the two shook hands again and Sly exited his office.

"How'd it go?" the girl at the desk asked. Sly looked at her and shook his head before he left the office. He started towards Jackson Hall, then opted to keep straight, and headed for the waterfront instead. He took a seat at the lone bench and watched the sailing team go by as he attempted to gather his thoughts.

*Scene 31*
# Such a Swell Guy

Sly walked out of the double doors of the Student Center and was met with the bright, beaming, Springtime sunlight. He squinted as his eyes transitioned, looking around before ultimately heading back in the direction of Jackson Hall. Sly really hadn't found anything to do with his newfound free time. He decided during his stroll that he would walk past the basketball court, while trying to determine what he would do for the remainder of the evening. He looped around the upperclassmen dorm and slowed his walk as he passed the waterfront. He really enjoyed the serine view and wanted to take advantage of its calming effects. As he rounded the corner, he saw there were a few people on the courts, but not enough to run a game.

"Aye, y'all know if anybody coming out this way after dinner?" Sly called over to the courts as he approached.

"I doubt it," Melo responded as the two dapped up.

"You know don't nobody come to the courts after we got off curfew," DJ added.

"Shit, I'm just here 'til I get a call about what's happening tonight," Melo pointed to their friend, agreeing with his point.

"Damn, ok. I was hoping it would be people over here since there hasn't been much talk about anything happening this weekend," Sly responded, sharing his thoughts on the upcoming weekend.

"Shidd man, you gotta make your own fun here. Or have a car," DJ said as they all laughed.

"Well shit, guess it's Madden for the night," Sly said, as he dapped up Melo and DJ before heading through the gap in between the dorms to get back to Jackson.

Sly opened his door to see Eugene and Kevin playing a game while Corey, Mack, and Daryl watched a video on Mack's phone. Sly walked in the room, looked around at all of his friends, then asked the group, "Y'all niggas not bored?"

Eugene looked up for a moment while the play was going on, "Uh, nigga if you got a move, we listening."

"Nah, fuck that. I'm not going nowhere else Sly said 'we' are invited to. Gon' have me standing outside lookin' stupid," Daryl said as the room laughed.

"In my defense, I didn't know she was gonna do that," Sly argued as it just further fueled the laughter.

"Doesn't matter, there isn't anything to do right now. I guess it's the quiet before all the big parties at the end of the year," Mack said as they all thought about his words.

"Wait, don't we have finals though? Do they throw parties while people are taking finals? Did they do that last semester?" Sly asked, puzzled by the concept.

"I'm sure someone did, but it's warm now and school is about to be done for the year. I know there is going to be at least one," Daryl chimed in as the room debated the topic.

"Well that still doesn't resolve the issue for tonight," Sly chirped, and just then, there was a knock at the door. Sly leaned over from his computer desk and twisted the knob.

"What's good, you filthy animals?" Dre announced as he and Melo walked in the door.

The room laughed as the two came in dapping everyone in the room.

"So y'all on the same thing over here I see," Melo quipped and leaned over to see the score of the game.

"Wait, what y'all 'bout to do?" Corey asked Dre, who just shrugged before responding, "Got this chick over at ODU I might go fuck with, so we gon' see."

Corey hopped up with anticipation. "She got friends? We going over that way?" he asked eagerly.

"I mean, that was the plan."

"Can I get a spot?" Corey asked quickly.

"Sure," Dre said before Sly and Kevin also blurted out, "I'm going," "Shit, me too."

Dre looked at both of them before shrugging and stating, "Welp, car's full. Y'all niggas ready? I told ole girl I was already on the way and that was about thirty minutes ago," Dre said as all the guys laughed.

"I'll meet y'all downstairs," Corey said and sprinted out of the room.

"You better hurry up, because we ain't waitin'," Dre yelled down the hall as they all started to leave the room.

As the four reached the first floor and opened the door, they could hear a voice behind them, "Y'all was really about to walk out?" Corey asked and without turning around, Dre responded, "Oh, you thought I was playing? Nah, I was dead ass serious. Nigga, I'm not 'bout to let me waiting on you stop me from getting some cheeks. How that sound?" Dre asked as they walked out the dorm.

Sly, Melo, and Kevin all looked at Corey for a response. When they heard nothing but crickets, they walked on, bursting into laughter.

"Apparently, it doesn't sound like anything," Sly quipped as the group continued to laugh.

"Are you still parked in bumblefuck?" Sly asked as the group started walking towards the Student Center.

"Where else I'm supposed to park, Sly? The campus security so damn scary. They don't even let people on campus after the school week is over. Like what the fuck y'all hiding on campus that I can't get on?" Dre argued his case amongst his friends.

"Pretty bitches," Melo said with a shrug as everyone laughed.

"I mean, y'all do have them in abundance here," Dre admitted as everyone agreed.

The group made their way to the furthest parking lot on campus, and just as the car became visible, Melo blurted out, "Shotty!!"

With the first seat gone, the other three looked at each other before Sly and Kevin both yelled, "Window!!!"

Corey looked at everyone as each of them started to laugh.

"Looks like you stuck in the middle," Dre said laughing.

"Come on, Sly. Let me get the window."

"Hell nah. And why you ask me?" Sly answered while looking at Corey.

He shrugged and turned to Melo and Kevin who both just shook their heads.

"You the shortest one in the car. Why should you not ride in the middle? You don't need no leg room," Sly said as the rest of the fellas started laughing.

"Ok funny guy. But I bet I still complete the mission tonight," Corey snapped back.

"And that's fine. You can sit in the middle and swing ya feet 'til we're there," Sly clapped back, before Melo added, "Sly said this nigga gon' be swingin' his feet like 'Weeee!!!'" Melo impersonated Corey as the whole group laughed and got into the car and on their way.

The group pulled out of the parking lot and Dre sped as fast as he could over the intermittent speed bumps on the back side of campus. The car reached the stop light and they noticed the veterans hospital dimly lit beside the car to the right. Everyone in the car stared at the light until it turned green. Once the light changed, Dre took the entrance ramp onto the highway and was soon on a bridge.

"Man, I hate this fucking tunnel," Dre commented.

As they approached it, the car lit up with a red glow from the brake lights in front of them. As the car crawled slowly into the traffic, Melo commented, "This is the most ass backwards thing in Virginia. How do y'all have a tunnel in the middle of a bridge? And there is traffic before the tunnel, and in the tunnel, but not after the tunnel? Virginia makes no sense...But I'm still staying here over Detroit," Melo said as the guys in the car cracked up.

"Nah, for real though. Where does all this traffic come from and disappear to once we get on the other side of the tunnel?" Kevin asked, genuinely confused.

"I don't think you have to worry about that given your current driving situation," Corey said as the car broke out in laughter again.

The car made its way out of the brightly lit tunnel and back into the darkness of the night while the boys' eyes readjusted. Traffic loosened up and Dre weaved through, making his way to one of the Norfolk exits.

The car came to a rolling stop as it approached the stop light off the exit. Dre looked left as he went to make the right turn on red. They turned the corner, headed down the road, and Dre prompted the riders, "Let me know when y'all see 49th Street."

"They got numbered streets over here too?" Sly asked.

"Every city pretty much has numbered streets. And typically, numbered streets are never a good thing," Melo chimed in.

"I can second that," Kevin said laughing.

"So are we in the hood?" Sly asked as he looked around.

"We're from Virginia, Sly. You ever heard about a good part of Norfolk?" Dre asked his cousin, who took a moment to think about the question before laughing.

"Damn, I guess you right," he concluded, still laughing.

The group continued to ride down the street, listening to different mixtapes while cracking jokes, before Melo pointed and said, "49th."

Dre approached the light and got into the left lane so that they could turn away from the main campus.

"Uhhhh, isn't the school on the other side of the street?" Corey asked, pointing to the sign for the school.

"I'm sorry, have you been over here before?" Dre asked in a sarcastic voice.

Corey paused, knowing he had walked into a joke, "...No."

"Den shut da fuck up. I know where the hell I'm going," Dre yelled, as the car laughed.

Sly texted a couple of people from his high school to let them know he was on their campus. Dre parked and the fellas got out of the car. He called the young lady he had driven over to see. While they were on the phone, Dre looked back at his friends, "Yea I'm here.....I mean, I got some of my boys with me......Oh, it's only you and your girl?" he asked as he gestured to the group.

"I'm good," Sly said, taking a step back.

"Yea, I'm good too," Kevin said as he stepped back towards the car.

Corey and Melo looked at each other.

"C'mon man, you already got to ride shotgun here," Corey pleaded his case as Melo laughed.

"Bro, what does that have to do with anything? You got it though."

Dre, still on the phone while simultaneously watching the selection process, relayed to the girl, "Oh nah, that's no problem. My other homies gon' go check some of their high school friends, so it'll just be two of us. We about to head your way and I'll let you know when we're outside."

Sly nodded as he pointed to his phone and gave him the ok signal.

"Look, a couple of the girls I went to high school with said we can hang with them until Dre and Corey done. Nigga, don't have us out here all night though," Sly announces to the group.

"Shiiiddd, get in, get out like an OG classic," Dre said, laughing as they all dapped and went their separate ways.

As the two groups went different ways, Dre walked ahead of Corey as the latter tried to keep up. "Look bro, you gon' know which one is for you, so please be cool," Dre explained to his wingman as they approached the building.

"You act like I've never been a wingman before," Corey retorted, annoyed with his friend.

"Not saying that you haven't, but you haven't been one for me," Dre explained to his friend right before calling the young lady, "Aye, we're outside."

He hung up the phone and the pair waited for the young lady to come down to the door. She arrived swinging the door open and leaping into Dre arms all in one motion. Corey grabbed the door as it started to close, and she detached from Dre's neck before speaking.

"Hi, I'm Paige," she shook Corey's hand as they made their way inside. The two stepped inside and waited for Paige to step in front and lead the way. She walked ahead of them and headed directly up the stairs to the second floor. As the guys walked onto the floor, she yelled, "Men on the floor." Some women peeked their heads out as they made their way to her suite. Upon opening the door, they saw another young lady sitting on the couch. "This is my roommate, Tara."

"Hi guys," Tara said while waving as the guys went into the room.

Dre followed Paige onto one couch, and to follow his lead, Corey went and sat on the other beside Tara.

"So where are you from?" Corey asked Tara who gave a short answer, "Philly."

"Oh ok, cool. I'm sometimes in the tri-state area, because I have family in New York," Corey responded, only to be heckled by Dre, "Corey likes to sometimes act like he's from St. Louis and other times, he's from New York."

The four continued their conversation until there was a small lull.

"Hmmmm..." Paige said as she stared at Corey and Tara sitting beside each other.

"What?" Tara asked.

"Nothing...but y'all do look cute next to one another."

Corey wrapped his arm around Tara, who pulled back slightly. "She's a good catch," Corey said as he leaned over to attempt a kiss.

"And you're such a swell guy," Tara responded with a soft punch on Corey's chin, knocking his face off course for the kiss.

Dre and Paige fought the urge to laugh, but lost as they laughed at the somewhat awkward interaction.

"Aye, we're about to go into the room. We'll be back in a minute," Dre said to Tara and Corey.

Tara responded, "I hope it's longer than that."

Corey and Tara shared a small laugh as Dre put up his middle finger and exited the room.

Sly looked down at his vibrating phone and noticed it's a little after eleven when he saw the message from Dre stating that they were headed back towards the car. "Aye, we gotta start heading back towards the car. Y'all remember my cousin from our prom?" Sly asked his former schoolmates as one of them blurted out, "The kinda hyped light-skinned guy, right?" Sly, along with Melo and Kevin, laughed, "Yea, that sounds about right," Melo added as the room laughed. "Yea......yea. Well we rode over here with him, and he said he about to dip. So I guess we are too," Sly said, as he dapped up and hugged his fellow Lions. Kevin and Melo did too.

"Y'all need me to explain how to get back out the way you came in?" La'sia asked, as the three guys gathered around the door to head out.

"I think we got it," Sly replied, only to hear La'sia laugh before she responded, "You can fool them Sly, but I know you have no sense of direction. I still remember you running into that pole in third grade."

Sly looked at his long-time classmate with a straight face before cracking a smile and responding, "Ok, ok, so you gon' make sure we don't get lost?" he asked, then Melo added, "Yea, cuz I don't wanna be lost in Norfolk. That's just not a wise decision." Everyone in the room agreed, while laughing, then said their farewells as the four left out of the room. When they reached the door of the dorm, La'sia gave the guys a hug and explained, "Y'all don't need Sly to come back either. Y'all are always welcomed." Sly looked at her before they both burst out laughing. "Aight, aight. We'll see you later La'sia." The trio walked onto the street, looking both ways and getting their bearings, before figuring out which way to go towards the car.

They approached the car and saw Corey leaning on the side as Dre and Paige talked. Melo joked as they walked up, "Guess somebody is still a Sahara desert."

Kevin and Sly laughed as Corey just looked at them with a straight face.

"Oh no, you didn't come up short, did you?" Kevin asked as Melo and Sly continued to laugh.

Corey never changed his face or responded other than, "Dre, you ready to go man?"

"Damn, why you gotta rush me? Just because you out here taking L burners to the chest don't mean we all have to," Dre said.

He kissed Paige one last time and walked around the car before Melo blurted out again, "Shotty."

"Nah, uh uh, I was already here and had already called shotgun," Corey said, explaining why he should get the front seat for the ride back.

"Hol' up, hol' up, hol' up. Everybody knows you can't call shotgun until you're actually leaving. And you also can't call shotgun until everyone who is riding is present. There are rules to this shit," Melo explained as Sly and Kevin both paid attention and nodded their heads in agreement.

"Window," Sly yelled out and Kevin did the same thing directly afterwards. Melo looked at both Sly and Kevin before looking back at Corey, "Well now that we're all on the same page, looks like you can take your seat in the middle of the back seat. Better luck next time, Champ," Melo said as he playfully punched Corey.

"Don't touch me," Corey snapped, only causing the guys in the car to laugh harder.

"Bruh, what happened? You seem mad," Kevin asked Corey as everyone quieted down to hear his response.

"She was weird, bro. And like hella passive aggressive, I think."

"You think?" Sly asked as they tried to make sense of the confusing response.

"It's hard to explain bro, but I'm super good on ever seeing her again," Corey added as everyone just looked at each other.

"But y'all seemed like it was all good when we left," Dre said, looking at Corey through his rearview mirror.

"Yea, I thought so too, especially with how she was talking to me," Corey responded again.

There was a brief silence before Dre's phone broke it as it rattled in the cup holder.

"Hello…" he answered the phone, listening to the person on the other line. "Uh huh, uh huh. Uhhh ok," Dre said as he looked back at Corey again and disconnected the call.

Seeing the clear change in his demeanor, everyone in the car looked at Dre before Melo asked, "Yo, what's wrong?"

Dre, looking into his rearview mirror, stared at Corey and said, questionably, "Ol' girl said you assaulted her."

Everyone in the car turned and looked at Corey.

"Nigga, what the fuck happened?" Sly asked as everyone really needed more details now.

"I didn't assault that girl. We didn't even have sex. I barely even touched her. I tried to kiss her twice. Once in front of Dre and Paige," Corey pleaded his case before being interrupted…"Yea, he did and got his ass played," Dre said laughing a little.

"Then, again when it was just us. I didn't do anything remotely close to assault. What the fuck is assault anyway? Like, what is she saying I did, exactly?"

The car grew quiet after the explanation for the next couple miles and the fellas endured the awkward car ride back to campus. Dre drove over to Roberts Hall to drop off Melo. As he was getting out the car, he looked back, "We know you ain't touch that girl, man. Don't sweat that shit too much." He closed the door, then Dre drove the next hundred feet or so to reach Jackson Hall. The guys all dapped up Dre before exiting the car. Not much was said upon entering the building, and the three went their separate ways and to their rooms.

The following Friday, Sly walked into his room where Kevin, Daryl, Eugene and Mack were all playing the game after classes. As he walked in, Corey walked in behind him, just nodding to the group, but still not saying much. "Aye, this the quietest you've been all year. You good?" Daryl asked Corey, who just nodded. As the first game went on, there was a knock at the door. Melo and Dre walked through after Eugene cracked it.

"What's good, niggas?" Dre prompted as he started dapping up everybody.

"Just the nigga I want to see," he announced as he turned his attention to Corey.

"Nigga, are you drunk?" Corey asked.

"I mean, maybe a little, but it's Friday. Nigga, you not?" Dre responded back, before continuing, "Look, you getting me distracted. I came over here to tell you that the same little bitch that said you assaulted her said the same thing about eleven other dudes in the past three weeks."

Everyone in the room looked around at each other, then to Dre, before focusing on Corey.

"Nigga, a bitch said you assaulted her? Oh nah, man," Daryl exclaimed, as he threw his arms in the air.

"She has zero credibility with the authorities on her campus at this point," Dre said, shaking his head before continuing, "But you in the clear, nigga. We know you ain't do that shit, and now we can make jokes about you for it."

"Ayyyye, cuz that's definitely gonna happen," Mack said as the room laughed and Corey finally joined in the joke, cracking a smile.

## Scene 32
# Shorty Shorts

Sly opened the door to hear the blaring music from the DJ. He looked down at his phone and could see that the time was twelve twenty something. He didn't care that much since he was done with his classes for the day. Walking through, he dapped up some of his classmates, some upperclassmen he'd met throughout the school year, and realized that he was no longer a stranger on his campus. He smiled as he reached the doors, before hearing, "Next week at the Legion, we'll be having the Shorty Shorts party. We're working with ODU and NSU, but the party will be at the Legion. This will be our biggest party of the year. Make sure you in the spot to be next Saturday." Sly listened to the whole message before he opened the door and held it for the ladies walking out behind him.

He made his way back to Jackson Hall and strolled through the lobby. He nodded at Gary who was in the office before heading up the stairs. He opened his door and saw the usual suspects sitting around the game.

"Yo, y'all heard about this Shorty Shorts party?" Sly prompted the room, though no one seemed to pay attention to his question.

"Yea nigga, you late," Daryl said, not looking away from the television.

"Yea, they throw that party every year. Supposed to be the last party of the year. Right around finals, I think I heard them say," Kevin added.

"Wait, so this is kinda like the High Rise, just off campus?" Sly asked, confused since everyone knew so much more than him.

"Nah, think of it as just a party for booty shorts that all 757 colleges are invited to. Like this year, it's over here, but next year it'll probably be over there," Mack explained further, before adding, "Yea, the older football players swear by it. They say it's usually the best party of the year."

Everyone looked at Mack. "That's a pretty high bar after the parties we've had this year," Sly chimed in as all of them took a moment to reminisce about the fun they had all year at different parties.

"Well damn, that gives us something to look forward to next week. Besides all this got damn studying," Kevin said as the room paused for a moment, only to resume with laughter.

"Well hopefully the next week will go by fairly fast," Sly commented as they all turned their focus back towards the game.

The following Friday, all of the guys were in Eugene and Sly's room playing Madden and talking shit. "Damn, that did go by fast," Sly thought out loud as he remembered his statement from just seven days prior. As he reflected, he asked the room for information he didn't know, "Aye, we gotta have tickets for the party tomorrow or is it just like paying at the door?" Sly asked as the group looked around at one another before looking to Mack. Feeling all eyes on him, he paused the game and looked back, "From what I know, there aren't any tickets. But y'all know this. If there were tickets, the sales would've started, and we probably would've had people walking around campus screaming the party name."

"I mean, that sounds good, but it's at the Legion, and there are three schools coming," Corey said, making a claim as to why there should be tickets.

"Have any of y'all ever seen the Legion even close to capacity?" Eugene asked as everyone shook their heads.

"That's why there are no tickets," he added flatly, making the reasoning that much more obvious.

The group all looked at each other before turning their attention back to the game. A moment or two passed before Sly interrupted the silence, "Wait, so I'm assuming the shorty shorts are for women to wear, but do we have a dress code? I feel like we've been told what to wear to the majority of the parties."

They all looked around at each other before Daryl spoke up, "If they don't mention anything, I'm sure you can go to it like it's an Opal gym jam. Plus, I don't think there's been a dress code at the Legion all year. But since it is off-campus, they may not let us in with basketball shorts and shit, but we are in Hampton. I feel like, as long as you not strapped or naked, you'll be able to get in."

The room laughed at the conclusion of his reasoning. The fellas continued gaming and throwing out theories about the upcoming party from the lore they had heard thus far.

The following morning, Sly rolled around trying to gather the energy to get out of bed. When he finally sat up, he glanced at the clock to see it read 9:58. He looked across the room and saw Eugene awake with a smirk.

"Oh, so you can sleep in like a normal person," his roommate said mockingly.

"Ha ha ha, but I messed around and missed breakfast," Sly said, making his case for being an early riser.

"Chick-Fil-A ain't stopping until 11, and you don't really wanna go to the café on the weekend."

Sly gave Eugene a side-eye before he cracked a smile. "You right though," he said as he reached across the room to dap up his roommate.

Sly got out of bed and looked for a fresh pair of socks. As he stumbled around the room, looking for this and that, he found a pair of basketball shorts he hadn't seen since the first semester. "You think we gon' be able to wear basketball shorts for real?" he asked Eugene, turning to just see him shaking his head before he rolled back over. Sly looked at his roommate, "Thanks Eugene," he said sarcastically as Eugene raised his hand out of the covers to give a thumbs up before covering back up. Sly chuckled as he left the room and headed downstairs. When he entered the lobby of the dorm, Sly was still undecided about whether he wanted to go and try to make breakfast at the café or if he would just go spend the last few dollars he had in his dining bucks account. There was a small group in the lobby studying for an upcoming exam. As he walked past the group, he caught a whiff of the chicken fried in that peanut oil, and he immediately made a right towards the Student Center after walking out of the dorm. While he grabbed breakfast from the Student Center, Sly was reminded that it was the weekend that there wasn't anything happening on campus because of the upcoming finals. He walked out of the building and headed towards the academic side of campus. As he strolled, eating his biscuits in quick succession, he realized how much he enjoyed just being on the campus.

Sly looked around at all the different spots he had recently learned about with Next Class Up and the different events that had occurred as the semester wound down. He rounded the sign in the front of campus before heading back towards Jackson Hall. As he passed by the library, Sly noticed more students going in there than he had all year. Looking on as a few more headed in, he understood their logic for getting their work done early so that they could have a good time later. He smiled as he walked past the different buildings, reciting the information that had been provided to him by the Student Ambassador Team. As he looped back towards Jackson Hall, he casually walked around the women's dorms, speaking as the ladies came in and out, and as he made his way to the waterfront. Sly walked along the water as he looked out and reflected on the past twelve months. He reached the point where the school's sailboats were docked before heading back towards the basketball courts. Cutting between the honors dorm and Roberts Hall, Sly approached Jackson Hall's door. When he reached for the handle, the door swung open to a few guys rushing out, running out of the dorm in different directions. Sly paused and watched them scatter, then looked around the lobby of the dorm from the door before walking in. As he entered slowly, he looked into the office and saw Mr. P looking at a paper. "Aye, Mr. P, do you know what just happened?" Sly asked his dorm director. Though he never looked up, Mr. P responded, "I try not to guess what you guys are doing, so I have no clue." Sly laughed at the answer under his breath as he made his way up the stairs.

When he walked into his room, Daryl and Eugene were playing Madden. "Where's everybody else?" Sly asked.

"Possibly studying, I guess. I don't know," Daryl answered as the ball was snapped.

Sly sat on his bed and thought about Daryl's answer. "So, are we bad students?" Sly asked, trying to understand.

"Do you feel like if you had to take your finals right now that you would fail?" Darly asked firmly, to which Sly responded promptly, "No!"

"Then you're not a bad student. If you know you're not prepared for something and choose not to prepare for it after the fact, then that would make you a bad student," Daryl summed up his response.

Then Eugene added, "Yup, that and getting bad grades."

They laughed as Sly responded, "Thank you, Eugene, thank you."

The three laughed again as the game continued.

After some time, Kevin and Corey joined in calling next and talking general shit for the night's party.

Hours passed and Sly wiped his eyes as he allowed them to readjust to the light in the room that had just been turned on. He sat up on his bed and surveyed the room as he heard plans being made on how to get to the party. He leaned over to look at the clock, then asked everyone, "Yo, what time does that shit start?"

"Shit starts at nine," Corey answered.

"Word. They got a shuttle for this one too?" Sly asked, just to be met with laughter.

"If you trying to catch the shuttle over there, you should've already been where the shuttle was picking up. They about to start rolling out soon, and you know it's already packed over there by the Burger King," Mack explained to the group.

"Well damn, ok. Dre, can I ride with you?" Sly asked frantically.

"Relax no doze, you got a space in my whip," he responded, as everyone laughed.

"But you need to get yo ass up cuz we gon' be leaving soon," Dre said, only half laughing.

Sly hurried to get dressed as the water bottles made laps around the room.

"Wait, what is this?" Eugene asked after taking a swig.

"That there is E&J, or as we call it back home, Early Jesus. Cuz you gon' be calling for the Lord early in the morning, asking why you drank this shit," Dre explained as the room exploded into laughter.

Sly rushed to get dressed, noticing that no one, not even Daryl, had on basketball shorts. He quickly slipped on some cargo shorts, a t-shirt, and his Air Max sneakers.

"Y'all ready to roll?" he asked, only to be met with criticism.

"Damn, you in a rush? The pussy at the party ain't going nowhere," Daryl exclaimed as the rest of the room laughed.

Sly looked around the room again, counting the people before asking, "Uhhh, Dre, how many people you got in your car?"

A few hands shot up and Sly stuck his hand in the air too to make sure he was included. He noticed Eugene and Mack had never looked up for a ride.

"I'm assuming y'all riding with the other football players?"

Both nodded as they looked at the screen for the next play. At the end of the game, Mack stood up to stretch then bellowed, "Y'all niggas should probably go ahead and go. I just got a text from Big Luke that it's already swamped out that thang."

Dre looked at the rest of the group that was riding with him and announced, "We out!"

Sly, along with Dre, Melo, Daryl and Kevin, made their way down the steps. Corey brought up the rear, shouting, "Aye, can I still get a ride with y'all? Mack said they had room initially but someone took that spot."

"You definitely riding in the middle," Daryl said as they all laughed and Corey shrugged.

"Long as I get in the middle of something later," he said with a smirk as the group laughed.

"Amen to that, brotha," Dre chuckled as they made their way to the back parking lot.

The group walked into the dimly lit parking lot as they discussed logistics for seating. "Well, we already established that Corey is sitting in the middle," Sly stated as he looked at the others.

"I'm driving, so y'all niggas figure it out," Dre said as he hopped in the driver's seat.

Melo looked at the group, already having called shotgun, "Y'all niggas knees gone be hurt tomorrow."

"Kevin, you should go in the middle," Daryl exclaimed, then Kevin rebutted, "You shorter than I am. You should go in the middle."

"But you weigh like a buck ten soaking wet bro, you little. Just sit in the middle," Daryl continued pleading his case.

"Bruh, we literally just going up the street. Get y'all asses in the car," Dre yelled as Daryl and Kevin ended up playing rock, paper, scissors.

"Shoot!" the guys both yelled as Daryl threw out his fist and Kevin threw out his open hand.

Kevin cupped Daryl's fist laughing. "Nigga, don't do that," Daryl said, frustrated, as he got in the car.

"Nigga, you on my hip," Corey complained, as they all piled in the back.

"Y'all niggas shut up and pass this around. Actin' like we ain't never did this shit before."

"Easy for you to say nigga, you not the one bunched up in the back," Sly said as they all laughed.

Dre started the car and began to drive off as the bottle started making its rotations. The car pulled up to the first light and made a right turn into the flow of traffic from campus. Traffic crept down the street, gradually making the venue more visible. The fellas rolled the windows down as everyone looked out of the passenger side windows at the massive crowd that had gathered around the bingo hall. The car crawled slowly as they rode by, viewing the sea of women, some recognizable faces, and a few police cars. "Oh, this shit looks like it's already wild," Melo said. Dre continued the slow pace, scavenging for a parking spot before finding one about a quarter mile from the party.

More and more students filled the parking spots and everyone hopped out to take the walk to the party. As the fellas got out of Dre's car, Daryl and Corey stretched a bit more, relieving their joints that had been crammed up in the middle. Finally, the group walked amongst other partygoers, but soon, their stroll was interrupted by shots fired into the air. The sound of the gunfire sent people running back to their cars, if only momentarily. After a few seconds, the sound subsided and the group made its way back towards the party.

"Yo, you turned around kinda quick once we ain't hear the shots anymore," Melo said as Dre replied, "Man, that's a typical part of the weekend in Richmond," Dre said, only half joking.

They approached the building from behind, attempting to turn the corner and get in line, but then they heard more shots ring out. Not wanting to head back to the car again, Dre went across the street and the rest of the unit followed suit. As they crossed the mostly empty street, they went into a 7-Eleven parking lot. As the light jog turned back into a walk, the group approached the door of the convenience store. The crowded storefront boasted all kinds of partygoers, but there were two sitting right beside the door.

"Damn, what the fuck happened to y'all?!" Dre yelled out as he reached for the door.

One of the guys moved the pack of frozen vegetables from his eye and stood up while poking his chest out.

"I'm like ninety percent sure you don't wanna do that my guy," Daryl said firmly as the group turned all its attention to the gentleman. The guy's friend tapped him and shook his head as the frozen vegetables rustled against his face.

"Yea, y'all already took one L tonight, don't make it two," Melo pleaded with the fellas as they sat back down and the group walked into the 7-Eleven.

As they entered the store, the already packed establishment continued to let people in from across the street. Dre bought a Black & Mild and they walked back out of the store. Sly, looking around, saw those same two guys again, and laughed as he walked away.

"So we going back over here where the shots came from?" Sly asked, only to be met with, "Do you hear any shots now? Stop being so scary, Sly," Daryl said as the group laughed.

"You focused on the wrong thing my guy," Corey said as his head swung back and forth, checking his surroundings.

The fellas waded deeper into the crowd, mingling and trying to find a way to get into the party.

The group scattered for a brief moment, with Sly, Melo, and Kevin walking around.

"Oh shit, is that La'sia?" Melo asked, tapping Sly to turn around.

"Shit, yea I think it is."

The three made their way over to the young lady who was posted in the girls' line with her friends.

"What's going on y'all?" Sly said as he hugged his high school classmate.

"Not much. Should've known we'd run into y'all here. Y'all been in here before?" La'sia asked as they all nodded.

"It's just a big open space. Nothing too special or fancy about it," Melo explained before Sly blurted out, "It's a sweat box, but the parties are typically good."

Kevin nodded, agreeing with both sentiments. One of the bouncers was walking along the line yelling out instructions for all attendees. "Ladies and gentlemen, there are no lighters, drinks, weapons, or drugs going into this party. If you wanna keep your stuff, take it back to your car. Otherwise, we throwing it away. Durags, brushes, gum, take it all back to your car. If you get to the front of the line with it, we throwing it away. Fellas, you all's line is on the right side of the building," he said, looking at Sly and his friends and pointing to the other line before continuing, "Ladies, your line is to the left. If you're not in the correct line, you will not be getting into the party. That goes for ladies and fellas. No exceptions. You need to be eighteen to enter this party. If you don't have an ID showing that you're eighteen, you won't be getting into this party."

Sly looked over at Kevin who started laughing. "Nah, we in there now!" Kevin exclaimed as the group laughed.

They exchanged hugs and daps with the women before Sly confirmed, "We'll see y'all inside."

The three made their way back over to where the guys' line was. As the three of them stood in line, Sly took a moment to survey the parking lot. He noticed three squad cars, but hadn't really seen the officers. He also noticed that the Fulton-Harley ratio seemed to be showing its head at the party with the men outnumbered. He smirked at the idea of his chances being increased. The line moved gradually as he stared out across the parking lot.

"Y'all seen Daryl, Dre, or Corey?" he asked the rest of the group as they shook their heads.

"They grown and there is a lot better things to be looking at than looking for them niggas," Melo said, never turning his head from his gaze.

As he looked into the crowd, Sly scanned for his friends before he noticed an argument in the middle of the parking lot, maybe fifty feet from the line he was in. He tapped Kevin on the arm as the argument grew louder and louder, garnering the attention of everyone around. Sly turned his back for a second to speak with Melo and Kevin again before they heard shots ring out for the third time. The three started to run back towards the car again, along with the majority of both lines. Once the shots stopped, the mass crowd made their way back to the venue, but this time, there were officers standing in front. "There will be no more entrance granted into the party at this time. Any partygoer who is caught loitering on the property will be arrested. I repeat, there will no longer be any entrance granted into the party," one police officer broadcasted over a bullhorn. The three stood over by the end of the ladies' line, trying to find the other three fellas that they rode with. As the crowd started to get a little rowdy, there was another round of shots fired into the air. Sly, Melo, and Kevin sprinted back towards the car, as those shots sounded closer than the others. As they were approaching the vehicle, they could see Dre, Daryl, and Corey also running that way. They all hopped in the car before Dre exclaimed, "Well that was a lot of fun." Everyone in the car laughed as they pulled off back towards campus.

## Scene 33
# Going Home

Sly stared out of his window, bored, looking around the empty campus. He turned back to his near empty room to look at the powered off tv screen.

He glanced over at Eugene and asked, "Bro, how many finals you got left?"

Eugene raised his hand, gesturing two to his roommate.

"Oh ok, what day you leave?"

Eugene pondered the question before shrugging his shoulders. "Might just stay down here again."

"I mean, I wouldn't blame you. Ain't shit in Richmond anyway," Sly commented as they both laughed.

"How many you got left?" Eugene asked.

"I only have two, but one is on the last day of exams," Sly explained, shaking his head in the process.

As the conversation carried on, there was a knock at the door. Eugene leaned over from his computer desk and cracked the door to allow the visitor in. Mack walked in and dapped up both guys in the process.

"I ain't seen you wear a book bag all year. Where you about to go?" Sly asked Mack.

Mack's hands were full of books and notebooks. "Man, shut up. I have to take this math final and I've been struggling with it. This girl said she'd help me pass the final, so I'm bringing everything she told me to bring," Mack explained his circumstances and Sly and Eugene laughed at the case.

As they joked on Mack about his grades, there was another knock at the door. Kevin and Daryl walked in, took a couple seats and turned on the PlayStation.

"Uhhhhh, do y'all not have finals?" Sly asked, puzzled.

"I only got one and it's on the last day of finals," Daryl said as Kevin just shook his head.

"Wait, so you didn't have any finals this semester?" Mack asked as everyone focused on Kevin's answer.

"All the classes I had didn't require a final and the professors weren't making us take them if you had a B or better," he explained as everyone in the room reacted.

"Oh, so you Dean's List shawty now?" Eugene asked and everyone laughed.

"I mean, if they forkin' over some free money, why not?" Kevin explained as they all laughed.

"I'll catch y'all boys later," Mack said as he started out of the room.

"Aye, can you take this back with you? You going to the library, right?" Eugene asked as he reached in his book bag.

Mack stopped and looked back as Eugene rummaged around in his bag before pulling out his middle finger, making the whole room explode with laughter.

"Fuck you!" Mack said laughing as he walked out the door.

With each passing day, the semester and school year drew closer to the end. Sly found himself trying to make the best of the last days on campus. Sticking with the Student Ambassador Team route, he went through the interview process to become an Ambassador. He had gone by the office to pick up an envelope, but the current members hadn't told him the contents of what was inside. Sly figured he could wait until he got home to uncover the news. He guessed it had to be good since he had nothing but positive experiences with the team. As he returned to his dorm, he saw families moving their sons out of Jackson Hall. Cars and trucks lined the street in front of his dorm. Sly looked at the people leaving, dapping up his dormmates and greeting their families while they loaded up to leave. He headed back up to his room and waited for either the usual suspects to come by or for the next day to arrive, anticipating being able to take his exam and go back home. He attempted to study while the room was empty, but had a hard time doing so. All the memories from his first year of college kept replaying in his head. Sly had already determined that he was prepared for the exam and didn't want to confuse himself with additional studying. He decided to look over his notes again before heading into the test, but he had maintained a B average in this class with minimal effort, so he wasn't too concerned about how it would go. As the day wound down, Sly laid in his bed, while Eugene and Daryl played Madden.

"Y'all coming back next year?" Sly asked his friends as he sat up in the bed.

"Yea, why wouldn't we?" Daryl asked.

Sly thought about the reasoning himself. He reflected on how he felt when he first arrived at Fulton-Harley compared to how he felt now and he smirked.

"You gon' be back? Know how much you hated it here initially," Daryl asked and Sly replied, "I mean, you got a point. Why wouldn't I come back?"

Daryl nodded and laughed, "Yea, I bet yo ass comin' back."

The room laughed as Sly laid back down, reflecting on the new space he was in.

On the day of his final exam, Sly popped up out of bed and headed towards breakfast at the café. Since he had so much time to prepare for the day, he scheduled his day out. After getting dressed, he ran down the steps and into the lobby of the dorm. He slowed down to see Mr. P in the office organizing keys from dorm tenants who had already gone home. Sly waved as Mr. P threw up a peace sign as Sly walked past. He made his way into the bright sunlight that was already beaming before nine in the morning. He strolled past the other two freshmen male dorms, not seeing any motion in or out of the buildings. He then walked along the waterfront as he approached the café from the rear, still without seeing any other students. As he entered the café, he saw a few students who were on campus, but the numbers had greatly diminished. Sly enjoyed having his share and selection of food, since most of the student body was gone. He lavishly took advantage of the waffles and corn beef hash.

After leaving the café, he walked back towards the waterfront. He had about five hours to burn and he was trying to think of all the things he could do on campus other than going to just sit in his room. He looped around the women's part of campus before heading back towards the front of campus. Walking along the main street coming into campus, he again quizzed himself on all of the different facts and tidbits he had learned about the school, from the Student Ambassador Team or otherwise. As he passed the sign for the school, he made a right turn and strolled down the road that led to the Convocation Center. As he walked, he decided to turn onto campus by the Engineering School. The weather had come around, reminding students and faculty alike that summer was around the corner. Sly walked with his head down, trying to avoid the beaming sun, as he watched his shadow walk with him towards the Student Center. His pace slowed down as soon as he opened the door to the chilled ventilation. He looked around and observed the emptiness of the building. Sly could hear the clanking of a few weights upstairs as he noticed a couple students scattered through the Student Center, with one walking around the track on the third floor. He took his time walking through the building as he anticipated going back to the dorm for the next few hours before his exam. He slowly strolled until a moment occurred where he remembered that he would have to pack up his room and prepare for his parents' arrival. Sly raced back to Jackson and hastily made his way up the stairs, noticing how quiet the hallways were. He got to his door and turned to look down the halls, since he heard Gary behind him, "Kinda weird to not hear any kinda noise in here, right?" Sly turned to Gary with a smile, "Hella weird, but also kinda nice." The two nodded as Sly went into his room.

When he entered, he saw that Eugene was in the middle of packing his stuff up too. "I thought you were staying down here again for the summer?" Sly asked as Eugene shook his head.

"Nah, she won't feelin' it. I'll be home tomorrow though. I think the fam gon' spend a day at Virginia Beach."

Sly shrugged before asking, "Wait, aren't you playing ball again next year? You gotta be here for the summer, right?"

"They only keep scholarship players. Everyone else would have to walk-on again."

Sly's mouth dropped with shock before he quickly gathered himself and added, "That's weak bro, so they not even gon' have a full team, probably."

Eugene shook his head, "Nah, between the people who wanna go through that process again, the scholarship players and incoming players, they'll have enough. But I ain't going through that shit again."

Both gentlemen laughed as Sly concurred with Eugene's position.

Sly sat on his bed and glanced at his notes while also looking out the window and watching the time. As 2 p.m. approached, Sly dapped up his roommate as he headed out the door.

Sly hurried across campus and into the T-Sci building. He rushed into the classroom and took a seat where Mr. Newman was sitting at the head of the class. "Good afternoon scholars, and welcome to your final. If you've studied what I provided you all with, you should be good to go. If you didn't…well… may God have mercy on your grade." Sly looked at his professor after he made that ominous announcement and he second guessed his preparation. Mr. Newman walked up and down the aisles, handing out the exam to each individual student. After he handed the last test out in the class, he returned to the front of the class. "You all have two and a half hours to complete the test. You may leave if you finish early, but I would encourage you to make sure that you're checking your answers and making sure that you're answering thoroughly." Sly looked down at the test and smirked, realizing that he had prepared well as he answered the first question with a smile. After about an hour and some change, Sly double-checked his answers before he rose from his chair and made his way to Mr. Newman's desk. "All done?" the professor asked as Sly nodded his head in response. "Alright, Mr. Jones. It's been a pleasure teaching you this year, and I look forward to seeing you next year. Know that my class definitely won't be this easy next year." Sly nodded continuously before stating, "I'd bet on that," he said with a smirk as he and Mr. Newman shook hands before Sly's departure. Sly walked out of the front of the T-Sci building and let out a deep exhale as he took his time walking back towards Jackson Hall. On his way back to the dorm, he felt his pocket vibrate. When he pulled the phone out of his pocket, he noticed Duchess' name across the screen. Excited to hear from her, he opened the phone frantically to see her text message, "I think we should just be friends." Sly read the text, and then again, and again, and again. He thought about the year and all the mistakes he had made when it came to considering her. As he started to text her back, he would type out a few lines and then delete them. What could he say to her to change her mind? Did he want to change her mind? He contemplated his answers to those questions and others he came up with as he trekked up the stairs to his room. He opened the door and slowly walked in. Eugene looked up and saw his mopey roommate then asked, "What happened to you? You failed your exam?"

"I think Duchess just broke up with me," Sly explained to his friend.

He sat down at his computer desk, staring blankly at the screen in front of him before hearing Eugene, "Man, that's probably for the best. Think about it bro, you were trying to speak with her for like a whole semester after you made your mistake." He raised his hand doing the air quotes as he said mistakes. "But now, you're single, at a school with the most beautiful black women in the world. Now you can just enjoy yourself, guilt-free." He got up and patted his friend on the back before sitting on his bed and turning on the PlayStation. "Come get this last L before we leave this building." Eugene tossed Sly the second controller.

"Last session in the building for sure, but I've already taken my L for the day. Bout time for me to hand a couple out," Sly laughed as he sat with Eugene and they waited for the kickoff.

# Acknowledgements

**Ashley & Ronnie Bland**
**Facebook**: @s27designs
**Instagram**: @s27designs
*Congratulations on completing your first book. May this be the first of many. Continue to push forward and be the best man you can be. God Bless!*

**Yao Thompson**
**Facebook**: https://www.facebook.com/nriventures
**Instagram**: https://www.instagram.com/nriventures/
**LinkedIn**: https://www.linkedin.com/company/nri-ventures
*Super Excited for the drop; I know it will be fire! You've always put your heart and soul in everything so I expect this will show the same!*